MW01241716

MAGI JOURNEY _ PERSIA

Terry Garner

BrodRo Publishing

Copyright © 2022 Terry P Garner

BrodRo Publishing, Phoenix, AZ

All rights reserved. No part of this publication may be reproduced, distributed, or transmitted in any form or by any means, including photocopying, recording, or other electronic or mechanical methods, without the prior written permission of the publisher, except in the case of brief quotations embodied in critical reviews and certain other noncommercial uses permitted by copyright law. For permission requests, contact Terry Garner at tpgarner@magijourney.com.

This is a work of fiction. Any resemblance to actual events or persons, living or dead, is entirely coincidental.

Paperback ISBN 9798351546414
Hardcover ISBN 9798352775028
Ebook ASIN B0B53ZRY6C

Book Cover and maps, Nick Bolton on Instagram @rainandcinder
Edited by Teresa Crumpton, AuthorSpark, at authorspark.org

CONTENTS

TERRY GARNER

CYRUS

Magi Camp – West Of The Euphrates – Day 87

In the center of the Magi camp, the teacher Rahim stood on his speaking platform, ready to teach the evening class. They were close to the Euphrates River, and the cloying odor of old vegetation permeated the desert air. Tonight, the children all had smiles on their faces.

"I know you all have many questions about what happened at the slave-trader camp two days ago; we all do. We will be with Tiz, Navid, and the others tomorrow, and they will answer all your questions. Tonight, I have one of your favorite lessons." Rahim unrolled the ancient Magi scroll and began to read....

Agradates – North Of Ecbatana – 590 Bc

It was April, and wildflowers of red, violet, white and bright yellow filled the large valley north of Media's capital city, Ecbatana. A slight breeze came from the north, and the temperature for April was slightly chilly, but the sun warmed the boys playing there.

Agradates, ten years old and tall for his age, with high cheekbones and penetrating black eyes, spoke to the children surrounding him. "I shall need a castle built as quickly as possible. Fravarti, see to the working party." Agradates had never seen or met a king, but he was sure of one thing, when a king gave orders they were to be obeyed. At least that was always how it was in their King Game.

Fravarti, also ten, was the son of Artembares, a nobleman from Ecbatana, whom King Cyaxares, King of Media, had sent to the village to take a census of people and cattle. Artembares had decided it would be a good learning experience for his son Fravarti to accompany him. But two days of the census had been more than enough learning for Fravarti, and he decided to play with the village children today. Agradates knew little about Fravarti, and that made him nervous. Fravarti's father was rich and powerful, and he reminded the boys of this constantly. Agradates had grown up with and knew the village children, but this boy was not to be trusted; Agradates knew thin instinctually.

"I know we elected you king, Agradates," said Fravarti, "but you must remember I am the son of a nobleman, and I do not take orders from a cowherd."

Agradates studied the boy. "I understand, Fravarti. You and the other boys elected me king for the day, and if you have changed your mind and would rather not play the game with the children of cowherds, you may go to your father."

Agradates was good at reading people.

"Very well, you are king, but remember: when you speak to me, you are speaking to a nobleman." Fravarti pointed to five boys. "You boys, gather limbs and grasses to build a castle. We will build in the center of the clearing." He pointed to a flat spot.

The boys gathered limbs and grasses, and in short order, a modest hut stood in the center of the clearing.

Agradates reviewed the castle, inspecting it inside and out, and pronounced it, "Excellent."

"Men, we have a castle to protect us from the weather and our enemies, but we have nothing to eat," Agradates stated as regally as possible. "Gather your weapons. It's time to hunt."

The boys cheered loudly. This was their favorite part of the game. The younger boys all had slings and stones. They formed a group and would hunt hares and birds. Agradates and the older boys picked up spears. They would hunt a Carpathian wild boar, a dangerous animal— usually weighing more than 300 pounds—with large tusks.

"What of me?" demanded Fravarti. "I do not have a weapon."

"Have you hunted with a sling before?" asked Agradates.

"Of course not. Noblemen do not use slings. We train with swords and spears."

"Have you hunted boar before?"

"No, but I have hunted tigers with my father. I'm sure a boar will be little trouble compared to a tiger."

Agradates looked at Fravarti's hands, they were small and soft. This boy's hands never handled a spear, but Agradates did not want to shame him in front of the other boys. He pointed at one of the boys. "Give him your spear. You are a beater today."

The boy looked down at his spear, hesitated, and finally gave it to Fravarti.

The two groups split up, and the older boys crossed the clearing and entered the woods to the south. The forest was not dense, but it had areas of thick undergrowth. The boars would lay in the thickets during the day and hunt for food at night. The boys needed no instruction. They spread out and formed a large circle. When everyone was in place, they began to walk toward the circle's center, yelling and banging their spears against nearby trees. Fravarti walked to Agradates's right.

A large hare jumped out of a thicket and raced at Fravarti, and he jumped but never raised his spear. The boy's eyes were wide; he was pale and sweating. He had never hunted before. Agradates moved closer to Fravarti to protect him. They continued walking, and the circle narrowed.

The boys were now slightly hunched over with their spears pointing forward and leveled. They stepped forward with their left foot and kept their right foot planted and pointing outward. They were bracing themselves. They then dragged their right foot forward and stepped with the left again. When the boar broke cover, they would have little time to react. Everyone was tense and ready.

Fravarti imitated the other boy's motions. Agradates was

pleased, the nobleman's son was learning.

The boar broke cover one hundred feet in front of them and ran full speed in three steps. The animal was running at a boy to Agradates's left. The boy dropped to one knee, planted the butt of his spear in the dirt, and prepared to receive the boar's charge.

Suddenly the noble Fravarti threw down his spear and ran from the racing boar. The boar saw the motion and turned and chased the fleeing boy. Agradates threw himself in front of the boar and barely had time to ground the butt of his spear. The boar ran onto the spear, and the point sunk into his chest. Agradates did not have his weight behind the spear, and all he could do was hang on and press the butt of the spear into the ground as the boar continued to grind forward. Agradates was dragged along, unable to regain his feet. The butt of the spear finally slammed against a small tree trunk, and the boar's momentum drove the spear deep into his chest, slicing his heart in two. In his death throes, his face was just inches from Agradates face, and spittle and boar blood covered Agradates's head. The other boys ran in, stabbing the boar and dragging him away from Agradates.

Agradates rose unsteadily. He was scratched but otherwise unhurt. The boys needed no instruction. They tied a rope around the boar's hind legs, hoisted him in a tree, and were bleeding him. They danced around the tree as the boar bled, ululating and cheering. The boar was dead. They were alive, and soon their bellies would be full. As the boys danced, they dipped their fingers in the boar's blood and painted stripes and circles on their faces, turning the scene macabre. Agradates did not paint his face, he never had. The hunt, the kill, and the food; that's all he needed. The others felt the need to celebrate they had survived the hunt. Agradates knew the boar would never win.

Fravarti had stopped running and was watching the wild village boys. Agradates knew Fravarti had never seen anything like this before. His eyes were wide. Agradates glared at him and pointed. "You," he yelled, "gather firewood and take it to the castle. Have a good fire going by the time we finish dressing the boar. The warriors are hungry."

Fravarti glared back. "Gather it yourself, peasant. Enough of this stupid game. You have forgotten that you are speaking to a nobleman."

Agradates yelled, "Bodyguards, arrest that man for insubordination."

Four boys designated bodyguards for the day rushed forward and grabbed Fravarti by his arms.

Agradates turned to another boy, designated as his cupbearer, and asked, "What is the punishment for insubordination, Cupbearer?"

Without hesitation, the boy answered, "Ten lashes, my King."

Agradates pulled the stock whip from his belt. The whip had a long handle and a single leather lash about three feet long. Agradates walked behind Fravarti and gave him ten firm lashes. Fravarti screamed as if he was being killed and cursed Agradates and the other boys with every lash.

"Release the prisoner," said Agradates.

Fravarti was shaking with fury as he backed away from the boys. "You will all live to regret this day," he screamed. Then he turned, ran from the forest, and raced back toward the village.

The boys finished butchering the boar and had enough meat to take to their families. They built a large fire by the castle hut, roasted a nice ham, and enjoyed the waning sun. Sated, they lay back, staring at the small white clouds forming various animal shapes in the clear blue sky. Periodically a boy would point at a cloud and name an animal or person the cloud resembled. The other boys would either agree or throw small pebbles at the speaker.

Early evening, someone called Agradates, and he sat up. Walking across the clearing was his father, Mithradates. Mithradates never came to the valley without the cattle, and Agradates knew this must be about Fravarti. His heart beat faster and his palms sweated.

His father reached the group of boys. "Come, Agradates, we need to talk."

His father suddenly looked old and tired, and Agradates's heart sank, "Yes, Father," he said, and they crossed the clearing, through the small forest, and climbed a hillock that overlooked the valley and the village.

At the top of the hillock, Mithradates stopped and scanned his world. He was a cowherd and had been all his life. He cared for the large cattle herds of Prince Astyages and the other nobles of Ecbatana. He was forty years old, and he loved his simple life. Agradates looked at his father then at the valley below and the village beyond. He looked north and saw the large herds pastured with four men surrounding the herd, keeping them safe from predators. This was his father's world, and what more could a man want? Yet he feared his actions today had changed everything.

Mithradates sat on a large rock and told Agradates to sit. "You beat the son of a nobleman today."

"Father, we played the king game, and the boys elected me king, including Fravarti. First, Fravarti almost got me killed when he ran from the boar during the hunt, and then he refused a direct order."

"He left me no choice. If I had left the insubordination go unpunished, I would have lost the respect of the other boys. Everyone knows the rules."

"Apparently, Fravarti thought he was exempt from the rules, and so does his father, Artembares, counselor to Prince Astyages and one of his closest friends. He wants you flogged or worse, but only the prince can give the order. He has commanded that you and I appear before the court in Ecbatana in one week. King Cyaxares, the prince's father, is campaigning in Lydia, but the prince will hold court."

"I understand, Father. I am sure the prince's punishment will be equitable to my offense. I am only ten years old. He may flog me, but I can accept that."

Mithradates' shoulders slumped, his head drooped, and then he looked up, "There is much you do not know, and I can hide it from you no longer. Everything will come out in Ecbatana. Have you ever wondered why you do not look like your mother or me?"

"I never thought about it, Father. I just thought I must look like my grandfather."

"You do not. You do not look like us because I am not your father."

Agradates jumped up and took a step back. "What are you saying? You are my father. I am your son...I am your son. I have never known anyone other than you and mother." Agradates closed his eyes and put his hands over his ears. He did not want to hear anymore. He did not want to look at the man who was the only father he had ever known, telling him he was not his son. His head spun, and his legs felt weak.

Mithradates stood and took Agradates hands away from his ears. "You will have to be brave, son. I am about to tell you things that will shake your foundations, but you must know all this before we get to Ecbatana. Please sit. Let me finish the whole story, and then you can ask questions. Everything I am about to tell you is the truth. I swear on my life and the life of your mother."

The man and the boy sat, and Mithradates told the story that had happened eleven years before:
• •

8

Prince Astyages 601 Bc

"Prince Astyages awoke in a cold sweat. This was the third night in a row he had the same dream. This was no simple dream. It was a message from his god Ahura Mazda. He called for his servants and told them to bring the magi.

Two magi entered the prince's bed-chamber, and the prince told them about his dream. 'I dreamed that water poured from my daughter Mandana and flooded Ecbatana before going on to flood all of Asia.'

The two magi conferred for a moment. One stepped forward and said, 'Your dream is significant. It means your daughter will rule over your kingdom and all of Asia, not you.'

'Are you sure? There can be no mistake,' said the prince.

'There is no mistake, my prince. Your daughter will rule.'

'You may leave,' the prince said, pacing his bed-chamber for the rest of the night. He dearly loved his daughter, but he had no intention of letting his kingdom slip from his hands. Mandana was of age, and he had intended to marry her to one of the strong Median noble houses, possibly to his friend and counselor, Artembares, but that was out of the question now. He could not take the chance that one of his Median nobles would supplant him. He could not bring himself to kill his daughter, but she could not marry a Mede. In the morning, he called for his counselor, Artembares, to discuss the situation.

The prince dressed and went to the Throne Room; Artembares was there.

Artembares smiled at the prince. 'How may I serve you this morning?' he asked.

'I have a problem, Artembares, and I need your advice.' The prince explained his dream and dilemma.

Artembares mulled the information and issue, then spoke. 'There is one who comes to mind. Cyrus, King of Anshan, is a king but is mild-mannered and weak. Cyrus is the leader of the Pasargadae tribe, the largest in Persis. He has a son named Cambyses, who is also mild-mannered. They appear to have no political ambition. Your daughter would marry royalty but would not be a future threat to your kingdom, since her children will be half Persian.'

Prince Astyages smiled at his friend. 'Excellent, I knew I could rely on you. Would you take care of arranging everything?'

'It would be my pleasure, my Prince.'

Artembares was as good as his word. Cambyses was summoned to Ecbatana, married Mandana, and took his new bride home to Anshan in the southwest Zagros Mountains. Problem solved.

Three months after the marriage, messengers informed Astyages that Mandana was expecting a child, and the prince was delighted. Several months later, the prince dreamed again and summoned the magi.

The same magi, plus their leader, entered the prince's chamber, and the prince told his dream. 'I dreamed last night that a vine grew from Mandana's womb and filled all of Asia. What is the meaning of this dream?'

The three magi conferred for a considerable time before the aged leader of the Ecbatana magi stepped forward. 'This is the same dream as your previous dream, my Prince. The son of Mandana will rule your kingdom and all of Asia, not you.'

In the morning, the prince summoned Artembares. He explained the dream and interpretation and instructed him to go to Anshan and bring his daughter back to Ecbatana. He was to tell her that her father wanted the Royal Physicians to attend her, not some midwife in Anshan.

Once again, his faithful friend carried out his duties, and late in her pregnancy, Mandana arrived in Ecbatana.

The time came, Mandana birthed a healthy baby boy, and Astyages called for his most trusted and loyal staff member, his cousin Harpagus. No one could ever know what he was about to do. What Astyages required now would take someone of total loyalty.

'My Prince, the hour is late. What is so important it couldn't wait till morning?' Harpagus asked as he entered the prince's bed-chamber.

'Harpagus, Mandana has borne a son.'

'Congratulations, Prince Astyages. I'm glad you didn't wait till morning to share such wonderful news.'

'I am ordering you to do something, Harpagus, and you may never speak of it. If you ever share what I am about to tell you, I will execute you. Do you understand?'

Harpagus's features showed nothing, but he began to sweat lightly. 'I understand, my Prince. What do you require?'

'You live a little over a day's ride from the Capital, Harpagus. That should be far enough away. I need you to take Mandana's child to your home, kill him, and bury him secretly. No one must know what you have done.'

This time, Harpagus could not keep the shock from his face. 'My Prince, I will do whatever you command, but he is your firstborn grandson and the heir to the Anshan throne. You want me to kill him?'

'Harpagus, the child is a threat to the Median throne. You will have to take my word for this. Yes, you are to take him, kill him in the middle of the night, and personally bury him.'"

Mithradates – 590 Bc

Mithradates placed his hand on his son's shoulder. "You were that child, Agradates. When Harpagus got home, what the prince required him to do mortified his wife. Harpagus could not bring himself to kill you, so he called for me. He ordered me to bring you to the village and leave you in the woods to die from either animals or exposure. Your mother, Cyno, was also pregnant, and when I arrived home, I found her mourning. While I was away, our son was stillborn. When I showed you to her and explained what Harpagus required me to do, she snatched you out of my arms and began breastfeeding you. She told me to take our stillborn son into the woods and leave him."

"You didn't bury your son? How could you do that?" asked Agradates.

"It was the hardest thing I have ever done in my life. I left my son in the woods lying on a rock. I sat there for hours mourning him and finally went home. Two days later, one of Harpagus's eunuchs came to the village demanding to see the dead body of Mandana's son. I took him to the rock. The body was there, but animals had eaten the baby's face, and he was unrecognizable. The eunuch was satisfied and reported to Harpagus that he had seen the body."

"I don't understand the problem, Father. Everyone thinks Mandana's son is dead. Why are you worried?"

"We will have to stand before the prince next week, and he will see you for the first time.

"When the prince sees your high cheekbones and piercing black eyes, he will know who you are. You are an exact image of him and his daughter, the same age as his supposedly dead grandson. No, when we get to Ecbatana, the prince will not think about the beating Fravarti received. He will take one look at you and be furious or terrified or both. If I thought we could run, I would try, but he would find us. We have no choice. We must face him in Ecbatana."

"Have faith, Father. I do not believe the prince will see me as a threat anymore. It has been ten years, and his kingdom is still intact."

"I pray you are right, Agradates. I could not bear to lose you."

Agradates also prayed that he was right. His world was hanging by a thread. He understood that his life and the lives of his parents lay in the hands of Prince Astyages who had once condemned him to death.

◆ ◆ ◆

A week later, man and boy approached the city of Ecbatana on their shaggy herding ponies. Seven massive walls ringed the city, each taller than the previous as the cowherds moved inward. The first wall was white, then black, scarlet, blue, orange, silver, and a golden wall surrounded the King's Palace. *How could people build such things?* Behind the magnificent city, a major stop for Asian-bound caravans, the Zagros Mountains rose. Agradates's eyes could not stop moving. There was too much to see. Agradates and his father entered the city, and the noise assaulted their ears. Various souks filled the city, selling every type of food and spice from hundreds of miles around. Agradates did not recognize many of the languages spoken. He and his father rode by other souks selling gold, jewelry, weapons, clothing, rugs, and furniture. It was a cacophony of sounds, and strange new odors permeated the air.

"I had no idea the city would be anything as grand as this, Father."

"I know," replied Mithradates. "I have worked hard to keep you away from the city. I have never wanted to take the chance of the prince or king seeing you. Royalty marries royalty, son, and many of the features of a royal family – eyes, cheekbones, eyebrows, ear shape, etc. are peculiar to the royal family. Your facial features are easily recognizable by those in the king's family."

"Is King Cyaxares still away on the campaign?" Agradates asked.

"I wish he were here. I am sure he has no idea the prince attempted to kill you at your birth. Unfortunately, only the prince is here."

They rode through the golden gate and entered the palace grounds. They tied their horses to a rail and walked to the Throne Room.

A guard stopped them and eyed their peasant clothing warily. "What business do you have with the prince?"

"I am Mithradates, and this is my son Agradates, the nobleman, Artembares, has summoned us," Mithradates stated.

The guard turned to the clerk, who scanned his list of appointments and nodded at the guard. The guard raised his spear and let them pass.

The man and the boy entered the Throne Room, which was full

of petitioners. and Mithradates stood silently in the back, head down as the morning passed, attempting to be as inconspicuous as possible. The Chief Counselor called their names just before noon, and the two strode forward and bowed to the prince.

The prince called the nobleman Artembares and his son forward. Artembares pointed at Agradates. "This slave, my Prince, dared to raise his hand to my son." Artembares turned his son so everyone in the room could see and bared his shoulders to reveal the welts that remained. A shocked gasp filled the room.

"Did you, the lowly son of this man," the prince said, nodding at Mithradates, "dare to raise your hand to the son of a nobleman of this court?"

"My Lord," replied Agradates, "I only treated him as he deserved. I was chosen king in a game by the boys of our village because they thought I was the best for the role. Fravarti was one of the boys who chose me. The others followed my orders, but he refused and made fun of them until he finally got his due reward. If I deserve to suffer punishment for this, here I am, ready to submit to it."[1]

Prince Astyages leaned back; eyes narrowed. The response was too elegant, the boy too composed for a simple village slave boy. He studied the boy carefully, the raised cheekbones, the deep black eyes. His aid had told him the boy was ten. Was it possible? The room was eerily quiet as the prince stared at the boy for more than five minutes.

The prince jerked upright. "Clear the room. I would speak to this man and boy alone."

Artembares protested, but the prince held his hand up. "Have no fear, my friend. I assure you I will deal with this matter."

Artembares bowed and left the room.

Red-faced, the prince rose and pointed at Mithradates. "Where did you get this boy? This is not your son. Who gave him to you?"

Mithradates wrung his hands. "My Prince. This is my son, born to my wife Cyno and me ten years ago. He is my flesh and blood."

"Do you take me for a fool?" the prince screamed, and he pointed to his guards. "Question him until he admits who gave him the boy."

The guards grabbed Mithradates and began to drag him away.

"Stop, stop," yelled Mithradates, "I will tell you the whole story." And so, he did, revealing that he had received the boy from Harpagus, who had instructed him to leave the boy in the woods to die. He told of his stillborn child and his wife's desire to switch the two babies, which they did.

"Easy enough to confirm this story," said the prince, and he called for his aid to bring in Harpagus.

Harpagus entered the Throne room and took in the scene before him. He saw Mithradates's bowed head and a boy standing beside him, erect and proud. He studied the boy carefully, noting the high cheekbones and black eyes, and he turned pale.

"Mithradates has been telling me an interesting story about how you gave him a child to kill ten years ago," the prince said calmly.

Harpagus said, "That is true, my Prince. I could not bring myself to kill the child and gave him to Mithradates to leave in the woods. I sent my eunuch to verify the boy's death, and he found the partially devoured remains of a baby in the woods. I had no reason to believe that the boy was not dead."

Prince Astyages pointed at the boy. "Does that look like the child of a peasant to you?"

"Clearly not, my Prince. He could be none other than your grandson."

The prince stood. "This is my decision. Mithradates, you failed to follow the commands given you by a noble, but in so doing, were used by fate to save my grandson. Therefore, you may live. You are no longer in my employ. Return to the village, gather your wife and leave. You may go where you will. The boy will remain with me. Harpagus, you attempted to carry out my commands, but not in the manner prescribed. Your failure has led to my grandson's preservation, so I will honor you at a banquet tonight, which I will hold, celebrating the return of Agradates."

Agradates's father and Harpagus backed from the chamber, and Prince Astyages commanded an aid to groom Agradates and dress him, befitting a prince of Media.

The prince had not yet settled the matter in his mind, and he called for the magi. Once again, the same three magi appeared before him. The prince related Mithradates's story and the event Agradates had described, and the magi consulted.

The elder magi stated, "Events in dreams often have various outcomes. We believe the kingship-play the boy was involved in was the act that your dream revealed. We believe the boy is not a threat to you, and if you relegate him to the backwoods of Persis, you will hear from him no more."

The prince studied the three magi for a moment. "Make sure this time, magi. All of our fates are bound up in your interpretation."

The threat was clear to the magi, and they conferred again. "My prince," said the elder magi, "we are sure of our interpretation, and we stand behind it. The boy is not a threat."

Cyrus – 590 Bc

Two days after the banquet, Agradates, dressed in princely clothes, riding a coal-black Arabian stallion, and surrounded by a troop of Median cavalry, traveled southeast through the Zagros Mountains. Riding next to him was the captain of the guard, Diomede. Agradates had never been this far from home, and he had no idea where he was going or what would become of him. He would never see his mother and father again, never see his friends. No one had told him anything. He was lost and alone.

"Where are we going, Diomede?" asked Agradates.

"Has no one told you anything?" the old soldier asked.

Agradates shrugged. "I will tell you what I know. We are going to Anshan, the capital of Persis. You are the heir to the throne of Anshan."

Agradates felt speechless.

"The King of Anshan is Cyrus I, your grandfather," the captain explained. "His son, Prince Cambyses, married your mother Mandana, the daughter of Prince Astyages, whom you met. He is the son of King Cyaxares and is heir to the Median throne."

"What is Persis?" asked Agradates.

"Persis is a vassal of Media," the captain said. "It is comprised of three primary tribes and several smaller tribes. Your grandfather leads the largest tribe, the Pasargadae, and is the king of the capital city of the Pasargadae, Anshan. Your father, Cambyses, is heir to the throne of Anshan!"

Agradates was silent for the next mile as they rode. "Who named me Agradates? And if Agradates is not my real name, what is my name? I don't know who or what I am, Captain Diomede. One moment I was the son of Mithradates and Cyno. I was a villager, a slave of King Cyaxares, and a cowherd. Herding cattle is all I know. I cannot read or write, and I have no formal training. How am I suddenly becoming the king's son and heir to a throne? This makes no sense."

"I understand your confusion," the old warrior said, "your old world and your new world couldn't be more different. Fortunately, you are young. There will be people to train you. You will learn to be a king. I know it is not my place to say, Prince, but your humble beginnings may make you a special kind of ruler. You will understand how the people you rule live and how they feel. You will look at them differently than most kings. Your first ten years may turn out to be your greatest blessing."

"I hope you are right, Captain. Right now, I just feel empty and lost. I wonder how my parents feel about my sudden reappearing?"

"I need to prepare you, Agradates," the captain said. He looked uncomfortable. "Your parents do not know you are alive. Prince Astyages did not send a messenger ahead of us. I am to tell them what has happened when I arrive."

"Are you going to tell them my grandfather ordered my death, and only fate spared me?" the boy said angrily.

"Listen to me carefully, Agradates. One of the midwives serving your mother substituted her sister's stillborn child for you, which is why everyone thought you had died. The midwife's sister was Cyno. The rest of the story will remain the same. Do you understand me? Mithradates and Cyno's lives depend upon you supporting this story. Can you do that?"

"You want me to lie?" Agradates said furiously.

"I want you to protect the man and the woman who saved and raised you. Your parents' lives will end horribly if the true story emerges. It will be a slow, painful death. Do you understand?"

They rode in silence as Agradates struggled to control his emotions. "I understand. My silence is a small price to pay for their safety."

The trip to Anshan from Ecbatana was a little more than 560 miles. The weather was mild, and they had no delays along the way. Agradates had never been in the mountains, so everything was new and wonderful to him. He studied the terrain, the animals and flowers, trees, and scrub brush, recording everything in his mind. They completed the journey in 11 days.

Agradates saw the city walls, built on a mound almost 200 feet high. The walls were 40 feet high, made of stone, and had a circumference of approximately 5 miles. The architecture was plain and simple, the effect being nothing like the impression Ecbatana made. The city gates stood open, as the guards had recognized the standard carried by the Medes.

Agradates and his escort entered the city, stopped in front of the palace, and entered the throne room. King Cyrus I was seated on his throne, and standing below the dais with his wife, Mandana, was Prince Cambyses I.

Captain Diomede and Agradates bowed and waited for King Cyrus to address them.

"Who represents Media?" the king asked.

"I do, King Cyrus. I am Diomede, Captain of the King's Guard. Prince Astyages sends his greetings and best wishes to you, and I bear a message for Prince Cambyses and Princess Mandana. I bear good news for the prince and princess."

"What new is that?" asked the king, "And who is this young man with you."

"He is the 'good new,'" said Diomede, "this day I am bringing your son, Prince Cambyses, and Princess Mandana, whom you believed to be dead. The boy standing with me is your son. Prince Astyages has verified the truthfulness of this attestation through various means. The boy was named Agradates by his false parents and was unaware of the circumstances of his birth until two weeks ago."

Everyone stood as if in a frozen tableau, and the throne room was silent for several moments.

The princess was the first to speak. "But how? How can this be?"

"I will make the explanation as brief as possible. One of the midwives who attended you switched the baby with her sister's stillborn child. The midwife died several years ago, and she alone knew the child's identity. The midwife's sister, Cyno, was married to a cowherd named Mithradates. They were unaware of the child's identity and raised him as a slave for the past ten years. Only through an act of fate was the boy brought in contact with Prince Astyages, and the prince recognized his royal lineage immediately."

The princess looked at the boy, the high cheekbones, the piercing black eyes, the erect carriage. She rushed to him and threw her arms around him, her tears wetting his hair.

She stepped back and held him at arm's length. "I am your mother, Mandana, and you are Cyrus II, named after your grandfather," she said, nodding toward the throne.

It was too sudden and confusing for the boy. "But I am Agradates. I have been Agradates my entire life. Why can I not keep my name?"

Prince Cambyses joined his wife. "Agradates is a slave name. You are in the line of succession to the throne of Persis. You must bear a name befitting a king. Your name is Cyrus."

King Cyrus rose and addressed his aid. "Sound the trumpets and raise a flag on the battlements. We have found Prince Cambyses's son and heir. We will hold a feast for the city for the next three days. Prepare everything. Send notices throughout all of Persis. Prince Cyrus is home."

Agradates looked at the king and his parents. *They may change my name, but they will be greatly disappointed when they discover I don't know how to be a king.*

Magi Camp – Day 87

Rahim rolled up the scroll. The scent from the river was still heavy, even this late in the day. "Tomorrow will be exciting; you will all need to be well-rested. You are dismissed."

Parents gathered their children and headed to their tents for the night.

BABYLON

Magi Camp – Euphrates River – Day 89

Fardad, the leader, sat in the Council Tent, surrounded by the other members of the Family Council. He was almost sixty, with a gray beard and a large hooked nose. Next to him sat his son, Jahan, a bear of a man who headed the Family's school and daily operations, second in command to his father.

To Jahan's right was Ram, responsible for the Family's animal husbandry, flocks of goats and sheep, and herds of horses, mules, and camels. Next in the circle was Kevan, a few years older than Jahan and leader of Military training. Then came Marzban, Kevan's son and understudy to his father.

Rahim sat to Marzban's right, responsible for teaching the Family's children. He was tall, slender, and had soft brown eyes. The last Council member was Navid, the youngest Council member at eighteen. Navid was the son of Jahan, extremely bright and mature for his age, and the leader of the Scouts. Next to Navid lay an empty cushion immediately to Fardad's left.

Fardad patted the empty cushion. "It has been many years since the Council has lost a member, but one of our own, my son, Sasan, sacrificed his life to save Navid. He was lost to us for many years as he pursued fame and power, but he returned to his family and faith. He willingly laid down his life for his nephew, and there is nothing more pleasing to God. His selfless act saved the life of Navid."

"I owe him my life," said Navid. "The storm's noise was so loud I did not hear Khalil sneak into the tent. I would have been defenseless if Sasan had not shouted. I am proud that he was my uncle. I will always honor his memory."

"Jahan, will you open the Council with prayer?" Fardad asked.

"We come before you, Jehovah God, and recognize You as Creator, Sustainer, and Redeemer. You have brought us far, and we still have far to go before finishing our journey. We have lost Family members from betrayal and death, but you have preserved us from every threat. Great is your faithfulness, Father. You have called us to worship your Son, the Messiah, the Redeemer of mankind. What a privilege and honor, Father. We seek your wisdom and guidance today as we seek to lead the Family safely to Jerusalem. Lead us, guide us, and protect us. We thank you that Sasan is safely in your arms, as are the other Family members who gave up their lives in Your service. Thank you, Father. We will see them again. Amen."

The whole Council responded, "Amen."

"I talked to several other 'older' members of the Family last evening," said Fardad, "and they recalled that when Israel returned to Jerusalem at the end of the Babylonian captivity, they followed the Euphrates River as far as they could. There is a bend where the river turns to the north. The Israelites turned west and proceeded a short distance to Aleppo at that bend. At Aleppo, they turned south and followed the coast to Israel. I recommend we follow this route."

Jahan replied, "I agree, Father. We made the mistake of following a guide we did not know, and we will not make that mistake again. If we follow the river, we will have water and grazing and not get lost."

"Is there any other discussion?" asked Fardad.

"I agree with you both," said Navid. "As soon as we finish, I will lead the Scouts north and begin looking for potential issues."

"Are you sure you can ride?" asked his father Jahan. "The slave traders gave you quite a beating over the past week. The whip marks on your back have not healed."

Navid smiled at his father. "Father, have you forgotten Mother's secret poultice? She doctored me last night. Unfortunately, that stuff stinks so bad, that Ava almost refused to sleep with me."

"I've had that poultice more than once," said Jahan. "I smelled so bad the dog ran away. Don't push today, Navid; it's more important you heal."

Fardad scanned the Council. "Are we in agreement on the route?"

Everyone responded *aye*, and the men rose and left.

Fardad walked next to Jahan as they left and said softly, "Keep a close eye on Navid, Jahan. He has been through a horrible ordeal, and I fear seeing Sasan murdered will haunt him."

Jahan nodded, and the two men separated.

Navid walked to the corral, and the Scouts were there. They had tacked their horses, but no one had mounted. As Navid approached, all conversation stopped.

Navid looked at the twenty-four Scouts, men he had ridden with and trained for years. They were the best of the best, known for their tracking, stealth, and combat skills. Many tested to be a Scout, but few could pass the tests.

"Well, what do we have here?" asked Navid.

Tiz said, "The men wanted the details on what happened in the desert, and I told them to wait for you so that we could do this once."

24

"Good idea. Let's discuss this once, and then we'll not discuss it again. Why don't you begin?"

"The first part you already know," Tiz reported to Navid in front of the whole group. "The slave traders captured you, Utana, Nura, and five others. I picked eight Scouts and Sasan to form a rescue party. Your sister, Fahnik, refused to be left behind, and she joined us carrying Baildan's ancient sword."

"How could father have let her go?" asked Navid.

"There was no stopping her, and he knew it. He had Smithy stay up all night modifying the sword for her."

"I thought it looked different."

"For brevity, I will condense things," Tiz said. "Sasan did all of the planning, B and Hugav did all the tracking and scouting, and I executed Sasan's plans. We focused Days One and Two on eliminating outriders and killing their guards at night. The slavers responded by sending out a party to hunt us, which we eliminated, and the next morning we burned the tents of the slavers. Through death and desertion, after four days, the slave traders had decreased from 200 to around 60."

"How did you know the slaver trader's numbers?" asked Navid.

"Hugav scouted the camp on Day Five and had a pretty accurate count. As expected, on the evening of Day Five, a massive sandstorm formed west of the slave-trader camp."

"What do you mean, 'as expected?'" asked a Scout.

"Before I left, I asked Pari to pray for a sandstorm in five days. I knew we would need a diversion and cover when we attacked. What we got was not what I expected. The storm was massive, and without hesitation, the men rode straight into the teeth of that storm. It was supernatural. After we entered the slaver camp, the storm surrounded the camp, but within it was calm. Fahnik went to the slave pen and freed the prisoners. The rest of us fought the slave traders. They attempted to surrender, but the freed slaves killed any still alive."

"Fahnik didn't just free us," said Utana, "she killed the blacksmith. We needed tools to get the chains off, so Fahnik went to the blacksmith shop. The smithy was there, and he was huge. He used a long-handled sledgehammer, but Fahnik was so fast he couldn't hit her. Finally, he tried to grab her, and she cut off his hand. She continued to dance around him. She got behind him, jumped up, and cut his head off. She cut off his head."

Utana stood there shaking his head from side to side in bewilderment, "How did she do that? I couldn't have done that. One blow."

"I think that covers our events," said Tiz. "Now tell us what happened to you, Navid and Utana."

"You all saw the capture," said Navid. "And things were extremely uncomfortable in captivity. Six of us, including Utana and me, were kept in the slave pens and targeted to be slaves on rowing ships when we reached Sidon. Fortunately, they kept Nura and Hayat with the slaves destined for harem duty and treated them well. My hatred of Khalil and Sheikh Malek grew daily, and I became angrier and angrier. Then on Days Four and Five, I was chained to a slave named Liyana, a Zulu from southern Africa. Some of you have met her. I mentioned the Messiah, and she wanted to know all about Him. I spent the next two days explaining the Scriptures to her, and I was no longer angry. I remembered the Psalm: 'Be angry, and do not sin, ponder in your own hearts on your beds, and be silent.'"[2]

"How could your anger have gone away? If they had beaten me, as they did you, I would have been furious," said one of the Scouts.

Navid smiled. "God brought to my mind His prophets, who had suffered much in His service, and I realized God was using me. What right did I have to be angry? Then, as Tiz said, there was a supernatural sandstorm on the evening of Day Five. I looked east and saw the Magi riding toward the camp. I looked to the heavens and felt total peace. I felt the Spirit of God moving within me. I reached down, grabbed my chains, and pulled them apart. I don't know how I did that. You know the rest of the story—we killed Sheikh Malek and Khalil, and now we are together again."

"He pulled the chains apart," mumbled Utana. "He pulled them apart as if they were a single strand of hair. He pulled them apart. Then Fahnik cut off a man's head, and I sat there helpless. I did nothing."

Navid walked over and put his arm around Utana. The other Scouts mounted and left the corral.

"Utana, God chooses whom He will. We do not choose: He does. You have nothing of which to be ashamed, and I have nothing about which to brag. God was working, and He accomplished His will."

"Still, I wish He had chosen me to do something."

"He did, Utana. You gave me courage. He used your kind heart and strength to inspire me. All I could think about was saving you and freeing the others. We all played a role, my friend."

The family gathered for the evening meal and kept an empty cushion where Sasan would have sat. Fardad led the family in prayer, Jahan and his wife Asha, with their three children, Navid, Pari, and Fahnik, and their respective spouses, Ava, Tiz, and Utana, along with Pari and Tiz's adopted son, Nura, were all there. The family's servant, Gul, ate with them, and tonight, Liyana joined the family for the first time. The family was together again.

"Navid, please introduce Liyana," said Fardad.

"Everyone, this is Liyana. She asked if she could join us on our journey to find the Messiah. And who knows, she may decide to join the Magi Family. Liyana and I were chained together for two days, and I had a chance to share Scripture with her and tell her about the Messiah. Liyana is from a tribe named Zulu in southern Africa and has no way to get back to her home. She does not speak Farsi, but she understands Aramaic. Perhaps Nura would agree to help teach her Farsi?"

Nura smiled at Liyana. "Nura," he said in Farsi, pointing to himself. "Pari, Tiz, Asha, bowl, goat stew…"

Navid laughed. "Nura, maybe you want to wait till tomorrow to begin your lessons."

Nura smiled at Liyana again and said in Aramaic, "We will begin our lessons tomorrow."

"Thank you, Nura," said Liyana, smiling at the boy and patting his head.

"What did you find today, Navid?" Jahan asked.

"We scouted the river for thirty miles. There is a cliff for the first ten miles, then it falls off, and for the next five miles, there is a flood plain that is dry now but has thick scrub brush and forage. Shale deposits in some places will make for firm travel; the rest is sand, and there is little grazing until we reach the flood plain. We will mark a trail across the flood plain tomorrow to avoid any bogs we find. We talked to a shepherd we met, and he told us the ancient city of Mari is about a week from here, and there are traders there."

"Our supplies are in good shape since we replenished at Ctesiphon," said Asha, "but we will top off anything we can. After Mari, there will be no large cities until we reach the coast."

"Excellent, Navid," said Fardad. "We will rely on your judgment to get us to Mari safely."

"Who is teaching tonight, Pari?" Tiz asked.

"Rahim is teaching tonight on the Babylonian captivity. There's not much action in this lesson, but I'm sure Rahim will find some way to keep the children's attention," said Pari.

Her son Nura piped up, "I haven't heard the story before. I love all of Rahim's stories. I'm sure I will love it."

Pari smiled at him. "I'm sure you will love it, Nura. You are an excellent student."

Nura puffed out his chest and beamed at everyone seated around the circle. Nura loved praise. When the meal finished, Tiz picked up Pari and carried her to the clearing for the evening's lesson.

Again, Rahim stood on the teaching platform and gazed out at the children. They had left Persepolis, Persia, 89 days ago, and he and Pari had taught almost every evening of the trip. Rahim wanted to teach the history of Israel from the time of the Prophet Isaiah to the release of Israel from Babylonian captivity, to cover it all by the time the Family reached Israel. He thought it was important that the children understand what the Scriptures taught about the Messiah and redemption. It would take another eighty days to reach Jerusalem, leaving him plenty of time to finish the lessons.

"Good evening, children," Rahim began. "This is the first lesson since the return of Navid and the other people the slave traders captured. First, I want to greet Liyana, the newest member of our Family." He nodded at Liyana. "Tonight, I want you to ask any questions about what happened during the past week or tell us how you feel about the things that happened."

One of the children stood. "I want to ask Navid if the slave traders hurt him?"

Navid stood. "The slave traders are not like anyone you have ever met. Their minds are twisted, and they are cruel. They beat all of us, except Hayat and Nura, thankfully." Navid turned his back to the children and lowered the top of his robe. There was an audible intake of breath from the children.

"It looks worse than it is," said Navid. "We all survived, which is more than I can say for the slave traders."

"Those are whip marks on Navid's back. We would not treat an animal the way the slave traders treat people," Rahim said. "Are there other comments or questions?"

A young boy stood. "I would like a pony like Nura's. Would Pari pray for one? God gives her everything for which she prays."

"I'll take that one, Rahim," Pari said. "Children, we need to talk about prayer. God doesn't give me things. He answers prayers that fit His purpose and will. God gives only good things. I prayed for God to save us from the Immortals when they attacked, and he saved the

Immortals and us. It was a wonderful answer to my prayer, but not one I expected. Then we all prayed for a sandstorm to help the Scouts when they attacked the slave traders. Again, God answered that prayer, and in this case, he used the Scouts to bring judgment on the slave traders. They all perished."

"Are you saying God does not answer every prayer, Pari?" asked Rahim.

"There are two parts to that question, Rahim. God tells us that first, we must confess our sins and seek Him, and then he will hear our prayers. God hears only the prayers of those who seek Him and seek to be obedient. Proverbs says, 'If one turns away his ear from hearing the law, even his prayer is an abomination.' And Isaiah says, 'When you spread out your hands, I will hide my eyes from you; even though you make many prayers, I will not listen; your hands are full of blood.' The second part of the question is, does He answer every prayer? Yes, but perfectly, and the answer may not be immediately clear to us." Pari looked at the boy who had asked the question. "What if you asked God for a sword like the one Tiz carries, and you did not get it? Does that mean God didn't answer your prayer?"

"If I really wanted that sword, God did not answer my prayer," the boy said.

"What if God loved you so much, and He knew that because you are too young if He gave you that sword, you would injure yourself or someone else? Which would be the more loving thing to do, give you the sword, or wait and give it to you when you are ready?"

The boy nodded in understanding. "Is it all right if I pray for a pony?"

"It is fine if you ask God earnestly for something you want," said Rahim, "and then wait on Him. You accept that He loves you; that's why you went to Him, and then you wait for Him to answer your prayer in His perfect way. Before Fardad's wife died, he and I prayed on our knees night and day for God to deliver her from her illness. After five days of praying, she died. The answer to our prayer was that God took her home to Paradise. We wanted to keep her here, to see her healed, but God chose the best thing for her, and He took her. We mourned our loss. Fardad is lonely without her, but we thanked God for His love and perfect wisdom. That is what it means to pray. Are there any other questions?"

One of the older girls stood. "Did Fahnik really cut off a man's head?"

Rahim saw Fahnik stand and leave the clearing. She was crying.

Rahim waited until she was out of sight, then continued. "There are some questions that we do not ask. Combat is a horrible thing. To take another person's life, regardless of how evil the person may be, leaves a scar. It's not a scar other people can see. It's deep inside the person's heart. Fahnik and the others who raided the slave trader camp do not want to talk about what they did. If they want to talk about it, it will be with people close to them. If they don't bring it up, then do not ask."

Rahim scanned the clearing, and there were no more questions.

"In a previous lesson, we talked about the fall of Jerusalem and the destruction of the city and the Temple. Tonight, our lesson begins after Jerusalem fell and the Babylonians took the Israelites into captivity to Babylon." Rahim opened the ancient scroll and began to read....

Babylon – Magi Compound – 586 Bc

Davi was thirty-eight and had been head of the Magi school outside Babylon for the past three years. His father, Natan, had been the Babylonian ambassador to Judah and had sent Davi, his sister, and his mother to Babylon before the siege of Jerusalem began. Natan had survived the siege and had decided not to stay in Babylon but had taken his wife and daughter to the Magi school in Persepolis, Persia a few weeks ago.

Today, Davi was copying some of the older Family scrolls. The Family had begun recording the history of Judah, Assyria, and Babylonia almost 150 years ago. Every month, Davi reviewed the scrolls kept in storage and copied any showing signs of aging. He had two assistants, who helped with the copying, but Davi still enjoyed doing some of it himself.

There was a knock on the office door, and Pera, fifty-three and with strong accents of gray in his hair and beard, came in. Pera was head of the Magi Family in Babylon. "Copying again, I see. You have helpers; why do you still copy scrolls?"

Davi smiled at Pera. "For one thing, it relaxes me, and I always find something new whenever I copy a scroll."

"You have an almost perfect memory," said Pera, "I have never seen anything like it. You remember almost everything you read."

"Almost everything," Davi admitted, "but not everything. Also, when I reread a scroll, I think about the events and what the people must have felt. My memory is like a picture. All the words are there, but I must add the emotions and the feelings.

"Today I copied the scroll of the battle at Mizpah 148 years ago. There were almost 500,000 men in that battle. Judah lost 120,000 men that day, Syria and Ephraim lost 50,000, and untold more were wounded. It was a horrible slaughter, and the battle lasted almost a day. Baildan did an excellent job describing the horror of what he saw. Reading these ancient scrolls is good; it reminds me of the importance of what I am teaching— not just facts, but important stories of real men and women."

"We are fortunate to have you, Davi. The students love your teaching, and you add wisdom to the Family Council."

"Thank you, Pera. What brings you to my humble office today?"

"We have news from Persepolis. Seena has died, and Bareil is now head of the school and Family there. He died peacefully in his sleep. Bareil said his father was fine when he went to bed, but when Bareil checked on him in the morning, his father was dead. I know this will hit your father hard. He and Seena were close."

"Will you pray with me, Pera?" Davi asked. The two men knelt in Davi's office, thanked God for Seena, and prayed for Bareil and Natan, who would now lead the Magi Family in Persepolis.

"Is there any other news from Persepolis?" Davi asked.

"The school has a new student."

"A new student doesn't seem newsworthy. They have new students all the time," said Davi.

"True, but not one named Cyrus II," answered Pera, "Cyrus's father is Prince Cambyses, and his grandfather is King Cyrus," Pera told Davi the complicated story. "Young Cyrus is starting school late, but your father said he is bright, if not a bit unusual."

"Unusual in what way?"

"A slave family raised him, cowherds located north of Ecbatana. His parents didn't raise him as a nobleman. They kept his identity from him for his safety. He has been at the court in Anshan for the past three years and has acclimated to the fact that he is nobility. However, at times his views of the nobility are not always favorable; he is torn between two worlds. He has strong empathy toward those who serve him."

"Do you think he is the Cyrus of Isaiah's prophecy?"[3]

"I am certain he is," said Pera, "His age fits the 70-year captivity prophecy of Jeremiah."[4] "Any other news?"

"Your father, mother, and sister are well and send you their love," said Pera. "Other than that, it's mostly administrative issues."

"I'm going to ride into Babylon today," said Davi. "I want to visit Daniel, check on the captives, and see how they adjust. Would you like to join me?"

"I would love to, but there are too many pressing issues today. Take your son; I'm sure he would love to get out of here for a while."

Pera left; Davi rolled up the scroll he was working on and walked home. His wife, Sarah, two years younger than her husband, tall, slender, with delicate features and light brown eyes, greeted him when he entered.

She asked about his morning, and Davi recounted what Pera had shared. They called the children, Manoah and Elka, and shared the news of Seena's passing. The four of them knelt and prayed, as Davi and Pera had earlier.

"Grandfather Natan will be lonely," said Manoah, twelve. He

looked like his forefather, Meesha, tall and slender, and was gentle and scholarly like his father.

Davi smiled. "That's the same thing Pera said. Yes, they were good friends. Father will miss him. I'm going to Babylon this afternoon. I need to see Daniel, and I want to check on the exiles. Would you like to go, Manoah?"

"I want to go, Father," said Elka, thirteen and short like her father, with coal-black hair and eyes.

"I know what she wants," said Sarah, "and it has more to do with shopping at the Souk than seeing Daniel. If you don't mind, we will all go, Davi. I am running low on spices and would like a new rug. Manoah has spilled food all over the one we have. I can't get the stains out anymore."

Davi smiled at them all. "Excellent, we will all go, and if we are blessed, Daniel will ask us to eat with him. Do you want to take a cart, or do you want to ride?"

"The cart shakes my teeth loose," said Sarah. "Elka and I will ride the mules."

They walked to the Family corral, and the grooms tacked two horses and two white mules. They mounted and rode the twenty miles to Babylon.

As they neared the city, Manoah pointed to the southwest corner and asked, "Father, what are they erecting?"

Davi did not need to look. "It is a golden image. Its head will be gold, and based on the beard and hair, it is Chaldean. In the third year of Nebuchadnezzar's reign, fifteen years ago, Daniel interpreted a dream Nebuchadnezzar had. There was an image in the dream with a head of gold, and I believe that is one reason the king is building the image. The golden head represents Babylonia. The statue is almost finished; it will be ninety feet tall when completed."

"Why would he do that, Father?" asked Elka.

"He is a foolish, arrogant man, Elka. He wants to unify his kingdom by requiring everyone to worship the image and only the image. He has forgotten that God gave him the dream, and God gave Daniel the interpretation of the dream."

"What will the king do to those who will not worship the image?" asked Manoah.

Davi looked at Sarah, who nodded her head. "He has not announced the punishment yet, but knowing the king, the sentence for disobeying will be death."

"But Father, we cannot worship the idol," said Manoah, his face reddening.

"I know, children. We cannot worship the idol, nor will Daniel, Hananiah, Mishael, or Azariah. Many hate the Jews being in power. Daniel and his friends hold four of the highest offices in the province of Babylon. They will use this as an opportunity to destroy these men and possibly us. We will get Daniel's thoughts when we talk to him today."

They rode through the city gate, and Davi closely examined the idol. At the current rate of construction, they would finish in a week. Davi dropped off Sarah and Elka at the souk, and he and Manoah continued into the city. Davi wanted to visit some of the captives before seeing Daniel. The Babylonians put some of his distant Magi relatives to work building the Military Temple. Davi rode to the work site and saw two of the men he sought. He and Manoah dismounted and approached the men. The overseer, a Jew who had come to Babylon with Daniel, intercepted them.

"What is your business here?" the overseer asked.

"I know two of those men, Kedem and Heber. I would like a word with them," Davi said.

"They are busy. They don't have time to talk."

Davi reached in his robe, took out a gold piece, and placed it in the overseer's hand.

"I suppose a short conversation won't put us too far behind," said the overseer, smiling as he turned his back and walked away.

"Kedem, how are you doing?" asked Davi.

Kedem held up his bloody hands. "I have never done work like this before, Davi. We have poor tools; we start before sunrise and work till sundown. My wife and children work for a tanner and constantly cough from the fumes they breathe. The food they feed us is barely enough to keep us alive. I don't know how long we can survive."

"Can you move us to the Magi school?" asked Heber. "When we met in Jerusalem, your father said there was a place for us."

Davi fought to keep the emotion from his voice. "I wish it were possible, Heber, but it is not. Gilad and my father warned everyone of what was coming and urged them to flee before the city fell. If you had left then, we would have been able to move you into the Family Compound. Now, you are the slave of another man, and I can't free you. But I will talk to Daniel to see if he can do anything to improve your food and conditions."

"I understand," said Kedem. "Thank you for coming to see us, and we appreciate anything you can do to help."

Davi embraced both men, then turned and walked from the construction site.

"Do you think Daniel can help the slaves?" asked Manoah.

"He is a powerful man, Manoah. He may be able to help. Why don't we ask him?"

Father and son made their way to the palace complex, where Daniel had an apartment and an office.

There was a guard outside Daniel's door, who recognized Davi and let him pass with his son. But Daniel was not there. Only his disciple Lem was there.

"Greetings, Davi and Manoah," said Lem, "Daniel will be sorry he missed you. He and the king are at the construction site of the golden image. Which, by the way, Daniel finds abhorrent, but then you already know that. But here I am prattling away. How can I help you?"

Lem was a funny little man, barely tall enough to see the top of his desk. He was joyful and talked nonstop. Every time Davi saw him, he smiled. "There are two things, Lem. I need to know more about the image. When will it be completed, and what will the king do with it?"

Lem was not smiling now. "Our enemies are at work, Davi. The king will require everyone to worship the image. The king will protect Daniel and not require him to attend the dedication, but Shadrach, Meshach, and Abednego will have to attend. Our enemies will point out that they did not worship the image."

"What will the punishment be?" asked Manoah.

"The king has commanded that anyone who does not fall and worship, will be thrown into a fiery furnace. And the king erected a furnace next to the idol to remind everyone attending of the consequences. What is the second thing you wanted to discuss?"

"I visited two exiles working on the Military Temple, and conditions are deplorable. They need tools and food; they and their families are starving. Is there anything Daniel can do?"

"Daniel has already seen the problem. The influx of exiles was sudden, and many people purchasing them were unprepared to care for them properly. Daniel will set up a commission to monitor public worksites and establish regulations requiring certain minimum standards for all builders. However, there is not much he can do for those slaves owned by individuals or private businesses. Life will not be pleasant for the slaves, but it will be better."

"One last thing," said Davi. "I hoped to eat with Daniel tonight. I have Sarah and Elka with me. Can you recommend someplace to eat?"

"There is a new inn not far from the palace. An immigrant from

India owns it. The food is a bit spicy, but it is excellent. I have eaten there twice."

"Thank you, Lem. I will stop by next week. Tell Daniel of our visit."

Davi and Manoah left, found Sarah and Elka loaded with packages, and went to find the new inn.

Magi Camp – Day 89

"Off to sleep, everyone; we begin traveling again tomorrow," said Rahim as he rolled up the ancient scroll.

NEBUCHADNEZZAR

Magi Route – Day 91

Navid rode point with Tiz and Utana, marking the route through the flood plain, looking for bogs or other issues.

"You are unusually quiet today, Utana," said Navid.

"It's nothing," said Utana. "I guess I'm still recovering from being a captive and a slave. That was an experience I never expected."

"That would have shaken anyone," agreed Tiz.

"There's more, Utana," said Navid. "Fahnik is so touchy; she takes everything I say as an attack. She's as bristly as Marzban's beard. What's going on?"

"I don't know if this is something I should talk about," said Utana.

"Utana, Tiz and I love you. Anything you say will stay between the three of us. We have all been married a short time, and we can learn from each other," said Navid.

Utana hesitated and then began. "Fahnik has been angry with me since we left the slaver's camp. She blames me for getting captured, for not breaking my chains as you did, and for almost anything else she can imagine. Then two nights ago, one of the children, during the evening lesson, asked if it was true that she had cut off a man's head. That triggered a flood of emotions. Now she doesn't want me to touch her. I'm sleeping on the other side of the yurt. I don't know what to do."

Tiz and Navid looked at each other, at a loss for words. Finally, Tiz shrugged and said, "Utana, I cannot imagine the horror of your captivity and the fear of ending as a slave on a trading ship, chained to an oar. Khalil beat and mentally abused you, leaving a scar inside you that has to heal. I think the same is true of Fahnik. All she ever wanted to be was your wife and a mother, and events turned her into a warrior. She did things she never thought possible. You don't know all of the details. The first night, she stood watch at the camp's latrine while the rest of us killed the sentries. She killed three people, including a young woman, and saw B rip out a man's throat. When the slavers sent out a search party to find us, she fought and killed a man with Baildan's sword, and when we attacked the slavers, you saw her cut off the smithy's head."

"I didn't know that," said Utana, looking shocked. "no one told me. I thought she just watched the horses. Why didn't she tell me?"

"I talked to her after that first night," said Tiz, "and I knew the killing, especially of the young woman, had shaken her. I gave her the option of not fighting anymore, but she wouldn't hear it. She said she only cared about freeing you and would do whatever it took."

"No doubt, you have identified the problem," said Navid. "The question is, how do we help her?"

"I fear that is far beyond us," said Tiz. "I think you and Utana need to talk to Fardad, Asha, and Rahim tonight. They are the wisest people I know."

Navid knew the scars he carried, and they were deeper than the whip marks on his back. But Fahnik had always been full of joy and love. Navid had never seen her utter a cross word to another person. He knew that killing another human was a burden she was not equipped to carry.

"I don't think this can wait," said Navid. "You two finish mapping the route. I am going back to the main column to find Fardad, Asha, and Rahim. Fahnik is with the flocks today, and I can talk to them without her knowing. Is that all right with you, Utana?"

Utana was visibly relieved. "That's perfect, Navid. Go, go, Tiz and I can handle this. We will see you tonight."

Navid turned his horse and galloped back to the main column. He saw his mother first and rode up to her. "Mother, where is Grandfather?"

"He's farther down the column. He decided he wanted to walk today. Why?"

"I need to talk to you, him, and Rahim. Will you meet us at Rahim's wagon?"

"Of course, but what is this all about?" asked Asha.

"I'll explain it when we are all together," said Navid. "I will bring Grandfather to Rahim's wagon."

Navid found Grandfather, and they joined his mother and Rahim in Rahim's wagon.

"What is so important that you left the Scouts in the middle of the day?" asked Fardad.

"It's about Utana and Fahnik," said Navid.

"I knew it," said Asha.

"What do you mean, 'you knew it?'" asked Navid.

Asha shook her head at him. "Do you think a mother doesn't know when one of her children is hurting?"

Navid nodded. "Of course, you would know, but you need to know the extent of the issue," Navid explained all of the things Utana and Tiz had disclosed.

"The young woman and the brutal way she killed the smithy are troubling her," said Fardad.

"Why just those two?" asked Rahim.

"The three men she killed were armed and were a threat, but the young woman she had to kill reminded her of herself. The woman was young, unarmed, possibly innocent, and her life was in front of her. Fahnik's arrow ended all of her hopes and dreams. The smithy was already dying. Fahnik had cut off his hand, and he was bleeding to death. She could have crippled him, but instead, she took out all her anger over the past week's events on the smithy. She murdered him."

Asha looked bewildered. "If all of that is true, why is she so angry at Utana?"

Rahim looked at Fardad and shook his head, understanding, "Utana is a reminder of everything that happened, and he is also her greatest joy. She doesn't believe she deserves to be happy after what she has done. She believes God is angry with her."

"What are we going to do?" asked Asha.

"We?" said Fardad. "We are going to do nothing. On the other hand, you will spend some time with your daughter. For the next few days, you will become a shepherdess. Fahnik will talk when she is ready. Your presence will be a great comfort, and she will cry out to you and God when her soul is crushed beyond bearing. You will be there, and God will tell you what to say."

"Thank you, Fardad," said Asha. "What would the Family do without you?"

"The Family will be fine, with or without me. The Family is God's; He guides and leads us. When He takes me home, Jahan will be ready. Do not underestimate your husband."

Asha leaned over and kissed Fardad on the cheek, and a single tear rolled down her cheek. "No wonder I love you so much," she whispered to him.

Navid left the wagon, a great weight lifted from his shoulders, and rode back to the Scouts.

Rahim entered the clearing for the evening class and saw Liyana sitting with the children, three of them on her lap.

"I see you made friends quickly," said Rahim.

Liyana smiled back. "They have adopted me. I miss my children terribly, and I believe they sense that. It brings me great joy to be near them and to hear your lessons."

Rahim smiled too. "It brings me great joy to see you wanting to learn and grow." He hesitated a moment, wanting to say more, but finally managed to mumble, "I...I like having you in the wagon with me."

Rahim mounted the speaker platform and looked out over the children. As he thought about this moment, a great sense of love and peace filled him. He loved teaching the children during the day, but when he gathered them together in the evening, it was the pinnacle of his life. These nights under the stars, reading from the ancient scrolls and watching the wonder in the children's eyes, had meant more to him than anything he had ever done. He would be sad to see the journey end.

"Good evening, children," Rahim began. "Tonight, we will return to ancient Babylon again and talk about King Nebuchadnezzar and his pride." Rahim opened the ancient scroll and began to read....

Babylon – 586 Bc

Davi, the Family's teacher, and scribe was teaching a class to the young Babylonian nobility on military history when Pera, the Family's leader in Babylon, entered the room.

"May I see you for a moment?" Pera asked.

Davi left the classroom, and Pera said, "A messenger has come from the city, and the king has called an assembly of everyone in the city to commemorate the completion of the golden image. You and I will go, but we will leave everyone else here."

Davi nodded. "Let me get someone to take my class, and I will meet you at the corral."

***

As they rode toward Babylon, Davi asked, "What did the decree say?"

"What we expected," said Pera. He took the decree out of his robe and read, "You are commanded, O peoples, nations, and languages, that when you hear the sound of the horn, pipe, lyre, trigon, harp, bagpipe, and every kind of music, you are to fall down and worship the golden image that King Nebuchadnezzar has set up. And whoever does not fall down and worship shall immediately be cast into a burning fiery furnace."[5]

"Well, that seems fairly clear," said Davi. "What do you intend to do?"

"Stand on the crowd's edge, as far back as possible. We cannot bow to this image."

Davi agreed, and the two men rode into the city. A large crowd had assembled around the image. Davi and Pera dismounted and moved to the edge of the crowd. Next to the ninety-foot-tall golden image stood the open furnace. A ramp led from the king's platform to a stone structure in the center of the furnace. The walls of the furnace were ten feet high. A square stone structure was also ten feet high in the center of the furnace. There was a gap of ten feet between the stone structure and the furnace walls. The gap had been filled with wood and was blazing brightly.

At a signal from the king, all the musicians played their instruments. It was a cacophony of discordant sounds. The minute the music began, everyone fell and pressed their heads to the ground. The music stopped playing, and everyone looked up, but no one saw Pera and Davi because all eyes were on the front row, just below the king's platform. Shadrach, Meshach, and Abednego, as they were known to the Babylonians—but Davi knew as Hananiah, Mishael, and Azariah —stood unbowed. Davi was astounded at their faith and courage. He and Pera had made themselves as inconspicuous as possible, but these three men chose a position as prominent as possible. Davi raised his eyes to heaven and began praying.

Several Chaldean court officers gathered around the king, speaking and pointing at the three unbowed men standing below them. The king called for the three men to come onto the platform.

There was a short conversation, and the king became furious. He screamed at his servants and had the attendants add more wood to the furnace. Around the furnace, the builders had affixed bellows to the outside of the walls on all sides. Large shirtless men manned the bellows, and they pumped furiously. The heat waves rose higher and higher.

Davi looked on in anguish, the bricks of the furnace walls were glowing. He wanted to turn away, but he could not. His friends had chosen to stand for God, the least he could do was watch their death.

The king screamed again, and his bodyguards surrounded the three men and bound them with thick ropes. Six bodyguards dragged the three men to the furnace and rushed down the ramp, throwing them onto the stone structure in the center. The bodyguards turned to run back up the ramp, but the heat was so great that their clothes burst into fire, and they fell from the ramp into the furnace.

Davi wanted to cover his eyes, but he could not take his eyes off the furnace. The three men were still standing, but their clothes were not on fire. Suddenly a fourth man was standing with them. Hananiah, Mishael, and Azariah were unbound and walking and talking with the fourth man. Davi tried to process what he saw, but he could not reconcile the furnace, the three men, and now a fourth man.

Pera said in hushed awe with absolute surety, "He is the Angel of the Lord."

It was as if the piece of a puzzle had fallen into place, Davi understood what he was seeing, and he fell to his knees. The crowd was completely silent.

King Nebuchadnezzar jumped to his feet, conferred with his counselors again, and shouted, "Shadrach, Meshach, and Abednego, servants of the Most High God, come out from the fire![6]"

The three men walked up the ramp, through the raging inferno, and stood unbound before the king. The king looked into the furnace, but the angel of the Lord was no longer there.

The king walked to the front of the platform and decreed in front of the assembled congregation, "Blessed be the God of Shadrach, Meshach, and Abednego, who has sent his angel and delivered his servants, who trusted in him, and set aside the king's command, and yielded up their bodies rather than serve and worship any god except their own God. Therefore, I make a decree: Any people, nation, or language that speaks anything against the God of Shadrach, Meshach, and Abednego shall be torn limb from limb, and their houses laid in ruins, for there is no other god who is able to rescue in this way."[7]

Davi could not believe what he was hearing. The king stood next to the ninety-foot golden image he had erected, decreeing that he would punish anyone who spoke against Jehovah. The dichotomy could not have been stronger.

Davi stood. "Look at the king's counselors. They are furious. The outcome was the exact opposite of their expectations. Instead of destroying Shadrach, Meshach, and Abednego, they strengthened their position with the king. God is truly amazing."

"God has shown us many wonders in our lifetime," said Pera, "but I have never witnessed anything like this. Are you ready to head back to the compound?"

"Before we go," said Davi, "I would like to go by the building site for the Military Temple and check on Kedem and Heber."

"Excellent," said Pera, "I have not met them, but I remember you telling me about them after your last visit."

The two men mounted and rode to the Military Temple, and Davi saw Kedem and Heber. He and Pera dismounted and approached the men. A man coughed behind them, and Davi saw the same overseer he had met on his last visit. Davi reached into his robe, extracted a gold piece, and placed it in the man's hand.

"It's good to see you again, Davi," the overseer said. "Have a nice day." And he turned and walked away.

Pera was confused. "He's Jewish. I don't understand?"

"The Chaldeans appoint Jewish overseers who are bilingual. Most overseers came with Daniel eighteen years ago and speak Chaldean and Hebrew. To keep their jobs, they are more brutal than their Chaldean bosses. The Jewish slaves hate the overseers but are powerless to do anything about them. Most overseers have begun worshiping Marduk and are more Babylonian than Jewish now."

"I remember in Scripture, the overseers in Egypt were also Jewish. It seems to be the common pattern for conquerors," said Pera.

"Kedem, Heber," said Davi. "Has there been any change in conditions?"

Kedem showed Davi his hands. "They are beginning to heal. And they gave us new tools. The work is no easier, but the tools help, and the food quality and quantity have improved. Daniel set up a program allowing all building programs to buy food directly from the government storehouse at discounted prices. And he established inspectors to ensure the food is getting to the slaves. It is helping. Thank you, Davi."

"No need to thank me, Kedem. The thanks belong to Daniel. How are your wife and children?"

"They are getting worse. The tanning chemicals, long hours, and poor food is ruining their health. Daniel's programs didn't extend to the small business owners that own slaves. The program only covers large contractors."

"It grieves me, Kedem, but I fear there is little that Daniel can do for them. Small groups of slaves are held all over Babylonia, and it is impossible to regulate their treatment."

"I understand, Davi," said Kedem, "and thank you for helping us."

Davi and Pera walked away from the captives. "Where to now?" asked Pera.

"With everything going on, I know Daniel is busy. We will stop by the palace, talk to his disciple, Lem, and let him know what we have discovered."

They led their horses and walked to the palace. The two men wanted to see what was happening in the city. Public works were everywhere. The king was expanding the zoo, and animals from every corner of the empire arrived daily. Every type of creature sat in cages outside exhibits, which slaves hastily erected. Work crews were building public buildings on every spare inch of ground, and large crews of gardeners and slaves planted beautiful gardens throughout the palace area.

Davi had no idea what half of the plants were. In addition to the plants, they built a large aqueduct from the Euphrates to water the gardens. The slaves on these large projects, similar to Kedem, looked healthier than they were on Davi's last visit. Daniel's programs were working.

Davi and Pera arrived at the palace and found Lem outside Daniel's office. "Greetings, Lem," said Davi. "We have just walked through the city, and the slave conditions have improved on the public projects."

"Daniel is brilliant," said Lem, "God constantly solves problems for him. Not only are the slaves healthier, but they are stronger and more productive. The builders have reduced building times, and costs are lower. Nebuchadnezzar is thrilled."

"Where is Daniel?" asked Pera.

"He is praying, giving thanks to God for the deliverance of Hananiah, Mishael, and
Azariah. Not only did God save them, but God used them to allow us to freely worship Him without interference. Nebuchadnezzar has forbidden anyone from interfering with the worship of Jehovah. The Chaldeans hate it, but there is nothing they can do about it."

"We talked to Kedem and Heber, and they are much improved, but their families are not working on public projects, and their health is declining. Can Daniel do anything for them?"

Lem's shoulder drooped. "There is little we can do for them. As you know, God has told us we will be in captivity for seventy years. The adults who are captives will not survive to see the deliverance. Daniel's focus is on the children. He has established a school for them, two hours per day, and no one may stop them from attending. We teach Hebrew and Scripture, and we feed them. God judged our people because they turned from Him, but even God's wrath has not turned their hearts back. They are worshipping Moloch and Marduk, attempting to please their Babylonian masters. God uses Daniel to prepare a people who will willingly return to Jerusalem, rebuild the Temple, and worship Him. That is Daniel's focus."

"Marvelous," said Pera. "If there is anything our school can do to help, please let us know."

"Daniel has decreed that the children in our school would be excused from work for three weeks a year to celebrate Passover, Feast of First Fruits, and the Feast of Tabernacles. He would like you to host these feasts and do intensive training. Will you do this?"

Pera and Davi smiled at each other. "Gladly, Lem," said Pera. "There is nothing we would love more. Our primary focus will be worship and Scripture. Our secondary focus will be military training. They must be able to defend themselves when they return to Israel. We will prepare them."

"Daniel will be pleased," said Lem. "The children are coming to you next month."

Pera and Davi laughed. "Then we need to go," said Davi. "It looks like we have work to do."

Magi Camp – Day 91

Rahim rolled up the scroll. "Off to sleep, children. Tomorrow will be another long day."

REPENTANCE

Magi Route – Day 94

The Family had reached the floodplain and crossed it, following the trail Navid and the Scouts had marked.

Asha was on the left flank with Fahnik, helping herd the sheep.

"Keep the sheep tight through this section," said Asha. "Navid has marked the area to our left as a bog."

"Mother, I know how to read the trail," said Fahnik. "I have done this far longer than you. And what are you doing out here? You are not a shepherdess. Why the sudden interest in sheep?"

"It's not the sheep I'm interested in," said Asha. "You are the reason I'm here. You went through a horrible trauma, and I am here if you need to talk to someone."

Fahnik's face turned red. "Did Utana put you up to this? Has he complained about me?" she demanded.

"Utana has nothing to do with this. He and I have not talked. Why? Are you two having problems?"

Fahnik said nothing. She put her head down and walked faster. She pretended to chase stray sheep, obviously doing anything to avoid talking to her mother.

Asha watched her carefully. She had never seen Fahnik like this. Her daughter had always been one of the most joyful people in the Family. She was troubled.

They walked, separated by a chasm Asha could not cross, for most of the day. Late in the afternoon, Fahnik fell to her knees and sobbed uncontrollably.

Asha rushed to her and knelt facing her. "Fahnik, my love, talk to me. It breaks my heart to see you in so much pain. What is it?"

Fahnik sobbed for several minutes before she gained enough control to speak. "God hates me, Mother. He hates me."

"God hates you?" asked Asha. "Why would God hate you? He loves you."

"I am a murderer, Mother. A MURDERER."

"Fahnik, you are many things, but a murderer is not one of them. You and the Scouts saved this Family and freed the slaves. God used the Scouts to judge the slave traders. All of you killed people in the raid. Does God hate the other Scouts? Tiz, Esmail, Hugav—does God hate them?"

"No, God doesn't hate them. Just me. I murdered a young woman, Mother. She was beautiful, not much older than me, and I shot her. I see her face every time I close my eyes."

"Why did you shoot her, Fahnik? Did you hate her?"

Fahnik looked confused. "No, I didn't hate her. She walked up to the slit trench and saw the two men I had already shot lying in the trench. She turned quickly and looked around. I was afraid she was going to scream, so I shot her. It happened so fast that I barely had time to think."

"You didn't answer the question. Why were you at the slit trench? Why did you shoot her?"

"I was at the latrine to protect the Scouts. I was to kill anyone who left the camp. The Scouts were inside the slave trader camp, and if anyone returning from the latrine had seen them, they would have raised the alarm."

"How was shooting the two men different than shooting the woman?"

Fahnik shook her head, confused. "I don't know; it just was. They were men, warriors; they had attacked our family. I needed to kill them, but the woman had done nothing wrong."

"So, you were there as a judge. Deciding who had done right and who had done wrong. Is that what Tiz told you to do?"

"You are twisting things, Mother. You know what I mean."

"Yes, I do know what you mean. After the fact, you decided it was murder if you killed someone who might be innocent. But that is not the command Tiz had given you. You went with the Scouts willingly. You became a warrior and when you did, you agreed to follow orders. Tiz ordered you to protect the Scouts and keep anyone from sounding the alarm. That's what you did. You don't get to decide afterward, which people deserved to die and which ones didn't. You had one mission, to protect the Scouts."

"Then why do I see her face every night when I close my eyes? She haunts my dreams."

"She will for a while, Fahnik. You are a loving, sensitive person, and when you decided to become a warrior, you didn't suddenly become someone different. You are still a loving, sensitive person, and killing bothers you. Especially killing someone you believe to be young, loving, and innocent. When you picked up the sword to fight against evil, God decided who would live and who would die. You are not the judge; He is. As commanded, you did what you had to do to protect the Scouts. Those who you and the Scouts killed face God's judgment now. If the young woman you killed was innocent, she is with God in Paradise. If she was guilty, then she faced eternal damnation. You are not the judge. Now let's talk about the smithy."

"I murdered him, Mother."

"Why is he different from the others?"

"When I went to the blacksmith shop, I was looking for tools. Then the blacksmith attacked me. He was huge and had a long-handled sledgehammer. I didn't see how I would survive; I was afraid. I used my speed to keep away from him. He made the mistake of reaching for me, and I cut off his left hand. He was bleeding badly, he could only swing the big hammer with one hand, and he moved slower and slower. I got around behind him, and I knew I had two options. I could cut his hamstring, put him on the ground, or go for a killing blow. At that moment, all the hate in me boiled to the surface. I jumped up, swung as hard as I could, and cut his head off. I wanted to kill him. I didn't have to kill him; I wanted to kill him."

"And now you think God hates you," said Asha. "You think He could never love or forgive you, and therefore no one else should love you either." Asha leaned forward and pulled Fahnik to her, kissing her cheeks and forehead and stroking her hair. "Your mother loves you, Fahnik, and always will. God also loves you. You risked your life to save others. You never thought of yourself. He loves you, and He loves the fact that killing bothers you. You killed someone young and pretty, and that bothers you. Then hate boiled to the surface, and you killed the smithy. It was combat, Fahnik. The slave traders declared war on all mankind, and God ended their tyranny. You were His instrument. Let's tell all of this to God."

The two women knelt together, and Fahnik poured out her heart to God. Asha prayed for her daughter, thanking God for her safety and using her in a mighty way. They finished, and the two women stood.

"Tonight, you need to share this with Utana, pray together, and forgive him."

"Forgive him for what?" asked Fahnik.

"He feels guilty about getting captured and being unable to help fight against the slave traders. He doesn't understand why he couldn't break his chains like Navid. He needs to hear you say that there was nothing he could have done. That none of this was his fault. God will heal you both if you seek Him."

"I will, Mother. Thank you for shepherding with me these past few days." The words barely left her mouth when Fahnik glanced around. The sheep had scattered in every direction. The two women looked at each other, laughed, and dashed about gathering the flock together again.

The family gathered for the evening meal, but two spots were conspicuously empty.

Jahan asked, "Did anyone see Asha or Fahnik? I can't imagine what's keeping them."

Everyone shook their heads *no*. Jahan shrugged, gave thanks for the food, and they began eating. The two women appeared a few moments later, disheveled, sweating, and breathing hard.

"What happened to you two?" Jahan asked.

Asha looked at Fahnik, and they began laughing. "Long story, Father. The flock was scattered, and it took us a while to gather them again," said Fahnik.

Jahan looked concerned, "Was there a predator?"

"No predator," said Asha, "we just were distracted. I will tell you about it later."

Fahnik sat next to Utana, leaned over, hugged him, and kissed him on the cheek. "I missed you today," she said.

Utana was speechless, then he smiled, grabbed her, and kissed her. "I missed you too."

Jahan raised his hands and face to heaven. "Dear God, can we just eat? Thank you."

Asha elbowed him hard in the ribs, and his hands dropped. She grabbed him on both sides of his face and kissed him. "I missed you, too."

Jahan smiled. "That's more like it. Maybe we should skip Rahim's lesson tonight." He said, making his eyebrows go up and down as he looked at Asha.

This elicited another elbow to the ribs.

"Women," Jahan grumbled. "I never have any idea what is going through their minds."

"Of course not," Asha said, smiling, "and that is how it will always be."

The family laughed and had their first relaxed meal together since the slave trader incident.

When they had finished eating, Pari announced she was teaching tonight. Tiz picked her up and carried her to the camp's center, followed by Nura, who took his seat with the children, sitting on Liyana's lap, and Rahim sat next to Liyana. Tiz placed Pari on her cushions on the speaker platform.

"Good evening, children." Pari began, "Tonight, we will learn about the beginning of the Persian Empire."

The older boys in the back started jumping up and down, ululating and shouting, "Cyrus, Cyrus, **Cyrus, Cyrus.**"

Tiz rose to his full height next to Pari and looked at the boys. They quietly sat down, and so did Tiz.

Pari smiled, opened the ancient scroll, and began to read....

Magi Compound – Persepolis – 585 Bc

Bareil, the leader of the Family in Persepolis, had been working on small-arms training with the students all morning, and one student stood out among them—Cyrus, the son of Prince Cambyses. Cyrus had been at the school less than a year and was ahead of boys who had been there for three years or more. He was fifteen years old, well-muscled, and quick. He was also extremely intelligent and was always two moves ahead of the other students. This morning, they had trained with javelin, sword, knife, and spear, and Cyrus had mastered them all.

The school contained the nobility of the Medes and Persians. The Medes didn't know how to treat Cyrus. His father was Persian, but he was the grandson of Prince Astyages, who was heir to the throne of his father, King Cyaxares, King of Media. Persia was subservient to Media, and the Medes never let the Persian students forget it. Cyrus had lived the first ten years of his life in Media, and his ties and affections were strong to his native land, but one day he would be king of Anshan. He was a boy straddling two worlds.

"Enough training for this morning," said Bareil. "Head to the mess hall." For all meals, students and teachers ate together in one large hall. The teachers sat at one table, and the students ate at the others. The Medes and Persians did not comingle for lunch.

Bareil had just sat down when Cyrus came up to him. "May I speak to you for a moment, Teacher?"

Bareil smiled at the boy. "Of course, have a seat."

Without a second thought, Cyrus sat at the teacher's table. The other students were staring at him, awestruck. No student in the school's history had ever sat at the teacher's table.

"I would like to talk about creating a special force, and I want them trained here in Persepolis," Cyrus said.

"You would like us to create a special force and train them here?" Bareil said in wonder. "Who will authorize and pay for this training?

"My father will authorize and pay for it. I will write to him."

Bareil couldn't help but smile at the confident young man. "What will this 'special force' do?"

"They will be my bodyguard and the central force of my army. I want 10,000 men. They must all be large. Their training must be like nothing you have done before. They must be fearless. They will never retreat. They will win, or they will die on the battlefield. They will be called the Immortals."

For the first time, Bareil was uncertain. "Immortals? Do you think we can train them not to die?"

"No," said Cyrus, "The Immortals, because there will always be 10,000. You will train a reserve force. The instant an Immortal dies, another will step into his place, returning the number to 10,000. They will have the appearance of immortality. They will strike terror in my enemies. They will carry 12-foot spears with thick shafts. That is why they must be large and strong. Spear training will be the most important aspect of their training."

"Is that all?" asked Bareil.

"That is all for now," said Cyrus, "but I have something else I would like to discuss with you sometime. I want to redesign the chariot. I want to use it to smash holes in the enemy line, not just run around shooting arrows. The chariot will create gaps that my infantry will exploit. I need your help to redesign it."

"Who are you planning to fight, Cyrus?"

"One day, I will unite the Medes and Persians, and when I do, we will conquer the world. One day, everyone will have to choose a side. I need to know if you are with me, Bareil. Can I count on you?"

Bareil stared at the boy. A fifteen-year-old prince, not a king, a prince of subservient Persia, had just asked for his allegiance. Cyrus was a leader, unlike anyone Bareil had heard of or known. Bareil looked in his eyes, remembered the prophecy of Isaiah, and knew that Cyrus would do everything he had said. "You have my allegiance, Prince. The Magi will support you."

"Excellent," said Cyrus. "I will write to my father tonight. You will recruit the Immortals from the three main tribes of Persis: the Pasargadae, Maraphii, and the Maspii. There are seven other tribes, and these three tribes will recruit from them. Every recruit must be a volunteer. We will not force any man to be an Immortal.

"Set up a strict entrance test, and reject anyone who doesn't pass. Once training begins, they may not quit. They will succeed or die. These men must be hard as iron, trained for one thing—battle. They will train separately from the nobles. There must be no contact between them.

"Also, I will not organize my armies like traditional armies. The Immortals will be a regiment with a nobleman over it. There will be 23 companies, and each company will have 70 squads of six men each. The squad is the heart of my new army. They must all be from the same village. The squad will eat together, live together, and fight together. Their bond must be unbreakable. In training, the squad will be kept together and compete and train against other squads."

Bareil staggered under the concepts Cyrus threw at him. They were brilliant. "I see you have given this a lot of thought, Prince. Is there anything else?"

"There is one last thing," said Cyrus. "Who do the Magi worship?"

Bareil didn't like this question. "Why do you ask?"

"I do not see any idols or statues, and none of the Magi teachers wear an amulet," said Cyrus. "I have seen Natan climb up to a cave concealed by brush and trees on two occasions. I climbed up there one night. The cave is full of scrolls. Many are history scrolls, and I could read them, but others are in a language I do not know. I believe these strange scrolls have something to do with your religion."

Bareil felt his face flush and his pulse increased. "You have gone too far, Cyrus. You are a student at this school. I don't care what your rank is; you do not pry into the affairs of your teachers. What we believe or do not believe is none of your business. This afternoon, I have some special training for you to reinforce this point."

"My apologies, Teacher, if I have offended you. That was not my intention. My father in Media, Mithradates, taught me to worship Ahura Mazda. He is a spirit and the god of all gods. Since you do not wear amulets, I thought you might also worship him."

"We do not worship Ahura Mazda," replied Bareil. "It is none of your business who we worship. You have breached our privacy and broken an inviolable rule. We are the teachers; you are a student. You go where we tell you when we tell you, and that is all you do. I should expel you, but I will not. You will spend the afternoon running up the mountainside carrying rocks to the cave you found so interesting to reinforce this principle. You may begin now."

"Thank you for not expelling me, Teacher. Your punishment is appropriate. I know I have much to learn."

Cyrus left the mess hall, walked to the base of the cliff, found a large rock, and ran up the path that led to the cave.

Late in the afternoon, a rider rode into the Compound and asked for Prince Cyrus. They brought him in to see Bareil.

"What message do you bring for Cyrus?" asked Bareil.

"I do not know the content of the message," said the courier. "King Astyages gave me the dispatch and told me to deliver it to the prince."

"King Astyages?" inquired Bareil.

"Yes, King Cyaxares has died. Astyages is the new king, and one of the first things he did was send me with this dispatch for Prince Cyrus."

"I see," said Bareil. "Wait here, and I will fetch the boy."

Bareil left his office and walked to the base of the cliff. Cyrus was running down the path. He had stripped off his outer robe and was running in a loincloth. Bareil could see his feet and hands bleeding, but the boy still ran. Bareil knew there was something special about this young man.

Cyrus reached the bottom. "I believe that is enough rocks for today," said Bareil.

"There is still light, Teacher. I can carry more."

"No, I believe you have learned your lesson. A courier has arrived from Ecbatana with a dispatch for you. King Cyaxares has died, and King Astyages has sent you a dispatch. Wash up, put on your robe, see the physician, and have him attend to your hands and feet, then report to my office."

Cyrus arrived in Bareil's office, clean, dressed, and bandaged. The courier handed him the dispatch pouch, and Cyrus extracted a small scroll. As he read, he arched his eyebrows, but his face did not change expression.

"My grandfather has ordered me to attend him in Ecbatana. He says he has a role for me in his new government."

"Does he say what your role will be?" asked Bareil.

"Interestingly, he does not," answered Cyrus. "King Astyages says that he needs family around him whom he can trust, and that is all he says."

The courier spoke. "I have already notified your parents that you will not be returning to Anshan. King Astyages has ordered me to accompany you to Ecbatana."

"We will prepare a room for you," said Bareil. "It is too late to start today. You may leave in the morning."

"Thank you for everything, Teacher," said Cyrus. "I will not forget the things you have taught me."

"And I will not forget your request. Everything will be as you requested when you are ready for it," said Bareil.

Cyrus smiled. "Thank you. When I am ready, we will change the world."

<u>Magi Camp – Day 94</u>

Pari rolled the ancient scroll and saw Rahim looking at Liyana, who was busy with the children. There seemed to be more than just friendship in his gaze. Pari smiled to herself.

"That is all for tonight children. I will see you tomorrow.

OMID

Magi Camp – Day 95

Navid and the Scouts had found a lovely piece of grassland just south of Mari, where the Euphrates River's banks were low. The had sounded halt around noon. The Family and the animals were tired, Rest would do them all good, and the animals would love the good grazing.

The mood in the camp was lighthearted this afternoon. Many of the women were at the river washing everything that needed washing, from clothes to rugs. Men had erected several stout poles and strung ropes between them. Rugs of every color hung from the ropes and women were beating the freshly washed rugs with wood dowels.

Men were repairing tents, wagon wheels, and tack. They rubbed sheep's fat into every piece of leather they owned. The desert sucks the moisture out of everything, and the leather needed attention.

Navid was oiling his saddle and reflected on the journey to this point. They had been traveling for 81 days, and the journey was nothing like he expected.

Utana joined him and began mending a torn seam in his tent, "You seem deep in thought."

"I was thinking about where we were 96 days ago. Seems like a different lifetime, Utana."

"It was a different lifetime," said Utana. "Think about it. On that day we were both single. You were planning to marry Leyla and become Satrap of southeast Persia. We were trainers and teachers, and you were destined for leadership of the Family, and possibly chief tactician of the Persian army."

"Now only two things are still the same. You are still my best friend, and I will be the leader of the Family one day if they will have me. Once everything was perfectly clear. I thought I was in control of my future. Now God is in control of my future, and I am at peace for the first time."

"I know," said Utana, "I can see it in you. Every day brings us closer to the Messiah. You are like a hunting dog with a faint whiff of the game ahead. He begins to strain at his leash, he wants to be let loose to run as fast as he can to find that which he desires. The scent overwhelms him, and it is the only thing he can think about. You, who once scoffed at the thought of the Messiah, are now that hunting dog. You want to find Him more than anything else in the world."

"You know me too well, Utana. But you are right. I am no longer the man I was 96 days ago, and I thank God for that. He has changed me Utana. All I can think about is meeting and worshipping the Son of God. What a privilege, that we have been chosen for such an honor.

The men chatted through the afternoon and were joined by other Scouts. It was the most enjoyable day Navid had in a long time.

The day ended with the usual evening meal, and the Family gathered for the evening lesson.

Pari was teaching again tonight. She opened the ancient scroll and began to read...

Babylon - Magi Compound – 564 Bc

Davi entered the room. Pera lay on his sleeping mat, face pale, breathing shallow, a slight sheen of perspiration on his forehead. Pera's face was gaunt and sunken; he had not eaten in several days. The once-magnificent warrior had lost his muscle mass, and the skin on his arms hung slack. Age and death came to all, but it was hard to see in a man who had been Davi's hero his entire life.

Davi sat on a cushion next to Pera, and a few moments later, Pera's son Omid entered the room. Omid was forty-five and a mirror image of his father, slightly less robust and gentler. He was a man of character and strength, and he loved Jehovah. Davi respected him greatly and knew the Magi Family was in good hands with Omid as its leader. Omid sat next to Davi, just as his wife, Elham, hurried into the room carrying a water basin.

"How has he been?" Omid asked.

"I have been with him most of the night," said Elham. "His breathing has become shallower, he is cold to the touch, and yet he perspires. I do not think he will be with us much longer. I have been gone just a few moments to get some water, and he looks worse than when I left him."

"He has suffered long enough," said Davi. "I will miss him greatly, but I cannot bear seeing him like this."

Omid was silent for a moment. "What happens to Father after death, Davi? I know what happens to his body; we will carry him to his burial cave, but what about his soul?"

"This is a difficult question, Omid. I believe the Tanakh teaches that there are two possibilities. The Psalmist says, 'But God will ransom my soul from the power of Sheol, for he will receive me.'[8] He also says, 'This is the path of those who have foolish confidence...Their form shall be consumed in Sheol, with no place to dwell.' Sheol is the destiny of both the righteous and the unrighteous, but God ransoms one from the power of Sheol and not the other. The Proverbs also say, 'Do not withhold discipline from a child; if you strike him with a rod, he will not die. If you strike him with the rod, you will save his soul from Sheol.'[9] I cannot find a clearer explanation, and I believe God will save Pera's soul from Sheol."

"Thank you, Davi. That is a great comfort. I agree with you. I believe God will save Father's soul from Sheol," said Omid.

"Yes, thank you, Davi," agreed Elham, "and now I am grateful to Omid for disciplining the children. He is always kind and gentle with them, but they know the difference between what is acceptable to God and what is not. I will make sure I am equally diligent. I cannot imagine them facing the horrors of Sheol because we failed to discipline them. They may choose not to follow God one day, but it will not be because we failed to train them. Thank you."

The three sat quietly by Pera's bedside for the next hour, listening to his labored breathing. Omid was the first to notice the silence. He looked up; his father's chest was no longer moving up and down. Omid reached over and closed his father's eyes. Elham began a soft keening cry, and Davi began to pray. The household heard the mourning, and others came in and joined them in their grief. Word spread through the Magi Compound that Pera had died, and the women of the Family came in and prepared him for burial.

When they finished, Omid, Davi, Davi's son Manoah and three other men carried Pera to his burial cave, placed him on his bier, and rolled a large stone over the cave opening. The Magi Family gathered outside the tomb of Pera and mourned until sunset.

The following morning, Davi joined Omid for the morning meal, and the two men began to plan for the future.

"It has been more than twenty years since we began to educate the children of those held in slavery," said Omid. "How many have we been able to train?"

Davi thought for a moment and did some calculations in his head. "To date, we have trained more than 20,000 children. As you know, we have taught them to speak and read Hebrew and the Law of Moses. There were 5,000 children under the age of ten who came as captives to Babylon; some of them may live to return to Jerusalem. Most of those who return will have been born in slavery.

"Ezekiel and Jeremiah prophesied that we would serve the King of Babylon for seventy years.[10] If we count from the time of Daniel's captivity, we have been slaves for forty-one years. We have roughly thirty more to go. We should be able to train a sizeable group by then.

"The question will be, how many will choose to return to Israel? The children born here do not know the country or city of Jerusalem. They never saw the Temple, the magnificent walls, or the King's Palace. They will return to ruin; there is no city and no Temple. The fields have had no one to work them. I don't know how those who return will survive."

"Try not to paint too rosy a picture," said Omid, laughing. "But

I understand your point. In our training, we need to be clear about the condition of the land they are returning to, but we need to be equally clear about what God is calling them to do. They need to know God has called them to return to rebuild Judah, Jerusalem, and the Temple. They need to understand that God will accomplish through them something marvelous."

Davi smiled. "You are correct, Omid. I shall amend our curriculum immediately."

"What else is on your mind, Davi?"

"Do you remember what happened eight years ago?"

Omid looked quizzical. "Eight years ago?"

"King Nebuchadnezzar had a dream eight years ago, and Daniel interpreted that dream. Do you remember?"

"Of course, I remember. Has it really been that long?" asked Omid.

"Yes, the dream was eight years ago, but God gave King Nebuchadnezzar a year to repent and worship Him, but he would not repent. Therefore, God fulfilled the prophecy, and for the past seven years, the king has slept outside in the rain and mist and has eaten grass like an ox.[11] I want to visit the city today to see if the prophecy has ended and see some of our friends. But I will understand if you are not up to it."

"No, I think the best thing for me is to get away from the compound for a while. It will do me good to visit some of the captives and see if we can help. Would Manoah like to join us?"

"I think that would please him. We will meet you at the corral."

The three men rode through the outer gate of Babylon. In the large grazing area to their right, King Nebuchadnezzar had spent most of the last seven years, hair and beard uncut, barefoot, wearing rags, his fingernails and toenails ranging from broken to inches long. It had been horrible to look at him. There had been guards around him to protect him, but the field was empty today.

"Let's start at the palace," said Davi. "It looks like something has happened to the king." The men dismounted outside the palace and saw several groups heading toward the Throne Room.

"The Throne Room it is," said Omid, and he led Davi and Manoah in. On his throne sat King Nebuchadnezzar, scepter in hand. The past years had aged him; his skin was dark brown and weathered. He had lost weight, and the royal tailors had not had a chance yet to take in his clothes. The Throne Room was filling, and the three men were pushed toward the front by newly arriving groups. Standing next to the king was Daniel, and in the front of the room were Mishael, Hananiah, and Azariah, whom the king had thrown into a furnace years ago.

The Chief Eunuch slammed the butt of his staff against the marble floor three times. It sounded like thunder, and the room grew quiet.

The king rose from his throne. "I stand before you today," he thundered, his voice undiminished by his recent ordeal, "and declare that there is one God, and His name is YAHWEH. He is the creator of heaven and earth, and everything is subject to Him, including the King of Babylon. I declare to you today that all His works are right, and His ways are just; those who walk in pride, He is able to humble.[12]"

The king resumed his seat, and the Chief Eunuch began the business on the day's calendar. Davi saw Daniel's disciple Lem standing by the wall. Lem looked over and saw Davi. Davi motioned his head toward the door. Lem nodded, and all four men made their way to the Throne Room entrance.

Once outside, Davi asked, "When did the king recover?"

"Two days ago," said Lem. "His recovery was just as God had revealed in the king's dream eight years ago. The guards told me that one minute he was eating grass, and the next minute he stood, lifted his eyes to heaven, and began praising God. Then he walked back to the palace and was greeted by his counselors as if nothing had happened, and his servants cleaned him up. How is your work coming with the Jewish children?"

"Very good," said Davi, "We have focused on language and the Law, but we must prepare them to return to Jerusalem... When this captivity ends, people will be going to Judah who have never been there before. To go back will be a difficult decision for them to make. We need to give them a reason to return."

"Have you found any promising children we should be preparing for leadership?" asked Lem.

"Two so far," answered Manoah. "A young man named Zerubbabel, the son of Shealtiel, and a young Levite boy, Jeshua, the son of Jozadak. They show significant promise. We will spend additional time with them."

"Excellent," Lem replied. "I will tell Daniel. Also, Jerusalem will need prophets. The Lord will show you those He has chosen. Please inform me, so they may become disciples of Daniel. We will train them. Where are you off to now?"

"We want to visit a few families to see how they are doing.

Daniel has greatly improved their condition, but life is still hard for them."

Lem embraced the three men, and they left the palace.

"Where to, Father?" Manoah asked Davi.

"I'm not sure; most slaves move from project to project. We will ride through the city and see what we find. We will stop by the tannery to see how Kedem's family is doing."

The men rode through the city past several public-works projects, the king's new library, an addition to the ziggurat, and a larger granary for the king. At each site, men and women were cutting blocks of stone to size, dragging the stones to the building, and raising the stones to set them in place. The labor was cruel and hard, and they had little rest.

The worst part was the Jewish overlords, who whipped their fellow Judeans if their pace slowed or if the project was behind. At the granary, they saw Heber. They dismounted and walked next to him as he dragged a newly cut stone toward the building with several other men.

Manoah stepped forward and grabbed the rope Heber was pulling, "Take a rest and talk to my father. I will help drag the stone to the wall."

Heber looked relieved and dropped the rope. "Thank you, Manoah. Thank you."

The overseer saw the exchange, but since the work continued, he did not interfere. Heber bent over with his hands on his knees, catching his breath. Omid took a waterskin from his horse and handed it to Heber, who drank greedily. Omid also removed bread and cheese from a saddlebag. Tearing off a large piece of bread, he spread the soft cheese and handed it to Heber. Heber devoured the bread; he was famished. After eating and drinking, Heber embraced both men, tears in his eyes.

"God bless you," he whispered. Slaves were not allowed to talk, and his voice had lost strength from lack of use. He had no body fat. Every muscle on his body stood out. His hands were heavily callused, his shoulders were broader, and there were whip marks on his back. It was amazing that he was still alive after all these years of hard labor.

"How is your family?" asked Davi.

"My wife died last month," said Heber. "It was a blessing. She'd cried herself to sleep every night because of the hard work and abuse. Now she has rest. Thank God my children are household slaves. They work long, but the work is not hard. They are also fed well. They will survive this captivity. They also attended the Magi school and are excited about going to Judah one day." Heber hesitated for a long moment. "Davi, do you believe God will release us from captivity after seventy years?"

"I know that His people will be released. They will return to Judah and rebuild Jerusalem and the Temple. Prophecy is clear." Davi put his hand on Heber's shoulder. "You will not see Judah again, but your children may. Pray for them. Where is Kedem, Heber?"

"He is performing repairs on the city walls. I have not seen him in several days."

"We will visit his family," said Omid.

Heber looked at the granary. Manoah and the other slaves had left the stone at the wall and run back to get another stone. Heber said, "Time for me to go. Manoah has done enough. Thank you for stopping." Heber ran to the stone cutters and motioned for Manoah to leave.

Manoah joined his father and Omid. "I have no idea how he has survived this long, doing that kind of labor." Manoah showed them his hands; they were red and beginning to blister. "We don't even work animals that hard."

"One day, the Babylonians will pay for their cruelty," said Omid. "Until then, the Judeans will continue to suffer."

The three men mounted and continued their tour of the city. They finished by riding to the outer wall; the tannery was located as far as possible from populated areas. Long before the three men saw the tannery, they smelled it. When they arrived, they saw several groups working different jobs. The hides arrived on wagons, were unloaded, and went to vats filled with water, where people scrubbed them with stiff brushes to soften the hide. After the water bath, another group pounded the hides with wooden clubs to remove excess fat and flesh.

The next process was the lime pit, the worst job in the tannery. They covered the outer side of the hide with a paste made from lime and water. This process loosened the hair follicles. The lime irritated the worker's skin, causing horrible rashes and dehydrating the slaves. Slaves did not last long in the lime pit.

After the lime coating, came the scudding process, where men and women used dull tanner's knives to scrape the skin, removing hair, hair roots, and the thin layer of skin on the inner side of the hide. The next step in the process involved vats of water filled with the brains of various animals. The oils from the brains softened the skins and made them supple. Slaves in this area kneaded the hides in the oily bath till they were soft. The last step was the actual tanning process, a compound made from tree bark and plant leaves. The slaves in this process stretched the leather on frames and dipped them in large vats filled with tannin.

Davi saw Kedem's wife and children working, dipping the hides in tannin and then placing them on racks for drying. The three men dismounted and walked over to the woman and her children.

Kedem's wife recognized them. "Davi, how wonderful to see you. What brings you to this awful place?"

"You and the children," Davi replied. "We wanted to check on you and ask you why the children have not come for training."

"We are much better now that we are no longer working the lime vats. I thought we would all die, but they moved us to tanning when we became too sick to work. Tanning chemicals are hard on the skin, but we are not sick anymore. And the reason the children have not been allowed to attend the school is the tannery owner. He decided in the king's absence to ignore the law."

"That's what I feared," said Davi. "I will report this to Daniel. He will get it corrected." Davi smiled at the children. "I look forward to seeing you in school next week."

Kedem's wife hugged them, and they mounted and rode back to the palace to find Lem. At least they'd found one thing they could fix today.

Magi Camp – Day 95

Pari closed the ancient scroll. "The lives of the slaves were very difficult in Babylon. None of the adults who entered into captivity returned to Judah. Their children would one day journey to a land they had never seen before. God works in miraculous ways. King Nebuchadnezzar died two years after he recovered from God's judgment on him, 562 years ago. Amel-Marduk, one of the king's younger sons, succeeded his father. No one knows why the king chose him, since he was not the oldest son, and the king had never shown much inclination toward him. But enough for tonight, children. It is time for all of us to get some sleep."

Tiz began to pick up Pari when Liyana approached. "May I speak with Pari, Tiz. I will bring her to your tent after we finish."

Tiz looked at Liyana's thick arms. "Of course, Liyana." He gave Pari a quick kiss, began to walk away, felt a tug on his robe, and looked down at Nura.

Tiz smiled, squatted, and said, "Put your arms around my neck and hang on tight." Nura beamed, put his arms around his father's neck, and wrapped his legs around his waist. Tiz rose to his full height and carried his son to their tent.

"What did you want to talk about, Liyana?" asked Pari.

"I know this will sound foolish." Liyana looked down at her hands. "But do you think I could learn to be one of the children's teachers?"

Pari put her hand under Liyana's chin and lifted her head. "Liyana, you would make a wonderful teacher. I have seen you with the children, but you must work very hard. You are making excellent progress learning to speak Farsi, but you will need to learn to read and write the language to teach. Can you do that?"

Liyana smiled. "I can do that."

"Good. Starting tomorrow, you will ride in the wagon with Rahim and me. In the morning you will learn with the younger children. In the afternoon, Rahim and I will teach you. How does that sound?"

"That sounds like the most wonderful thing that has ever happened to me."

Liyana effortlessly picked up Pari and carried her to her tent.

70

REBELLION

Magi Route – Day 98

"Mari turned out to be disappointing," said Navid. "I expected it to be larger. It was barely more than a village."

"I agree," said Utana, riding point with Navid today. "But at least they had all the trading goods we needed. I was hoping they would have some honey, but there was none. I would love to have some sweetened rice. We have been out of honey for weeks. My mother's Shirin Polo is the best in all Persia."

"I agree on your mother's sweet rice, but don't let Fahnik hear you say that. She is pretty handy with a sword, you know."

Utana's expression hardened. "Not funny, Navid. She is like Tiz, a fully capable warrior, but they are too tender for killing. Freeing us took a horrible toll on her. Your mother helped greatly, but she still has days she is troubled."

"Utana, I am so sorry. That was a stupid thing to say. You have my deepest apology. It will not happen again. I know how much you have both been through; I can't believe I was that thoughtless."

"All is forgiven," said Utana. "It was just a careless comment."

"But speaking of Fahnik, how are you two doing?"

"Now that she is through the worst of it, we are closer than ever. I experienced the horror of being a captive, and she experienced combat. It changed us both, and we can talk about it now. Also, I have learned when she needs quiet time by herself or time with Ava or Pari. I cannot be everything to her. The women in her life provide things I can never provide. I am learning, Navid."

"I understand, Utana. I have thought about that lately. Have you ever thought about how blessed we are? We know the word of God, and the Family has many who know, love and follow Him. All of those people have different gifts, and they share their gifts freely. Just think of the men who have trained us. From Fardad—wisdom; from Jahan—strength, value, and courage; from Rahim—learning, sensitivity, and spiritual values; from Ram—the treatment and care for animals and outdoor skills; from Kevan—warrior skills, from the Scouts before us, how to survive in any condition. Then there are the women of the Family. From Pari, we learn how to love the Lord with all our heart, soul, and mind; from Fahnik—joy, and our mothers— love and respect. We are blessed beyond measure."

Navid had barely stopped speaking when several horns sounded alarm on the left flank. Navid scanned the area to their front and did not see signs of danger. He and the Scouts turned west and kicked their horses hard. The Scouts lay flat on their horses; hooves thundered, and the wind whipped their hair and clothes. Anosh flattened and lengthened his stride; he flew by the other horses. Navid's heart hammered in his chest. Navid loved being a Scout. When there was danger, they rode straight at it. Not one man hesitated.

When the Scouts arrived, a group had already gathered. The Scouts reined hard, and their horses skidded to a stop. Navid jumped down and ran to his father, who was there.

"What is it?" Navid asked.

Jahan pointed to a shepherd staff lying on the ground.

"Whose is it?"

"You're not going to believe it," said Jahan. "It's Hayat's."

"Not again," said a stunned Navid, "not after everything she has been through; it just can't be. First, the slave traders stole her, and now she has been taken again? Is there a sign of a struggle, animal tracks, blood, anything?"

"We haven't seen any blood, but we were waiting for you to arrive to tell us what you think happened. We have tried to stay out of the area."

"Hugav, Tiz," Navid called, "tell us what has happened here."

The two men walked in ever-expanding circles until they had covered 100 yards in every direction. Then they walked back to the group.

Hugav gave the report. "Hayat and the sheep came from the south to this point," Hugav said, pointing to the staff on the ground. "From here, the sheep scattered in every direction. A set of tracks, single male, 170 pounds based on the depth, came from the west. There is a shallow ravine fifty feet from here. He lay in the ravine, watching her approach. After she passed, he came up behind her. There was a struggle. Then the male left carrying Hayat. Follow me."

One hundred yards from the ambush site, Hugav pointed to a depression in the sand. "The man had a camel and made it lay down here. The tracks are clear, and there is little wind today. We will not have a problem following them. Tiz, did I miss anything?"

"No, your report is accurate, although I would say he's closer to 165 pounds, and I also found the prints of either an upright bear or Jahan. Nothing else could have made tracks that deep." Tiz heard a deep bass growl and quickly apologized.

Ram arrived with the three war dogs, B, Arsha, and Bendva.

"There are forty of us, and the captor doesn't have more than a two-hour head start," said Jahan. "Let's try to catch up with him before he joins a larger group."

Hayat's father was furious. "When we catch up with them, whoever has stolen her is mine. I will kill him with my bare hands."

Jahan glared at Hayat's father, "There will be no talk of murder; if judgment and justice are required, Fardad will be the one to pass the sentence. We are the Magi, not a mob. Mount up; we have a hard ride in front of us."

Hugav, Tiz, and the dogs led the way, the dogs ranging in close. These were war dogs, trained to stay close to their handlers. They never ranged far ahead unless instructed. Not wanting to lose the trail, the men rode at a slow, steady pace. The man they were pursuing was on a fast camel, pulling farther away every hour.

Jahan rode up to Hugav and Tiz. "Unless I'm mistaken, the man we're after is on a racing camel. Look at the length of his stride. We must pick up the pace; he's pulling too far ahead."

Tiz nodded and yelled, "Up B, Up Arsha, Up Bendva." The three dogs needed no more encouragement; they leaped forward and were racing across the sand. The riders put their heels to their horses, and soon men, horses, and dogs flew across the undulating landscape.

Navid grinned at his father. "Nothing like an invigorating chase, I always say."

Jahan grunted back, not totally in agreement with his son's enthusiasm.

Late in the afternoon, Hugav saw all three dogs drop to the ground at the top of a sand dune. Hugav held up his hand, halting the men behind him. Hugav and Tiz dismounted, walked to the top of the dune, and lay down next to the dogs. After a few moments, they crawled backward, then rose and returned to the group of men.

"There is a camp about half a mile ahead. I counted thirty tents and large herds of camels and goats. We saw several groups of women and children, but there were at least fifty warriors. They are definitely not slave traders."

"How do you want to proceed, Father?" asked Navid.

"Let's go in friendly, but keep your weapons ready, bows over saddle horns, and two arrows in your hand. Ram, put B on a leash; we don't want any accidents."

They rode forward and topped the dune at a walk. They were

giving the camp in front of them plenty of time to see and assess them. Six men and Hayat walked forward to meet them as they neared the camp.

A tall, well-kept man in a beautiful robe and turban stepped forward, clearly their leader. "Greetings, and welcome to our camp. I am Sheikh Nadeem." He pointed to a young man standing next to Hayat. "And this is my son, Taalib, who has caused your arduous ride. I will explain this misunderstanding if you join me for tea and refreshments."

"I am Jahan, leader of the Magi, and this is my son Navid, and the angry man on my other side is the girl's father. We will be glad to join you for tea. Racing across the desert works up quite a thirst."

"If your men would follow my other sons, they will ensure they also enjoy tea and refreshments."

Jahan, Navid, and Hayat's father, Vasil, followed the sheikh, his son, and Hayat to the sheikh's tent. They entered. The tent was large and well-appointed, with beautiful rugs covering the ground. The sheikh's servants had placed cushions around a low table and set out various fruits, breads, curries, and rice dishes. Another servant stood behind the table holding the largest teapot Jahan had ever seen. The group sat around the table, and the servant poured tea.

"Let me apologize for causing you such worry," said Sheikh Nadeem. "My son, Taalib, is used to our customs. He had never seen people like you before and never thought that your customs might be different than ours. He saw your caravan trail three days ago, and out of curiosity, he watched you. That is when he saw this beautiful young woman," the sheikh said, pointing to Hayat, "and decided he wanted her as his wife. He trailed you for another day and then kidnapped Hayat this morning. Among our tribes, it is not unusual to find brides this way. Young men kidnap a woman, and if she is willing, they marry; if not, they return her to her tribe."

"You are correct, Sheikh Nadeem; that is not our custom. Hayat was captured by slave traders a few weeks ago, and they almost sold her into slavery. So, you can imagine our concern when we found someone had taken her again."

Taalib's face paled. "My deepest apologies," he said, looking at Vasil. "I had no idea. I never meant you or your daughter any harm. She did not tell me about the slave traders, or I would have brought her back immediately."

"Taalib has shamed us," said the sheikh. "You have the right to beat him with a rod if you choose, Vasil. That is your right. You may not kill him, but you may beat him."

Vasil looked at Taalib and softened. "No, there is no need for me to punish Taalib. He did not harm Hayat; in fact, Hayat doesn't seem upset at all."

Hayat spoke for the first time. "I was furious at first, Father, but I knew this was different from the slave traders. Taalib was gentle. As we rode, he explained their custom of kidnapping brides, and I told him that was not our custom. He offered to take me back immediately if I chose, but he begged me to meet his family first. Then, he would take me if I still wanted to go back. I agreed to come with him. He told me about his family and how they lived. They are spice traders, Father, constantly on the move. They travel to countries far to the east, where they purchase the spices, then sell them in large cities along the sea coast. He told me of the wonders he has seen, the people he has met, and his family's care and respect for each other. I will marry him, Father."

Vasil was too stunned to speak. "Marry him?" asked Jahan. "You have only known him for a few hours. How can you possibly marry him?"

"He is kind and gentle, Jahan, and he thought enough of me to track me for three days. No Magi boy has shown that much interest in me. Father has not picked anyone for me. The best boys are taken; there is no one in the Family I am interested in marrying. I think being Taalib's wife would be wonderful."

Taalib smiled, and then Vasil found his voice. "Out of the question," he sputtered. "He's a pagan."

"A pagan?" asked the sheikh.

"We are followers of Jehovah, the God of all creation. Vasil means that Hayat may not marry someone who is not a follower of Jehovah," said Jahan.

"I agree, Father," said Hayat, "I already told Taalib that we could not marry until he receives instruction in the Tanakh and bows to Jehovah. He has agreed to receive instruction and understands we may not marry without your approval."

"Here is what I propose," said Jahan. "Hayat and Taalib will return with us. This will give Vasil, his wife, and Hayat time to learn everything they need about Taalib, and Taalib will receive instruction from Rahim, the Magi teacher, for five days on the Holy Scriptures. If at the end of this time, Taalib agrees to follow Jehovah, and Vasil approves, there will be a wedding, and the Magi will host it."

A strong female voice spoke behind them. "I have an

amendment to your proposal. I will accompany my son. I want to meet Hayat's mother to learn more about the Magi, and I will also receive instruction from Rahim. Agreed?"

The sheikh grinned sheepishly. "Mother has spoken. How can it be otherwise?"

Jahan turned to see the source of the voice and saw a beautiful, tall woman in her mid-thirties. "Of course, that is an excellent proposal. Don't you agree, Vasil?"

It looked as if things were moving way too fast for Vasil; his head seemed to spin. "Yes, an excellent idea. We would love to host Taalib and his mother."

The sheikh stood. "Excellent, it is settled. If you leave now, you have enough daylight to reach your camp. I will bring our tribe to your camp in five days, and hopefully, there will be a wedding."

The Wedding – Day 103

The family discussed the week's events as they ate the morning meal. Navid glanced over at Vasil's family; Taalib and his mother seemed to enjoy the meal and the conversation. Hayat was not eating with them; she was busy preparing for her wedding tonight.

Liyana spoke, "How wonderful to see young love. It will be nice to see a wedding."

"You are not too old for marriage," said Pari. "There are a few men in the Family whose wives have died. Father would be glad to talk to them if you are interested."

"Oh no," said Liyana shocked. "I could never. I am learning to be a teacher. That is my dream now. I love being with you, Pari, and Rahim. It is the happiest I have ever been." She was quiet for a moment. "Why has Rahim never married?" she asked innocently.

Jahan's eyebrows went up. "There was someone once, but she died before they could marry. After that, Rahim dedicated himself to the children, and everyone has always thought he enjoyed his bachelorhood. Why do you ask?"

Liyana blushed. "No reason. He is such a kind, loving, wonderful man. I would think many women would love to be with him."

"Would you like me to ask him why he has not married?" asked Jahan.

Now this is getting really good, thought Navid.

Liyana waved her hands frantically. "You must not do that, Jahan. Please do not ask him. It was a foolish question. I don't know why I asked it. I am glad he is not married. I am glad he has dedicated his life to the children and teaching, and I am thrilled to be part of that."

Navid saw Jahan nod, but he knew this was not over.

The evening was bright and clear; a gentle breeze cooled the guests. The entire Arabian camp had come for the wedding and brought curries, dishes native to their culture, and barrels of excellent wine. Taalib and his mother and father, along with Vasil, Hayat's father, were at the head table. Hayat and her mother would be the last to arrive.

Navid saw Hayat approaching; her robe was scarlet with gold thread, her turban, was scarlet, and her dress was pale yellow with an intricate pattern of deep green. Around her turban, Tiz had woven a strand of golden wildflowers. Navid looked at Taalib; the boy's eyes were alight as he smiled at his bride, and he wore a white robe, shirt, turban, and pants; even his boots were white. *What a beautiful couple,* Navid thought.

Hayat and her mother sat, Fardad prayed, and the Persian and Arabian women rushed to the head table to offer their dishes to the wedding party. Navid was concerned that war might break out; there was a lot of jostling, but everyone took it good-naturedly, and the Arabian and Magi women laughed as they jockeyed for position.

Taalib and Hayat barely ate; they sat with their heads together amidst the talking and laughing. They focused on each other, an island in the stormy sea of noise.

When they finished eating, Fardad called Taalib to the center of the clearing.

"Before we begin the marriage ceremony, I need to ask if you believe Jehovah alone is God and that He is the creator of Heaven and Earth. Do you also believe God called Israel to be His chosen people through covenants made with Abraham, Isaac, Jacob, and King David? And do you believe that the Messiah is the Son of God, that He comes to redeem mankind from sin, and that He is present in Israel today?

Taalib did not hesitate. "I profess today that Jehovah is God, and there is no other. He is the Creator of heaven and earth, and I willingly choose to follow Him from this day forward. I further profess that the Messiah is the Son of God and has come to save all mankind."

Fardad turned to Vasil. "Do you give Hayat to be Taalib's wife, Vasil, based on his profession?"

Vasil rose and said, "I do."

"Hayat, will you join us?" asked Fardad.

Hayat joined Taalib, and they clasped hands. Fardad performed the ceremony in the Magi tradition. Taalib kissed his bride.

Post ceremony is when things became truly wonderful. The Arabians had brought their musicians, and the Family also had musicians. They decided to alternate playing, and the two groups performed their traditional folk dances. The Arabian men performed a version of the sword dance, and not to be outdone, the Scouts performed a faster and more intricate form of the dance. The dances rotated, and blending the two cultures made the evening magical. When it was time for the bridal couple to retire, the Arabian musicians played the Shamadan, and one of the male dancers placed a candelabrum on his head. The dancer and the musicians, followed by the wedding party, wound their way through the Magi camp to Taalib's new tent. In the Arab culture, this was the transfer of the bride to her new home. Taalib and Hayat retired, and everyone else returned to the clearing to continue the celebration late into the night.

On Day 104, the Magi and the Spice Traders rested, exhausted from the previous evening's celebration. Both groups had gathered again this evening to share a final meal and hear Pari teach.

When they finished the meal, Tiz carried Pari to the clearing and placed her on the platform.

She unrolled the ancient scroll and looked out at the mixed assemblage. Smiling at everyone, welcoming their Arab guests, Pari said, "Tonight's lesson is about King Cyrus and the creation of the Persian Empire. Cyrus was a fearless warrior and military leader...."

At this, the Arabs in the gathering began jumping up and down and ululating, which naturally encouraged the Magi boys to join them. They had found kindred spirits, and the two groups competed to see who could ululate the loudest or jump the highest. There was pandemonium in the clearing.

Rahim and Tiz joined Pari on the platform and waved their arms. After a few moments, the ululating and jumping ceased, and everyone regained their seats.

"Let's try this again," Pari said, laughing. "The story of King Cyrus." She unrolled the scroll, lowered the tone of her voice, and began to read...

Ecbatana – 553 Bc

"Oebares, what is on the schedule today?" asked Cyrus. Cyrus was bored and restless, he was 47 years old, and had been serving his grandfather, King Astyages, in various capacities for the past 32 years. He had lived in the palace in Ecbatana in opulence, and his best friend and faithful servant, Oebares, was with him daily, but he had not seen his wife in years.

"The king is holding court this morning. The Cadusians are here. You can probably tell by the stink of fish in the air," said Oebares.

"Not a nice comment about people from your own country," said Cyrus. Oebares had been with him for almost twenty years. Cyrus had met Oebares when he visited the Cadusians as the representative of King Astyages. Cadusia was on the southwest coast of the Caspian Sea. It was known for two things, fish and horses. Oebares was a horse groom with the temerity to offer Cyrus horse dung in a basket when Cyrus had asked him to gather firewood. Cyrus had laughed at Oebares, not realizing the Cadusians used horse dung as fuel and took an immediate liking to him. Cyrus purchased him from the Cadusians and gave him fine clothes, a robe, and a magnificent stallion to ride.

Due to the poor grazing in Persis, the horse herds were small in the area. Cyrus knew that if Persis was going to overcome Media one day, he would need cavalry and chariots and that required horses. Cyrus tasked Oebares to find solid war horses for Anshan and send the horses south. Oebares also created a group of suppliers, who annually provided fodder for the horses. Over the past twenty years, Oebares had furnished enough horses for a 4,000-man cavalry for Persis.

Oebares smiled. "Not nice, but true. They arrived yesterday with a cartload of dried fish, enough to last while they are here. Every cat in the city followed them to the palace."

"Anything else on the schedule?"

"Just your normal cupbearer duties. Speaking of which, the king will be eating soon. You need to get to the kitchen to perform your tasting duties."

Cyrus had become the king's cupbearer two years before when King Astyages's friend and cupbearer, the nobleman Artembares, had died. He was the same Artembares whose son Cyrus had whipped during their childhood 'king' game. Not only had Cyrus become the king's cupbearer, but the king had given him Artembares's estate and wealth. Artembares's son, Fravarti, had received nothing and had left

Ecbatana for Amandia to beg a living from his mother's family.

"Then I best be off to the kitchen," said Cyrus. "Is there anything else?"

"You received a letter from your wife. She says that she and Cambyses II are fine, and the boy looks just like you. Why don't you bring her to Ecbatana? You have only seen her once since she left for Anshan 10 years ago."

"You know the answer to that question. Cassandana and Cambyses cannot come here. Cambyses is heir to the Anshan throne. I cannot take the chance that King Astyages might have some strange dream and try to kill the boy. She is my love, Oebares, yet I cannot be with her. I hate this."

"I'm sorry, Cyrus. I knew the answer to that question. Please forgive me for asking," said Oebares.

"Who knows, Oebares. Maybe we will all be together in Anshan soon. We can hope, but for now, I'm off to the kitchen."

Cyrus entered the kitchen and tasted each dish prepared for the king. Cyrus thought it was a foolish ritual, but King Astyages insisted that Cyrus sample the food at least thirty minutes before eating. Cyrus finished and was about to leave the kitchen when a servant of Harpagus entered the kitchen, carrying a freshly killed hare. Instead of taking the animal to the cooks, he brought it to Cyrus.

The servant leaned close and whispered, "Harpagus suggest that you gut this one yourself." And he handed the hare to Cyrus.

Cyrus took the hare; it was unusually heavy for a small animal. He nodded knowingly at the servant, "Tell Harpagus I will attend to this personally."

The servant breathed a sigh of relief and exited the kitchen. Cyrus took the hare and went back to his room in the palace. He shut the door and blocked it with a chair. He put a heavy cloth on his desk and used his knife to open the hare. Inside the animal was a thin clay tablet. Cyrus had a flagon of wine by his desk, and he used it to clean the tablet. He took his time and read the message carefully. When he finished the message, his hands were shaking, his heart was racing, and he was breathing heavily. Harpagus was offering to give him the kingdom. Cyrus was the only nobleman in the line of King Astyages who was both Mede and Persian. Cyrus alone could muster an external force, so Harpagus and the other generals were willing to support him to overthrow King Astyages.

A noise jolted Cyrus from his thoughts. Someone was trying to get into his room. He walked to the window, threw out the hare and the cloth on which he had opened it, and put the clay tablet inside his robe. He strode to the door, moved the chair, and opened the door.

"I thought maybe you had a woman here," said Oebares.

Cyrus grabbed him by his robe and pulled him into the room, shutting the door behind him. Cyrus handed Oebares the clay tablet. "I received this from Harpagus's servant this morning."

Oebares read the tablet, then whistled softly. "Harpagus is going to have his revenge, it looks like."

"Those were my thoughts," said Cyrus. "No one can do what King Astyages did and not expect it to come back on him sometime."

"I'll say one thing for Harpagus, he is a patient man," said Oebares. "He has waited thirty-six years for his revenge. I was never sure if the story was true, but based on this, it was."

"It's true," said Cyrus. "The day then-prince Astyages discovered I was alive; he threw a banquet in honor of me. Little did I know the banquet had two purposes, to honor me and punish Harpagus."

"Harpagus had a son my age," Cyrus continued. "So, Prince Astyages asked Harpagus to send him to the palace to entertain me until the evening banquet. The king sent for Harpagus's son before the banquet; that was the last time I saw him. Harpagus sat at Prince Astyages' right hand, thoroughly enjoying the banquet. After the banquet, the prince asked him if the meat was to his liking. Harpagus said, 'it was excellent.' The prince said, 'it should be; it was your son.' He killed Harpagus's son and fed him to Harpagus. Harpagus never batted an eye. He thanked the prince for being just."

"Now what?" ask Oebares.

"Now we go home," said Cyrus.

It had not been easy, but plied with enough wine, King Astyages had agreed to let Cyrus go to Anshan to make sacrifices to the gods on behalf of his sick father. But Cyrus was not going to Anshan. He had sent riders to the heads of the three tribes of Persis, the Pasargadae, the Maraphii, and the Maspii. The message said that King Astyages had appointed him as his general, and he needed to talk to the three men concerning future military campaigns. He also sent a messenger to Persepolis requesting Bareil meet with him. The meeting would occur at Hyrba, on the Media/Persia border.

Cyrus arrived at Hyrba and met with the city leaders, informing them of the coming meeting. Within two days, King Cambyses, the head of the Pasargadae, arrived with a delegation from Anshan, and the leaders of the Maraphii and Maspii arrived with their retinues. Bareil did not arrive, but a lone rider appeared on the third day and asked for Prince Cyrus.

"Who has sent you?" asked Cyrus of the stranger.

A man of about thirty-five, bearing a slight resemblance to Bareil, answered, "I am Kia. My father was Bareil; he died in a hunting accident last year. I am head of the Magi Family and the school in Persepolis."

"I am sorry to hear the news concerning your father, Kia. He was a good man and taught me much in my short time at the school. Did he pass on the request I made him all those years ago?" asked Cyrus.

Kia smiled, "We have been training Immortals since you left the school, as your other guests will be able to attest. They easily exceed 10,000 men at this time. We have trained them in the six-man squads you requested, but there is no nobleman over them. In addition, I have a design for a new chariot that you discussed with my father." Kia unrolled a scroll and handed it to Cyrus.

Cyrus studied the scroll for a moment and smiled. The drawing showed four horses in the traces of the largest chariot Cyrus had ever seen. They had designed fish scale armor for the horses that covered all vital areas. The chariot's sides were high, completely covering the driver, and there was no space for archers. The wheels were extra-large and thick, enabling the chariot to roll over most obstacles, including men.

"Perfect," said Cyrus. "It needs only one modification. I want four two-foot-long blades attached to the axle of each wheel. Then, the chariot will have the smashing effect I desire."

Cyrus dined with his guests, and the conversation turned to why King Astyages had gathered them.

"I know you're eager to discover the news I bring, but I will ask for your patience. Humor me for the next two days, and you will have the answer to all your questions."

The leaders of the three tribes and their retainers ate with Cyrus the next morning. When they had finished eating, Cyrus led them to the town square. Lined up on the wall of one of the buildings were scythes, farm implements used to harvest wheat and straw.

"Everyone take a scythe," said Cyrus, "and follow me."

"Does King Astyages want to turn us into farmers?" the leader of the Maspii asked.

"Indulge me," said Cyrus. "Everything will be clear tomorrow."

Cyrus stopped in the center of a large field two miles from the city. The field was half a mile on each side and overgrown with weeds and brush.

"We are going to clear this field today," said Cyrus.

"You expect your father to do common labor, Cyrus?" asked King Cambyses.

"Yes, Father. This is important," said Cyrus. "I cannot command you since you are my king, but I ask you."

King Cambyses looked at the leaders of the other tribes and knew that if he refused to work, so would they. He swung his scythe and began to clear the field. Cyrus smiled and also began working. The other leaders shrugged, removed their robes, and began to work. The men were not farmers, but they were warriors. They had strong, calloused hands, and they were proud. No one wanted to be the first to quit. They worked through the day. Servants from the city brought them food and water, and they finished clearing the field by sunset. Cyrus led a tired, weary group back to the city that evening.

The men ate together, and the leader of the Maraphii asked, "Now are you going to tell us what is going on?"

"As I promised you, tomorrow, you will have the answer to all your questions. Bear with me one more day."

The next morning, Cyrus led the men back to the field they had cleared the day before. In the center of the field was a large pavilion. Beautiful carpeting covered the pavilion floor, and Cyrus had filled it with cushions.

"Gentlemen," said Cyrus, "please have a seat."

Once everyone was seated, servants brought wine, curries, stews, bread, and cheese. There was even a whole goat roasting on a spit.

Cyrus excused himself and walked back to Hyrba. Late in the day, Cyrus returned to the clearing. Everyone was in a great mood. They had eaten and drunk their way through the day.

Cyrus held up his hands for quiet, and all eyes were on him. "Which did you enjoy more," Cyrus asked, "yesterday or today?"

The agreement was unanimous that today had been wonderful.

"Yesterday is what slaves experience every day. Today is what free men enjoy from the fruits of their labor. As a slave, all your hard work is for another man's benefit. Your master allows you to keep very little. Today I am offering you a choice; continue living as slaves to the Medes, or rise with me and overthrow the yoke of Media. There is no love for King Astyages. He has grown harsher every year, and the Generals of Media have promised to join us when we invade Media. I do not offer you an easy victory. They will outnumber us two to one, they will have more chariots and more horses, and they will be better equipped. But we will be fighting for something—freedom. Our backs will be to the wall. For us, it will be victory or death. That is what I have to offer you. Will you join me?"

There was a stunned silence in the clearing; this was not what the tribal leaders had expected to hear.

King Cambyses was the first to speak. "You, the grandson of King Astyages, have served in his court all these years. Why now? Why do you want us to break from Media?"

"The thought had been in my mind for years, Father," Cyrus replied. "Then, a few weeks ago, I was approached by General Harpagus, the King's cousin. The general proposed that I consolidate the Persians and revolt from Media. Since I am both Mede and Persian, he believes I am the only person who could successfully unite the two peoples. King Astyages murdered Harpagus's son thirty-seven years ago. Harpagus has waited all these years to exact his revenge. He sees me as the best hope for Media. The King's son is even worse than the father. The nobles fear for the future." Cyrus scanned the chieftains sitting around him, reading each of their faces, and smiled. He could see it in their eyes. "What will it be? Will you be Princes of Persia or slaves to the Medes? Choose now; the chance will never come again!"

There was a roar as they leaped to their feet. They pulled their swords and chanted, "WAR."

Cyrus's expression grew grim, his eyes narrowed, and his lips were a thin line on his face. "If it is a war that you want, it is a war you will get. Send out runners to every tribe. We will need every warrior of Persia, and the Medes will still outnumber us. But I promise you. Those who live and die will be long remembered in the new Persia."

Cyrus and the tribal chieftains returned to Hyrba and had no sooner arrived than the watchmen on the wall announced that a large group of Median cavalry was approaching. Cyrus ordered the city gate closed and instructed the city headman to gather all the men with whatever weapons they had.

Cyrus climbed to the parapet and saw the cavalry arrive. The cavalry leader rode forward and saw Cyrus on the wall. "Prince Cyrus," he called loudly, "King Astyages has commanded you to return immediately to Ecbatana."

"You may tell the king that the five-month leave he granted me is not up. I will return four months from now."

"Prince Cyrus, I have my orders," the cavalry leader replied, "I must bring either you or your head to the king."

"Very well," said Cyrus, "I will come out, but it will not be my head that is sent back to Ecbatana."

Cyrus descended, and Oebares met him carrying his arms and armor. The city headman had gathered 400 men armed with scythes and ox goads. He sent half of the men with Oebares out the back gate of the city and led the gathered chieftains and the rest of the villagers out the front gate.

Cyrus led his 200 villagers out the city gate and taunted the cavalry leader. "Here is my head. Come and take it."

The cavalry leader's sole focus was on Cyrus, and he did not see Oebares leading men into the rear of his formation. Cyrus stood his ground as the horses bore down on him. He reverted to his boar-hunting training. He planted the butt of his spear in the ground and aimed the spear at the oncoming horse of the cavalry leader. The horse refused to run onto the spear and reared at the last moment unseating the cavalry leader, who lay on the ground unconscious. Cyrus stepped over the cavalry leader and strode into the oncoming horses. He blocked a sword blow from the next rider and thrust up with his spear. The point entered under the man's chin and killed him instantly. Cyrus ducked under another blow and hamstrung the horse. The horse screamed and fell, crushing the rider's leg. Cyrus looked for another opponent, but the few cavalrymen who remained seated had thrown down their weapons.

Cyrus strode back to the cavalry leader, who was now sitting up. Cyrus walked behind him without a word, swung his sword, and beheaded him. Cyrus bent, picked up the severed head by the hair, and walked back to one of the riders. He threw the head to the man. "You may tell King Astyages that I will return to Ecbatana, but I will have an army behind me when I come. Tell him that his days as king are numbered."

Cyrus looked at the chieftains. "We have our war."

After a few days, men trickled in daily. Some were well-armed and armored, others carrying farm implements converted to weapons, but in every group, there were six men, dressed in black, carrying twelve-foot-long spears and large black shields. The Immortals that Bareil had promised him were coming. At the end of six months, 65,000 men had gathered in Hyrba. A tent city had grown outside the city walls.

Cyrus organized his new army and built the chariots Bareil and his son Kia had designed. Cyrus had enough horses to field 3,000 cavalry, and by the end of the first year, he had built 100 chariots. Each chariot required 4 horses, plus a backup for each horse.

Training the chariot horses was time-consuming, and not every horse passed the training. Cyrus set up straw men in a field, and the horses had to charge straight into the obstacles without hesitating. If a horse refused to charge more than once, they disqualified it.

Cyrus divided the army into six regiments of 10,000 men. Cyrus, his father, and Oebares served as the generals of three divisions, the chieftains of the Maraphii and Maspii served as the generals of two divisions, and Kia commanded the last division. Cyrus divided each division into companies of 420 men, led by a captain, and he divided each company into six men squads. The squad was the heart of Cyrus' army. Squads ate, trained, and slept together. Squads competed against other squads in combat drills and athletic competitions. The squad became a brotherhood. No squad mate would ever leave his brothers on the battlefield. The squad was the soul of the Persian army.

But if the squad was the soul of the army, the Immortals were the heart. Cyrus led the Immortals. On the first day of training, Cyrus formed the 10,000 Immortals into a formation by company, with a squad forming each row. They ran 10 miles fully armored and armed. At the end of the run, they did combat training for four hours and then ran back to Hyrba. The training was grueling, but no man ever thought of quitting; they would rather die.

Other divisions trained and sought to match the Immortals, but none came close. At the end of each day's training, Cyrus allowed a division to compete against the Immortals in weapons training. The challenging division chose the weapon. They competed squad against squad. No one ever beat a squad of Immortals. The men loved the competition, and they revered the Immortals. There was never animosity. The Persian army believed they were unbeatable with the Immortals in their center.

In addition to the Persians who had joined Cyrus, Kia brought twenty-five Magi Scouts, men specially trained in stealth and tracking. Cyrus deployed the Scouts in layers around Ecbatana to monitor the activity of the Medes as they prepared for war.

Hyrba – 551 Bc

It was late fall when the Scouts came in, one by one, to report the Median army was on its way. The Scouts estimated there were 220,000 men with 300 chariots and 10,000 cavalrymen.

Cyrus pulled his force inside the city of Hyrba and shut the gates. By now, many of the wives and children of the officers and men had joined the army in Hyrba, including Cyrus' wife, Cassandana, and his nine-year-old son Cambyses II.

Cyrus watched from the wall as the Median army approached. They were colorful, dressed in greens, reds, and yellows. They did not march, and there was little organization. From his years in Ecbatana, Cyrus knew the lack of organization and leadership would be the great weakness of the army he was facing. They were well-armed and armored, but Cyrus was confident the gods were with him. The Median army stopped on a hillock a mile from the city. King Astyages had his throne set up on the hilltop and sat with his scepter in his hand and his crown on his head. He signaled, and half of the army moved into the valley in front of Hyrba. The advancing army of 110,000 men stopped a half-mile from the city and formed ranks.

Cyrus turned his back on the attackers and looked down on the army massed below him, "Men of Persia, today we begin the battle for our freedom. We fight for the right to live as free men, to live securely in our homes and villages, and to reap the wealth and benefit of our labors. We fight for our wives and children. The men you are facing are not fighting for anything. They fight because their king has forced them to fight. Maybe not today, and maybe not tomorrow, but they will break. They cannot stand against a determined foe who will not quit and will not stop. Men of Persia, will you fight with me today?"

The men below bellowed, ululated, and beat their shields as they roared their assent. Then they began an ancient Persian war chant that grew louder and louder.

Cyrus raised his sword above his head and shouted, "**MEN OF PERSIA, WILL YOU FIGHT?**"

The chant grew louder as the men raised their swords and spears. Cyrus turned and took a last look at the Medes. It was obvious they had heard the war song, and Cyrus saw men shifting from foot to foot in nervousness. He smiled, descended, mounted his horse, and led his army out of the city gate. The Persians formed with King

Cambyses's division on the far right, Oebares on the far left, and Cyrus and the Immortals in the center. The Persians were in dull brown and tan, wore floppy wool caps, and carried round shields with a half-moon cutout through which they thrust sword, javelin, or spear. They did not have armor. They wore hardened leather vests and leather guards on their forearms and shins.

Once the Persians were in formation, the Medes sent out their chariots. The chariots charged the Persian line, then turned at the last moment, and the chariot archers fired at the Persians. The Persians returned fire. They targeted the horses, not the men. Soon there were horses down and chariots overturned. Other horses were running wild with arrows protruding from shoulders and flanks.

The Medes sent their cavalry against the Persian flanks, and Cyrus released his cavalry to meet them. The Median front began a steady march forward, and as they neared; the two armies exchanged arrows. When the Medes were two hundred yards from the Persians, Cyrus sent his chariots forward at a trot, with all of the divisions running behind them. Unlike the Medes, the Persian chariots did not veer. The chariot was massive, and the driver and horses were armored. The chariots smashed into the Median front and drove straight through the stunned infantry, the horrible blades on the wheels dismembering man after man. The Persian infantry ran into the gaps created by the chariots and enveloped group after group of Median infantry. It was a slaughter. Hour after hour, they fought with Cyrus and the Immortals in the thick of the fight.

King Astyages sent wave after wave of reinforcements against the Persians. Late in the day, Cyrus rode out of the battle and up and down the front to assess the condition of his army. The flanks had suffered severely, and his father was wounded. Cyrus sounded the retreat, and the army fought an organized withdrawal. The Medes did not pursue them. Cyrus saw King Astyages on the hill screaming and waving his scepter forward, but the army would not move. Cyrus withdrew behind the city wall, and the Medes set up camp.

Cyrus called the division commanders and captains together. "We lost 10 percent of our force today, either dead or severely wounded. We inflicted ten times those losses on the Medians. The problem is they still outnumber us. I believe this will be a running fight over a long period. From this point forward, we will hit, then withdraw, hit and withdraw. We will move high into the mountains. The mountains will eliminate their horses and chariots and put us on even footing. We are mountain fighters; they are not. I am sending

Cassandana and the other women and children to the fortress at Pasargadae tonight. Does anyone disagree?"

There was no disagreement. "Good, notify the men, and get the women and children ready to leave in one hour."

An hour later, the group was ready to travel, and Cyrus said a tearful goodbye to Cassandana and Cambyses. Cyrus has selected ten lightly wounded men to accompany the group as guides and protection. Cyrus watched the group disappear into the night out of the back gate. The Medes hadn't bothered to surround the city, further confirmation to Cyrus how poorly organized they were.

In the morning, Cyrus went to see his father. Cambyses was in pain and running a fever. "How are you, Father?" Cyrus asked.

"I don't believe I can fight today, but maybe tomorrow," he replied weakly.

"I think your fight is over, Father. There is a good chance I will take the army into the mountains today, and if I do, I will be unable to take the wounded. I'm so sorry, Father."

"You are the future of Persia, Cyrus," said Cambyses clutching his son's forearm tightly. "Do what you must do. You are doing the right thing; you are the only one who can unite Media and Persia. Remember to rule well. Be just and rule wisely. You will not fail. The gods have chosen you."

"I may not see you again, Father. If I do not, I want to tell you that you are a man I admire. You have ruled well. I will honor your memory by doing the same." Cyrus turned so his father would not see his tears and left the room.

The commanders had assembled the army behind the city gate. Cyrus mounted and led them out, as he had done the day before.

Cyrus was in the center again today and would lead the 10,000 Immortals. Cyrus had replaced any Immortals who had fallen with men who had been through the Magi's school and had fought in other divisions yesterday. There would always be 10,000 Immortals. They dressed in black, with black wool hats. The Immortals carried their 12-foot-long spears, scimitars, and black round shields with the half-moon cutout.

Cyrus saw the center of the Median line trying to edge left or right to avoid the Immortals, and their officer used whips to keep them in line. Cyrus knew he would break these men. Maybe not today, but they would break.

The day's battle began just as the day before with a chariot attack by the Medes followed by their infantry moving forward. Cyrus sounded the charge, and the massive chariots surged forward with the Persian infantry running behind. The results were the same. The chariots cut gaps in the Median line, and the infantry surrounded and slaughtered the Medes. Then things changed. Cyrus saw King Astyages' signal, and 100,000 men held in reserve moved to surround the Persians. Cyrus sounded the retreat, and again the Persians fought an organized retreat, but this time Cyrus bypassed the city and led the men into the mountains.

Oebares rode up. "Cyrus, give me the Immortals, and we will serve as the rear guard. You lead the army to Pasargadae."

Cyrus hesitated, then nodded. "You are right. You have command of the Immortals. Thank you, Oebares."

Cyrus turned in his saddle and shouted, "Immortals go with Oebares."

Oebares gave a command, and the Immortals stepped to the side of the trail and watched as the army streamed by. As each division passed, they beat their shields and yelled encouragement to the Immortals. The Immortals stood at attention, heads up, chests out, spears upright and centered on their chest, to show respect to the passing men.

The Persians marched for five days. At every narrow pass, the Immortals stopped and engaged the pursuing Medes, holding them in the pass for hours. Then the Immortals would break contact and run through the mountains till they reached the next pass and repeat the process. The Immortals created a significant separation between the two armies which allowed the Persians to easily reach Pasargadae, high in the mountains and not far from Persepolis. The mountain fortress was small, but it was adequate to house Cyrus's army when they arrived.

The day after Cyrus arrived, Oebares and the Immortals arrived, dropping to the ground, exhausted, and the army brought them food and wine.

Cyrus called the tribal chieftains, Kia and Oebares, together. The only difference was that Cyrus now stood as the King of Anshan since his father was either dead or captive. "Oebares, what can you tell us about the Median pursuit?" asked Cyrus.

"Good news," said Oebares, "We were pursued by 100,000 men. They had to abandon their chariots and most of their horses. We took the roughest ground we could find. King Astyages returned to Ecbatana with the rest of the army. It appears he will winter in Ecbatana and leave the 100,000 men here as a blocking force. We watched them pitch camp. They have no intention of climbing this mountain to fight us. That gives us the winter to prepare for the spring campaign."

"Excellent news, Oebares," said Cyrus, grinding his fist into his hand's palm. "When spring comes, we will be ready for them."

Cyrus looked at the other tribal leaders. "I need runners sent to your tribes, to the other Persian tribes, and to anyone you think may be willing to support a rebellion against King Astyages. Tell everyone we need as many men, food, and weapons as they can send."

Everyone nodded in agreement, and Kia said, "There is one more thing we can do, King Cyrus. Would you permit my Scouts to harass the Medes during the winter? I believe we can greatly discourage them."

Cyrus grinned. "What do you think your 25 men can do against 100,000?"

"Why don't you come with us tonight and see yourself?" replied Kia.

"I will," replied Cyrus. "When do we leave?"

"Now, my men are ready to go."

Cyrus drew on a warm robe and grabbed his weapons. "Lead the way."

Kia gathered the Scouts. Cyrus was shocked. They wore black from head to foot, including a black turban, and they had covered any exposed skin with charcoal to reduce glare. They were almost invisible. Kia led the way down the mountain, and they arrived at about midnight.

Kia pointed at a spot behind a log with a good view of the valley. "You and I will remain here. After this point, we would be a liability. You are about to see a special demonstration."

The two men lay next to each other. The Scouts took two or three steps and disappeared. Cyrus could not see them or hear them. "How many guards would you say the Medes have posted?" asked Kia.

Cyrus estimated the distance between each guard and the circumference of the camp and said, "I would say just over 200."

"That is my estimate also," said Kia. "Keep your eyes on the guards."

The guards were barely visible in the firelight from the camp. Cyrus could see thirty guards, and for a long period, he saw no activity. Suddenly in his peripheral vision, he saw a guard slide slowly to the ground, then the next guard, until none of the guards within sight were standing. An hour later, a voice whispered, "It's time to leave."

Startled, Cyrus leaped to his feet, drawing his sword and looking around in confusion. There stood the twenty-five Scouts; he had not seen or heard them return.

"They will be changing guards soon," said Kia, "And we don't want to be here when they do. I believe they will be upset."

The men ran up the mountain for thirty minutes and then slowed to a fast walk.

"How many guards did you kill?" asked Cyrus.

One of the Scouts shrugged and replied, "All of them?"

"How could each of you kill eight men in a little over an hour?" asked Cyrus.

Another Scout answered, "We train for this. Many nights we train in the dark. We are fast and quiet; the best part is that the Medes will not know what killed the guards."

"What do you mean they will not know what killed them? I would think a slit throat would be fairly obvious."

"There are no slit throats," a third Scout answered. The man held up a weapon; it was six inches long and the thickness of a large needle, "we insert this in the ear or under the jaw, straight into the brain. Death is instant, silent, and undetectable. A few nights of this and half of the Medes will desert within a month."

Cyrus looked at Kia. "These men are terrifying; where did you find them?"

"We didn't find them," replied Kia. "We trained them. The Magi have developed these techniques over the past fifty years. They come originally from the Far East. Very few men can pass the training; that's why the number of Scouts is so few."

Cyrus turned to the Scouts. "Make this a long winter for the men in that valley."

It *was* a long winter. The snows were particularly heavy, and the temperatures were bitter, but that did not stop the tribes of Persia from delivering food and war material. Fresh supplies came in weekly, and men came too. When the snow melted, and the army of the Medes returned, the Persians were ready for them. Cyrus now led an army of 80,000 men but was still outnumbered by the 200,000-man Median army assembled in the valley.

The army was in formation in the city center when the Scouts rushed into the fortress and informed King Cyrus that King Astyages was sending 150,000 men up the mountain.

"Men of Persia," Cyrus thundered, "today, we begin the final battle for our homes and freedom. Behind you stand your wives and families. They are counting on you today. Today there is only victory or death. There will be no surrender and no retreat. There is no place we can go. We will end the war today on this mountain."

Without another word, Cyrus turned and led the Persians out of Pasargadae. Cyrus led the Immortal down the broadest trail coming up the mountain. The Medes would send as many men as possible up this trail. The other divisions each covered smaller trails that led up the mountain. There were no straight trails; they wound up the mountain through thick forests and rock-strewn fields. Cyrus and the Immortals ran down the mountain; he intended to make the Medes fight for every inch of this mountain. Cyrus had the advantage of the high ground.

The Persians reached a spot 300 yards from the mountain's base and ran into the lead element of the Medes. Cyrus drew his sword, screamed, and charged into the Medes. The Immortals took up their terrifying war chant and followed their leader. The Immortals, with their twelve-foot-long spears, slaughtered the Medes.

Cyrus faced a thickly built Mede, a man with great strength but little skill. Cyrus parried two clumsy overhead blows. Then on the man's third attempt, Cyrus dropped to one knee and thrust upward. His sword went under the man's chest plate, up through the stomach, lungs, and heart, and the big man toppled backward. Cyrus stepped over the dead man and faced a tall, thin warrior. There was fear in the man's eyes, and the man hesitated. Cyrus took advantage of the man's indecision and thrust quickly over the shield and into his neck. The man fell to the ground and drowned in his blood.

With the front ranks engaged, Persian and Mede archers fired into those following. The Immortals raised their large shields to protect themselves and the men engaged in the front ranks. The battle continued hour after hour, Medes pouring up the mountain, and the Persians giving ground grudgingly.

Every twenty or thirty minutes, the front ranks would part to allow the men behind them to surge forward and take the brunt of the Median attack. The front rank would fall back for a brief rest and to take water. Cyrus moved back up the trail to check his men's condition and encourage them.

Late in the day, the Medes had not made it halfway up the mountain, but the Persians had run out of arrows and javelins. Men were throwing rocks at the Medes; others had taken slings and become slingers. The fight was desperate, and Cyrus feared it was the same for all his divisions.

As night drew near, the Medes withdrew down the mountain, and Cyrus' army returned to Pasargadae. As they neared the fortress, Cyrus stopped at a stone hut outside the city wall. The building contained an altar and shrines to various Persian gods. Cyrus entered the building and knelt at the altar. Out of respect, the Persian army knelt outside the shrine. Cyrus prayed, and his men watched. As he prayed, thunder rumbled, lightning flashed, then a murmur began outside the building, which Cyrus ignored at first, and then it grew louder, "Look, look, **LOOK**." Cyrus left the hut and saw men staring and pointing at the roof of the building. A large falcon was sitting on the roof peak, staring directly at Cyrus.

Cyrus turned, faced the army, and raised his hands, "The gods have spoken. They have sent us a sign. I will be king of the Persians and the Medes. Tomorrow you will be free men." There was a roar as men leaped to their feet and pounded the shields with their spears.

Cyrus watched the men and smiled. This war was over. These men believed; there would be no stopping them tomorrow.

In the morning, Cyrus and his army ran screaming down the mountain, chanting their war song. As they neared the valley, a lone Mede approached under a flag of truce. "King Cyrus," the man said as he kneeled, "Commander Harpagus and the other generals offer their surrender." The man proffered a parchment bearing Harpagus's seal. Cyrus opened the parchment and read.

Cyrus turned to the army following him, "The Medes have surrendered. If they have laid down their arms, there will be no more bloodshed. We will welcome into our army anyone who wishes to join us. You will embrace them as brothers. From now on, we are one people. Welcome to the new Persia."

Cyrus turned, continued down the mountain, and cautiously entered the valley, still concerned about Median treachery. He entered the valley, and no more than 20,000 Medes were left. The army had mutinied and deserted en masse. They ran away in a panic, leaving everything behind. King Astyages, alone and terrified, had also left everything behind, including his throne, scepter, and crown.

Cyrus approached Harpagus and the other generals. They were kneeling with their necks bared as a sign of their submission to Cyrus and recognition of his power and authority over them. Cyrus walked up, grabbed Harpagus by both shoulders, and lifted and embraced him. He commanded the other generals to rise and embraced each of them. He offered them a generalship in the Persian army, and they all accepted.

Cyrus told his men to sack the Median camp and keep anything they found. He ordered the Immortals to take control of the king's possessions, including a large chest of gold he had left behind. Cyrus then sent runners up the mountain, informing the women and their families of the victory and telling them to come down. They would be leaving for Ecbatana immediately.

Over the next week, the Persian army approached Ecbatana. King Astyages met the Persians in a small plain outside the city with a small army and was quickly defeated. Astyages fled back into the city, and Cyrus found him hiding in a storage room. Much to the dismay of Harpagus and Oebares, Cyrus did not order the death of King Astyages. Instead, he announced that Astyages would become provincial governor of Barcania on the Caspian Sea and that he would marry Amytis, Astyages's daughter, Cyrus's mother's younger sister. Cyrus was now both the grandson and son-in-law of Astyages, thereby firming his right as King of Media. A new Persian Empire had been born.

Magi Camp – Day 104

Pari rolled up the scroll, and the Arabians, men, and women, rose, ululating and jumping. They had never heard a storyteller like Pari, and they were showing her their appreciation of a well-told story.

When things quieted, Pari looked at the children. "Our bride Hayat will be leaving us in the morning to begin her new life. Would you like to gather around her and Taalib and pray for them?"

Without a second's delay, the children surrounded Hayat and Taalib. They placed their little hands on them and poured out their hearts. They thanked God for Hayat, for letting them be a part of her life. They prayed for Taalib and future children. They prayed for safety when they traveled, good health, good friends, and God's love, grace, and mercy. Their sweet prayers rolled on and on as tears ran down Hayat's and Taalib's cheeks.

THE ROMANS

Magi Camp – Day 105

Navid and Ava rode to Sheikh Nadeem's tent. The sheik had invited Hayat's and Navid's family to join them in a farewell meal. The couple dismounted, stooped to enter the tent, and saw that everyone else was already present. They sat on cushions between Navid's mother and Hayat. The table was loaded with food. Fardad gave thanks and blessed the sheikh and his family.

"I want to thank you for coming," said Sheikh Nadeem. "Taalib and my wife received excellent care and instruction in your camp these past days, and I wanted to show my appreciation. I also wanted to answer any questions you might have about what Hayat's life will be like."

"I also have something to say," said the sheikh's wife. "I went through the instruction with Taalib, and Rahim and Pari taught us about Jehovah and the Messiah you are journeying to see. Of course, we know of Israel and their beliefs, but we had never considered that their God might be different than all the other gods we see. You have opened our minds and hearts. Taalib is not the only one who has believed. My husband and I believe what you taught us is true. There is one God, and we will worship Him."

"We praise God," said Fardad, "and will pray for you as you seek His face. Sheikh, I do want to know more about what Hayat will experience. Tell us what you trade and where you go."

"We travel the Silk Road, but some call it the Spice Road," replied the sheikh. "We trade for spices, silk, or anything else of value. We travel approximately 3,000 miles each trip, southwest into India for spices, then northwest into Shangshung Tibetan for tea, spice, medicines, and silk. We once went as far as the Han Empire, but it was too far, and their resources were poor. Hayat's life will be a life of travel. She will see many new things and meet people she never knew existed. Being a trader has made me wealthy. I own ships based in Sidon, and they travel the world. I have an agent in Sidon, my younger brother. He manages my wealth and the shipping. Taalib will inherit a vast trading empire one day. I could stay in a large house, counting my money and living at ease, but I wander the world and love it. I will always be on a camel going somewhere. That's what Hayat will experience. We are on our way west now. We will pile our camels high, and next year we will return and sell everything, and then we will do it again. We are blessed. I have promised Hayat that we will stop in

Persepolis on our return every year to see you."

"Excellent," replied Fardad. "We will see you next year in Persepolis."

"Are you sure we will be in Persepolis next year, Grandfather?" asked Navid.

"Have faith, Navid; we will be in Persepolis next year."

"I apologize, Grandfather," said Navid. "You are right. I need to have more faith, but I'm getting there. I also have a question, Sheikh Nadeem. What is the best route into Israel from here?"

"Continue to follow the river as you have been. In two days, you will reach Resafa, a trading center, but with a Roman outpost. Sooner or later, you will have to deal with the Romans. A group of fighting men as large as yours will make them nervous, especially since you are going to Israel, where they have had more than one political uprising. If I might, I would like to make a suggestion. Reduce your guard force to ten men as you near the outpost. The rest can walk and help the shepherds. You will not look as warlike if you do that. Secondly, you cannot tell them a king is now in Israel, who will rule the world. You need a different explanation for your trip."

Navid looked at Jahan. "What do you think, Father?"

"The sheikh is right. Dealing with the Romans may be the hardest part of the journey. They are powerful, arrogant, protective, and do not like the Persians—an extremely bad combination for us," said Jahan.

"Leave the Romans to me," said Fardad. "It is a matter of appealing to their interests and desires. I will do the negotiating."

"I saw you negotiate at Ctesiphon," said Jahan, grinning, "I will gladly let you do the talking. If anyone can get us past the Romans, it is you, Father. You handled Trdat masterfully, and he had every reason to turn us over to Queen Musa."

The group ate for a while longer, and the sheikh's wife shared what it had been like for her, traveling, bearing children, raising children, caring for her husband, and learning languages. She loved her life and had many wonderful memories, and she expected the same for her new daughter-in-law. She summarized by saying she wouldn't change a thing.

Navid looked at the sheikh. "This has been wonderful, Sheikh Nadeem," he said, "thank you very much for hosting us this morning. I'm afraid we must leave you now. I want to scout ahead to see Resafa, which means I must leave now. I speak for the Magi when I say we wish you God's blessings and protection, and we look forward to seeing you next year."

The group stood; there was hugging, kissing, embraces, handshakes, crying, more hugging and kissing, and finally, the Magi departed.

Jahan rode next to Navid as they caught up with the Magi caravan. The caravan moved slowly, at the walking pace of the herds and children, so they were able to ride at a trot to catch up.

"When you near Resafa, I want you and Tiz to ride alone. If the Romans see you, I don't want them to see a group of twenty-five armed warriors. Also, you will ride camels; Anosh looks far too much like a war horse."

Navid laughed. "I agree about Anosh. He even terrifies the other Scouts. I hate to think what the Romans would think of him. It's hard to believe our journey is two-thirds over. Once we get past the Romans at Resafa, the rest of the journey should be manageable. We will have plenty of grass and water once we reach the coast. I'm also excited about seeing the sea, and I'm *glad* that I will not be seeing it chained to the oar of a ship."

"The slavers were never going to chain you to the oar of a ship," growled Jahan. "If Tiz had failed, I would have brought every warrior we have. None of you were ever going to be slaves." Jahan visibly relaxed. "But Tiz did not fail. Ten men plus Fahnik killed more than 100 men. I never thought that possible. I knew he would find a way to free you, but I never thought he would destroy the entire group of slavers. God performed a miracle, Navid. Do you realize that?"

"Father, God has performed so many miracles on this trip I cannot count them all. He led Hugav up a sheer cliff face in pitch darkness. God blinded the Immortals and kept us from a horrible battle. He restored Sasan to us. God gave Tiz victory, created a supernatural sandstorm, and gave me the power to break chains. Father, I was in the middle of every one of those miracles. Grandfather was right. God has called us to a special purpose, and His hand has been on us every step of the way."

They reached the rear guard of the caravan, and Jahan dropped out of the group of riders to join them. When they reached the main body of the caravan, the rest of the group stopped. Navid and Tiz swapped their horses for camels and continued riding to find the Scouts. The two men increased their pace. The camels could run faster than a horse's canter for hours. The Magi bred these camels for speed and endurance. The Scouts would now be several miles ahead of the caravan, but Navid and Tiz would catch them quickly.

The wind was blowing through Navid's hair, the temperature was cool, and the animal beneath him was strong and fast. The ride was more jarring than his horse, but Navid enjoyed the height advantage of being on a camel. He could see the river stretching into the distance on his right, the banks were green and filled with vegetation. He saw to his left the barren desert as far as his eye could see. Navid had grown to appreciate the beauty of the desert. It was a sea of sand, and the wind changed it daily, rearranging dunes and mounds until they resembled the waves of the sea. Navid scanned his surroundings, and the scene filled him with joy. God used the journey he had feared to turn him into a man. He knew that the strength and convictions he now had would be with him for the rest of his life.

"Tiz, do you think God has changed you on this journey?" Navid shouted to his friend.

Tiz rode closer so Navid could hear him. "God has changed us and confirmed us through His testing. I am troubled by the number of men I have killed on this journey. Yet, when I think of each instance, I do not see an option – at the Persian Gate, the first encounter with the slave traders, the last encounter with the slave traders, every death was necessary to protect the Family. God tells us in Deuteronomy to choose life.[13] However, in choosing life for one, the death of another was necessary. Pari and I have prayed about this several times, and she has helped me find peace with this dichotomy."

"Is that the only change?"

"Far from it," answered Tiz. "God gave me the woman of my dreams. I thought Pari and I were close before, but I had no idea what I was missing. She has completely changed the way I see prayer. 'God is a person,' Pari says, 'not some unseen force or power. He is a person. God creates, loves, feels pain and sorrow, and He hates.' He is a person, and she has taught me to speak with Him, to believe that He hears me, and to listen when He speaks to me. I see life differently now. Pari also sees life differently. She and I have talked about some things, but you must swear anything I say stays between us. No one else may know."

"Of course, Tiz. You never have to worry about that. I will do it if you ask me to hold something in confidence. What is it?" asked Navid.

"We have talked about staying in Israel. We want to stay with the Messiah. Does that sound crazy to you?"

"I can't say I'm surprised," said Navid. "Pari has thought of little other than the Messiah her whole life. I can assure you Mother and Father have already thought about it. Once she finds Him, she will not be able to leave. It will be equally hard for Rahim to leave, but he loves the Family's children too much to leave them. He will want to stay with the Messiah, but he will not. He will return to Persia with us. I'm glad you want to stay. You and Pari will be our eyes and ears. You will be able to tell us everything about the Messiah. I will miss you both, but the Family will feel good about you keeping us informed."

"What a relief," said Tiz. "I never thought about the fact we will be representing the Family, but you are right. We will be. I can't wait to tell Pari about our conversation. I had reservations about your reluctance when we began the journey, but God has changed you. You are becoming a great leader, Navid. I am proud to serve you."

Navid felt his cheeks grow warm and was glad Tiz couldn't see his face under his scarf. "You are wrong, Tiz. It is I who am honored to lead men like you. I pray and work daily to be worthy of the Scouts' and the Family's trust in me."

They topped a rise and saw the Scouts camped in the valley below them. They cried "hut-hut," their camels flattened, and they rode full speed into the camp. Navid and Tiz used their riding crops to make their camels kneel, and they dismounted.

"Morning tea break?" Navid asked.

"Close, but no," replied Hugav. "You can see a fortress on the other side of that hill. I have watched it, and there are a large number of Roman soldiers stationed there."

"Good work, Hugav," said Navid. "Sheikh Nadeem told us that is the fortress at Resafa. It is a trading post, and it has a Roman garrison. Father does not want us to approach. He and Grandfather will visit the Romans tomorrow. The great news is, from here, we will turn west toward the coast and then south into Israel. We will spend the rest of the day scouting to the west to see what we will face after Resafa."

Esmail, stationed at the top of the dune, raced down, waving his arms. "Roman patrol, Roman Patrol."

"Slow down," said Navid. "Where are they, and where are they heading?"

Esmail panted. "They are a mile out and heading straight at us at a trot."

"All right, Scouts, you ride back and report to Fardad, tell him what you have seen, and tell him Tiz and I are riding to meet the patrol. If we do not return by evening, you may assume they have taken us to the fortress. Now, ride fast; they must not see you."

Everyone mounted, the Scouts racing back to the caravan and Navid and Tiz leisurely riding their camels up the dune. They saw the Romans when they topped the rise; they were much nearer than a mile. A Roman soldier pointed to them, and the patrol increased speed to a canter riding straight at the two men. Navid and Tiz rode down the dune to meet the Romans. The two Scouts had no weapons visible. They wanted to appear as welcoming as possible. The Romans were not as welcoming. They surrounded the two men with their lances leveled.

The officer in charge spoke to them in a language they did not understand.

Navid responded in Aramaic. "Greetings, I am Navid, and this is my friend, Tiz. We are scouting for a caravan that is following us."

The officer in charge responded in halting Aramaic, "Dismount." The officer pointed to two men and said, "You two search them and the camels."

Navid and Tiz dismounted, and the men performed the search. They approached the officer and showed him two bows, two knives, two quivers of arrows, and two waterskins.

"Traveling light," the officer said, "no gold, swords, or shields."

Navid tried again, "I am Navid, and this is my friend, Tiz. May I ask your name?"

The officer stepped forward and hit Navid hard in the stomach. "Here's how this works. I ask questions, and you answer questions. Let's try it again. Where are your gold, and weapons?"

Navid slightly nodded his head. "I am unfamiliar with your customs. I have not been in Roman territory before. We don't carry gold because we are merely scouts. We have no need. We do not have more weapons today because we left them with the caravan. We did not need weapons today. We knew we were in Roman territory, so we were not concerned about bandits. The legion's stance on law and order is well known."

"How far behind is your caravan?" the officer asked.

"They will arrive tomorrow."

"Good," said the officer. "They can do without scouts the rest of the day. I'm sure they can find Resafa on their own. You two will come with us to meet the Tribune. I'm sure he will have questions for you."

Navid and Tiz mounted and accompanied the patrol to Resafa. The fortress was 12 miles from the Euphrates. They had built the city and the fortress on a mound, and the fortress walls were 40 feet high and built in a rectangle of 500 feet by 300 feet. It was a formidable edifice. There were guard towers every 100 feet. Navid did not like the idea of entering that fortress.

They rode through the fortress gates, and Navid counted

ten large barracks that would house around fifty men each. Resafa contained a cohort, which fit the fact they were meeting with a tribune. In the city's center was a large stone building with thick wooden doors with iron cross braces with an X on each door. They rode to the stone building, dismounted, and the patrol officer led them inside. They were taken to a small anteroom, told to sit, and the door was closed behind them.

"I would say this is going well. What do you think, Tiz?"

Tiz looked at his friend and shook his head. "Feels a little too much like a prison to me, and I don't think that patrol officer liked you very much."

"Oh come, Tiz, I think I was starting to grow on him, but I agree with you about this place. I don't like it. I don't like it at all," replied Navid.

Tiz laughed softly. "I must have missed that subtle change in your relationship. It went right by me. What do we do now?"

"We wait. There is nothing else we can do. The tribune will make us sit here for a while to demonstrate Roman power and authority, and then the grilling will begin."

The two men looked around the room. There was nothing, no chairs, table, cushions, nothing. They sat on the floor in opposite corners and made themselves as comfortable as possible. Navid trained the Scouts to clear their minds, be still, and block out their environment, and that's what they did now. They closed their eyes and waited. They heard the door open, and both men were immediately on their feet. Navid knew they had been there for quite a while, but it had seemed like only moments. He was refreshed and ready to meet the tribune.

A guard escorted them into a large room, where a young man, whom Navid believed to be the tribune's clerk, sat behind a large desk. The man was writing when they entered and continued to write without looking up. The guard left the room, and Navid and Tiz waited patiently.

When he finished writing, the youth looked up and announced, "I am Tribune Pilot. Commander of Resafa, and who are you?"

Navid was too stunned to speak for a moment. "I am Navid, and this is Tiz. Our caravan is passing through your territory on our way to Israel. We were scouting when we encountered one of your patrols."

"That leads me to several more questions, Navid. Where did your caravan originate? How large is the caravan? And what is your business in Israel."

Navid thought quickly – truth or lie and finally decided on mostly true. "We are Magi, and our caravan originated in Persepolis, Persia. We are going to Israel on a religious journey to meet a new prophet. Our caravan has 200 men, women, and children. We are traveling with flocks of sheep and goats and a herd of horses and camels. We are a peaceable people."

"Magi, you say? How interesting. I didn't know many Magi were left. Can you show me a magic trick, make something disappear, turn my water into blood, anything?"

"We are not that kind of Magi, Tribune. We are teachers and astronomers. We do not practice divination or other secret arts. Some do such things, but not us."

"How disappointing. Things are rather dull in the desert. I was hoping for some entertainment. But you still have not answered the reason for your trip. If you are who you say you are, simple teachers, why a journey of 1,000 miles to meet a Hebrew prophet in Israel? It appears you have uprooted your families to make this trip. That is astounding. Why would you do that?"

Navid knew he had reached a critical moment and wished Fardad was here, but he was not. "I will be honest with you, Tribune. Not all of us were in favor of this journey. I am a member of the Family Council, and I voted against making this trip. My Grandfather, Fardad, whom you will meet tomorrow, is considered a very spiritual person. Grandfather had a vision, the Council believed we should heed his vision, and the Family voted to make the trip. Again, I voted to send three or four people, but the Family wanted to meet this prophet. And, so here we are."

"Tiz, you have been quiet," Pilot said. "Did you want to make this trip?"

"I did, Tribune," Tiz replied. "Navid is my brother-in-law, and I respect him, but I felt he was wrong. The Magi have existed for hundreds of years. Our ancestors recorded old predictions made by the prophets of Israel. The Magi are knowledgeable of the prophecies, and these prophecies point to someone special who will come at this very time. Fardad is the most respected man in the Family, and if he had a vision, then I would follow him."

"Ah," said Pilot, "a true fanatic. Are you a fanatic, Tiz?"

Tiz's eyebrows scrunched together, and he tilted his head. "I don't know what you mean by fanatic, Tribune."

"I will tell you what I mean, Tiz. Israel is full of men like you. They call themselves Zealots. They hate Rome, and they kill Roman soldiers every chance they get. They are looking for a prophet too. They call him the Messiah. They believe this Messiah will be King over the world and restore Israel to power. Is that who you are looking for, Tiz? Are you going to find this Messiah and join him?" Pilot's face turned red, and he rose, "Do you want to kill Romans, Tiz."

Tiz stepped back, a look of horror on his face. "No, Tribune, absolutely not. I have never heard of these Zealots. That is not who we are. Ours is a mission of peace. We will go to Israel, meet with this prophet, and then return to Persia. I assure you we want nothing more than that. Speak with Fardad; you will know I am telling the truth. I am not that kind of fanatic, Tribune."

Pilot sat back down and shrugged. "You seem like a nice young man, Tiz. I want to believe you; I do. This is what we will do, you and Navid will be my guests tonight, and tomorrow I will speak to this Fardad. If the Magi are as you say, I will give you a pass allowing safe passage through Roman territory. If the Magi are not who you say they are, well...I am afraid you will not like the results. Guard," Pilot yelled, and the same guard stepped into the room. "Please find our guests a comfortable room for the night and see they are well fed."

The guard nodded, pointed to the door, and Navid and Tiz exited the room with the guard following. They left the stone building, and the guard led them to a stout wooden building next to one of the barracks. It had ten cells with thick iron bars. Prisoners occupied several cells. The guard placed them in a cell by themselves and locked the door.

When they were alone, Navid said. "That could have gone better."

"I'm sorry," said Tiz. "I think I messed everything up. I didn't know how to answer his questions."

"You did great, Tiz. Our imprisonment was always going to be the outcome of that meeting. We didn't know what was happening in Israel. There is unrest there, and apparently, these Zealots are at the heart of the problem. The Roman authorities are nervous, and this Pilot is young, which makes him doubly nervous. If he was suspicious after meeting us, just wait until he sees ninety-five Magi warriors. We don't look much like school teachers, with calloused hands, broad shoulders, and skin like leather. Do we look like we sit in a school room all day? I fear for Fardad; he will have a difficult time with this man. I wish I had a way to get a message to him. We are doomed if the word Messiah comes out of his mouth."

A man two cells from them said something to them in Latin,

but neither Navid nor Tiz understood.

Navid responded to the man in Aramaic, and the man nodded to his cellmate.

"I speak Aramaic," the man said. "We heard you speaking. Where are you from?"

"We are from Persia, on our way to Israel," said Navid. "We are part of a caravan, and the tribune is holding us overnight until they talk to the caravan leader."

The prisoners in the other cell grinned at each other, poking each other's ribs. "Is that what they told you? Your caravan may eventually make it to Israel, but you will be a few men short," the man said.

"Why do you say that?" asked Navid.

"The tribune is from Rome," said the man, "and he loves the Coliseum. He never misses the chance for a gladiator match when he has the opportunity. The problem is he cannot afford to lose a soldier. There is too much explaining to do. He will pick the smallest, weakest-looking man in your group. It will not be a fair fight. No one has ever beaten a Roman soldier in one of these matches. The tribune is bored out here, and you are about to be the entertainment."

Navid looked at Tiz; the men said in unison, "Hugav."

Resafa – Day 106

The caravan approached the fortress at Resafa and stopped half a mile from the gate. A squad of cavalry rode out and approached the Magi. Fardad and Jahan rode out to meet the soldiers. The officer in charge spoke. "Tribune Pilot instructed me to bring Fardad to see him." The officer spoke in Aramaic, assuming that Fardad could not speak Latin. Fardad was surprised and could have responded in Latin but chose not to. No reason to reveal too much too early.

"I am Fardad," he said as he rode forward, "and this is my son, Jahan, and I believe you have met my grandson, Navid."

"Yes, I have met Navid. He decided to spend the evening with us, but my instructions are to bring you, Fardad. Jahan may wait here."

Jahan was about to protest, but Fardad waved his hand. "That will be fine; lead the way. I am anxious to meet the tribune and to see my grandson again."

The officer led Fardad to the same anteroom where they'd held Navid and Tiz the day before. Fardad made himself comfortable until the guard came for him an hour later. When Fardad entered the room, the tribune was leaning back in his chair with his fingers steepled.

"Fardad," Pilot said, "I have looked forward to meeting you after the interesting conversation I had with your grandson and Tiz yesterday. Tell me about this journey and how it came about. Persepolis, Persia to Israel, that's a long trip."

"Yes, it is a long trip, and we are anxious to be on our way. It all began with a vision I had. In the vision, I saw an angel, and he told me to go to Israel to meet the prophet."

"This angel said, 'the prophet.' Not very specific, was he?"

"I know. I thought that strange. The Magi know a lot about the prophets of Israel, and there is an expectation that Elijah, the prophet, will return at some point. I am sure the angel would have assumed that I would know that. Elijah was the most powerful prophet in the history of Israel. The Magi Family knows these prophecies. So, when I told the Family, they all wanted to go. It was almost unanimous."

"Almost unanimous?"

"Yes, Navid was against the Family going. He thought we should send some representatives. A few other families decided to return to Persia in the middle of the trip. So, no, it was not unanimous."

"So, your grandson told me. But he mentioned something about a Messiah. You didn't mention that."

Fardad paused and looked at the tribune carefully; there had been a twitch in his right eye. He was lying. So Fardad said, "You mistook the word Messiah for Elijah. Simple enough, they sound much alike. No, the Messiah and Elijah are two different things entirely. The angel would have never referred to the Messiah as a prophet. Heavens no." Fardad laughed.

Pilot pressed on, "This Tiz fellow seems a bit of a rabid believer. He admitted to being a Zealot."

Fardad was not laughing now. "Tribune, I honor and respect your position. I understand your need to protect Roman territory from those who seek to harm Rome. But it does not further our conversation when you lie to me. I have never heard the word Zealot in my life, which means Tiz has never heard the word Zealot. Tiz is also among the kindest, gentlest people in the Magi Family. There is nothing he said or did that should arouse this level of vitriol. We are a peaceful people; on our way to Israel, we are on a quest for truth. God has revealed many truths through His prophets. We are eager to meet this newest prophet. There has not been a prophet in Israel in over 400 years. We will not stay in Israel long. We must return to Persia as soon as possible. We will stop and tell you about the prophet and what he said on our way back. This prophecy may be very important information to your superiors."

Pilot sat up straight. "I believe you, Fardad, and it will be necessary for you to stop here on your return since one of your Magi Family will be staying with me when you leave. I believe your grandson said you have a Council that is over the Family. One of the Council members will stay with me, and if you do not return in six months, I will kill him."

"I see," said Fardad, "one of the Council will be glad to stay with you, but can we agree on eight months? It may take us a while to find the prophet. Is that the only condition?"

Pilot nodded. "I will agree on eight months, and there is one more condition. We will have a contest tonight between one of your men and one of mine. It's boring on a remote outpost, and the men need entertainment. Whenever a caravan comes through, I arrange a contest between a Roman soldier and a caravan member. The men enjoy it tremendously, and they have come to expect a match whenever a caravan stops. I will accompany you to your camp and select one of your men for the competition."

"That won't be necessary," said Fardad. "I will select someone."

Pilot grinned. "That is not up for negotiation, Fardad. Lead the way. I will select your fighter."

Pilot, Fardad, and the same cavalry squad rode to the Magi camp. Jahan came out to greet them.

"This is my son, Jahan," said Fardad, "Jahan, the tribune has informed me there is to be a match tonight between one of his soldiers and one of our men. He wants to select our combatant."

"That is correct, Jahan," Pilot said. "Please gather all the men between twenty and thirty and line them up."

"That won't be necessary," replied Jahan, "I will fight. I will represent the Magi."

Pilot looked at Jahan. He looked like a bear with clothes on. His hands were massive and calloused, and his forearms were scarred from hours of sword training and combat. Pilot shook his head. "You will not fight, Jahan; just gather your men between the ages of 20 and 30 as I have commanded."

Jahan's face turned crimson, but he strode away and returned in a while with thirty men. The men lined up, and Pilot walked down the line examining each of them carefully. "I thought you said you are teachers, Fardad. These are not teachers The only way they could look like this is through years of sword and bow training and a lot of time outdoors."

Fardad smiled. "I never said what they taught. Many of them are military trainers. They train the Persian nobles and the elite Persian military."

Pilot gritted his teeth and continued down the line until he came to Hugav. Hugav was a foot shorter than the other men. Pilot smiled. "What is your name?"

"Hugav, Tribune."

"Hugav, you will have the opportunity to fight a Roman soldier tonight. What do you think of that?"

Hugav looked at Pilot. "I don't think you care what I think of that."

"You are right, Hugav; I don't care. You will come with me."

Jahan approached, "Tribune, I strongly encourage you to select someone else. Hugav is the deadliest fighter we have. I won't be responsible for the safety of your man if you pick Hugav."

Pilot laughed. "Nice try, Jahan. Hugav will fight. He will return to the fortress with me now."

"What of Navid and Tiz? When will you release them?" asked Fardad.

"They will join you tonight to watch the contest," said Pilot. The fortress is small; you and Jahan may attend, but no one else. We will see you tonight at sunset."

As Hugav passed him, Jahan leaned down and whispered, "Try to wound your opponent if you can. If you kill him, we may all be in danger."

Hugav nodded and followed Pilot back to the Fortress.

Fardad and Jahan entered the Fortress just before sunset and found Navid and Tiz standing behind a group of Roman soldiers, who had formed a square.

"Did you have a nice visit with the Tribune?" asked Jahan.

"It couldn't have been more pleasant," said Navid smiling. "We had a lovely room, and they fed us like kings."

Tiz snorted and shook his head.

"I can see Tiz doesn't agree with you completely," said Jahan. "Where is Hugav?"

Tiz pointed to the square of Romans, and in the middle of the square, chained to a post with his arms over his head, stood Hugav.

"They staked him in the sun and gave him nothing to eat or drink today," said Tiz.

"Not good," said Jahan, "Hugav will be very upset. I wouldn't want to be the Roman facing him. I asked him not to kill the man, but this may change things."

The Romans had set torches on poles around the perimeter of the square. One man with a burning brand was moving around the perimeter, lighting them, casting everything in long yellow shadows.

The tribune and one of the guards entered the square. The guard was carrying a set of old, well-worn armor, a sword, and a makhaira. The guard dumped everything at Hugav's feet, and the Tribune unlocked his chains.

Hugav slowly lowered his arms and rubbed them to restore circulation. To the amazement of everyone, he ran around the square several times and then began leaping as high as he could, then squatting and leaping again. Finished, he looked at the tribune and pronounced that he was ready.

A Roman soldier entered the square. He was in his early thirties, a seasoned veteran, helmeted with a face plate, and he wore full armor. He was six feet tall and was at least fifty pounds heavier than Hugav.

Jahan gritted his teeth; he knew this would be a difficult test for Hugav.

Hugav looked at the pile in front of him, but to the amazement of everyone, instead of putting on the armor, he took off his robe and pants and stood in his loincloth. He picked up the sword and knife and looked at his opponent.

Hugav spoke loud enough for all to hear, "In our culture, we fight in the tradition of Baildan, our founder, who fought the giant Zikri in this fashion. We fight with weapons only. We do not hide behind armor. But I will understand if the evocatus is afraid to fight without armor. Romans are not known for their courage."

The goad worked, just as it had for Baildan 700 years before.

The Roman ripped the helmet off his head, threw it to the ground, then stripped off his armor, picked up his sword and knife, and declared, "For the glory of Rome, I will give you a slow death, little man. A dog like you does not insult the greatest empire the world has ever known."

Hugav struck his knife against his sword and began circling the Roman. The Roman went on the attack immediately. He rushed Hugav and began furiously reigning blows with sword and knife. Overhead blows, knife thrusts, sword thrusts, sweeping cuts at Hugav's legs and torso.

Hugav stayed defensive and focused on parrying everything. Jahan knew he was biding his time, letting the Roman wear down a little.

The Roman's attack lasted almost thirty minutes. He was in magnificent condition. Hugav had suffered a minor nick to his shoulder, but it was nothing. The Roman stepped backed, sweating and breathing heavily. It was Hugav's turn.

Hugav circled right, then left, constantly increasing his speed. The Roman matched him turn for turn. The Roman was fast, but not quite fast enough. Like a cobra striking, Hugav would flick knife or sword, and small cuts appeared on the Roman's arms and thighs. The cuts were not crippling, but the Roman was bleeding freely. Hugav continued circling and cutting for almost twenty minutes.

The Roman was tired from exertion and blood loss. Hugav kept his eyes on the Roman's eyes and saw a slight loss in the Roman's concentration. Hugav stepped in and, with the precision of a surgeon, took off the Roman's left hand. The hand, still clasping his knife fell to the ground.

There was complete silence in the Roman ranks. Then several men lowered their spears and advanced on Hugav. The disabled soldier stepped in front of Hugav and yelled, "Halt." He looked at the advancing men, "This man could have killed me any time he wanted. I have never seen a more skilled fighter. He did not kill me. He kindly took my left hand, which means I will live to fight again. You will not dishonor me by killing this man. Stand down."

Hugav threw down his sword and knife, walked over to his pile of clothes, and dressed. He walked toward Jahan, and the Romans parted to let him through.

"Nicely done, Hugav," said Jahan. "You left him with his honor and his fighting hand. This is the best outcome we could have hoped for."

Pilot approached the group. "Please do me the honor of dining with me. We will celebrate your victory."

"Thank you," said Fardad," we accept."

They followed the tribune to the stone building, and he led them into a beautifully appointed dining hall. The servants had prepared the meal; they just hadn't anticipated that it would be the Magi who would be enjoying it. The Magi sat, and two Roman officers joined them. The servants poured wine, and the men ate. Hugav devoured plate after plate of food, but the wine went to his head because of dehydration. His head began to lower toward the table, and Navid jabbed him gently in the ribs. His head shot back up.

"It is clear," said Pilot, "you are much more than you have led me to believe. Can all of you fight like Hugav?"

Jahan answered, "I cautioned you, Tribune, not to select Hugav. I told you he was one of our best fighters. The only people I know who can beat him are Navid and Tiz. We have other excellent warriors, but we also have men dedicated to teaching and studying mathematics, astronomy, medicine, and literature. We are teachers and trainers. We are who we said we were."

"I could use Navid, Tiz, and Hugav if they want to enlist," said the Tribune.

"I can speak for all of us, Tribune," said Navid, "you do us great honor, but we are Magi. The thought of being separated from the Magi Family is unimaginable. Your offer is most generous since it comes with Roman citizenship, but we must decline."

Tiz and Hugav nodded in agreement.

"Pity," said Pilot, "I could use men like you, but I will not force you."

A clerk came in bearing a parchment and handed it to Pilot, who reviewed and signed it and then handed it to Fardad. "As agreed, here is a pass that gives you eight months to visit Israel, and at the end of that time, you will return the pass to me, and I will give you your Council member back. Have you selected who will be staying with me?"

Navid was about to volunteer, but Fardad cut him off. "The Council will meet tonight to select someone. Whoever we select will join you in the morning, and we will depart."

The group spoke for a while, and the Magi left and returned to camp. Fardad had Navid gather the Council members, and he and Jahan went to the Council tent.

The Council arrived, Kevan, his son, Marzban, Ram, Rahim, and Navid. They sat in a circle around Fardad.

Fardad wasted no time. "The Roman Tribune has demanded we leave a Council member with him as surety for our return. If we do not return in eight months, he will kill the hostage. We will spend the next few minutes in silent prayer, and then I will hear your opinions."

The Council collectively bowed their heads as each sought God's will in this decision.

Fardad was the last to finish. He raised his head and looked at the Council members. "I hate this. One of us will not meet and worship the Messiah. I cannot ask anyone else to do this. I will stay in Resafa."

"Is this a Council decision or not?" asked Jahan. "This is not something you decide on your own. We will hear from everyone, then vote, and the Council's decision will be final. Agreed?"

Fardad looked at each of them. "Agreed. Therefore, I want to offer to be the one who remains behind."

Over the next several minutes, Jahan, Navid, Kevan, Marzban, and Ram all argued vehemently and persuasively about why they should be the one to remain. After the third cycle of arguments, Rahim finally spoke. "You are the bravest, noblest, and most faithful men I know. You have risked your lives countless times over the years in leading and defending this Family. I have sat safely by, learning and teaching under your protective wings. Today, my time has come. This is my day, my time. I will stay in Resafa. All of you are needed to complete this journey and return to Persia. I am not needed. Pari can teach for the rest of the journey. Her skills with the children and her knowledge far exceed mine. She can also document the trip and share every small detail with me when you return. It will be as if I was there, but I will be seeing through the eyes of an angel. Please, please let me do this. For the first time, I get to be the hero. Please do not deny me this. I will never have the chance again to serve the Family like this."

Fardad spoke, "I do not think there is anything more to say on this matter. Everyone has made a strong and impassioned argument on why they should remain behind. But Rahim is correct; he has earned the right. He is also right in that each of you is necessary for the remainder of the journey. Therefore, there are only two logical choices. All those who favor me remaining in Resafa, raise your hands."

Fardad raised his hand, but there were no others. Fardad shook his head knowingly. "Those in favor of Rahim remaining, raise your hand." Everyone raised their hands, and Rahim smiled.

"Thank you," said Rahim, "by the time you return, this will be the first Roman garrison to become believers in Jehovah."

Later that night, the tribune was sleeping soundly when suddenly a strong hand clamped over his mouth. His eyes flew open, and in the faint moonlight from his window, he saw Hugav.

Hugav leaned close and whispered, "In the morning, we will send you one of the most beloved men in the Magi Family. I am holding you personally responsible for his welfare and care. When we return, he must appear well rested, well fed, and content or I will visit you again. Please don't make me visit you again. You have seen me fight, but that is just a small sample of what I can do. I will sit over in the corner while you consider what I have said, and then you can give me your answer."

Pilot's mind was racing. This fool had gotten into a guarded fortress and past the guards at his door. *What kind of man was this?* He thought about screaming for the guards, but then he thought better; he had seen Hugav's speed. Finally, he called, "Hugav...Hugav," but there was no answer. The Tribune unhooded the candle by the bed. The room was empty, and a chill ran up his spine.

LYDIA

Magi Camp – Day 107

Rahim joined Fardad's family for the morning meal. The mood was somber, and everyone was quiet. A guard detachment had arrived to collect the selected Council member, and Fardad had told them to wait.

"Why the long faces?" asked Rahim. "They aren't going to execute me. They are holding me as surety. In their place, we might do the same thing. They have already seen what our most diminutive warrior can do. The Tribune must be terrified about what one hundred Hugavs could do. I will see you all in a few short months."

Pari had fidgeted with her food the entire meal and looked as if she would burst into tears any moment. "But Rahim, you will miss seeing the Messiah. You have dreamed of this more than anyone your whole life, and what will I do without you? I cannot teach everything. You know so much more than I do."

"Little one," Rahim said affectionately, "I will see and worship the Messiah through your eyes. You must record everything, then tell me what you saw and felt in the minutest detail. I will miss nothing, and God will use me to pray for all of you. I will be on my knees daily."

"This will be our last chance to speak of the Messiah, Rahim," said Pari. "Please tell me Who we are going to see."

Rahim was thoughtful, then began. "I will tell you what I believe. Early in Isaiah, God tells us that a virgin will bear a child named Immanuel, God with us.[14] A child will be born with no earthly father. That means God will be the Father of the Messiah. Next, Isaiah tells us a boy is born, the government will be on His shoulders, and He will be called 'Wonderful Counselor, Mighty God, Everlasting Father, Prince of Peace.'[15] Finally, Isaiah says He is despised and rejected by men, a man of sorrows, and He will give His life to bear our sins.[16] That is what I believe."

Fardad's eyebrows went up. "Rahim, all Israel has believed for hundreds of years that the Messiah will establish kingship over this world. How can he die?"

"This is one of the most confusing questions, Fardad, yet I believe we find the answer in Leviticus. What concerns God most—our earthly conditions or our spiritual condition? He established the Day of Atonement in Leviticus, which Israel holds annually. The High Priest sacrifices a bull to atone for his sins, and then the High Priest sacrifices two goats and a ram for the people's sins.[17] Isaiah tells us that the Messiah intends to act as the High Priest and Lamb of God.

He intends to cover the sins of all mankind, including the Gentiles[18]. How are we to avail ourselves of His sacrifice? Isaiah does not say, but I firmly believe the baby you will worship will lead a difficult life. He will be rejected, persecuted, and killed, and His blood will cover our sins. That is what Isaiah teaches. His kingship is confusing, but He will reveal all in good time."

Fardad looked stunned, then recognition dawned, "I forgot," he said, smacking his forehead. "I forgot. I think I forgot it because I did not understand. As you spoke, it came to me. When the angel visited me, I said he told me only one thing, we were to go and worship, but he said something else. We are to gift him with frankincense and myrrh, burial spices. Rahim, you may be right."

Navid spoke softly, "The Magi will not reject Him. We will show him the love and honor he deserves. He is coming to do something only He can do, redeem mankind. Thank you, Rahim, for sharing. That is a great comfort and a compelling reason to complete this journey."

"Rahim, I could take your place," said Liyana, "I will wear your robes and cover my face, and the Family will be gone before they discover me. This would work, Rahim. Please let me stay in your place, please." Liyana was sobbing so hard at the end; Rahim could barely understand her."

Rahim pulled her close, holding her head against his chest and rocking her. Rahim stroked her hair, soothing her. "Never, my love. Never. The Romans would kill you when they discovered the deception. I love you too much ever to let that happen. Jahan asked me a few days ago if I ever thought about marrying. I laughed and told him no one wanted an old man like me, and he said he knew of someone who thought I was wonderful. That person happens to be the woman I love very much. I know I am a foolish old man, but when the Family returns, we will be married if you will have me. I want you to be my wife, and as we grow old and sit beside the fire, you will tell me again and again about the Messiah. That will be far better than having seen Him myself."

Navid couldn't tell who was more shocked, the family or Liyana. There was a moment of stunned silence before Liyana put her arms around Rahim's neck and kissed him hard.

"Of course, I will marry you," said Liyana. "You have been my life from the first day I joined the Family. My heart aches every day until I am in the wagon next to you, watching you teach the children and learning from you. Yes, I will marry you, but not when we return, right now. When we return, I will return to my husband, and if the Romans harm one hair on your head, I will kill every last one of them."

God has a marvelous way of turning sorrow into joy, thought Navid.

The family was suddenly ecstatic. Everyone jumped to their feet, hugging Liyana and pounding poor Rahim on the back. Navid managed to interject himself between Jahan and Rahim, just as his father was about to pound Rahim's back.

Jahan announced the good news to the Family in the clearing, followed by more hugging, kissing, and pounding. Fardad finally calmed everyone and conducted the fastest marriage ceremony anyone could remember.

The Magi Family formed parallel lines between Rahim and the waiting Roman soldiers when Fardad finished the ceremony. Rahim and Liyana passed between them, and every man, woman, and child embraced him. Rahim stood tall, head up as he walked toward the Romans. There was a light in his eyes and a smile on his face. Liyana kissed him goodbye and then told the Roman commander she held him personally responsible for her husband's safety. She then explained that if any harm came to Rahim, she would cut off the commander's appendages. Navid wasn't sure if the commander understood her words, but her graphic gestures were clear.

The Scouts mounted and rode out. They would head due west today. Their next objective was Apamea, sixty miles away, and then it was a short ride to the coast.

Esmail asked as they rode out of camp, "Do you think Rahim will be safe with the Romans?"

Hugav grinned. "Perfectly safe. They won't harm a hair on his head. I assure you."

Navid shook his head. "Oh no. What have you done, Hugav? I don't like the sound of this."

Hugav tried to look innocent. "I have done nothing. Although I admit, I had a brief conversation with the tribune, who assured me Rahim would be safe."

"I don't recall this conversation coming up at dinner, Hugav. When did you have this conversation? Navid asked.

"It may have been a little after dinner," Hugav stated.

"How much after dinner?" Navid continued to press.

"Okay, fine," Hugav said in exasperation. "I visited him in his bed chamber in the middle of the night. The tribune understood the message perfectly. He knows that not his walls nor his guards can protect him from the Magi if anything happens to Rahim. I believe I made that message clear."

Navid grinned. "Well done, Hugav. I would have loved to see the Tribune's face when he saw you in his room. Why didn't I think of it?"

They scouted to the west all day, and Navid saw a small mountain range to the south, but the area they were in was flat plains and grasslands. There would be adequate grazing for the flocks and herds. Navid was relieved. They met a few groups of shepherds that day, a good sign they were approaching populated areas. The shepherds told them that after Apamea, they would run into mountains, turn south at the mountains for two days, and there would be a valley that led to the sea. "Follow the sea south until you reach Israel," they said.

Navid was beginning to get excited. He believed they would make it to Israel with all of their people. *What a miracle,* he thought.

Tiz was riding in the lead with Navid. "That was a foolish stunt of Hugav's. It is never a good idea to give away too much information about us."

"I agree," said Navid, "but it was a good idea in this case. The tribune will think twice before he abuses Rahim. I assure you; the tribune is sitting at his desk today wondering how Hugav got past that many guards. The tribune is pagan and very superstitious. I'm sure he believes Hugav has supernatural powers. That would explain how he defeated his best warrior and made it through multiple levels of security. No, in this case, I'm glad Hugav left him guessing."

Tiz nodded. "I hadn't thought of it that way. It seems everyone is always a step ahead of me. Am I slow, Navid?"

"Do you mean, are you a slow thinker? No, it is just that you always think about doing the right thing, in the right way. Most of us believe others are devious; therefore, it is good sometimes if we are also devious. You do not think that way. You think everyone is telling the truth; therefore, you always tell the truth. You are not slow, naïve, or overly cautious. You merely want to see the best in everyone. We all wish we were more like you. You keep us balanced, Tiz. Always tell us what you are thinking or how you feel. You help everyone else reassess their actions and decisions. That is good, not bad."

Tiz smiled. "You always make me feel better, brother. How do you do that? You always know what to say. I tell the truth, and you are an encourager. We make a great pair."

Navid laughed. "We do make a great pair, brother."

They rode for the rest of the day and did not encounter anything concerning. The evening horns sounded, and the Scouts rode back to the main encampment. Cooking fires had started, people were erecting tents, and those selected for the first watch grabbed a quick bite and headed back to the flocks, herds, or perimeter security. This was the pattern of their life, and Navid was comfortable with it.

Tiz had found the only tree in fifty miles and set up their blanket under it. Pari, Nura, and he was seated along with Fardad and Ava. He saw Utana and Fahnik approaching and knew that Mother, Father, Liyana, and Gul would not be far behind. This nomadic life was becoming too familiar, with meals in a different spot every day, constant scenery changes, and a different night sky. *I love* this, thought Navid, who sat, kissed Ava, and waited for the others to arrive.

When everyone had gathered, Fardad prayed, and they ate. Everyone's eyes were on Pari. She was depressed, concerned, and missing Rahim.

Asha spoke, "It is all right, Pari. We all miss Rahim, but you will be fine. The children love you and love your teaching. Ava, I saw you talking to your mother today. What were you talking about?"

Ava blushed. "Not much, really. Just some womanly issues."

Asha nodded. "Did she tell you that you are pregnant?"

It was hard for Asha to tell who looked more shocked, Ava or Navid.

Ava stammered, "But how would you know, Mother? How can you be sure? It is too early; even my mother said we must wait longer to be sure."

Asha shrugged. "I have dealt with pregnant women my whole life, Ava. You are pregnant. It is a sixth sense. I don't know what changes, but something does, and I can always tell."

Jahan roared and began pounding Navid on the back, knocking him into the curry and causing multiple contusions. Navid leaped to his feet and bear-hugged his father to save his own life. Pari laughed for the first time since Rahim had left. Utana and Fahnik hugged Ava. The others eating in the clearing came over to see what the ruckus was about and, upon hearing the news, began beating Navid on the back and hugging Ava. When the congratulating finally ended, Navid could not remember a battle or training session in which he had incurred more damage.

Navid backed away from everyone, wiping curry from his face and clothes, and said, "I believe it is time for the evening lesson." Everyone agreed and began wandering toward the clearing. Navid walked over to Ava and took her in his arms. "Have I told you today how much I love you?" he asked.

"I believe you may have," she said, smiling up at him, "but I wish your mother hadn't said anything. It is so early. What if something happens to the baby?"

Navid held her tighter. "Nothing will happen to the baby. You will be fine, but maybe you need to ride in one of the wagons for the rest of the trip."

Ava laughed. "The last thing I need is being bounced around in one of those wagons. I will walk. It will make me stronger, but I will make sure to drink plenty of water and eat properly. And you can massage my back every night and maybe my feet too."

"You don't need to worry about that; I will fuss over you like a doe with her fawn."

They both laughed and walked to the clearing for the evening lesson. Tiz had already placed Pari on the platform.

"Good evening, children," Pari began, "as you all know, Rahim will not be with us for the next few months. He is staying with the Romans in Resafa, and we will pick him up on our return to Persia. Tonight, we return to King Cyrus. In our last lesson, he defeated the Medes and has now consolidated the nations of Media and Persia. Tonight, I will teach you how he created an Empire that would end up conquering the known world. Pari opened the ancient scroll and began to read...

Ecbatana – 547 B C

A runner from the king knocked on Kia's door; King Cyrus had summoned him. Cyrus had made Kia his cavalry commander. The Scouts were too valuable to send back to Persepolis. In addition, Cyrus trusted Kia, and Cyrus loved to surround himself with men he trusted.

Kia entered the Throne Room, and several generals were present. Kia bowed to the king and waited for him to speak.

Cyrus nodded at Kia, "Your Scouts have proved invaluable once again, Kia. They have brought word that Croesus and the Lydians have invaded Cappadocia and have laid siege to Pteria. Croesus thought he would bite off one of our best agricultural areas, but I don't think I am willing to give it to him. I have sent riders throughout Persia to summon the Persians to war. The Median army is also gathering. We are going to war."

"My King," said Kia, "did the Scouts give you a report of enemy strength?"

"Why would you even ask?" said Cyrus smiling, "They are your Scouts. They miss nothing. They estimate Croesus's force at slightly over 400,000 men. The bulk of his force is infantry, archers, and slingers. He has 10,000 cavalrymen and 400 light chariots. We will organize and fight, unlike anything Croesus has seen." Cyrus pointed at one of his generals; we cannot match the size of his cavalry. We don't have enough horses for both cavalry and baggage train. Therefore, I want you to remove the horses from the baggage train and replace them with camels. Your responsibility is to acquire those camels." The general nodded.

Cyrus walked to a large skin covering a portion of the wall. Cyrus had detailed everything about the organization of his army, the line of march, the camp setting, and the baggage train organization. His organization was meticulous. "We will maintain the same structure we used at Hyrba. The highest unit in the army is the division, comprised of 10,000 men and commanded by a general. Within the division will be10 regiments and 23 companies of 420 men, each company led by a commander. The squad will continue to be six men, led by a squad leader. The squad members must be from the same city or village. They will sleep, eat and train together. The squad is a brotherhood, and men fight harder to protect their brothers. The squad is our true advantage over our enemy. Kia, how many heavy chariots do we have?"

"King Cyrus, we have 300 chariots, and the cart makers continue to build. I have trained horses and reserves for 300 chariots. If we continue to build, I am not sure I will have enough trained horses for the additional chariots before we march," Kia said, shrugging and turning his palms up.

"Continue to build, Kia. You can train horses during the march. We need every chariot." King Cyrus walked over to another large skin hanging on the wall. "This drawing shows the order of march and the organization of the camp. Every regiment, 1,000 men, will have a baggage train. There will not be a baggage train at the rear of the army. There are several reasons for this; first, an enemy attack on our rear will not end up destroying all of our supplies, and hence the army. The second reason is efficiency. At day's end, the supply train is smaller and can set up and feed troops within an hour. And lastly, in battle, the arms and resupply for the division are traveling with them. The drawing below is the camp organization and order of march. Every division will camp in the same position every night, and I have marked the specific location for the general and each company commander's tent. The division closest to the enemy will lead every morning, the division to their right will follow, etc. When we stop at night, we will form a circle with my command tent in the center of the camp. This way, everyone knows where to find me, and I know where to find every general and commander. I have also marked specific locations for every latrine; there will be no deviation from the daily camp. Your thoughts, General Harpagus?"

"I have never seen such detailed planning, my King. The structure alone will give us a significant advantage over the Lydians. I would make only one recommendation: you have specific runners assigned to each division. The runner will stay with the general during battle to provide rapid information to you. Also, I would rotate the latrines and move them out another fifty feet."

Cyrus pointed to his aid. "Revise the drawings as General Harpagus has noted. I should have seen the advantage of both changes. Well done, General."

Cyrus continued down the wall. Leaning against it were forty spears with flags of varying colors. Each standard was a different color and bore the image of a sacred animal. The first and largest flag was Cyrus's standard, a golden falcon with outspread wings. There was an orb above its head representing the god Mithra, and in his talons were two more orbs representing the sun and moon. Cyrus walked down the wall, selected a green standard bearing the image of a tall, slender dog with a plaited mane, and gave it to Harpagus. "Yours is the Dog Division, General Harpagus."

Next was a yellow standard bearing the image of a large black raven, wings folded back and an orb in its mouth. King Cyrus called General Oebares, handed him the standard, declared his division the Raven Division, and reached for the next standard. "In addition," announced Cyrus, "the color on your standard is the color your division will wear in battle. On the battlefield, I will be able to identify every division, and I can adjust support as needed." The generals who had grown up in the Median army were astounded by the changes Cyrus made and the detailed level of his planning. Cyrus had thought of everything.

By October, Cyrus had gathered his western army and was ready to march. The army was well over 300,000 men with 350 chariots and 10,000 calvary. Kia received a message to report to the king early one morning and went to the Throne Room in the palace. King Cyrus and General Oebares were deep in conversation over a map.

The king looked up and saw Kia enter. "Kia, join us," said King Cyrus. "General Oebares and I were discussing the march route. Pteria is 800 miles from Ecbatana, and winter is approaching. We can be in Pteria, at 50 miles daily, in a little more than 2 weeks. You must find a route on which we can travel fast."

Kia looked at the map. "My King and General Oebares, I recommend we pass well to the east of Nineveh; the Babylonians have a division stationed there. We don't want to worry them. Once past Nineveh, we will turn west toward Melitine and northwest to Pteria."

"What about mountain passes and rivers?" General Oebares asked.

Kia leaned over the map and traced the valleys he would follow and the two river crossings they would make. "I have already discussed routes with the Scouts. They are confident those are the easiest routes and crossings for the army, and there is good foraging in most places. We will be in Pteria in no more than sixteen days."

"Good," said Cyrus, "because we leave today. Gather the Scouts and lead the cavalry out. The army will follow you in two hours. I also want to congratulate you on your new tunic, the silver looks very good, and the rearing black horse on your silver standard is perfect. Remember, when you stop at night, you will be the first division, the divisions following you will form a circle, and my staff and I will be in the center. Carry your colors proudly, Kia."

"I will, my King. I will see you tonight," said Kia.

Kia went to the cavalry camp and found his friend Vafa waiting for him. Vafa was five years older than Kia and was the Magi Family's military trainer in Persepolis. Kia had decided that Vafa was more useful in leading cavalry than teaching, so he sent for him. Although even if Kia had not sent for him, he would have come. Vafa knew this campaign was critical. If Cyrus defeated Lydia, he would have an Empire rivaling Babylonia.

"Good morning, my friend," Kia greeted him. "Have the buglers sound, 'Mount Up.' We're leaving." Without being commanded, Kia's aid was already packing his things, and others were taking down the tent. "I suggest we move, Vafa, unless you want to get rolled up with the tent."

The two men stepped from the tent to hear the ram's horns calling the army to war. Every division was summoning its men to arms. There was nothing like the sounds of an army preparing to march – officers shouting, men yelling encouragement and ribbing one another, thousands of feet rushing about, horses being harnessed and tacked, horses, camels, mules, and donkeys whinnying, braying, or grunting, spears, swords, and knives clattering, and leather creaking. Standards were unfurled and raised in every direction. There had never been an army like this before. It was a sea of colors, with every division sporting individual colors.

Cyrus was brilliant, thought Kia. These soldiers were no longer part of a massive army; they had an individual identity. First, they were part of a six-man squad, a brotherhood. Then they were the Wolf, Bear, Raven, etc. Division. They had a standard to defend and their colors. Kia had heard a general address his division yesterday, saying, "When the battle is hot, and men are dying, the Panther Division may run, but the Raven Division will never run."

And 10,000 men dressed in yellow tunics screamed their agreement and beat their shields. Brilliant! Cyrus had them; these men will never break. They will die before they run. Cyrus had his army.

Kia led the cavalry. The king, his staff, the 10,000 Immortals dressed in black, and the chariots followed the cavalry in the line of march. The rest of the army followed. A long steady climb faced them as they left Ecbatana. When Kia reached the summit, he rode to the side of the column with Vafa and looked back as the cavalry continued its steady pace.

Kia saw all the divisions making slow progress up the rise. King Cyrus wore a golden helmet with bull horns, riding his giant black war horse. Forty different colors followed in his wake, and a camel supply

128

train came after each regiment.

They watched for several minutes. Vafa was the first to speak. "I have never seen anything like this, Kia."

Kia smiled at Vafa. "Magnificent, one day you will tell your children and grandchildren that you were there when Persia became an empire. When we stop tonight, record what you saw today and your feelings. Everything about this campaign will be in the Magi scrolls. I will tell you what I see, Vafa. I see the best organized and motivated army history has ever seen. King Croesus made a big mistake. There was no reason for him to attack Pteria. King Cyrus would have been happy to develop treaties with Lydia, but now, he will attack and defeat the Lydians. Croesus will rue the day he attacked Persia."

They traveled for thirteen days and made excellent time. Kia's Scouts had watched the city of Pteria the past two days, and Kia knew King Cyrus needed the information he had received. Kia rode to the King's Pavilion. He was greeted outside by the King's Aide, the aide announced him, and Kia entered the pavilion.

"Kia," Cyrus greeted him, "this must mean you have news for me."

"I have news, King Cyrus. The Scouts tell me King Croesus has taken the population of Pteria captive and transported them to Lydia. The Lydian army has dug in; they are not going anywhere. It appears King Croesus's primary purpose was to draw you out. I'm sure he believes you too inexperienced and ill-prepared for war."

"You are correct, Kia. He has planned this carefully. The timing, he attacked in summer, knowing it would take me a while to get organized. He wants this battle to be late in the year. If things do not go as he wants, he slips back across the Halys River, knowing that with winter coming, we cannot follow. In addition, he selected the location perfectly. He picked a significant city at the point furthest from Ecbatana. He wants to stretch my supply line and make it difficult for me to reinforce. Kia, Croesus made several critical errors, and he shall pay dearly. Will we reach Pteria tomorrow?"

"Yes, the lead elements will arrive late in the day, but it will be well past dark before all divisions arrive."

Excellent," said Cyrus, "I will see you at Pteria tomorrow."

Battle For Pteria – 547 Bc

Cyrus stood on a grassy hill well past sunset, but the moonlight was bright enough for him to see the arriving divisions. They were not moving into the normal camp formation. Cyrus was directing each division into the line of battle, preparing for the coming conflict. Once a division was in position, the men rolled in their cloaks and slept.

The baggage trains lit fires before sunrise and cooked the morning meal. Servants for each regiment provided food to the waiting troops standing in formation. When the sun arose, the army, well fed and rested, stood facing the Lydian army as they came out of Pteria's City Gate. The Persian position was as expected; they would be fighting uphill. That did not bother Cyrus. The king mounted his charger and took the standard from one of his aides. Holding the standard aloft in one hand, Cyrus rode along the front of his formation. "Persians, we have not sought this war. King Croesus of Lydia wants war, but he wants more than that. He is testing us to see how much we like our freedom. He wants to know if we are willing to fight to be free men. We will build an Empire in which men are not slaves to the king but citizens of an Empire. You have lived the past three years in freedom. Is your freedom precious? Will you fight to be free men?"

The division in front of the king erupted into cheers and yells and ended by singing the Persian war chant Cyrus had first heard sung at Hybra. Cyrus repeated the message to every division and received the same response every time. These men were ready to fight.

Cyrus gathered his generals and ensured everyone understood his role in the battle. Cyrus led his troops through the valley in front of Pteria, leaving a group of 3,000 men in reserve in the rear. When Cyrus was within 200 yards of the Lydian troop, he saw Croesus send two infantry groups, one right and one left, in a circling movement to trap his rear guard. Croesus had done what Cyrus had wanted him to do. Now, Cyrus was about to give him another surprise.

When the Persians were inside 200 yards, Croesus followed traditional battle protocol. He sent his archers forward and released his chariots. Traditionally the chariot would ride parallel to the enemy line and fire arrows into the infantry. After both sides fired numerous arrows, the leaders would send in the infantry. That was not Cyrus's plan.

When the Lydians fired their first arrow, the entire Persian front sprinted at the Lydian front. Preceding the Persian infantry were the 350 heavy chariots. The chariots were into the Lydian archers before they could react, and the infantry poured into the gaping holes the chariots made. The Persians killed the isolated Lydian archers to a man.

King Cyrus fought in the middle of the Immortals' formation. In the center of the Lydian line were Greek mercenaries from Caria, wearing Greek helmets with a large helmet crest. Cyrus knew these Greeks would be a good test for the Immortals. Once the Lydians recovered from Cyrus's opening gambit, the battle settled into hard-fought inches. The Persians painfully fought their way forward, and the Lydians held them. Hour after hour, men died from exhaustion, loss of concentration, blood loss, and muscle fatigue. At some point in combat, the adrenaline is gone, and it's muscle memory and training. Both armies were well past the point of exhaustion.

As the afternoon was waning, Cyrus made a critical decision. He signaled to his bugler, who looked at him confused after he received instruction. Cyrus understood the unspoken question. "Just blow the signal, man. Do it now."

The signaler raised his horn and blew halt, not retreat, halt. The signaler repeated it over and over. The Persians crossed their weapons over their chests and backed up three paces. The Lydians didn't know what to do without a command. But Croesus knew what to do, and he had his signalers sound halt. The Lydians heard the signal and gladly backed up. Men standing, still alive, were either almost asleep on their feet or giddy with the knowledge they had survived this horrible day.

King Cyrus had shallow wounds on his forearms and thighs. None were deep, and they had stopped bleeding. He sent out runners to bring in the generals; 35 of the 40 generals reported, and the other five reports were by their second in command. Cyrus appointed those second in command to general and continued the meeting. "I need to know two things in one hour. First, send support teams to the field of battle and search for recoverable wounded. If a man is dying, help him to the next world. If he can recover, whether or not he will fight again, save him if you can. This team is also to count our dead and the enemy dead. Your second responsibility, generals, is to perform a roster check. I want every commander, including immediate replacements, to visit every squad. I want to know any squad that suffered significant losses. That is all, generals, be back in one hour."

An hour later, everyone assembled in the King's Command Tent. The generals all reported. General Oebares suffered the highest casualties, with 1,800 dead and 200 severely wounded. General Oebares had the left flank during the battle and faced opposition from two sides. When all the generals had reported, the Persians had suffered 25,000 dead or severely wounded. And if his generals had a good count, the Lydians had suffered more than 40,000 dead or severely wounded. It was the bloodiest battle Cyrus had ever seen. Corpses littered every foot of the battlefield.

"Support personnel will work through the night. Arrange them in two parties, one cutting trees and gathering wood for the funeral pyre, the other collecting the dead from the battlefield," commanded Cyrus.

A general in the back of the tent asked, "Will we attack at first light, King Cyrus?"

"We will not attack at first light. We will not attack at all. I have a feeling King Croesus would love to find a way to extricate himself from this battle. No, we will sit tight tomorrow and see what the Lydians do."

Kia asked, "Do you want me to put the cavalry between the Lydians and the bridge over the Halys River?"

"That is the last thing I want you to do. I'm counting on Croesus's attempting to slip his army back into Lydia tomorrow night. Croesus is counting on the fact that we will go home and not follow. That is where he made his mistake. Three days after Croesus leaves, we will follow. He will feel safe when he is back in Sardis. He will dismiss his mercenaries and send much of his army home for the winter. By the time he realizes we are coming, it will be too late; he will have disbursed his army. Lydia is ours."

The generals in the room smiled at each other, proud that they had backed the right king. Cyrus was brilliant. They would follow him anywhere.

Sardis – The Battle Of Thymbra - 547 Bc

Cyrus had crossed the breadth of Lydia. Sardis sat on a rocky promontory twenty miles from the Mediterranean Sea. Cyrus approached across the broad flat plain of Thymbra northwest of Sardis and halted his army in sight of the city. He wanted the Sardinians to see the size of the army facing them. Cyrus watched a flurry of activity on the city wall all that day and knew that the Lydians would come out to face him tomorrow. Cyrus called for his generals, to hear any input they might have on the upcoming campaign.

"Kia, give us a scouting report," the king commanded.

"Things are not as expected, King Cyrus. The Greeks have left, and the king sent much of the Lydian infantry back to their farms for the winter. But King Croesus received reinforcements during his absence. He has 120,000 Egyptians, 60,000 Babylonians, plus Greeks, Phrygians, and some of the Cappadocians he impressed at Pteria. He has approximately 400,000 men, 300 chariots, and 60,000 cavalry, and the rest are infantry, archers, and slingers. He outnumbers us two to one."

"No matter," replied King Cyrus, "we are here and we will fight. King Cyrus outlined his battle plan for the generals, and asked for comments."

General Harpagus stepped forward. "King Cyrus, I recommend we convert the baggage train camels into cavalry tomorrow. It will increase the number of mounted men, and horses hate the smell of camels. Put the camels in the center of our formation; the Lydian horses will not like it. We have been having problems with our horses whenever they are near the baggage train. I have had more than one rider thrown from his horse at the smell of those foul beasts."

Cyrus grinned at Harpagus. "Brilliance in simplicity. That is what we will do. General Harpagus, I will put you in charge of the Camel Corps since it is your idea."

The sun rose, warming the backs of the Persians arrayed in battle formation. The wind had picked up and was blowing from the north, which would serve General Harpagus's plan. The camel stench will be in the faces of the Lydian horses.

Kia looked up at the city of Sardis, perched on its rocky hill.

The morning sun was glinting off the ice on the stone walls. The city glittered like a star field on a moonless night. *It seemed a shame to ruin such a beautiful morning with the impending horror.* Kia had no sooner finished this thought when the Lydian cavalry and chariots rode out through the City Gate followed by their infantry. *Pity* thought Kia, *death, and bloodshed for no purpose.*

King Cyrus deployed his forces with the flanks drawn in. His army was in a large square. King Croesus did as Cyrus expected, he pivoted his left and right wings to envelop the Persians. When King Cyrus saw the enveloping move, he sounded the attack and sent his cavalry and chariots into the hinge points of each wing. The Lydian army had been split into three pieces, and Cyrus quickly destroyed both of the exposed wings. With the Lydian cavalry and chariots in shambles, Cyrus attacked the main body of the Lydian army with all of his forces. Harpagus's prediction of the effects of the camel odor on the Lydian horses was accurate. As the camels closed with the Lydians, horses refused to advance; some bucked, unseating their riders, and other horses ran for the rear of the formation. The Lydian cavalry lost adhesion and effectiveness. Many cavalrymen were fighting on foot, destroying their mobility advantage.

The battle lasted less than four hours, and Cyrus had destroyed over half of the Lydian army. The Lydians rode from the field. King Croesus would keep his army behind the walls of Sardis, and wait for Cyrus to attack King Cyrus knew they would not come out again.

Cyrus summoned Kia. "Position Scouts at all gates. If any riders try to get out, ride them down."

Kia rode to the Scouts and picked four men, including his son, Azad. "The king wants us to cover the city gates and ensure no messengers escape. If anyone comes out of those gates, chase them down and kill them. Are there any questions?" There were none.

"Azad, take my Arabians," said Kia, "they are both fresh. Nothing can outrun those two."

"Have no fear, Father," said Azad, "no one will get past me."

Azad raced to the corral and tacked up the two Arabians. He mounted the big black and had the white on a trail rope. Azad positioned himself on the northwest corner of the city. To the north, the city sloped down to a narrow valley, and within 300 yards, the ground sloped up into a series of heavily wooded hills. Azad knew if he didn't close with a rider fast, the probability of losing him in those woods would be fairly high. Azad had dropped unnecessary equipment at the corral. He carried his knife, bow, a quiver of arrows, and a water skin. He had a pouch containing bread and cheese, and when he finished eating, he would dispose of the pouch.

An hour before dark, a group of four riders burst from a rear gate of the palace. One man rode northwest, and Azad rode in pursuit. He had to trust that the other Scouts would each ride down their man. Azad did not intend to make this an endurance race. He dug in his heels and began to close the distance. Azad could not make any mistakes. The Lydian had two beautifully matched dun horses with black manes and socks. Azad did not think the Duns could match the speed of his Arabians, but the Lydian was an excellent rider, and he knew these woods.

The Lydian rider looked back at Azad. They were less than 200 yards apart. The Lydian turned and focused on a narrow opening in the trees. He lay on his horse's back and whispered to him. The big dun lengthened its stride and was flying toward the safety of the woods. Azad matched him, he gave the black Arabian its head, and Azad was flying over grass and rocks, wind streaming through his clothes and hair. His eyes watered from the force of the wind.

As they approached the woods, neither rider slowed. The Lydian rider reached the trees, and in moments, Azad lost sight of him. Azad had expected that. He reached the woods less than a minute behind the Lydian. Azad could not see him but could hear him and did not slow. The Lydian rode a zigzag pattern through the trees, hoping to negate Azad's speed advantage. The Lydian had miscalculated the agility of the Arabians. The turns reduced the speed of both horses, and Azad gradually cut the distance between them. Azad saw an upcoming tree; the tree branches were so low the Arabian had to flatten out to get under the branch. Azad threw himself to the horse's left side, clung to the horse's mane till they were past the tree, and then threw himself upright again. The Lydian was full of tricks and surprises, low tree branches, sudden log jumps, and even a couple of streams to negotiate.

Azad could hear the Lydian and knew he would be visible in a few more minutes. Azad made a quick decision and threw himself from the back of the black onto the white Arabian. He dropped the black's lead rope. Azad was fully committed. The white had to get the job done, and she did not disappoint. The white threw herself into the tight turns, and Azad could see the Dun ahead of him in less than a minute. The Lydian looked back, saw Azad and the white Arabian, and realized the Dun was no match for the Arabian. The Lydian slowed and threw both hands in the air. He lowered one hand, removed the bow and quiver from his saddle horn, and dropped them on the ground. Next, he removed his knife from his robe, held it with two fingers, and let it drop.

Azad rode up behind him, bow in hand, with an arrow nocked, "Slide off the left side of your horse, then turn and face me."

The rider did as instructed, keeping both hands raised. "Take the sash off your robe, let it drop, then open your robe," Azad instructed.

Again, the Lydian did as instructed. Azad saw that the man had no other weapons and nimbly jumped down. He approached the Lydian, bent down, and picked up the sash the man had dropped. He ordered the Lydian to turn around and tied his hands behind his back using the sash.

"Why did you surrender?" Azad asked.

The man smiled. "I am a scout. I watched your army approach Pteria. I have never seen such organization and discipline. I was in the battle at Pteria, and you Persians fought intelligently. You fought in small groups, and your men protected each other. I have never seen that before. So, I had a choice: die here in these woods for no reason or live to fight in the Persian army. Cyrus will create an Empire to rival Babylonia, and I want to be there when he does."

Azad smiled back at the man. "Welcome to the Persian Empire; my name is Azad." Azad untied the man's hands, took his courier pouch, and the two men mounted.

Azad and the Lydian courier rode into the cavalry camp, and Azad found Kia.

"I see you have brought a guest," said Kia casually. "Introduce me to your new friend."

Azad made introductions and asked, "Have any other Scouts returned? Four Lydian couriers rode out at the same time. They split up. I followed this man," Azad said, pointing at the Lydian, "has anyone else reported back?"

"No one has returned but you," said Kia, "but that is understandable. I knew you would be the first to return. I knew you wouldn't make it an endurance race; the Arabians are too fast for that."

"Let me introduce our new friend to his company commander, and then I will return," said Azad. "The hard part, until we have a few more Lydians in the command, is to fit him into a squad. The squad must vote to accept him, and they may not be willing to take a Lydian."

"True," said Kia, "but if you vouch for him, the squad may be more willing."

Azad led the man away and returned quickly. "That wasn't as hard as I thought it would be. One of the commander's squads had two Greek speakers from northern Lydia, who had left years ago. They took him into their squad since they were down two men."

"Still no sign of the other riders," said Kia. "Sit with me; we haven't talked since this campaign started. You should not be here. You should be back in Persepolis getting married, not out here riding with me. You are betrothed. The Family exempts you from military service until six months after your wedding."

"We have talked about this, Father. I am here because Cyrus is forging an Empire. I believe Cyrus is the greatest military leader and statesman the world has ever seen. There is no way I can sit back in Persepolis while you and Cyrus are making history."

"Your betrothed and her father did not see it that way. I am not sure she will be waiting for you when you return."

"Her father started shopping for a new husband the day after I announced I was joining you," said Azad. "So much for true love. But I have a feeling she will still be available when we return. The Family is loyal to you; none of the fathers are willing to talk to her father."

Kia nodded, "I thought that might be the case, but I do feel bad for the girl. I have some bad news and some good news."

"Better give me the bad news first," said Azad, "it makes the good news all the sweeter."

"The bad news is I lost two company commanders in the last action. The good news for you is I'm appointing you, company commander. You are young for the position but mature and the best qualified. You see the battlefield the same way I do, which makes my job much easier. That is something I cannot train into a new commander quickly."

"Thank you, Father," said Azad. "I will not let you down. Which company are you giving me?"

"The company you are currently in," said Kia. "You already know the men, and they respect you. It will make the transition easier."

The two men talked for a while, and later in the day, two Scouts came in. One was leading his horse, which had come up lame during his chase. "General Kia, I failed to stop one of the riders. He was heading southwest but could have gone anywhere after losing me. I did get a shot at him and hit him high in the shoulder, but he did not fall."

The horse was favoring its right foreleg. Kia lifted the leg; the hoof had split. He had probably stepped on a sharp rock. Kia shook his head. "Nothing you could have done. I'm not sure we'll be able to save the horse. Wonderful news on wounding the Lydian courier; unless he can get help, he won't be riding very far." Kia looked at the other Scout who had returned, "What happened to the man you were pursuing?"

"He outran me, General. His horse was very fast. I pursued him for hours, but he constantly gained distance on me. My horse was foundering, so I gave up the pursuit."

Kia's eyes narrowed, and his color deepened. He walked to the man's horse and circled it twice. He put his hands on the horse several times, put his ear against the horse's lungs, and listened. Kia walked back to the Scout.

"You pursued the man for several hours. Is that correct?" asked Kia.

The rider looked at the ground. "Yes, General."

"You will look at me when you speak!" barked Kia.

The man's head shot up. "Yes, General."

"The pursuit started ten hours ago. You pursued the man at top speed for three to four hours. Is that correct?"

"Yes, General."

"You broke off the pursuit, and since you were southwest, you had to retrace your original route to return. You rested your horse for an hour, then had to ride at a canter for five hours to make it back here, yet your horse is barely sweating and is not breathing hard. Now, why don't you tell me what happened?"

"I couldn't decide who to pursue, and I hesitated. My companions each picked a man to pursue, and the remaining man had a good lead on me. He got into the woods, and I followed, he twisted around trees, and I had to slow to track him. After the first thirty minutes, the rider entered a stream, and I tracked upstream and downstream to find where he exited the stream. I never found another track."

"I appointed Azad as Commander of a cavalry company today, and I am assigning you to his company. I am removing you from the Scouts. You have demonstrated that you are willing to lie, which is an unacceptable trait in a Scout. Let's see if you can do any better as a cavalryman. But I warn you: if you fail, Azad, I will kill you. Am I clear?"

"Clear, General."

Azad and the ex-Scout left, and Kia went to the King's Tent. The attendant at the tent door announced him, and he entered.

"What news, Kia?" asked the king.

"The Lydians sent out four Couriers. My son Azad captured one, and he is now a Persian cavalryman. A second Scout's horse went lame. He was able to put an arrow into the Lydian rider, but the man rode on. A third Scout lost the Lydian's trail in a stream and gave up the pursuit. I have disciplined him appropriately. The fourth rider has not returned. Word of the siege will reach the Greek allies of King Croesus, my King. The Scouts failed you."

"Kia, there is no one who loves perfection more than I do. You have seen my planning and organization. There is no detail too small. I try to anticipate every need and possibility. But when a battle begins, the number of variables increases to the point where I have to focus on major decisions and let generals and commanders worry about the details. You have stopped two or three of the riders; that is excellent. You have exceeded my expectations. Word may be out, but it will spread slowly with only one courier."

"Thank you, my King, but it doesn't make me feel better," Kia replied.

The king turned to the cup bearer. "Call for the generals; we have decisions to make."

The generals gathered within twenty minutes. The old and the new generals were all in attendance.

"Generals, how is work going on entrenching?"

General Harpagus stepped forward. "I have assigned a division to each section of the wall. The men will dig in where possible, but if an area is too rocky, they will build stone walls for defense. Initial defenses will be complete tonight."

"Thank you, General Harpagus. The Lydians sent out four couriers today, and at least one of them has escaped. I have decided not to sit here and wait to be surprised by a Greek army. Generals Adousius and Hystaspes, take your divisions to Halicarnassus and Phrygia, respectively. Seek treaties with the Greeks and Phrygians if possible, and if not possible, subdue them and put satraps over the new territories. You will create a courier station every 100 miles on your route. You will leave two fast horses and a courier at every station. I want daily reports from both of you and not just military reports. I want to know the conditions for every location. Are people adequately fed, clothed, and housed? If anything is lacking, seek to help the settlement or city. How is morale? I want to know what is affecting the people where it is low. To build an empire that lasts requires the support of the people. They must see Persia as benevolent, not despotic. I don't need people to love me. I want them to know there is justice in Persia for every man. Where justice exists, people will accept reasonable taxation. That is your message and responsibility, Generals."

Both generals saluted and left the tent.

General Oebares stepped forward. "That leaves a problem, King Cyrus. We have two large gaps and a reduced army. This knowledge may incentivize King Croesus to attempt to break out. I recommend we create a 'ghost army.'"

Cyrus smiled. "A 'ghost army?'"

"Yes, my King. I will send out men to gather large sticks. We will create crosses, drape them with clothing, and intersperse them around the camp. They will be mixed in with the remaining divisions to give the appearance we are still at full strength. As long as there is movement around the still figures, it will give the appearance of animation. If the divisions leave during the night, King Croesus will have no idea they have left."

"Brilliant, General Oebares. It's your plan. You are responsible for implementing. Generals, please ensure the 'ghosts' are in place before morning. Is there anything else?"

There was nothing else, and the Generals disbursed.

Toward the end of winter, Cyrus became frustrated with the siege and sent couriers throughout the army promising great wealth to the first man who could find a way into Sardis. There was nothing more alluring to a soldier than the promise of wealth.

Hyroeades's entrenchment on the western side of Sardis faced a sheer rock precipice. The reward news disappointed him because there was no way into the city up that precipice. He watched the sunlight rise slowly up the rock face, and the glare off the ice embedded in the rock made seeing difficult this early. Hyroeades blinked; he thought he saw something shiny bouncing down the cliff. He looked closely. It was a helmet. How odd. Then he saw something even odder. A bare-headed Lydian soldier slipped over the city wall and descended a twisting path, hidden by rock, and invisible from below. The soldier retrieved the helmet, climbed the rock face, and slipped back over the wall.

Hyroeades walked down to the next man on duty. "Did you see

that?" he asked the man.

"Did I see what?" the man responded

Hyroeades smiled. "Did you see the heavens open and gold pouring like rain?"

"You have been on duty too long," the man said. "It happens. I once saw a man chew off his hand. He thought it was trying to strangle him. You stay in this army long enough; you see a lot of strange things. Probably best if you get out of the sun for a while."

Hyroeades turned and walked back to his station, humming a tune in his head—a song his mother used to sing. He looked at the wall above and began to draw a map in his head of how to get to the King's Citadel. When his shift ended, he called his squad together and told them what he had seen and what he planned to do. He said he needed four more squads to help attack the city, but they had to do it quietly. The men suggested four other squads, and they sent men to speak with each of them. A short while later, they reconvened; they had their men. Hyroeades took a deep breath. Now for the difficult part. He left his squad and walked to the General's tent.

Hyroeades approached General Harpagus's tent. The guard stopped him and asked him his business. Hyroeades said he needed to talk to General Harpagus. The guard refused him entrance until, frustrated, Hyroeades blurted that he knew a way into the city. The guard spun on his heels, announced the man to the General, and led him into the tent.

Harpagus glared at the man. "What is so important that it can't wait till after my meal?"

The man bowed. "My apology, General Harpagus. My name is Hyroeades, and I know a way into the city. Also, I was a slave in this city many years ago, and I know the way to the King's Citadel. I have gathered six squads who are willing to attack the city tonight. Once inside, we will open the city gate on the northwest corner of the precipice and capture the king in his citadel."

Harpagus leaned back in his chair, temporarily speechless. "I see, and am I to refer to you as General Hyroeades? Will we share command of the division, or am I reporting to you?"

Hyroeades fell to his knees. "Great General, I am but a flea, and I know it. King Cyrus offered a reward to the first man over the wall. I have gathered thirty men willing to go over the wall with me. The only thing we want is the reward the king offered. I will split the reward with the men going with me. We will open the city gate to you, and you will receive the glory for capturing the city and King Croesus. No one will remember my name tomorrow, but everyone will speak of General Harpagus and his capture of Sardis and King Croesus."

The general let out a bellowing laugh and slapped his knee. "You are a shrewd man, Hyroeades. Very well, you shall lead your thirty men over the wall and open the gate to me. Then tomorrow, you may bask in your wealth and your promotion, Commander Hyroeades. I have one company for which I have not announced a replacement commander. You will be that commander. Congratulations. What time will you begin your raid?"

"We will attack at the end of the third watch. Half of the guards will be sleeping. It will take us fifteen minutes to get the gate open. Then everything will be in your hands, General Harpagus."

The general rose from his chair and stood before Hyroeades. Harpagus extended his right arm. Hyroeades looked up, grasped his forearm, and arose. "Thank you, General. We will not let you down."

At sunrise, General Harpagus strode into the King's Meeting Tent and told the cup bearer he had news for the King. The cupbearer asked if it could wait, and Harpagus told him it could not. The cupbearer left, and almost immediately, the king appeared.

"I was up and dressed, General. I'm assuming any news this early and urgent must be good news. Bad news can always wait. What is it?"

Harpagus removed his helmet and smiled. "I took Sardis this morning, my King. Sardis is yours. I have King Croesus locked in a dungeon awaiting your pleasure, and I have secured all of King Croesus's treasure rooms."

The king leaped down from the dais and hugged Harpagus. "My dear friend, it seems like a long time ago you offered to aid me if I rebelled against King Astyages, and here we stand today in an Empire that will rival any in this world. This is the beginning, my friend, just the beginning."

Magi Camp – Day 107

Pari rolled up the ancient scroll and looked at the children. "We are not in Israel yet, children, but it will not be long. Soon you will smell ocean breezes and see fertile valleys. In a few days, we will take the same road Abraham took when he left Haran. I will talk with Fardad and Jahan and see if they will let us stop in Bethel to find the altars that Abraham and Jacob built for the Lord. We will worship where God's anointed worshipped Him. Other than worshipping the Messiah, nothing could be more glorious. Off to your tents, and lift a prayer for Rahim. I assure you that he is praying for all of you at this very moment."

NABONIDUS
(BELSHAZZAR)

Magi Route – Day 110

Navid and Utana rode point as the coastal mountains loomed before the Scouts. "It's nice to be riding on grass again," said Navid, "even if it is a little sparse. But do you see that valley ahead on the left, Utana? It looks like a paradise."

"I see the valley," Utana said. "I have looked at nothing else for the last thirty minutes. Can you imagine the game we will find? All I can think of is a nice haunch of venison roasting over a fire. My imagination is making me salivate."

Navid laughed; he had not felt this good in a long time. They had reached the coast. They were so close now to Israel that it made him ache. He could not believe he had ever doubted that God would carry them all this way. Navid took the ram's horn from his saddle and blew three quick notes, 'Assemble.' The Scouts raced up and formed ranks in front of Navid.

Navid pointed at the lush valley to their southwest. "Scouts, we are going hunting!" Then he whooped, and dug his heels in, and he and Anosh flew over the steppe toward the valley. He heard the thunder of hooves behind him, the creak of leather, and the jangle of tack. He leaned low and put his head next to Anosh's ear. "We have done it, boy. We have done it!"

The Scouts were all ululating, laughing, and making wild boasts about their hunting prowess. They were young and full of life, it was a beautiful day, wind in their hair, and life was good. They were going hunting. They reached the entrance to the valley; the Scouts slowed and then stopped. To the southwest was a thick stand of trees at the base of a gently sloping mountain. To the north were a thinner stand of trees and a steep rocky slope. They could see wild goats and Nubian ibex higher on the slope. Ahead, in the center of the valley, lay a small lake surrounded by marsh and trees.

"Divide into pairs or small groups," said Navid. "We will meet back here later today. Utana and I will see what is in the marsh ahead." There were several brief conversations, and the Scouts split up, with Hugav and Esmail heading for the wild goats, of course. Heaven on earth to Hugav was a tall mountain.

Navid and Utana entered the marsh, an area of tall grasses and reeds. In a short period, they came across a herd of wild pigs. They used their javelins to dispatch three pigs, weighing 200 to 300 pounds each. They threw ropes around the hind feet of the pigs, dragged them to a short tree nearby, hung them, and bled them. They would come back for them later. They continued through the marsh and saw roe deer and gazelle tracks near the water.

Navid knelt and ran his hand gently over the deer track. He looked up at Utana, "Remember our last deer hunt?"

Utana smiled wistfully. "The day before we saw the star. I will never forget it. I also remember our conversation after the hunt." He smiled at Navid. "You are not the same man you were 111 days ago. I like the new you even better than the old you."

"I was a selfish, ignorant brat, Utana. I have no idea why the Family elected me to the Council. I did everything I could to stop this trip."

"The Family elected you because they knew the man you would become. They knew one day you would be the future of the Family. Greater than Jahan and wiser than Fardad. Everyone knew. You were the only one who didn't know. And we were right."

"Utana, I don't deserve you. You always believe in me. You never doubt. I think you have more faith in me than even Ava."

"That would be impossible," said Utana. "That woman adores you. We have different roles. My responsibility is to challenge you, when necessary, counsel you, and always support you. Every great man must have a great companion. That is my role, and I love it. I would give my life for you, Navid, because this Family needs you." Utana was thoughtful for a moment, "That is why I was so upset when you broke your chains and attacked the slavers. I just sat there chained to the ground, helpless. You fought by yourself, and no one had your back. I screamed for you to come back and get me, but you couldn't hear me over the noise of the sandstorm."

Utana broke down and cried. "Don't ever do that again. I am your man. You never fight without me," he said as he pounded his fists against Navid's chest. "Never. Where you go, I go. Do you understand?"

"I understand, my brother," Navid said as he gently pulled Utana into his arms. "I will never leave you behind again. I promise."

After a moment, Utana stepped back and wiped his cheeks with his sleeve. "Good," he said gruffly, "now let's get that deer."

Navid smiled and slapped Utana's back. "Let's get that deer."

Utana led, and Navid followed, but soon Utana stopped and pointed at the tracks. A set of smaller tracks followed the larger tracks. Utana shook his head and whispered, "Doe and fawn." The two men turned and walked back to the water. They would never kill a doe who was nursing. They found the gazelle tracks, and Utana followed those.

They found two gazelles laying up in a small stand of trees. When the men approached, the gazelles leaped, heading in opposite directions. Utana and Navid shot simultaneously and neatly brought them down.

Utana grinned broadly. "Meat over the fire tonight, boss."

Navid grinned back. Life was good. They hung the two gazelles and bled and gutted them. They had hunted for hours, and both men were famished. They sat as the gazelles bled out and had bread, cheese, and water with a little wine in it. It was wonderful. When they finished eating, they each draped a gazelle around their necks and walked to where they had left the pigs. They left the marsh, placed the gazelle on the ground, and then went back and dragged the pigs out of the marsh. Other Scouts had finished their hunts, and everyone brought their game to Navid and Utana. When all the Scouts were present, there was a mountain of meat, more than enough for the Family. They had deer, pig, gazelle, wild goat, two Nubian Ibex, several Arabian Oryx, hare, squirrels, a medium brown bear, and a jungle cat.

Navid scratched his head and looked at the Scouts, "Which one of you thought we needed a jungle cat for the stew pot?"

One of the younger scouts grinned sheepishly. "I wasn't hunting the darn thing," he said, "I was just trying to stop it from eating me. I thought I might as well keep the hide."

Navid laughed, "Well, I'm glad we didn't lose you to this ferocious predator," he said, looking at the small cat.

The Scout replied defensively. "You can get a serious infection if one of those things scratches you."

The Scouts erupted in laughter and gutted and cleaned the animals they had killed. They started fires and roasted meat. They cut the bear into thin strips and smoked it. It would make good jerky. When the Family arrived, they were treated to the wonderful aroma of cooking game.

Spirits were high when the Family gathered in the clearing for the evening lesson. The Family was spending the evening in a cool valley with clean water, and they had eaten fresh game for the first time in months. Pari looked out at the eager faces, covered with grease from the fresh game. The grease felt wonderful on their dry skin. Pari was about to begin the lesson when Navid approached the platform. He was carrying a package wrapped in skin. He approached Pari and whispered to her.

Navid stepped onto the platform and looked at the children and Family members. "I want to thank the Scouts for their excellent hunting today. After sixty straight days of lamb and goat, we all appreciate the wild game." The Family cheered and ululated, and the Scouts bowed deeply in mock acknowledgment. "One hunter distinguished himself above all others today. He faced one of the fiercest animals in the desert and singlehandedly killed the ferocious beast to save himself and his hunting partner. Scouts are known for their prowess as trackers and hunters, but to my knowledge, no Scout has ever singlehandedly brought down an animal of this size, strength, and ferocity. From this day forward, this Scout and this Scout alone will be known as The Hunter. His fame will be spread from campfire to campfire as long as the Magi exist."

Navid removed the skin from the package he carried. Tiz had polished a piece of wood and mounted the head of the small jungle cat on the plaque. The Scout's eyes, who had killed the cat, widened in horror. Before The Hunter could react, the other Scouts surrounded him, picked him up, and carried him to the platform, where Navid presented his trophy. The clearing roared with laughter. Jahan knelt before the platform, tears streaming down his face as he repeatedly bowed to The Hunter. The only one not laughing was The Hunter, who leaned toward Navid and yelled, "You wouldn't be laughing if that thing had scratched you," which caused Navid to collapse on the platform, unable to breathe from laughing.

The Scouts carried The Hunter to his place, and when the laughter had died, Pari resumed the lesson. "The Babylonian empire is coming to an end. Tonight, we will study the last king of the Babylonian Empire, King Nabonidus." Pari opened the scroll and began to read...

Magi Compound – Babylonia - 541 Bc

Omid and Manoah sat together discussing the king's summons. It didn't seem that long ago that it had been Pera and Davi sitting at this table; now, it was their sons. Pera had died twenty years ago, and Davi is blind, and his once infallible memory was now all too fallible. Omid and Manoah led the Family in Babylon.

"We need to be unified and consistent when we meet with the king," said Omid.

"Which king?" asked Manoah.

"Excellent question, Manoah. King Nabonidus. Babylon is in disarray and confusion. King Nabonidus has been in Arabia for the past ten years. He has only come home to deal with the chaos created by his forcing the people to worship the moon god Sin. He stopped the annual festival of Marduk, the most beloved event on the Babylonian calendar, and the priests of Marduk have been sowing dissension for years. But the real reason he has returned is Cyrus."

"No doubt," agreed Manoah, "King Cyrus has consolidated Lydia, Cappadocia, Cilicia, Lycia, and the northern parts of Assyria. He's coming, and Nabonidus knows it."

"He has been agreeable these past years in letting his son, Belshazzar, lead Babylon and the military, but if Cyrus is coming for Babylonia, I am sure Nabonidus wants to lead the military."

"I agree," said Manoah, "people and priests are upset about failing to observe the Festival of Marduk, and Cyrus is coming. Do you think there are any other issues?" he asked.

"For us," said Omid, "a big one. We are in a precarious position. Things could go poorly for us if we are not careful. King Nabonidus will want to know why the Persepolis Magi are supporting Cyrus and where the Babylon and Persepolis Magi will stand if Cyrus attacks. The safest thing is for me to respond, and you remain silent. Agreed?"

"Absolutely," said Manoah. "I will gladly let you take those questions. I'm ready to leave whenever you are."

The two men rode out of the compound on the all-too-familiar road to Babylon. When they reached the palace, they entered the Throne Room, where Nabonidus was holding court. Belshazzar was seated to his father's right, clearly indicating his rulership position. Nabonidus glanced at the two Magi as they entered the crowded room, and his face darkened. *Not a good sign,* thought Omid.

Nabonidus was receiving a report from one of his spies, who had been in Pasargadae where Cyrus was relocating his capital. Cyrus was now confident enough in his Median support to relocate the capital to Persia, to Pasargadae, where it had all begun. The spy reported a great amount of courier and troop movement and said it appeared King Cyrus intended to launch a major campaign the next year.

King Nabonidus turned to his cupbearer and Belshazzar. "Have we heard from the Egyptians or other allies? Will they stand with us?"

Prince Belshazzar looked at his feet, and the cupbearer reddened. "My King, Pharoah Ahmose II states that he is preparing to defend Egypt against an attack by King Cyrus and cannot weaken his army with a campaign this far north. Cyrus's armies have been in the field for years. He has brilliant generals and has absorbed the armies of every territory he has defeated. None of the coastal states had an army that could survive more than an hour against Cyrus. We have no other allies. No one will stand with us."

"Prince Belshazzar, how many men can we field next year?"

"With full conscription, Father, we can field 550,000 infantry, archers and slingers, and 30,000 cavalry. We may be able to get 50,000 more from the Chaldeans, and that should give us enough to defeat Cyrus."

Nabonidus mulled over what he had just heard, then fixed his gaze on Omid. "And what of my Magi servants?" asked the king. "You seem to have your feet in both camps. Do I need to be concerned about your loyalties?"

Omid did not hesitate. "King Nabonidus, the Magi have always been loyal servants of Babylonia. The Medes and Persians have been allies of Babylonia since King Nabopolassar and his son, King Nebuchadnezzar, established the Magi school in Persepolis to support and train the Medes and Persians. If conflict comes, I cannot speak for the Magi in Persepolis; I can only speak for the Magi Family in Babylon. We will stand with you. We are servants of Babylonia, and you are our king. You command, and we obey. This is how it has always been, and this is how it will be. I will write to the Magi leader, Kia, in Persepolis tonight and ask him not to participate if there are hostilities between Persia and Babylonia. At this time, there is no way to extract the Magi Family from Persepolis."

The king asked his son, "Is that satisfactory, Prince Belshazzar?"

"During your absence, Father, the Magi have been loyal servants to Babylonia. I know Omid, and I accept his word."

"Very well, Omid, your services will continue as usual, but I expect detailed reports of Cyrus's preparations from Kia. Is that understood?"

Omid cringed inwardly. "That is understood, King Nabonidus. I will include that in my letter to Kia."

The two Magi backed from the Throne Room. "Let's see if we can find Daniel or Lem," said Manoah. "I would like an update on Daniel's status and the slaves' conditions."

The men mounted and rode to a large building that housed sellers of cloth, fine merchandise, and furnishings. Above the sales floor on the second story, Daniel had an apartment. The men climbed the stairs and knocked on Daniel's door; Lem answered.

"Omid and Manoah," Lem said, hugging each man. "How wonderful to see you. Daniel is out with the owners. They may not return today."

"Not a problem, Lem," said Manoah. "You can tell us everything we want to know. We are checking on you, Daniel, slave conditions, and morale in the city. Cyrus is coming, Lem. I believe your time in Babylon is short."

Lem smiled ruefully. "The time for the young people is short, Manoah. I am too old; Daniel and I will not see Jerusalem again. We will die in Babylon, but we have obeyed God and have prepared His people for their return. That is what He called us to do."

"Does Daniel regret not being a part of the government? He did so much for those in slavery; it's not the same without him managing the affairs of Babylonia. Does he still work for the men who own this building?"

"Yes, four men own the buildings and the shop below. When Daniel became available, they grabbed him. He has made them rich. Daniel manages everything; they don't have to do a thing. And no, he is thankful he is not serving the present king or his son. The monarchy has worsened since Nebuchadnezzar, and Nabonidus and Belshazzar are the worst. Nabonidus enslaved the city of Tayma in Arabia when he relocated there. He worked the people to death. Their life was unimaginable. That is what will happen to the slaves in Babylon if Cyrus does not come quickly. Nabonidus is self-centered and heartless and deludes himself into thinking that he is Adam reincarnated. He believes he is a god. The sooner Cyrus comes, the better."

"What of the slaves, Lem?" asked Omid.

"So far, things are unchanged. Nabonidus is distracted with preparing for war and is too busy to start any major projects.

Concerning morale, people are angry. There are plots, counterplots, and conspiracies. People are furious that Nabonidus stopped celebrating Marduk's festivals. The people have celebrated these festivals for years and are not just unhappy; they are angry. When Cyrus comes, he may have quite a bit of support. Nabonidus may need to be more concerned about his people than the Persians."

Omid and Manoah looked at each other and nodded. "Just as we thought," said Omid, "but we wanted you to confirm it. I am writing to Kia tonight. I will update him on everything. Please let Daniel know we came and relay our conversation."

The men embraced, and Omid and Manoah rode back to the Magi Compound. They rode through the compound gate, and Omid looked at what had been his home his entire life. He sighed heavily. "It's almost over, Manoah. He's coming."

Magi Camp – Day 110

Pari rolled up the scroll and looked at the Magi Family. Her eyes misted. "Tonight, I can say the same thing Omid said, 'It's almost over.' Tomorrow our route takes us south into Syria and then into Israel. It is the route Abraham took when he left Haran all those years ago, the route the Babylonian captives took as they returned to Jerusalem. It is also the same route our founder, Baildan, took as he rode with the Assyrian army to bring God's judgment on Israel. Remember every step from this point on; imprint everything you see in your mind. You are entering the land God gave to His chosen people for all time. It doesn't matter who occupies it now. It is Israel's land, and they will possess it again one day. We have exciting days ahead. Now, off to sleep."

SYRIA

Magi Route – Day 125

"Will these mountains never end?" asked Navid.

Tiz, riding point with him, looked at the peaks to both the west and east of the valley they were in. "It doesn't look like it, and yet we know that Damascus is getting close. Why don't you and I ride ahead to see how much farther to Damascus?"

Navid grinned and took Anosh to a trot. Tiz put his heels to his horse, and they kept pace. These two men loved nothing more than the wind in their hair and new vistas on the horizon. They were at the peak of their strength and endurance. They felt invincible.

They had ridden for an hour at a trot when suddenly Navid pulled back hard on his reins, and Tiz followed suit.

"What is it, Navid?" Tiz asked.

Navid pointed to a spot on the southeast corner of the valley.

Tiz saw two things: the mountains to the west ended, and the standards of a Roman cohort were barely visible. The two men dismounted and dropped their reins to the ground; both horses would remain where they were. The Magi had taught their horses to ground-tie. Ram was excellent at this training; he started when the horse was young. Using a long lead rope, he would drop split reins to the ground and progressively walk farther from the horse, correcting the horse if it moved. When the horse learned to stand, Ram, eliminated the lead rope and used only the split reins. He would walk farther away and stay away for longer periods until he was certain the horse would stay.

Navid and Tiz moved on foot toward the Roman camp. There were low scrub bushes in this area, and the two men walked bent over to reduce their profile. When they were within 200 yards, they lay flat and crawled toward the camp. It was a cohort—almost 500 men. They crawled close enough to hear guard conversations, but most of it was Latin, which they did not understand.

Finally, a pair of guards who were not from Rome came on duty, and they conversed in Aramaic. Navid and Tiz observed everything they could, listened to the guards, and then slowly crawled to a safe distance before rising to a crouch and moving away. They rose to a slightly bent position 400 yards from the camp and ran to their horses, threw themselves in the saddle, dug in their heels, and galloped back to the Scouts.

When Navid saw the first Scout, he blew a single blast on his ram's horn, and the Scouts galloped to him and reined. When everyone was present, Navid said, "We have trouble ahead, and there is no way around it. There is a Roman cohort at the exit of this valley. Tiz and I got close enough to observe the camp and listen. They have been camped for several days and are waiting for the Magi. The Tribune in Resafa sent word to the Roman Legate in Damascus, Gaius Caesar, and he is interested in meeting us."

The light-hearted mood of the morning and the feeling of invincibility suddenly disappeared.

"What do we do now?" asked Esmail.

"We warn the Family and let Fardad decide how to proceed."

The Scouts raced back to the main camp, signaling a halt on their ram's horns as they rode. When they arrived at the main formation, the Family had halted, erected tents, and started cooking fires. Jahan rode in from the rear guard to Navid. "What's happening, son?" Jahan asked.

"Romans," Navid replied.

Navid and Jahan dismounted and went to find Fardad. Fardad called for the Council, and the Family had erected the meeting tent by the time the Council arrived. The Council filed in, and everyone sat in their usual places.

"Romans," Fardad announced to the Council. "I'll let Navid tell you what he and Tiz observed."

"Ten miles from here, the mountains to our west end. At the exit to the valley, there is a camp containing a Roman cohort of five hundred men. They have been there for several days. We overheard two guards and heard them use the word Magi several times. They are waiting for us. I believe the Tribune in Resafa sent word to the Roman Legate in Damascus that we are coming. We also heard the name, Gaius Caesar. I believe he is the legate."

"If it is the same man," said Fardad, "Gaius Caesar is the man who negotiated the peace treaty last year between Rome and Persia with King Phraates V and Queen Musa. Sasan was with them for the negotiation and signing. This meeting will not be like the one with the Tribune in Resafa. Gaius Caesar is an educated, powerful man who knows Persian Royalty. I am sure he will ask many difficult questions."

"How do you want to proceed, Father?" asked Jahan.

"The Family will travel tomorrow but will not approach the Romans. Navid and I will ride ahead to meet with the Romans and accompany them to Damascus. The journey is over if I am not successful in negotiating with Caesar. If we do not return, you will take the Family back to Persepolis, Jahan. The Family cannot fight the

Roman Empire. That is why you will not accompany me to Damascus."

Faithful Kevan spoke, "God has brought us this far. He will take us the rest of the way. He called us to worship the Messiah; nothing will stop us. You will be successful, Fardad."

Fardad gripped Kevan's shoulder. "The simplicity and absolute confidence of your faith always astound me, dear friend. That is what I needed to hear. Thank you. You are right; we will see the Messiah."

Everyone nodded, and Fardad dismissed the Council.

Damascus – Day 127

Fardad and Navid rode to the Roman camp. The cohort stayed in place, and a squad was detached to escort Fardad and Navid to Damascus. They arrived in Damascus late in the day, and the Romans quartered them in a room in the legate's palace.

Navid woke refreshed. It was the first nice room he had slept in since leaving Persepolis. He woke his grandfather. Servants had placed a bowl for washing in their room, and both men washed and then had morning prayer. When they finished praying, Navid opened the door. The legate had stationed a soldier outside the door.

The soldier smiled. "If you are ready, the legate has requested you join him for something to eat."

Navid was shocked; the man had smiled at him. He had never seen a Roman soldier smile, and food too! Navid hid his amazement. "We would be delighted. Lead the way."

Fardad and Navid followed the soldier to an elaborate dining hall, where the legate sat at the head of a large table. Several senior officers and other officials were already seated. Fardad and Navid were the last to arrive and were seated on either side of the Legate.

Navid stared at the exotic array of foods piled on the table. The presentation was beautiful, and the aroma was breathtaking. He would have difficulty controlling himself if they didn't eat soon.

"Gentlemen," the legate began, "let me introduce our guests. The senior gentleman, Fardad, heads the Magi Family, and I assume this young man is Navid, his grandson. Fardad leads the Magi Family, some 200 people, on their journey to Israel to find a new Jewish prophet. Do I have all of that correct?"

"Legate Caesar," replied Fardad, "Tribune Pilot has briefed you very well. Everything you said is true. We are on our way to meet this new prophet. We are a peaceful people. We will visit Israel; spend a few months, then return to Persia."

The Legate leaned back in his chair and stared at Fardad and then Navid. "Fardad, let's examine your journey before we conclude you are a peaceful people. First, the Uxians attempted to rob you at the Persian Gate, and you defeated them. Then the Immortals, some 400 of them, attempted to stop you from leaving Persia, and you defeated them with almost no deaths on either side. Finally, you encountered a group of 200 slave traders led by Sheikh Malek, and you killed them all. Lastly, your smallest warrior, a man named Hugav, defeated the best

Roman soldier in Resafa, and from the report, I heard he toyed with the man for almost an hour before cutting off his hand. Did I miss anything?"

Fardad was silent for a moment. "Legate Caesar, the facts you state are accurate, but you are missing key information. Over four months ago, we saw a sign in the heavens announcing something of significant magnitude had occurred in Israel. The same night we saw the heavenly sign, an angel visited me. I will tell you, Legate, that the Magi worship the same God Israel worships. We believe Jehovah is the Creator of heaven and earth, and He is sovereign over the affairs of men. We are not converts to Judaism; we are Gentile believers. We have studied the ancient Hebrew Scriptures and believe they tell the truth.

"This is important because it relates to the miraculous events to which you refer. God called us to go to Israel, and He assured me He would guide and guard us on our journey. That is what He has done. He temporarily blinded the Immortals when they attacked us, and He created a supernatural sandstorm that allowed us to defeat the slave traders. I freely admit the Magi have trained the military leaders of Persia and the Immortals for hundreds of years. Many of our men are highly skilled warriors, but we are not a military force. We are teachers and trainers and fight only when we must."

"So, you would have me believe, Fardad, that God fights for you," said the Legate, "the way He fought for Israel when He defeated Pharoah, or Gideon when he defeated the Midianites, or with Joshua at Jericho. You would have me believe that God has fought for the Magi."

Fardad smiled. "You have made my case for me, Legate. Sometimes the facts speak for themselves, and when there is no possible natural cause, a supernatural cause is the only possible explanation. The defeat of Pharoah is incontrovertible. Many people saw the waters covering his chariots and Pharoah's army destroyed. The same is true of Joshua, Gideon, and even Hezekiah when he prayed and the Angel of the Lord killed 185,000 Assyrian warriors in one night. The facts speak for themselves, as you admit, and there is no possible natural cause for any of these events. And there is no possible natural cause for the defeat of the Immortals or the slave traders. You have stated the results correctly, and you are correct; there is no natural explanation for either event, which leaves the Hand of God as the only possible explanation."

The Legate abruptly changed direction without a pause. "You know I met your son, Sasan, last year. He was with Queen Musa and King Phraates V when we negotiated and signed the peace agreement with Persia."

"I am aware of that, Legate. Sasan told me he had met you and was highly complimentary of you."

"Is he on the journey with you, or is he in Susa with the Queen?" asked Caesar.

"He was on the journey with us. He died in the battle against the slave traders. He gave his life to save Navid."

The Legate became serious. "I am truly sorry, Fardad and Navid. Sasan was a great man; his death is Persia's loss. I'm sure it is no surprise to either of you that neither Queen Musa nor her son/husband could lead the nation down a straight road on a sunny day. I believe that for Rome and Persia to have lasting peace, the Satraps must address the incompetency and evil of your monarchy. And to that end, I have a surprise for you."

A soldier led a man and woman into the room, and for the first time, Fardad noticed two empty seats at the table. Navid leaped to his feet, knocking over his chair, "Leyla," he shouted without thinking, "what are you doing here?"

"All in good time, Navid," said the Legate. "Please sit; we still have much to cover."

The soldier led Leyla and her companion to their seats and then left.

"Well," the Legate said, smiling. "I can't remember the last time I had this much fun. I take it you know the young lady, Navid."

"Legate Caesar," replied Navid, "not one fact has escaped you so far. I am sure you know that I am acquainted with Leyla and her father, Baraz, Satrap of southeast Persia. Who I do not know is the gentleman with her."

"Leyla," said the Legate, "would you please introduce your companion."

Leyla smiled at Navid. "I would like you to meet my husband, Mirza."

Navid looked at the man closely; he had a slightly rounded face, flat nose, and narrow eyes. He was clearly Asian. Navid couldn't think of anyone in the Royal Family who resembled this man. Navid sat there speechless, mouth agape.

"It is a pleasure to meet you, Mirza," said Fardad, covering for Navid. "I don't remember meeting you before."

Mirza glared at Navid and broke his stare to look at Fardad. "You would not remember me, Fardad, but we have met. I was a courier rider for Baraz, Leyla's father."

"Of course," said Fardad, "I remember you now; you came to the compound in Persepolis last year to bring us the wedding invita…"

"Correct, Fardad," replied Mirza glaring at Navid, "to bring the invitation to the wedding of your grandson, Navid, and Leyla. A betrothal which he broke by hitting my wife," screamed Mirza, leaping to his feet.

Leyla jumped up, punched Mirza in the stomach, and knocked him back into his chair. "Oh, for heaven's sake," said Leyla, "that is ancient history. I don't need you two fighting. We have a common enemy, and that needs to be our focus." She turned to Navid as her eyes narrowed. "But you did hit me."

The Roman officers roared in laughter. "Legate, this is the best meal you have ever hosted," roared one of the officers. ": These people are great. Are you sure you didn't hire actors?"

"No," the Legate said, laughing. "These are real people. Isn't this just wonderful? I have never seen anything like it."

Fardad was dumbfounded, realizing that they were the unwitting participants in a Greek tragedy that he and the other Persians played out for the amusement of the Romans.

"I'm glad we could provide entertainment," said Fardad, "but that doesn't explain what Leyla and Mirza are doing here."

Leyla gave Navid one last glare, then turned to Fardad. "When the Immortals returned to Susa, after their encounter with the Magi, Queen Musa lined them up and crucified every other man. The Immortals and the Satraps are furious. My Father met with several Satraps and decided it was time to do something about Queen Musa and her son. They want the Magi to return. The Magi are the most unifying force in the country. That is why Mirza and I have ridden a thousand miles; to bring this message."

"There you have it," said Caesar. "The needs of Rome and Persia are both served by the return of the Magi to Persia. That is why my cohort was waiting for you to bring Baraz's message to you. I had no idea the process was going to be this entertaining. Thank you all very much."

Navid leaped to his feet. "I wouldn't have hit you," he screamed, "if you hadn't attacked me first."

Mirza and Leyla both jumped to their feet and screamed back at Navid, eliciting a new eruption of laughter from the Roman officers, some of whom fell to the floor gasping for breath.

When the room began to quiet, Fardad stood. "Navid, you will apologize to Leyla and Mirza. You acted foolishly and rashly, breaking in on Leyla, and your actions resulted in her injuries. You will apologize to them both."

Navid was about to protest when he saw the look in his grandfather's eye. "Yes, Grandfather. You are correct. I hoped I would have this opportunity one day."

Navid walked around the table and bowed deeply to Leyla and Mirza. "I ask your forgiveness for my actions. I was inappropriate, and I caused your injury. Please forgive me."

Leyla stepped forward and hugged him. "I forgive you, Navid. Thank you for your apology."

Mirza hung back, fists balled till Leyla elbowed him hard in the ribs and nodded toward Navid. Mirza reluctantly extended his hand, and the two men grasped forearms. "I forgive you," Mirza mumbled.

"Thank you, Mirza," Navid said, smiling.

As Navid walked around the table toward his seat, Roman officers stood, clapped him on the back, and said, "Well played."

"Outstanding."

"Good finish."

"I can't wait to tell my wife."

Fardad put his head in his hands, thinking *they still thought it was a Greek tragedy*.

The legate stood. "Thank you, Magi, for providing excellent entertainment. I can't remember a more memorable occasion in this dining hall. Now there is plenty of food. Let's eat."

Everyone dug in with relish. Attendants circulated, filling wine glasses, and the good humor continued. The Roman officers peppered Navid with questions about the battle with the slave traders. They were astounded when they learned that ten men and one woman defeated the slave traders. There were numerous arguments between officers on tactics and defensive positions they would have used at the Persian Gate and against the Immortals. It was a rousing meal.

When they finished eating, the legate stood again. "I know you still have a long journey ahead of you, but if you will indulge us just a little longer, I would like to see Navid fight. If your smallest warrior defeated the best soldier in Resafa, I would love to see Navid against the champion of Damascus. Of course, you will use training swords."

Fardad nodded yes to Navid. "Gladly, Legate, but I prefer to use my weapons. I am used to their weight, and I'm sure your champion feels the same. I believe we can do it without injuring each other."

"Your choice, Navid," said the legate. Legate Caesar commanded his orderly to assemble the garrison. The officers around the table pounded their fists on the table and roared approval.

Damascus had a coliseum, and the Roman Legion gathered to watch the exhibition.

Navid stripped off his robe. He wore a tunic, linen trousers, and his deerskin boots. He unsheathed his sword and knife and was ready. He walked to the center of the coliseum and waited for his opponent.

A large black warrior over six feet tall emerged from the tunnel at the other end of the coliseum. He wore a loin cloth and carried a Roman sword and knife. The Romans erupted when he walked into the coliseum. Navid looked at the man and hoped he understood it was an exhibition. The Roman strode to the center of the coliseum and stopped. The two men saluted each other.

The legate stood in his box and introduced the two combatants. Navid and the Roman saluted the legate and the legion, then squared off against each other.

Navid took a deep cleansing breath and focused on the center of the Roman's body. The mistake most fighters made was watching moving hands and flashing weapons. Arms and feet followed the torso. The man and his weapons would go wherever his hips and chest pointed. That was Navid's focus.

He let the Roman press the action. He had excellent technique and came at Navid from every possible direction. Navid stayed defensive. The Roman pressed forward, and Navid backed up. Once Navid understood the Roman's attack technique, he began circling right.

Navid's change forced the Roman to adjust, but he was still fairly effective. Then Navid switched his sword to his left hand and circled left. The Roman was uncomfortable, his attack slowed, and Navid went on the offensive.

Navid heard murmuring going through the crowd. He and the Roman had been fighting for almost an hour. Navid had reserved much of his strength by being defensive the first half of the fight. The Roman was sweating heavily and breathing hard. Navid's feet moved faster and faster, first left, then right, then back to the left. The Roman was confused, and that's when he hesitated. Navid had been waiting for this; he faked an overhead stroke, then dropped to one knee and thrust upward with his knife, stopping less than an inch from the Roman's heart.

The Roman looked down, nodded, and dropped his weapons. He reached down, grabbed Navid by his right arm, and lifted it into the air. The coliseum erupted in cheers. Navid accepted the cheers, and when they quieted, he addressed the legion.

"Always remember, massed combat is not the same as individual combat. In massed combat, it's strength and forward motion. You have a man on your right and left and a spearman at your back. The objective is to kill quickly and keep moving forward. But, if you are separated and fighting one-on-one, your strategy changes.

"At the beginning of the fight, I stayed defensive and focused on his torso and hips, not his arms. His core determines where he is going. Once I learned his preferences, I moved right, assessed my opponent's effectiveness moving right, and then moved left to see how well he fought moving in that direction. I also switched sword arms. We train the Magi to fight with either hand. That is critical in a long fight, plus you will find that your opponent will be more comfortable fighting against either the right or left hand. Once you know this, you are ready to attack. Forward and backward are not enough in individual combat. The Magi fight with their feet. If the feet quit moving, you die. That is the secret to Magi combat."

The legion pounded their spear shafts on the stone steps of the coliseum. It was like being in the middle of a thunderstorm. These were men devoted to combat, and they appreciated everything they had seen and heard.

Navid saluted the legate and his opponent, bowed to the legion, and strode from the coliseum to the sound of spears pounding stone.

Navid found Fardad, Leyla, and Mirza. The leader of the squadron who had brought them to Damascus was standing with them, and he led them to the waiting cavalry squad, where they mounted and rode from the city. When they rode into Damascus, Navid had not noticed a caravan of fifty men camped outside the city gate. These were not traders. There were no women or children, and every man was heavily armed. Leyla signaled one of the men as they rode past, and the caravan leader called to his men. They mounted and fell into line behind the Roman squad.

"Friends of yours?" Navid called to Leyla.

"Mercenaries hired by my father," she called back. "The world is a dangerous place."

When they reached the Roman camp, the squadron leader reported to the cohort tribune. Navid did not hear the conversation, but he saw the tribune nod. The tribune called for the cohort to break camp and assemble, and they rode back to Damascus, leaving the Persians.

"Will you accompany us to Israel, Leyla?" asked Navid. "Or are you returning to your father?"

"Father and the Satraps need to know that I found you, and they will also want to know if you will support them in overthrowing Queen Musa. Will you support them, Fardad?"

Fardad did not hesitate. "Tell your father that the Magi will stand with the Satraps, but it is too late to begin your journey today. Come, eat with us. I know the Family will want to meet Mirza, and I apologize for not speaking earlier, but congratulations on your marriage."

"Thank you, Fardad," said Leyla. "We would love to join you. Wouldn't we, Mirza?"

"That is most generous of you, Fardad," said Mirza. "I would love to meet the Magi Family. Leyla has told me much about you."

"There is one thing you need to know before you meet the Family," said Navid, blushing, "I also have married. My wife is Ava."

Mirza smiled broadly, and Leyla looked shocked. "Congratulations, Navid," said Mirza, "I can't wait to meet your wife."

Leyla's mercenaries made camp next to the Magi camp, and Leyla and Mirza accompanied Fardad and Navid to the Magi camp. They left their horses with the grooms and joined Jahan and the rest of the family on a rug in the clearing. Steaming pots of curry and rice sat on the rug and a platter of Tandoori lamb. The newcomers sat, and Fardad made introductions.

Fardad smiled at everyone. "Most of you remember Leyla, I am sure, and this is her husband, Mirza."

The following silence was deafening. Great, thought Navid, here we go again. Jahan was the first to recover and said, "We have prayed all day for the return of Fardad and Navid, but God has certainly exceeded our expectations. What in the world are you two doing in Damascus? Oh, where are my manners? It is wonderful to see you again, Leyla. Congratulations, Mirza, on your marriage, and it is nice to meet you. Now, what are you two doing in Syria?"

"Thank you, Jahan," said Mirza, "but before I begin our story, why don't you introduce the rest of your family?"

"Gladly," said Jahan, "to your right is my daughter Fahnik and her husband Utana, then my daughter Pari, her husband Tiz and their son Nura, my wife Asha, Liyana, who joined the Family during the trip, our servant, Gul, and Navid's wife, Ava."

Ava leaped up at the mention of her name, pointed at Leyla, and yelled, "You attacked my husband."

Leyla jumped up and glared at Ava, "He hit me first, and he was **my** betrothed," she said, jutting her chin out.

Fardad threw up both hands and looked heavenward.

Navid stood and gently encouraged Ava to sit. She did, but her stare never left Leyla. "We covered all this in Damascus, to the delight of the Roman officer corps," said Navid. "I have apologized to Leyla and Mirza for breaking into Leyla's room and hitting her. We all need to move on."

Ava's eyes teared up as she looked at Navid. "You wish you hadn't broken up," she cried, "I knew it. You're still in love with her. How could you?"

Ava ran sobbing to her tent. Navid rose to follow, but Fahnik stopped him. "Men are such boneheads," she said. "You have done enough. You stay here; I'll go talk to her." As she followed Ava, Fahnik mumbled, "Morons."

A short while later, Ava and Fahnik returned. Ava sat next to Navid and, without looking at him, said, "I forgive you."

Navid was about to protest when he saw the death stare Fahnik gave him. "Thank you, darling," said Navid, and he kissed her tenderly on the cheek.

Ava smiled and arched her eyebrows at Leyla.

They ate, and Mirza explained why Baraz had sent Leyla and him to find the Magi. Mirza inquire about their trip and Navid summarized the slave trader encounter, Hayat's second capture and subsequent marriage, and the encounter with the Romans in Resafa. When they finished eating, Pari explained the evening lesson to Mirza and Leyla. They thought it sounded great fun and said the mercenaries might enjoy hearing a story. Pari said that would be wonderful, and Mirza went to tell the men.

Tiz carried Pari to the clearing center and placed her on her cushions on the platform. Then Tiz handed her the scroll with the evening lesson and sat next to her. The Family had gathered and were seated when Mirza entered the clearing leading the fifty mercenaries. They were rough-looking men, heavily armed and scarred from many fights.

Pari smiled at them. "Children, we have guests with us tonight.

Leyla, the daughter of Satrap Baraz, her husband Mirza, and their traveling companions have joined us. Will you please welcome them?"

Nura stood, walked over to one of the mercenaries, took his hand, and led him to the children's area. Nura asked him to sit, then sat on his lap. All the younger children thought this looked like great fun, retrieved a mercenary, and sat on their laps.

Pari looked at the strangest sight she had ever seen from this platform. She could explain the supernatural sandstorm easier than she could this odd gathering.

"Welcome to you all," said Pari, "and we have the perfect lesson tonight for our visitors, the Battle of Opis between Persia, under King Cyrus, and the Babylonian forces led by King Nabonidus." Every mercenary's face lit up at the mention of a battle story. Pari unrolled the ancient scroll and began to read…

Pasargadae – 540 Bc

Just a year before, Cyrus had turned Pasargadae, thirty miles from Persepolis, Persia, into the capital of the Persian Empire, and he had greatly improved the city. He erected a Palace and attached a Persian Garden for his wife, Cassandana—the largest structure in the capital. The Palace portico opened onto the garden, and in the center of the portico, Cyrus built a large stone throne facing the garden. The architects divided the garden into four quadrants with water-filled channels forming an X to separate each quadrant. Each quadrant contained planting for a specific season: the deciduous winter quadrant and quadrants for spring, summer, and fall. There was something to enjoy in every season. It was beautiful and peaceful.

Today, Cyrus held court on the Portico. It was a beautiful fall day, and the garden was blooming in soft golds and browns; a warm breeze blew through the garden. But amid the garden's beauty, Cyrus was planning war and destruction.

This war council was the first Cyrus had faced without the ever-present Oebares, who had killed himself last year after a bitter conflict with Cyrus's second wife, Amytis, the daughter of former King Astyages. Cyrus had banished Amytis because of the incident, but that did not ease the pain of the loss of Oebares. Cyrus's son, Cambyses II, stepped into the vacancy, but Cambyses was only twenty and lacked Oebares skills, knowledge, and connections. Cyrus felt vulnerable and exposed without his trusted lieutenant.

Therefore, as he planned the campaign that would solidify his Empire as the largest and greatest the world had ever seen, he felt uncomfortable. He had already prepared a stone tablet and placed it in the garden declaring, "I am Cyrus, king of the universe, the great king, the powerful king, king of Babylon, king of Sumer and Akkad, king of the four quarters of the world." Compared to everything he had accomplished, mopping up Babylon would be a minor inconvenience, not a major event.

"Generals," asked Cyrus, "Are you prepared to march?"

Kia was the first to respond; he now commanded the largest cavalry ever assembled, 40,000 men and over 100,000 horses. "I have sent 10,000 men into Elam, along with the Scouts. They tell me that Susa is so disgruntled with King Nabonidus that it will fall without much of a fight. The Babylonians have a force of 30,000 men at Susa, but morale is low. I believe Susa is a mere formality on our way south;

as you know, Elam is Nabonidus's easternmost border. After Susa, we will face the Median Wall; once we have taken that, it is on to Babylon. This campaign will be over in two years."

The rest of the generals reported that they had assembled 200,000 infantry, archers, and slingers, 500 hundred heavy chariots with scythes attached to the axels, and 3,000 heavy horses to pull the big chariots. They had six siege engines and twenty missile flatforms for use against the Median Wall. Cyrus would again use camels and mules in his supply and support groups to free up horses for combat.

"We march in five days, Generals; make sure you have your supply groups stocked and ready," Cyrus commanded.

The generals bowed and exited the portico. Cyrus sat with Cambyses, contemplating the garden's beauty, and Cassandana joined them.

"Are they ready?" she asked her husband.

"They are ready, and so am I. I will not underestimate the Babylonians, but their leadership is weak, their military poorly organized, and their king a fool. I have taken all of northern Assyria from Nabonidus, including his birthplace and the site of his sacred moon temple, Haran, and he has not lifted a finger. He is either a coward or a fool. I will crush him and his idiot son, Belshazzar."

"Are you taking Cambyses on this campaign?" Cassandana asked.

"Of course," Cyrus replied, "how else will he learn to fight and lead if he is not with me?"

"You know I worry about him," she replied. "He still has fits periodically, and his eyesight has not improved, despite the Egyptian physicians."

"Mother," Cambyses said, obviously exasperated, "I am fine. I cannot show weakness. Men will not follow a weak leader. Never mention those issues again."

"He is right, Cassandana," agreed Cyrus. "The generals and satraps cannot think Cambyses is weak. He is the only one with the strength and intelligence to assume the throne when I am gone. Never mention his medical issues, not even in the palace. Even the palace walls have ears."

The Persians marched on Susa the following week. The small Babylonian force came out, offered token resistance, then quickly surrendered with almost no loss of life. Cyrus folded the Babylonians into his army.

Next, Cyrus decreed that the citizens of Elam could choose which deity they wanted to worship, and he re-established the festival of Marduk. Previously, they'd held the festival in October. The people and the priests of Marduk began immediate preparations, and they held the festival for the first time in ten years. People came from all over Elam, and the festival was a huge success. The people were ecstatic. Cyrus knew that word of the festival would be broadcast in Babylon, further increasing dissatisfaction in that city. He could have proceeded against Babylon but chose to winter in Susa. He built a winter palace and sent for his wife, Cassandana. Pasargadae would be the capital city of Persia, but wintering in Susa was far more pleasant.

Cyrus let spring and summer pass and called his war council in August.

"Kia, update us on the activity of King Nabonidus," Cyrus commanded.

"I have had Scouts out for the past two months. Nabonidus is ready for us. He plans to defend the Median Wall that King Nebuchadnezzar built as protection against the Medes. It's 70 miles long, running from the city of Opis in the north, protected by the Tigris River, and the city of Sippar in the south, situated on the Euphrates River. The wall is 100 feet high and 20 feet thick. Prince Belshazzar leads the troops at Opis, and King Nabonidus leads in Sippar. The king wants to be as close to Babylon as possible when he has to run for it."

This comment elicited a murmur of laughter among the generals.

"The problem is the Babylonians are trying to defend too long a front for the number of men they have," Kia said. "We will attack in concentration, and they will not be able to move men from the wall fast enough to support the army we attack. Pick your target, my King, and we will defeat it."

"Opis is closest. We will attack there," said Cyrus.

"To reach Opis, we have one obstacle to overcome," said Kia. "We must cross the Gyndes River. It is normally fordable this time of year, but there were late rains, and the river is high and fast. I have had the engineers look at the river."

The general over the engineers stepped forward and said, "We looked at two options: building a pontoon bridge or digging relief canals. The river's current makes the pontoons a poor option, but if we conscript everyone in the area and use the infantry, we can dig relief canals in two weeks. We will dig 180 channels on the east and west banks of the river, 360 total channels. The relief channels will lower the river enough to allow the army to cross."

"Let it be done as you say, General. When will you start?"

"We will conscript the local villages tomorrow and begin digging the next day," the general responded.

Cyrus waited a week and then rode out with Cambyses to inspect the canal project. The engineers had groups working on both sides of the river, 360 groups of men. Each canal they dug was 100 yards long, 30 yards wide, and 30 feet deep. The general over the engineers approached Cyrus and Cambyses.

"Explain this process, General. How does this work?" the king asked.

"My King, each canal will displace at least 24,300 cubic feet of water or almost 9 million cubic feet in total. But many canals are in areas that slope away from the river, meaning they will form large pools. We will displace more water than our original calculations because of the pools. We will cross safely at the end of next week."

"Why are some groups farther ahead than others?" asked Cambyses.

The general smiled. "Two reasons, Prince Cambyses. The soil is not the same in every area; some are loose, some stony, some compacted. The soil condition affects the digging rate. The other factor is 'The Incentive.'"

"The Incentive?" said Cyrus, his eyebrows going up.

"Yes, my King. You are paying a year's wage to each man in the group that finishes first. 'The incentive' has cut a week out of the digging schedule. The men won't stop for breaks and will punish any man who slows down. There is nothing like a group incentive, my Lord."

"How generous of me," said the king, looking amused. "I am sure this is in an order I issued."

"Of course, my King, I believe the clerk included the order in the middle of a long supply provision you signed."

"Remind me to talk to the clerk when we return, Cambyses. But even if I had known, I would have approved the order to save a week. Well done, General."

In the nearest canal, the men had stopped working, and men on top of the canal threw ropes that they were tying under their arms.

"What are they doing? Why have they stopped working?" Cambyses asked.

"They are the winners," the general said. "Look closely. Do you see water beginning to seep into the canal? The wall separating the river and the canal is about to give way. This is the most dangerous time. We want all of the canals to open at once. These men will wait until all of the canals have seepage, and then everyone will dig furiously until the wall thins enough to collapse. There is an engineer at the top of each canal with a flag. When he waves his flag, the men climb the canal walls as fast as possible, with the men at the top pulling them up. They are racing against the water."

Ram's horns sounded, and the infantry gathered on the river banks, 200 yards downstream from the last canal. Stacked on the banks was a mountain of logs. Every log was 20 feet long. When the water level dropped, the men would carry the logs down the bank and line the river bed. The army would be able to cross without becoming mired in the mud.

Cyrus scanned the many canals. Only one group was still digging, and then they stopped, received a rope end, tied it off, and waited for the signal to begin digging again. The engineers signaled the diggers, and there was a flurry of activity. Men attacked the thinning walls.

Engineers began waving flags furiously up and down the bank, and men scrambled for their lives up the canal banks. Men popped over the tops of the banks and lay sweating and panting on the ground, completely spent. Here and there, a man was too slow, and the water caught him, but in almost every case, the men above hauled him to safety. But in one canal, the engineer had been inattentive, inexperienced, and who knows what, but all the men were at the bottom of the canal when the wall collapsed. The massive wall of dirt buried them, and the force jerked the ropes out of the hands of their rescuers. Every man died.

Cyrus was furious. "Bring that engineer here, General," he said, pointing to the engineer staring in horror into the canal.

The General's aide ran to the canal and summoned the man, and they ran back to King Cyrus. The engineer fell to his knees before Cyrus, blubbering and apologizing. With the speed of a cobra, Cyrus unsheathed his sword, took one step forward, and beheaded the man.

Cyrus whirled and glared at the general. "The men in that canal deserved a competent engineer, General. Make sure you choose wisely next time, or there will be two executions. Now throw this man into the canal with the men he killed."

The general's aide bent to retrieve the body, and Cyrus stopped him. "No, this is something the general will want to attend to personally. Am I correct, General?"

"You are correct, my King." The General picked up the body, covering his uniform in blood, and carried it to the canal.

One of the mercenaries jumped up and interrupted Pari. "He should have chopped that man into little pieces and fed him to the dogs. He didn't deserve to share the canal with those brave men."

The child sitting next to the mercenary rose and took his hand, pulling him down. "We never interrupt the teacher," she said softly. "It is disrespectful."

The man's eyes grew wide; he looked around the clearing. Everyone was staring at him, aghast. He blushed and looked at Pari. "I am so sorry, teacher. It is a wonderful story. Please continue. Is Cyrus about to kill those Babylonian dogs?"

The child next to him looked up, put a finger in front of her lips, and said, "Shhhh."

The mercenary nodded and looked down at his hands.

"An excellent question," answered Pari. "Let's read on and see if Cyrus is about to kill those Babylonian dogs." ...

The army had crossed the Gyndes River, and Cyrus rode at the head of the Immortals. The Median Wall that had been a thin line on the horizon an hour before grew in height as they neared Opis. Cyrus had expected Prince Belshazzar to stay behind the wall and force him to lay siege, but for a reason, Cyrus could not understand, the prince had come out.

Arrayed in front of the wall near Opis stood Belshazzar's army of more than 300,000 men. If the Babylonians lost that army, the city of Babylon would be indefensible. There would be nothing to stop him. Cyrus signaled for his generals.

"Belshazzar has come out," Cyrus said. "Opportunities like this seldom present themselves. If we destroy that army, Babylonia is finished. We will save many months and lives if we crush that army today. We will throw everything we have at Belshazzar, no reserves. Every man will attack straight into their arrow storm at the run, and we will close as quickly as possible. Kia, you will attack the flanks with the cavalry, then slip behind the Babylonians and keep them from fleeing to Opis. We will kill them all here today, in this one battle, and Babylonia is ours."

"For Cyrus and Persia," the generals screamed in unison and raced back to their men.

Kia gathered the cavalry generals and commanders and explained the plan. He split the cavalry in two to attack both flanks. Their mission was simple, destroy the Babylonian cavalry, harass both flanks, and slip behind them as quickly as possible. Kia would lead the group attacking the right flank. His son, Azad, would lead his cavalrymen in front of the army to the left flank.

The Persians closed to within 300 yards of the Babylonians, and the Persians began to jog.

Prince Belshazzar sent out his chariots and cavalry.

Kia's force outnumbered the Babylonian cavalry two to one and easily shattered them; then, he turned the cavalry on the Babylonian chariots and drove them from the field. The army was now 200 yards from the Babylonians, and the Persians increased from a jog to a run. The sky filled with arrows from both sides, but still, the Persians ran. They knew that the faster they ran, the fewer would die. At 100 yards, they sprinted, the heavy Persian chariots came to the front, and the cavalry galloped straight at the Babylonians.

Kia rode at the front of the Persian cavalry. Men were screaming, horse hooves thundering, and the wind in his eyes blurred his vision. An attack of this magnitude was an assault on one's senses. The smell of sweat from men and horses combined with churned dirt, dust, and fear; you smelled everything all at once. The smell mixed with the sounds of men and horses screaming, hooves thundering, arrows whistling, chariots rumbling, feet running, weapons and tack clanging. And the sights made it impossible to focus—banners of every color with gods and animals portrayed, multicolored clothes and uniforms, the contorted faces of men as they screamed, or the looks of fear and horror, the sight of hundreds of arrows coming straight at you, glistening spearheads and swords. If you were new to combat, the sights overwhelmed you. Veterans like Kia learned to focus.

He focused on a large Babylonian General on horseback who was directing infantry. Kia rode straight at the man, nocked an arrow, pulled, and released. The arrow entered the man's neck, under his helmet. The big man pitched from his horse, and the men he was leading looked about, wanting someone, anyone, to tell them what to do.

Kia led his men along the flank, and they killed as many as they could. Once they cleared the flank, Kia led his cavalry behind the Babylonians and saw Azad riding toward him from the left flank. The massed Persian cavalry was now behind the Babylonians, and when the Babylonians broke, it would be a slaughter.

Kia kept his eyes on the front of the Babylonian ranks. The heavy chariots hit the front ranks and drove through the massed infantry without slowing. Men were trampled or chewed up by the spinning scythes. The Persian infantry poured into the gaps created by the big chariots and quickly penetrated the Babylonian infantry and broke it into manageable pieces.

At the center of the fighting were the Immortals, methodically killing everyone in their path. They were a terrifying sight, and in the center of them streamed the Falcon banner of Cyrus with its crimson background. Kia saw the king on his massive black war horse, golden helmet with bull horns, crimson tunic, and cloak. He was magnificent.

On schedule, the troops facing the Immortals broke. At first, there was nowhere for them to go; they ran into Babylonian troops trying to move forward. The fleeing Babylonians were compressed between the Immortals and their own troops until the dam broke. At first, it was a trickle running toward the rear, and often these men were killed by their officers, then those officers were dragged from their horses, and more began to run, and then everyone was running—straight at Kia.

He was ready. He screamed, "Fire," and thousands of arrows poured directly into the oncoming Babylonians. The Persians fired an arrow every eight seconds and quickly emptied their quivers. When the rate of fire slowed, Kia sounded the charge.

The cavalry went from a trot to a gallop. The Persians lowered their lances and rode into the fleeing Babylonians. The Babylonians didn't fight. Many had thrown their weapons down; they ran straight into the horses and spears. It was a massacre, and it was complete. Kia saw a group of Babylonian horsemen escaping toward Sippar. The group flew the banner of Prince Belshazzar. Kia regretted that

Belshazzar had escaped, but his reprieve was temporary. Kia would see him again soon.

Kia watched the Persians strip the dead. They were the victors, and theirs the spoils. It didn't upset Kia; the men laying on the ground had no use for earthly possessions any longer. What bothered him was the slaughter of lightly wounded men to take their possessions. But it was war. The Persians had been in a life-and-death struggle; the men they were killing would have gladly ended their lives. There was no mercy today.

The leaders in Opis opened their gates, and Cyrus would have liked to show mercy, but it didn't fit his grand strategy. He expected to take Babylon in a few days, and he did not want the men looting Babylon. Therefore, by letting them sack Opis and Sippar, they would not feel the need to sack Babylon. Cyrus turned the men loose. Kia did not enter the city. The things the Persians did in Opis demonstrated the depravity of man at his worst. Rape, slaughter, theft, and worse. To know the true heart of a man, watch him pillage a city. That will tell you everything you need to know about him.

The following day, the army followed the Median Wall southwest to the city of Sippar. King Nabonidus whose army had been stationed at Sippar had withdrawn to Babylon. The city knew the fate of Opis and opened its gates. Ugbaru, governor of Gutium, in which Sippar was located, was in Sippar and had sent word to Cyrus that he wished to defect and had brought 5,000 troops with him. Cyrus welcomed Ugbaru and appointed him general.

Cyrus and the Persian army now stood on Babylon's doorstep, just as Isaiah had prophesied 195 years before.

Magi Camp – Day 128

Pari rolled up the ancient scroll, and the mercenaries leaped to their feet. They drew swords and knives and banged them together, showing their appreciation. They ululated, yipped, and growled. But the children were thoroughly terrified. Tiz stood, gave the mercenaries a hard look, and then pointed down at the children. Realizing their error, the men put away their weapons and tried to console the children.

The mercenary leader spoke, "Please excuse my men. Few of them have families. We live rough and do not always do well in polite society. I want to thank you for your warm hospitality. It touched us deeply."

"Children, would you like to sing for our guests?" asked Pari.

The children stood and sang a Psalm:
Oh give thanks to the Lord, for he is good,

for his steadfast love endures forever!
Let the redeemed of the Lord say so,

whom he has redeemed from trouble
and gathered in from the lands,

from the east and from the west,

from the north and from the south...[19]

The children sang the whole Psalm, and tears stained the mercenaries' faces when they finished. The mercenaries bowed to Fardad and Pari, hugged the children, and exited the Magi camp without a word. *God works in mysterious ways*, thought Pari.

BETHEL

Magi Camp – Day 138

Navid loved the start of the day, eating with his family, sharing the previous day's events, and planning the day to come. Today he was eager to start. They would enter Israel today. Yesterday he scouted south to Lake Huleh and talked to some fishermen. They were shocked he spoke Hebrew, but it made them more trusting. They told him he had two choices, follow the Jordan and cross over into Israel south of the Sea of Galilee, or cross the river south of Huleh and enter Galilee. Navid remembered Baildan's journey with the Syrian army and was eager to retrace the route, but it may be important to visit Galilee. This decision was one for his father and grandfather.

"I need a decision, Grandfather. Do we cross the Jordan south of Huleh and enter Galilee, or continue south and cross after the Sea of Galilee? The fishermen we spoke to weren't very encouraging about visiting Galilee. They painted a poor picture of the place."

"We have very little information at this time and no idea where to start our search," said Fardad. "I wish the angel had told us more, but there is a reason God gave us so little information. So, let's use the information we do have. In the book of Isaiah, there is a vague reference to Galilee, 'But there will be no gloom for her who was in anguish. In the former time he brought into contempt the land of Zebulun and the land of Naphtali, but in the latter time he has made glorious the way of the sea, the land beyond the Jordan, Galilee of the nations.'[20] It's not much information, but I think it would be unwise to ignore it. So, we will start in Galilee. A much stronger reference is in Micah. 'But you, O Bethlehem Ephrathah, who are too little to be among the clans of Judah, from you shall come forth for me one who is to be ruler in Israel, whose coming forth is from of old, from ancient days.'[21] But Bethlehem is south of Jerusalem; it makes no sense to start our search there. We will start in Galilee."

Navid smiled. "Galilee it is. I will find a ford south of Lake Huleh for us to cross."

"You scouting mission changes today, Navid," said Jahan. "Before today, you scouted for a safe route, good grazing, and water. Now, you are scouting for information. Talk to everyone; if you find promising information, come find your grandfather or me."

"I have a better idea, Father. Tiz has developed into an excellent leader. Let him command the rear guard. We will let the Scouts ride with the main body, and you and I will ride ahead. A father and son riding together will not look very threatening. We will leave the war horses and switch to camels. We will look like traders or merchants. What do you think?"

Jahan looked at his son and smiled. "I think my son has turned into the man and leader we all knew he would be. That is what I think." Jahan looked at Tiz. "You have the rear guard. I will be riding with my son today."

Fardad smiled. "Father and son, searching for the Messiah. You have made this old man very happy. Go with my blessing."

Navid and Jahan tacked camels, and Esmail and Utana saddled two horses. Esmail and Utana would help them find a place to ford the Jordan River and lead the family across. Navid and Jahan would continue into Galilee while the family forded the Jordan.

They found a place to cross the river, and Utana and Esmail rode back to the main body. Navid and Jahan crossed and came to a small village with a well in the center. Shepherds were watering their sheep, and several women with jars were waiting for the shepherds to finish. Navid and Jahan dismounted and approached the shepherds.

"What is the name of this place?" asked Jahan.

The men looked at him suspiciously. "You speak Hebrew, and yet you do not know the name of this place. How can that be?"

"We speak Hebrew, but we come from far to the east. This journey is our first to Israel. We are seeking a child. A little over four months ago, we saw a star over Israel. It was a sign. We believe it was a sign the Messiah was born. Did you see this star, or do you know this child?"

The shepherds looked at each other and began to laugh. The elder among them responded, "You have traveled hundreds of miles because you think you saw a star? Are you madmen or fools? We are in these hills every night," he said, waving his arms to indicate the surrounding hills, "and we have seen nothing unusual. Do you not think that if some magical star suddenly appeared, we wouldn't see it? You are chasing smoke. Turn around and go home."

Not dissuaded, Jahan continued, "We thank you for the information, but you did not tell us the name of this place."

The elder said, "This village is Chorazin, and there is nothing here for you."

Jahan and Navid mounted and rode out of the village. "Not quite the welcome I expected," said Navid.

Jahan laughed. "We did receive some very important

information. We have not had Magi in Jerusalem for hundreds of years, and we do not know how it has developed since the people returned from Babylon. God will have revealed himself to those who seek Him or to others He chooses. We will know soon, but I believe this is a response we will hear often."

"This suddenly looks like a daunting task," said Navid.

"Not at all," said Jahan. "God has led us this far. We will find the Messiah."

They continued southwest and saw a small city perched on the northern shore of the Sea of Galilee. They entered the city and saw a souk filled with traders. They dismounted and approached a stall selling crockery.

"We are new to Israel," said Jahan. "Can you tell us the name of this place?"

The trader was a friendly man and smelled a profit opportunity. "Greetings, friend; you are in Capernaum. And if you are looking for bowls, vases, cups, or dishes, you have come to the right place. I have the best crockery at the lowest prices in all Capernaum, if not in all of Galilee. Look at this bowl," he said, holding up a large blue bowl glazed to a shiny, hard finish. "Have you ever seen anything more beautiful?"

Jahan smiled. "The bowl is lovely, but I am here seeking information. To be precise, we are looking for anyone who saw an unusual star or nighttime event 138 days ago. Or for any information about a child born on that date."

The merchant looked heavenward and scratched his chin, and then he scratched his head. "It was 138 days ago, you say? Hmm, my memory is not what it used to be; age, you know."

Jahan nodded knowingly. "How much did you say you wanted for that bowl?"

The merchant brightened. "For you, friend. Just for this one day, I can let you have this beautiful creation for five denarii."

"Five," Jahan almost shouted. "One would think you are a Midianite trader, five denarii. I will give you a denarius."

"One?" The merchant wrung his hands. "My family would starve if I sold work of such beauty for a denarius. My shame would be so great I couldn't go home to my wife if I sold my wares for such prices. I could accept four denarii, and that is my best offer."

Jahan turned and began to walk away.

"Wait," the merchant said. "Don't be hasty. My family needs bread today, and I have made no sales. I could let it go for three."

"Two, and we have a deal."

"Two and a half. I beg you, friend, have mercy on a poor man."

"Two and a half it is," said Jahan, taking the coins from his purse. "And now what can you tell us about the star or the child?"

"I do not have first-hand knowledge," said the merchant, "but I can tell you who does. See that tall building to the north? That is the synagogue. The priest there will be able to tell you."

The merchant handed Jahan his purchase, and he and Navid led their camels toward the synagogue. At every side street, Navid stopped and looked carefully up and down the street. The third time he stopped, Jahan, exasperated, said, "What are you trying to find?"

"I'm looking for someone selling wagons," said Navid. "We will need one to carry everything you buy between here and the Messiah."

Jahan narrowed his eyes. "Funny, very funny. I didn't hear you offering help back there. So, unless you have something useful to offer, please keep it to yourself. And Asha will love this bowl. It is very beautiful."

They stopped at the synagogue and went into the Court of the Gentiles. A man was sitting there. "Excuse me," Navid said. "We are looking for the priest."

"He is not here," the man said. "His house is the first one east of here. This time of day, he will be there."

Navid thanked the man, and they left the courtyard and went to the indicated house. Navid knocked on the door, and a woman answered.

"Excuse me," Navid said. "We are looking for the priest."

Without a word, the woman closed the door.

Navid and Jahan stood there, not knowing whether to knock again or wait. Waiting was the correct answer. A moment later, a man in his early fifties with a well-kept salt and pepper beard opened the door. He wore a robe and shawl and a black head covering.

"May I help you," the priest asked.

"I am Jahan, and this is my son, Navid. We are seeking information. One hundred thirty-eight days ago, we saw a star, which we believed to be the sign that the Messiah had come. We want to know if you or anyone you know saw the star or know of a child born on that day."

The priest stood there looking puzzled. "I'm sorry. Who did you say you are, and from where have you come?"

"We are Magi and have traveled from Persia; our journey has taken 124 days."

"You are Gentiles from Persia. Magi, you say, and you believe

God has shown you the Messiah's star, and yet I know of no one in Israel who has seen this star or knows about this child. In addition, the Messiah will not be a child. He is the King of Kings, the ruler of the world. You are talking nonsense. If the Messiah were in Jerusalem, His people would know it. He would not be in hiding. You are sadly delusional. You need to return to Persia."

The priest stepped into his house and closed the door. Navid was no longer dumbfounded, he was angry. God's people were completely unaware the Messiah had come.

Magi Journey – Day 144

Navid and Jahan had spent the previous six days questioning as many people as possible in Galilee and had come up empty, Navid and Jahan rode into Shechem, Samaria, in the foothills of Mt. Gerizim. Not only did the Galileans not know anything about the star or the birth of the Messiah, they knew nothing about Isaiah's prophecy that the Messiah would be a child[22]. The Galileans thought He would appear fully grown, ready to lead Israel.

As Navid and Jahan approached Shechem, they saw a group of women at a well drawing water. So, Navid dismounted and approached the women. "Greetings," he said. "I am Navid, and this is my father, Jahan."

All of the women turned their backs to Navid. The group's leader said, "Clearly, you are not Israelites, or you would know that men do not speak to women."

"My apologies," said Navid. "You are correct; you are the first women we have spoken to since entering Israel. We need information. Can you tell us where to find a priest or someone in authority?"

"My husband is the headman in Shechem," the woman said. "If you have questions, he is the person to ask. You will find him at the city gate this time of day. He judges disputes there every morning."

"Many thanks," replied Navid, "and again, I apologize for not knowing your customs."

Navid mounted, and he and Jahan continued toward Shechem.

"Women do not speak to men?" asked Jahan. "What a strange custom, but it is a good thing we discovered that now. I would hate to think what might have happened if a group of men had been present to witness our error."

"I have never felt so helpless," Navid answered. "We don't know their customs, and we don't know what they believe. I feel like I am walking on ice, and I'm not sure how thick it is."

"Stay patient, Navid. We are making progress. We will learn, and we will find the Messiah."

"I know, Father. I want to find Him sometime soon, without having to talk to every man, woman, and child in Israel."

Jahan laughed. "Come on, I can see the city gate," he said as he pointed. "See the small group of people gathered inside the gate? That is where we will find the headman."

They rode through the gate and dismounted. Navid saw a dignified, elderly gentleman sitting in a tall chair with a group of six petitioners in front of him. The current issue was about an injury to a man's ox, which he had lent to the other man. The man wanted compensation for the injury, and the other party thought nothing was due. The injury was described in lengthy detail by the aggrieved party.

When he had heard enough, the headman stopped the man's diatribe and ordered the other party to pay him one denarius for the superficial injury. One man was happy, and one man was not. The remaining four presented their petitions, one a dispute over ownership of a plot of land and the last a dispute over a burial tombs' ownership.

Navid and Jahan approached the headman after he'd heard the last petition. "Greetings, I am Jahan, and this is my son, Navid. We are new to Israel. We know we are in Samaria but do not know this city. Can you tell us a little about the Samaritans and this city?"

"Greetings, friend," the headman replied. "I have heard many accents, but I cannot place yours. Also, the Hebrew you are speaking is very old. Where did you learn it?"

"We are Persian, from Persepolis, the ancient capital of Persia. We are descendants of the Magi. Our founding fathers were in Israel before the Babylonians destroyed the city and the Temple. Our founders copied the Tanakh, we learned the Law, Prophets, and Writings from them, and the Hebrew we speak is more than 500 years old."

"You have come to the right place," said the headman. "I can tell you about Samaria, and I can also correct many of the things you may have learned in studying the Tanakh. Samaria is ancient; most of us are the remnants of the tribes of Ephraim and Manasseh. True, the Assyrians brought in mongrel gentiles from all over their Empire more than 700 hundred years ago, but many of them have converted to the true religion. Those who do not follow Jehovah live apart from us.

We Samaritans trace our lineage to Abraham, and Joshua placed us here. Joshua also designated Mt. Gerizim as the correct place to worship Jehovah[23], according to the priest Eli. We worshiped on this mountain for hundreds of years before the Judeans built the Temple in Jerusalem. Mount Gerizim is the true place of worship. We worshiped Jehovah on this mountain first, and this mountain is also higher than that little hill on which the Judeans worship. Everyone knows God chooses a place the closest to heaven on which to worship

Him. This is common knowledge. As to the second part of your question, you are in Shechem."

Jahan and Navid looked at each other surprised. "Shechem," said Navid, "where Syria and Israel joined together for their campaign against Judea."

The headman's face grew red. "I see you know your history. We defeated the Judeans near Mizpah and would have taken Jerusalem and all Judah if the Assyrians had not interfered. We beat them. Judah should have been ours, and one day it will be. This war will never be over."

"Thank you for the information," said Jahan. "That is a great help. Can you tell us where to find the souk?"

"But, Father," Navid began.

"We have taken enough of the headman's time," said Jahan. "He has better things to do than to sit here chatting with us all day. Come, we have enough daylight left to do some trading."

The headman gave them directions to a souk, and the two men walked away.

"I don't understand, Father…"

"We will talk later, Navid. Now is not the time or place," Jahan said.

They visited several vendors. Jahan bought some cloth he thought Asha might like and three brass lamps as gifts for each of his children.

Late in the day, they left the city and rode north to find the Magi camp. Five miles from Shechem, they found the camp. The Magi had set up the tents, and everyone began the evening meal. Navid and Jahan joined their family.

"You two look worn out," said Asha. "I take it you had another fruitless day."

"I wouldn't call it fruitless," said Jahan. "I bought you some beautiful gold and red cloth and three brass lamps." Jahan pulled the gifts from a bag he was carrying. He gave the cloth to Asha and the lamps to Navid, Fahnik, and Pari.

"The cloth is beautiful," agreed Asha, "but you know what I mean. Since your father is playing dumb tonight, Navid, why don't you tell us what you learned today."

Navid looked at his father and then back to his mother. "That's the strange thing. We were in the city of Shechem today, and when it came time to ask the question about the star and the Messiah, Father never asked. I don't know why."

Jahan patted Navid on the shoulder. "You have learned a lot on this trip, Navid, but you still have things to learn. We learned quite a bit today. First, men are not allowed to speak to any woman who is not their wife. That is a very important lesson. But, the most important thing we learned is that Scripture ends with Joshua for the Samaritans. They believe Joshua told them they were to worship on Mt. Gerizim, and therefore the Temple in Jerusalem is a false temple. The Samaritans believe the priest Eli, who Samuel describes as being the priest in Shiloh, is the one who confirmed they were to worship on Mount Gerizim and only on Mount Gerizim.

"The headman seemed to be ignorant of God's word after Eli died. The Samaritans are frozen in time. The other thing we learned is they hate the Judeans. The headman believes that one day Samaria will conquer Judah. So, based on all this information, why didn't I ask the headman about the star and the Messiah, Navid?"

"Of course," said Navid. "I can't believe I didn't see it. If the Samaritans believe in the Messiah, He is not the Messiah described in Scripture. Also, since their worship of God is false, He would not have revealed the birth of His son to them."

"And there you have it," said Jahan. "We will learn nothing of value in Samaria. We will continue to Judah. We need to quit wasting time. I want to go straight to Bethlehem. I believe that is where we will find valuable information."

"Before Bethlehem, I want to find the mount between Bethel and Ai, where Abraham and Jacob built altars to God and worshipped," said Fardad. "That mount is holy ground. Jacob said this about the mount: 'How awesome is this place! This is none other than the house of God; this is the gate of heaven.'"

"I understand, Grandfather," said Navid.

"Navid and I will find the mount tomorrow," said Jahan. "That will be a glorious day. The Magi Family will worship where Abraham and Jacob both received promises from God."

Magi Route – Day 145

Mid-morning, Navid, and Jahan found the village of Bethel and entered the city gate, but there was no elder at the gate. They rode in and found two men repairing farm tools using an ancient forge and anvil. The older man, barrel-chested with large arms, hammered the glowing metal on the anvil, while a younger man pumped the bellows. The air reverberated with the sound of the hammer on metal.

Navid and Jahan approached the man and waited. He beat the metal for several minutes, then used his tongs to put the piece into a bucket of water sitting beside the anvil. As the heated metal entered, steam hissed from the bucket.

"Finished." The smithy looked up. "How can I help you?"

"I am Jahan, and this is my son, Navid. We are looking for anyone with information about an unusual star that appeared 145 days ago. Did you see such a star? We believe the star announced the arrival of the Messiah. Can you tell us anything"

"My day starts before the sun rises," the smithy said, "and I am asleep as soon as the sun sets. The moon could have sat on the top of Mt. Gerizim, and I would not have seen it. But I always talk to shepherds who are up all night, and no one has ever told me of anything unusual. As far as the Messiah goes, you must be careful about asking that question. That can be a pretty sensitive subject. Is that all you wanted to know?"

"No, we are also looking for a mount between Bethel and Ai on which Abraham and Jacob built altars to God. We want to visit the site and worship there. Can you tell us how to find the mount?"

"I can do better than that; my son can guide you," the smithy said, pointing to his son pumping the bellows. "Of course, I will have to hire my worthless neighbor's son to pump the bellows while he is gone."

Jahan nodded in understanding and took five denarii from his purse and handed them to the smithy. "Will that be enough to cover your costs?"

The smithy's eyebrows went up. "For that price, you can keep him."

"I believe we will borrow him for a few hours. That should be adequate," Jahan said.

The young man looked visibly relieved.

The smithy's son mounted behind Navid and directed them to a mount southwest of Bethel. The top was broad and flat with no visible markings. The ancient altars had disappeared long ago.

"This is where Abraham and Jacob built their altars," the young man said. "Priests and holy men come here frequently, hoping to see the heavens open and the angels climbing up and down Jacob's ladder, but they never do. If God used to be here, He is long gone."

Natan looked quizzically at the boy. *God has not spoken through a prophet in so long that this boy thinks He is no longer present*, how sad, Navid thought.

They took the youth back to his father, and Navid and Jahan returned to the Magi main body and found Fardad.

"We have found the mount, Father," said Jahan. "It is not far. Do you want to camp there tonight?"

"Yes, we will set up camp early, leaving us time to worship."

They camped at the base of the mount and erected Pari's speaking platform on top of the mount. The Family ate early. Everyone removed their shoes, ascended the mount, and sat facing the platform.

Fardad ascended the platform and stood holding the scroll containing the Law of Moses. He opened God's Word to the beginning of Genesis. The Family stood to hear the reading of the Word of God, and Fardad read the Book of the Law – Genesis, Exodus, Leviticus, Numbers, and Deuteronomy. He finished reading and closed the scroll. He signaled for the Family to sit, and everyone sat on the rocky ground.

"We left Persepolis 145 days ago," Fardad said, speaking loudly enough for all to hear, "and God has safely bought us to the land of Israel. Abraham worshipped on this mount before and after he sojourned in Egypt. Tonight, we sit and worship on Holy Ground.[24] This mount is also the same mount on which Jacob worshipped God and saw the gate of heaven open and angels descending and climbing.[25]

"The Magi Family waited more than 500 years to see the Messiah's star, and God chose this time, our time, to send His Son. God has blessed us, not because of anything we have done, not because we have earned the right to see His Son, but because we were waiting and ready when He chose the moment.

"The Son of God has come, and in a few days, we will meet Him. We are close, very close. Tonight is a night of thanksgiving. We worship God tonight with our prayers of joy for all He has done. God has brought us through every hardship we have faced. We follow the

God of all Creation – Yahweh, Jehovah, Elohim, El Elyon, El Roi, El Shaddai, I AM. He is a God so great a single name cannot describe Him. Pray with me now, and give thanks to God."

The people prayed, some with bowed heads, others with faces and hands uplifted or kneeling with their foreheads touching the ground. Their position did not matter. For two hours, the Magi blessed every name they knew of God and thanked Him for His great love and guidance.

When they finished praying, Fardad spread his hands wide and blessed the people with the ancient blessing of Aaron: "The Lord bless you and keep you; the Lord make his face to shine upon you and be gracious to you; the Lord lift up his countenance upon you and give you peace."[26]

Tiz carried Pari and placed her on the speaker platform.

"Tonight, we will learn about the fall of Babylonia. The time of redemption for God's people is drawing close. I cannot think of a more fitting place to teach this lesson."

Pari opened the ancient scroll and began to read…

BABYLONIA

Surrounding Babylon – 539 Bc

"Today is October 1st," said Cyrus," and on October 12th, eleven days from now is the annual festival of Marduk. My spies tell me that to appease the people and the priests of Marduk, King Nabonidus is allowing the festival to take place. Everyone will be drunk and incapacitated at the festival. It is the perfect night for the attack. Now, all we need is a plan. Does anyone have a suggestion?"

The general over the engineers spoke first. "My King, the walls of Babylon are more than eighty feet high, and the gates are impenetrable. It would take a year to build siege mounds and penetrate the wall. I do not see an engineering solution to this problem."

Cyrus glared at the general. "Did I ask you to explain why you can't help, or did I ask for someone with a plan to get us inside Babylon in eleven days?"

The general shrank under the stare of Cyrus and stepped back.

Kia responded, "My King, the general is correct; breaching the walls or gates is impossible in eleven days. The Babylonians have more than 100,000 men on the wall. For protection, Babylon relies on the walls, gates, and the Euphrates River. But the engineering feat at the Gyndes River gave me an idea. What if we lower the river?"

The engineering general stepped forward again. "My King, you know how long it took us to dig the relief canals at the Gyndes. The banks of the Euphrates are much higher; it would take us more than a month to dig the canals."

"What if I were to tell you that the canals exist, and all we need to do is open them?" asked Kia.

"The canals exist?" asked Cyrus. "How do you know this, Kia?"

"I was born in Persepolis, King Cyrus, but I spent many summers in Babylon when I was young. A day north of here, Queen Nitocris dug a massive basin to divert the river's waters to construct the piers for the bridge that links east and west Babylon. The basin is still there; the only thing needed is to open the channel to the basin. We don't need to dig hundreds of canals, just one."

"I need to see the basin, My King," said the General. "But if what Kia says is accurate, we will be ready by the 12th."

"Excellent," said the king. "Leave some of your engineers here.

I want a full-scale effort to build siegeworks against the southern wall on this side of the river. The Babylonians must believe that our only focus is to breach the walls. They are confident in their defenses, which will cause them to relax and encourage them to enjoy the Marduk Festival.

"King Nabonidus desperately needs this festival to buoy the spirits of the people. They have been angry for the past ten years because Nabonidus would not celebrate the festival." King Cyrus looked at his other generals. "No one leaves that city," he commanded. "General Ugbaru is in charge of the army in my absence. I need to see this basin. General Ugbaru, if one person escapes, I will have your head. No one leaves or enters Babylon."

A day later, Cyrus, Kia, the engineers, and every non-combatant in the army, slaves, servants, supply workers, etc., arrived at Queen Nitocris's Basin. Cyrus, Kia, and the engineering general rode to the bank of the river above the basin and looked back. It was as Kia had described.

"What will you need?" Cyrus asked the general.

"Two things, my King. We need to dig a channel 100 yards wide, and I need as many 100-foot-tall palm trees as we can cut. We will build a levy with the trees to divert the Euphrates as quickly as possible when we open the channel. This project will be easier than I expected. We can finish this work in two days."

The general was as good as his word. Two days later, on October 4th, they completed digging the canal, and laborers had piled hundreds of trees on the river bank.

Cyrus remained on site to oversee the canal's opening and sent Kia back to the army to notify General Ugbaru that he was to lead the attack on Babylon on October 12th.

Prince Belshazzar

That afternoon, Prince Belshazzar had ridden with his father, King Nabonidus, in the procession carrying the god Marduk through Babylon. After the procession, the king held festivals in every quarter of the city, showering food and wine on the citizenry. Belshazzar knew the eating and drinking would carry on well into the night. His father hated the thought of holding a festival to Marduk but had done it to appease the people and demonstrate they could celebrate, despite the Persian presence outside their walls. He wanted the people to see there was plenty of food and wine. There was no need to fear.

Once the official events ended, King Nabonidus retired to his chambers in the palace. Belshazzar was free to host his friends and celebrate late into the night. He converted the Throne Room into a dining hall for the festivities, and 1,000 lords, wives, and concubines attended. With the king absent, Belshazzar was again king for the night. He had been the king for ten years in his father's absence. He might not have carried the title, but everyone had called him King Belshazzar. When his father returned, of course, protocol relegated him to the status of a prince, but not tonight. Tonight, he would be king, and everyone knew it.

As the night wore on, Belshazzar grew louder and drunker. He had one of his father's concubines sit next to him, draped his arm around her, and caressed her, kissing her in front of the Babylonian lords. He took a sip of wine from his cup and made a face.

Prince Belshazzar signaled the steward. "What is wrong with this wine?" he demanded. "Have you switched the wine?"

The steward paled and stammered, "No...No, my King. It is the same wine I have served all night."

Belshazzar grinned drunkenly. "I'll tell you what's wrong. We need cups made for a god. It's these cheap cups we're using. Go to the Treasure Room and bring all the gold and silver vessels King Nebuchadnezzar took from the Temple in Jerusalem. My guests and I will drink from those sacred vessels. That will make this wine taste better."

The drunken lords roared their approval, and the servants brought the Temple vessels from the Treasury. The Babylonian lords threw the cups they were using against the wall, splashing wine everywhere, sending everyone into a paroxysm of laughter.

When the servants returned, the guests took the Temple's

vessels, filled them, and drank. Prince Belshazzar took a large bowl with two handles, had the steward fill it, and drank. He stood unsteadily, lifted the bowl, and roared, "To BABYLONIA!!"

The lords tried to rise, but many of them fell. The response to Belshazzar's toast was muted and ragged, sending everyone into fits of laughter again.

Lampstands ringed the Throne Room, standing every twenty feet, casting long shadows toward the room's center. As Belshazzar stood weaving back and forth, holding the Temple's vessel, a wind disturbed the lampstand flames, and a hand appeared. The hand wrote on the plaster of the wall and then disappeared. Belshazzar turned white and fell into his chair. Everyone stared at the writing on the wall. No one was laughing now.

Belshazzar determined that no one in the room could read the writing and screamed for the steward. He ordered him to find all the enchanters, Chaldeans, and astrologers, every wise man left in Babylon. The steward obeyed.

It took a while before the wise men arrived, but none could read the writing on the wall.

King Nabonidus's wife, disturbed by the noise from the Throne Room, entered and saw the writing and the helpless wise men. The queen said, "O king, live forever! Let not your thoughts alarm you or your color change. There is a man in your kingdom in whom is the spirit of the holy gods. In the days of your father, light and understanding and wisdom like the wisdom of the gods were found in him, and King Nebuchadnezzar, your father— your father the king—made him chief of the magicians, enchanters, Chaldeans, and astrologers, because an excellent spirit, knowledge, and understanding to interpret dreams, explain riddles, and solve problems were found in this Daniel, whom the king named Belteshazzar. Now let Daniel be called, and he will show the interpretation."[27]

"Who knows this, Daniel?" demanded Belshazzar.

A wealthy merchant stood, "I know him, King. He works for me and lives above my store. I will send my servant for him at once."

The servant ran and brought the aged Daniel into the Throne Room. Daniel's eyesight was no longer strong, and he walked close to the wall to read the writing. It was shortly before midnight.

Daniel turned to Belshazzar and spoke, "O king, the Most High God gave Nebuchadnezzar your father kingship and greatness and glory and majesty. And because of the greatness that he gave him, all peoples, nations, and languages trembled and feared before him. Whom he would, he killed, and whom he would, he kept alive; whom he would, he raised up, and whom he would, he humbled."

"But when his heart was lifted up and his spirit was hardened so that he dealt proudly, he was brought down from his kingly throne, and his glory was taken from him. He was driven from among the children of mankind, and his mind was made like that of a beast, and his dwelling was with the wild donkeys. He was fed grass like an ox, and his body was wet with the dew of heaven, until he knew that the Most High God rules the kingdom of mankind and sets over it whom he will."

"And you his son, Belshazzar, have not humbled your heart, though you knew all this, but you have lifted up yourself against the Lord of heaven. And the vessels of his house have been brought in before you, and you and your lords, your wives, and your concubines have drunk wine from them. And you have praised the gods of silver and gold, of bronze, iron, wood, and stone, which do not see or hear or know, but the God in whose hand is your breath, and whose are all your ways, you have not honored."

"Then from his presence the hand was sent, and this writing was inscribed. And this is the writing that was inscribed: Mene, Mene, Tekel, and Parsin. This is the interpretation of the matter: Mene, God has numbered the days of your kingdom and brought it to an end; Tekel, you have been weighed in the balances and found wanting; Peres, your kingdom is divided and given to the Medes and Persians."[28]

Belshazzar was so drunk that he was thrilled with the interpretation. He put a purple robe on Daniel, placed a heavy gold chain around his neck, and declared him the third ruler in the kingdom. Daniel unsuccessfully attempted to refuse the gifts but finally smiled and walked proudly from the Throne Room. October 12th was the last night of Israel's Babylonian captivity.

Kia

At two in the morning, Kia sat on the riverbank with General Ugbaru, the Scouts, and 300 hand-picked men. He watched the waters of the Euphrates roll by inexorably. There was enough moonlight to see a root sticking from the far riverbank above the water line. For the past hour, the relationship of the water to the root was unchanged. Kia blinked and looked closer; the distance between the water and the root seemed to have changed slightly. He continued to watch and, inch by inch, saw the water lowering.

Kia slid down the bank. "General Ugbaru, the river is lowering," said Kia.

Thirty minutes later, the general gave the order to the waiting men, and they climbed the bank, then slid into the cold water of the Euphrates. The water was below hip level. Before the Babylonians noticed the receding river waters, they needed to be in the palace. Speed was now the key.

The men carried scaling ladders. When they reached the quays, they climbed the riverbank with the ladders—then scaled the brick fences separating the quays from the city. They were just south of the palace. Ugbaru and his men moved quickly and silently toward the palace.

They turned a corner, and Kia came face-to-face with five or six drunks. One of the men yelled, "Hey...," –his last words. Kia clamped a hand over his mouth and slit his throat. The man thrashed for a few moments before Kia lowered him quietly to the ground. The other drunks had met the same fate. Sooner or later, the Babylonians would find them.

General Ugbaru split his force, sending half the men under Kia's son, Azad, to the Ishtar Gate. Azad's responsibility was to open it and an outer gate to allow the Persian cavalry access to the city. Kia picked up the pace toward the palace as Azad and his men ran toward the gate.

Kia reached an intersection from which he could see the Palace Gate. There were ten guards, but two were passed out and leaning against a wall. Kia prayed the gate was not barred, but he knew if he rushed the guards, the noise would alert the guards inside.

He turned to General Ugbaru. "Didn't we pass a wine shop in the last block?"

"Yes," the General replied, "it was on the left-hand side."

"Good," said Kia. He chose one of the men and commanded, "Come with me."

The two men ran back to the shop, and Kia kicked in the door. The breaking door alerted the owner, who lived above his shop. He ran down the stairs and saw the two Persians.

Kia pulled a purse from his belt and threw it to the man, "We are not here to harm you or rob you," he said in Akkadian. "That should cover the wine."

The man opened the purse and smiled. "Take it all," he said, "I'm going back to bed. Shut the door behind you."

Kia and his companion grabbed a case of wine and hurried back to the waiting men. "Remove your weapons," Kia instructed his companion. "We're going to make a wine delivery." He turned to General Ugbaru. "As soon as you see us enter the palace, attack the guards. This man's life and mine depend on your speed."

Kia picked up the wine case and approached the gate.

The Guard Captain stopped them. "What are you men doing?" he asked. "You don't make deliveries through this gate. You should know that."

"Listen," Kia responded, "all I know is the steward sent a servant to our master demanding more wine for King Belshazzar. Got him up in the middle of the night. He told us to deliver this stuff. If you don't want it, fine, we'll take it back, but I wouldn't want to be you when the king finds out who sent his wine away."

The captain thought for a moment. "Take it in. Remember next time to use the gate on the north side."

Kia nodded his thanks, and the two men entered the palace. Five guards stood in the inner courtyard, sober and awake. The guards challenged why they were using this gate, and Kia repeated the same story. He was glad for the delay; it bought them a few moments. Then they heard the sound of screaming and fighting on the other side of the door, and two of the guards moved to put the blocking bar on the door. Kia grabbed a bottle of wine and hit one of the guards. The bottle shattered on his head. Kia held the broken piece and jabbed it into the guard's neck. The guard clutched his neck, and Kia grabbed the guard's sword before the man fell. Kia's companion, a large man, didn't bother with a bottle. He hit a guard with an uppercut, shattering the man's jaw and knocking him out. He also grabbed the guard's sword before the man fell.

The two Persians squared off against the three remaining guards. Then the gate slammed open, and Persians poured into the room. The Babylonian guards ran for the Throne Room. When the door opened, Kia could hear the sound of fighting and knew it was coming from the Ishtar Gate. The element of surprise was gone. Kia prayed Azad could open the outer gate, or they were all dead men.

The Persians raced after the Babylonian guards and entered the Throne Room. Belshazzar's guests had fled to any part of the palace where they could hide. The Persians faced Belshazzar and fifty palace guards. The fighting was hard but short.

The palace guards were the Babylonian military's elite and were excellent warriors. Kia wished they had surrendered, but these were not the kind of men who surrendered. Kia faced two men during the brief battle, and silence filled the room as the second man fell. General Ugbaru was down, and Kia rushed to him. He had two bad wounds, one to the thigh and another that may have nicked a kidney. The Persians had lost some men, but the palace guards had all been killed, along with Belshazzar.

Kia ordered the men to stay with the general, and he took twenty men and ran to the king's chambers. The door was barred. They took two large brass lampstands and used them to batter the door and gain entrance. King Nabonidus, the queen, and ten palace guards were in the king's chamber.

King Nabonidus looked at the blood-covered Persians, "Prince Belshazzar?" the king asked.

"Dead, King Nabonidus," said Kia. "He chose to fight, and he fought well. I am sorry for your loss."

The king waved for the palace guards to lower their weapons, and they laid them on the floor before the Persians. The news of his son's death crushed the older man, the realization he had lost his son and his kingdom in one night were more than he could take, and his legs gave out from under him. His guards picked him up and placed him gently in a chair.

"Are you here to murder me?" asked the king.

"No, never," replied Kia. "King Cyrus is not a murderer. He has spared every king he conquered. You will meet him in a few days, and he will tell you about your new position in his Empire. I am Kia, one of the king's generals. If you need anything, send word to me."

Kia turned to the palace guards. "Will you swear fealty to King Cyrus?"

The guard captain looked at King Nabonidus, who nodded.

"We will," said the captain.

"You cannot make that decision for your men," said Kia. "They must each swear."

All of the guards swore allegiance to Cyrus.

"Good," said Kia. "Pick up your weapons. You are responsible for the safety of King Nabonidus. Guard him with your lives."

Kia climbed to the top of the palace and went out on the parapet. He could see all of Babylon from here. The outer gate was open, and the Persian cavalry poured into the city. The riders in the lead spoke Akkadian and told the citizenry to remain indoors. They would be safe in their homes. The cavalry killed anyone in the streets. The Babylonian military offered no organized resistance, and it was the least violent overthrow of a city Kia had ever seen. Babylonia was no more.

Magi Camp – Day 145

Pari rolled up the ancient scroll. Little heads were nodding; it had been a long day. "Off to sleep, children. We need to be well rested tomorrow. Who knows, tomorrow may be the day we find the Messiah." The children perked up, ran to their parents, and descended the mount to the camp below. Tiz picked up Pari, and Fardad climbed the platform and sat on Pari's cushions.

Jahan came over. "What are you doing, Father?"

Fardad smiled at his son. "This may be the only time in my life I am on the very site Abraham and Jacob worshipped God and received a promise from him. I am going to stay a while longer."

"Would you like me to stay with you?" asked Jahan.

"No, you and Navid need to find the Messiah tomorrow, and I want to be alone with God."

Jahan hugged his father. He could not imagine life without this man. Jahan walked down the hill. A short while later, Navid came up the hill, carrying a robe for his grandfather.

Navid handed him the robe. "Don't stay too late, Grandfather. You will wear yourself out."

"I will be fine. All I need now is for you to find the Messiah."

Navid smiled. "Soon, Grandfather, very soon."

JERUSALEM

Magi Camp – Day 146

The family gathered for the morning meal, and everyone was seated, but Fardad's place was empty. The clearing grew quiet, and Navid looked around to see what had caught everyone's attention. Fardad was coming down the mount. He had been up there all night. As he entered the camp, a murmur started and grew louder. People pointed at Fardad; some began to pray, others to praise God. As he neared, Navid noted that Grandfather's face and hands were glowing. Fardad sat, prayed, and began eating.

"Father, what did you see? Can you tell us what happened?" asked Jahan.

Fardad's gaze grew distant. "Someday, I will tell you. I need to think and pray about the things God showed me. Someday," he said and continued eating.

The family finished eating, and Navid and Jahan rode out of camp and stopped in Bethel at the smithy shop they had visited the day before. The smithy was at the anvil, and his son was faithfully pumping the bellows.

When the two travelers entered his shop, the smithy looked up. "Hello, again," he said cheerfully. "How was your visit to the mount?"

"It was everything we had hoped it would be and more," answered Jahan.

"You didn't see any of those angels going up and down the ladder, did you?" he asked, laughing.

"We did not," replied Jahan, "but we had a wonderful time worshipping God. Today, we need more information. How far is Bethlehem from here, and what is the best route?"

"Jerusalem is fifteen miles due south," replied the smithy, "but you want to steer clear of Jerusalem if you're asking questions about a star or the Messiah. The priests and officials in Jerusalem are a touchy lot, and they would not take kindly to a gentile asking such questions."

"Then what is the best route to Bethlehem?" asked Navid.

"Bypass Jerusalem to the east; you will find Bethany. It's a nice village. Go there and then from Bethany, go southwest 10 miles to Bethlehem. That's what I would do. It's rough and hilly from here to Bethlehem. It will be slow going for your young ones and your flocks. I'd plan on a couple of days to reach Bethlehem."

Navid and Jahan left Bethel, and the smithy was correct. They were in the hill country, and the going was slower. In addition, they were in populated areas and frequently encountered travelers. Before arriving in Israel, they had taken pains to avoid all encounters. Now meeting others was inevitable and welcome. They gained information from every person they met.

In mid-morning, they stopped to rest and water their camels. They sat by the side of the road, and ten men riding camels approached from the south. Well dressed with expensive saddles and bridles, they looked like wealthy traders.

The man on the lead camel dismounted and approached. "Greetings, friends," the man said in Aramaic. "Where are you going?"

"We are on our way to Bethlehem," said Jahan, "and you?"

"We are coming from Jerusalem. We always expect profitable trading when we come to Israel. We sold our entire spice inventory to the Romans and Judeans. The merchants here are shrewd negotiators, but they know we are consistent, high-quality suppliers, and in the end, we receive a fair price."

"Where are you going from here? Back to the Far East for more spices?" asked Navid.

"No, our trading headquarters are in Sidon. My older brother makes the trip annually to India and Shangshung Tibetan for spices, tea, and silk."

Navid's eyebrows rose. "How coincidental," he said. "We met a Sheikh Nadeem a little over a month ago. He is a spice trader with a brother in Sidon."

"You met my brother," the trader said, looking startled. "Fate has brought us together. You must tell me everything." The trader gave several quick commands, and within minutes the other riders dismounted, set up an awning, laid a beautiful rug and cushions under the awning, built a fire, and unpacked food from saddlebags.

The three men sat on lovely silk cushions under the awning; the servants served tea and platters of cold meats, cheeses, and date balls.

Jahan shared the story of the kidnapping of Hyat, the subsequent marriage of Hyat and Taalib, and the time that Taalib and his mother had spent in the Magi camp learning about Jehovah.

Nadeem's brother asked, "So, are you telling me that Taalib and his mother are now followers of the Hebrew God, Jehovah?"

"Yes," said Jahan, "that is what I am telling you."

"I have visited Israel much of my life, but no one here was interested in telling me about Jehovah. I thought that only Israelites could believe or learn about Him. I have never given Him a second thought. But I know my sister-in-law; by the time they return, the entire tribe will be followers of Jehovah. There is a priest in Sidon. I will pay him to teach me. I need to know more. You have not said what brings you to Israel."

Jahan explained about the star, the angel, and the Messiah.

"I have heard of the Messiah," said Nadeem's brother. "The Jews believe He is a powerful ruler who will rule the world. Are you saying He is in Israel now?"

"Yes," said Jahan. "He is in Israel, and we will find him soon, but He may not be the person Israel expects. We will know more when we find Him."

"Will you do me a favor?" the trader asked. "After you find Him, will you stop in Sidon on your trip home? I want to know what you discover."

"We will gladly stop and tell you," said Jahan. "We will see you in a few months."

The men said their farewells, and Jahan and Navid continued toward Bethany. They met and talked with another man, a Samaritan, on his way home to Shechem. They didn't bother to ask him any questions. They met several groups of shepherds and some Jewish traders and questioned each group, but none had seen the star or knew anything about a baby. They also informed the Magi they were mistaken about the baby part. *Well, at least they are consistent.*

Late in the day, they arrived in Bethany, another sleepy village, like others they had seen in Israel. In the city center, a shepherd watered his flock. Navid approached him. "Greetings, I am Navid. I come from the East and am seeking information concerning a star that appeared 146 days ago and a baby born on the night the star appeared. Did you see the star?"

The question startled the shepherd. "How would you know about the star? Where are you from?"

"We are from Persepolis, Persia, and have traveled 1,000 miles to find the baby. We saw the star," answered Navid.

"You saw the star in Persia? How is that possible? I didn't see it, and I was only ten miles away. But my cousin saw it. He is a shepherd, and his flock and three others were outside Bethlehem the night the star appeared. I tell you; it almost frightened them to death. First, there was this blinding light, and then an angel appeared and talked to them. The angel said, 'Fear not, for behold, I bring you good news of great joy that will be for all the people. For unto you is born this day in the city of David a Savior, who is Christ the Lord. And this will be a sign for you: you will find a baby wrapped in swaddling cloths and lying in a manger.' Then all of a sudden, a bunch of other angels showed up and began singing and praising God. 'Glory to God in the highest, and on earth peace among those with whom he is pleased!'[29] That's what he told me. The shepherds ran to Bethlehem and found the baby, just like the angel said they would. The folks in Bethlehem accused the shepherds of being drunk, and that's nonsense. I know them. They would never touch a drop while they were tending a flock. My cousin knows what he saw. My flock was outside Bethlehem a couple of months ago, and I went in to see if I could find the baby, but his parents had left. But I bet someone there knows where they went."

Navid thanked the man profusely, then turned and hugged his father. Unfortunately, his father hugged back, and Navid thought he would pass out before Jahan finally released him.

"You look a little flushed," Jahan said. "Are you feeling, okay?"

Navid stood, trying to fill his lungs with air once again. "I'm fine. I think all my blood went to my head. It didn't have any place else it could go. Father, I don't know how to tell you this, but sometimes you don't know your own strength. Your normal hug is enough to break ribs, but your excited hug is enough to kill a normal human."

"Oh nonsense," said Jahan, slapping Navid on the back, sending him onto his knees. "Let's get back to the Family. I can't wait to tell them what the shepherd told us."

Navid got off his knees, the men mounted, and they rode back to the Family, outside Bethany.

Before Pari taught that night, Navid took the platform and told the Family what the shepherd had told them. Everyone was excited. After all these days and miles, they had their first confirmation of the star and the child. They were ecstatic.

Magi Journey – Day 147

At long last, today we will finally learn something, thought Navid.

Navid and Jahan rode into Bethlehem, and as they had seen in Shechem, a village elder was at the city gate, but there were no petitioners. They dismounted and approached the elder.

"Good morning, sir. I am Jahan, and this is my son Navid. We are seeking information and are hoping you can help us."

The elder's eyes narrowed. "You have an unusual accent and speak a very old dialect of Hebrew. Who are you, and where are you from?"

Jahan forced himself to be patient, and he explained who they were and why they spoke the old dialect.

"Interesting," said the elder. "We have someone in the village who claims he is a descendant of Magi who lived in Jerusalem hundreds of years ago. We always thought he was making it up. What is your question?"

"One night, 147 days ago, we saw a star or heavenly phenomena over Israel. We need to know if anyone here saw the star or if you know of a baby born on that date. We believe it was a sign the Messiah had been born."

The elder became nervous and twisted the tassels of his shawl. "There was a baby born here on that date; it was a young couple from Galilee, I believe. The man's ancestors are from Bethlehem, and he came here because of the census. No one in Bethlehem saw a star, but one man told me that several shepherds claim to have seen something about that time. We all dismissed the information. They were just shepherds."

"Who is the man who talked to the shepherds?" asked Navid.

"The man has a house and an inn on the outskirts of town, with a stable next to it. He can tell you about the shepherds and the young couple. They stayed with him."

Navid and Jahan thanked the man for the information and rode to the innkeeper's house. As they drew near, they saw the man in the stable mucking stalls. They dismounted and approached him.

"Greetings, friend," began Jahan. "Are you the owner of this inn and stable?"

"I am," said the man. "Do you want me to put your camels up?"

"No," said Jahan. "We are seeking information. The elder at the gate tells us that a couple stayed with you 147 days ago, and the mother gave birth to a child. What can you tell us about that?"

"Those camels look pretty hungry and thirsty. Are you sure I can't look after them for you?"

Jahan pulled some coins from his purse and handed them to the man. "You may feed and water them after we talk. What can you tell me about the couple?"

"As you said, I can't remember the exact date, but 150 days ago sounds right. They were a young couple from Galilee, here because of the census. There were several visitors then, and thankfully my inn was full. When the young couple arrived, the only thing I could rent them was a space in the stable. That's where she gave birth. They were young and poor; they barely had enough money for stable rent.

"My wife is a midwife for the village and helped the woman. She can tell you more about them. I remember the night the baby was born very well. Late at night, four or five shepherds came running into the stable, praising God and claiming they saw a star and talked to an angel. I had never heard such a ruckus. They were obviously drunk. I ran the lot of them off. They were disturbing my guests."

"Is the couple still here?" asked Navid.

The innkeeper looked at him quizzically. "Of course not. They had to purify the baby on the fortieth day[30]and took him to Jerusalem. That was the last I saw them."

"May we speak with your wife?" asked Navid. "Maybe she will remember something the couple said."

"She's fairly busy cooking for the inn's guests right now," the man said, scratching his chin.

Jahan withdrew another coin from his pouch.

The innkeeper smiled. "Let me go get her," he said as he scurried away.

The man's wife returned. She was short and thick and wore an apron covered in flour. "My husband tells me you want to know about that young couple who stayed with us in the stable. What can I tell you?"

"We want to know anything they said about themselves," said Navid. "We want to find them."

"I can't tell you much. I assisted her with the birth, a normal delivery, in labor for four or five hours, and I talked to her, trying to comfort her and reassure her. It's hard on a woman if her mother is not with her."

"Her husband was with her," said Navid.

The innkeeper's wife spit on the ground. "When it comes birthing time, men are as useless as a saddle on a pig. They run around wringing their hands and wailing. They do more harm than good. I've seen shepherds who have delivered hundreds of lambs faint when they see their wives deliver. What is wrong with you?" she asked, pointedly looking at Navid.

Navid stood there blank-faced. He had no answer to that question.

"That's what I thought," she said. "Anyhow, the woman's name was Mary, and the man was Joseph. They were from Galilee, and they had family there. She told me she had a cousin, Elizabeth, a slightly older woman, who had given birth a short while ago and survived the delivery. I could tell she took comfort from that. Said Elizabeth had named her baby John. I asked her what she was going to name the baby. Mary said, 'Jesus.' I asked her what she would name the baby if it were a girl. She smiled at me and said, 'It's a boy.' It was a boy. I bet her mother told her. A wife's mother can often tell the sex of the child. At least that's my experience."

"Is there anything else you can remember?" asked Navid.

"I talked to her several times before they left, but she never said much more. It was odd. It seemed like there was something else she wanted to tell me. Some secret, but she never did tell me. I asked her if she knew why the shepherds thought the baby was the Messiah. But she never answered. I think there was something she wasn't telling me."

Navid and Jahan thanked the innkeeper and his wife and rode out of Bethlehem. When they saw a shepherd on a distant hill, Jahan looked at Navid and shrugged. They rode to the shepherd and found out he had seen not only *an* angel but a multitude of angels and a pure blinding light. He said he and several other shepherds ran to Bethlehem and found the baby in a manger. They told Mary and Joseph everything the angel had told them, and then the innkeeper ran them out of town, but he couldn't stop them from singing and praising God as they left. Navid thanked the shepherd, and the men rode back to camp.

Right away, Navid and Jahan found Fardad. They shared everything they had learned, and there was a light in Fardad's eyes. "Tomorrow is the day," said Fardad. "You will find the information you need in Jerusalem. I know it."

Jerusalem – Day 148

Navid and Jahan rode into Jerusalem through the Water Gate. They made inquiries concerning the Temple and rode to the Temple Mount. They dismounted outside the Temple and entered the Court of the Gentiles and found a priest.

"Excuse me, Rabi," said Jahan. "I was wondering if you could give us some information."

They had to go through the usual explanations – Magi, Persian, ancient dialect, the whole story.

"What is it you need to know?" asked the priest.

Jahan rubbed his hands together eagerly. "We are looking for a couple who brought their child here 108 days ago. The couple was named Joseph and Mary. Do you remember them?"

The priest looked at Jahan as if he were mad. "We purify thousands of children yearly. Parents come, purchase the appropriate sacrifice, and we purify the child. Do you think we would remember one child? That's insane."

"But this child is special," blurted Navid. "Surely Joseph and Mary told you this was the Son of God, the Messiah. Didn't you see his star? It was in the sky 148 days ago."

The priest recoiled as if slapped; his face was crimson. "You are a stranger and a Gentile; I will make allowances, but never say that again. You are speaking blasphemy. Do you think you would know something about the Messiah before a priest of Israel? Are you mad?" The priest turned to Jahan. "Get control of your son before he gets you both killed."

Jahan apologized profusely and backed away. They walked quickly toward the Temple exit when an elderly woman stopped them.

"I am Anna," she said. "I did not see the child about whom you inquire, but He was here on the date you said. God filled me with His Spirit and told me the Redeemer of Israel is here. I prophesied and told everyone who would listen."

"I'm surprised they didn't stone you," said Jahan. "The priest over there was pretty excited when we brought up the subject of the Messiah."

"I am a prophetess. The priests would not touch me. They just ignore me. They are blind fools. I pray God will open their eyes, but I fear He will not."

"Did you hear anyone say anything about the Child or His

parents?" asked Jahan. "Or do you know where they went?"

"I wish God had told me, but He did not."

Jahan thanked Anna and began to leave, but not before he saw the priest, they had spoken with, talking to the Temple guards and several other priests.

"Time for us to leave," said Jahan nodding toward the priest. "It looks like trouble is coming."

They walked quickly from the Temple and mounted, but a steady stream of people walked toward the Temple, and the camels slowly picked their way through them. They heard shouts behind them and turned to see Temple Guards racing toward them.

Jahan saw Navid reaching for his sword, but Jahan shook his head, and the two men dismounted.

The captain of the guard arrived, breathless. "You two come with me," he demanded, "King Herod wants to see you."

The guard led the way to the palace, he did not take them to the Throne Room but to a small antechamber. The guard opened the door and ushered them in. A man was in the room, and the guard closed the door behind them.

The man smiled at them. He was of medium height, aquiline nose, thick eyebrows, and a six-inch-long curly gray beard. He plaited his hair and wore a gold wreath on his head. "I am King Herod. I hear you two have been stirring people up looking for the Messiah, the king of the Jews. The priest tells me you are Gentiles, Magi. Is this true? You have the citizens of Jerusalem very upset. They do not like Gentiles meddling in the affairs of Israel."

"We did not mean to upset anyone, King Herod. We are Magi from Persepolis, Persia, and 148 days ago, we saw a star over Israel. We believe this star indicated the birth of the Messiah, and we are searching for Him. We have come to worship Him and nothing more."

"Excellent and appropriate," Herod replied. "The chief priest and the scribes tell me the Messiah will come from Bethlehem. I suggest you start your search there, and when you find the child bring him to me so I may worship him.[31]

Navid was about to tell the king they had been to Bethlehem, but Jahan responded first. "King Herod, thank you. We will go to Bethlehem. No doubt the chief priest and scribes know best, and when we find the child, we will return and tell you where to find him. Again, we apologize for upsetting your citizens. We did not realize that inquiries about the Messiah by gentiles would be so upsetting. But we assure you, we will find the child, and when we do, you will be the first person we tell."

The king smiled at them "Go with God, Magi. I pray I will see you soon."

King Herod called for the guard, and they escorted Navid and Jahan from the palace. They mounted and rode toward the city gate. "Father, I would like to stop at a souk I saw on the way into the city."

Jahan looked confused. "The king just told us to stop asking questions, and you want to stop at a souk?"

"I don't want to ask questions," said Navid. "I saw a merchant selling wooden toys. I want to buy something for Nura. Something for him to remember Israel."

"We are searching for the Messiah, and you want to stop and buy souvenirs. Is that right?"

"It sounds worse when you say it. No, I want to buy something nice for my nephew. Is that so bad?"

Jahan laughed and pointed. "Is that the shop?" he asked.

Navid turned. "Yes, that's the one."

They dismounted and walked to the booth that contained numerous wooden objects. "What is that called?" asked Navid, pointing at an object with a pointed bottom, four square sides with a Hebrew character on each side, and a round wooden dowel on the top. In addition, the maker had painted each side of the square a different color.

"That is a dreidel," said the merchant "It is a children's toy. You grasp the top and spin it as hard as you can. Children love the spinning colors. Adults are known to use it to gamble, betting on which color will come up when it stops spinning."

Navid negotiated a price and purchased the dreidel.

Jahan saw a square block of unworked wood sitting in the corner of the shop. The wood was unlike anything he had seen. The color ranged from dark reddish-brown to yellowish-brown, and the grain was interlocked and formed an unusual stipe, "What is that wood?" he asked, pointing to the block.

"That is African Mahogany, very rare and expensive in this area. I only use it if someone commissions me to make something special. Why do you ask?"

"We have a man traveling with us who turns wood into art. I would love to see what he would create from that wood."

"I tell you what I will do," said the merchant. "Have your friend bring me a sample of his work, and if it is as good as you say, then I will discuss selling you the wood."

Jahan looked at the sky. There was time. "We will be back in one hour."

Navid and Jahan raced back to the camp outside Bethel and went to Tiz's tent, where he sat outside the tent, teaching Nura to carve.

"You're back early," said Tiz. "That must mean you have good news."

"I do have something good," said Navid reaching into his saddle bag and removing the dreidel. He handed Nura the toy. "That is for you."

"Thank you, Uncle Navid. It is beautiful," said Nura, scratching his head. "What does it do?"

"I will show you," said Navid. He grasped the dowel on the top, placed the pointed end on the ground, and twisted the dowel. The top spun, and the colors flashed. Nura squealed in delight, hugged Navid's neck, and kissed his cheek. "It's the best present I ever got. I love it."

"Go show the other children," said Jahan. "I'm going to borrow your father for a little while. Tiz, do you still have that eagle you made?"

"Yes, it's in the tent. Why?"

"Bring it. I want you to show it to someone."

"Who?" asked Tiz.

"Just bring it," said Jahan. "You will find out who soon enough."

Tiz retrieved the eagle, saddled a camel, and followed Jahan and Navid to Jerusalem. They entered the city and found the merchant's stall, where Navid had purchased the dreidel.

They dismounted, and Tiz brought the eagle.

"This is the man I was telling you about," Jahan said to the merchant. "His name is Tiz."

When the merchant saw the eagle, his eyes grew wide, and he held out his hands. "May I?" he asked Tiz.

Tiz handed the merchant the bird, who turned it and viewed it from every angle. He said he had never seen anything like it. It had a wing span of three feet, held a fish in its mouth, and perched on a tree branch. Tiz had painted the bird, and the colors were perfect. It was so lifelike you expected it to fly. The anatomy was detailed and exact.

"You said Tiz turned wood into art," the merchant said. "You are incorrect. This is magic, not art. I have never met anyone who could carve and paint this well."

The merchant walked to the corner with the African Mahogany. The block's diameter was three feet and it was six feet long. "I will make you a deal, Tiz. I will trade you this block for the eagle."

Tiz eyed the mahogany, and his mind raced with thoughts of what he could make with the wood. It was a simple decision. Possessing meant nothing to Tiz; creating was what he loved.

"You have a deal," said Tiz taking the wood block as if it weighed nothing.

"I have one condition," said the merchant. "You must sell me something you create with this wood. It can be something small, a bird or animal, but something."

"Agreed," said Tiz. "We will leave for Persia soon, but I know a trader who comes to Jerusalem every year. I will send it with him."

The merchant extended his hand, and Tiz grasped his forearm. "We have a deal," said the merchant.

The three rode back to camp, where the family was already eating, and the men joined them.

"Where did the three of you disappear to?" Asha asked.

Jahan recounted everything from the priest, Anna, and King Herod to the merchant.

But Pari was upset. "We have searched from the north to the south of Israel and have not found the Messiah. What are we going to do?"

"It's all right," said Navid. "We know things we didn't know before. The Messiah is in Galilee, His name is Jesus, and his parents are Mary and Joseph. We may have to go to every village and city in Galilee, but we will find them. We are closer, Pari. We will find them. God will show us the way."

Pari smiled at her brother. "You lead, brother. I will follow you anywhere."

Tiz nodded in agreement. "We all will, Navid. We trust God, and we trust you. You will find Him."

They finished eating, and Tiz carried Pari to the clearing and placed her on the platform.

"Not tonight," said Pari. "You and I will sit with Nura."

Tiz looked puzzled.

"Liyana is teaching. She is ready, but the poor thing is so nervous she memorized the scroll so she wouldn't have to read it."

Tiz and Pari sat next to Nura, and Liyana took the platform. She did not carry a scroll. She looked out at the wide-eyed children (and their parents). "I will teach the lesson tonight, children. I have read it over and over again. It is the story of the redemption of Israel from slavery. I, too, was once a slave, and God and the Magi redeemed me.

I asked if I could teach tonight because this story speaks deeply to me." Liyana lowered her already deep and resonant voice and began to teach...

ZERUBBABEL

Magi Compound – 538 Bc

Omid, Kia, and Manoah ate together for the first time since Kia had been young.

Several months had passed since the fall of Babylon. Cyrus was still organizing the government for his new territory, appointing Satraps for each major territory, and reorganizing the Babylonian military. He had also appointed a governor for Babylon, a Median general named Gubaru, whom Cyrus renamed, Darius because it sounded more Persian. Apparently, the man was a second or third cousin on his mother's side, but no one knew for sure.

"We wondered when you would show up, Kia. It took you long enough," said Omid.

"You know how it is, being an invaluable general under King Cyrus. He finds me indispensable," kidded Kia.

"That can't be the case," replied Manoah. "When you were young, you couldn't walk and think simultaneously. I think it took you this long to remember where the compound was."

The three men laughed. It felt good to be together again.

"What now?" asked Omid.

"I expect that question has several components. What now for the Magi, the Israelites, and each of us? I will tell you what I know. King Cyrus has decided he doesn't need two Magi schools. He likes control and centralization. Cyrus made Pasargadae the capital of the Persian Empire, and it is a few hours' journey from Persepolis. He wants us to move everyone from Babylon to Persepolis. The second question is about the Israelites. What will happen to them? We may hear the answer today; he has summoned us to the palace."

"I understand Cyrus has reinstated Daniel in the government," said Omid.

"True," said Kia. "Several people told Cyrus about Daniel's role under King Nebuchadnezzar and his interpretation of Belshazzar's message from God. Cyrus met with him and Darius, and the two agreed to appoint Daniel as one of the three officials over the Babylonian Satraps.[32] And, speaking of the king, if you are finished eating, we must ride to the city. He will be holding court soon."

The three men mounted and rode to Babylon.

"I assume you will be head of the Magi Family in Persepolis," said Omid.

"Once we are together in Persepolis, the people will elect a new Council. The Council will select a leader, who the Family will then approve," said Kia. "That is how it has always been. We will not change that now. But I will not be that leader."

"Why not?" asked Manoah. "What if the Council selects you?"

"I am withdrawing my name from the selection. King Cyrus has already told me he intends to conquer Egypt and wants me to continue as Cavalry General. Knowing Cyrus, that was not a request. I am sure the Council and the Family will want Omid as the leader. He has done an excellent job in Babylon."

"It doesn't seem fair," said Omid. "You have served Cyrus for twelve years. Isn't that enough?'"

"Fair and enough are not two of Cyrus's favorite words," laughed Kia. "The more he conquers, the more prideful he has become. I had hoped he would not, but he has. I am sure I will be with him until his last campaign. You must lead the Magi, Omid. It is God's will."

They rode through the outer and inner gates of Babylon and arrived at the palace mid-morning. If someone had told you that Cyrus had conquered the city a few months before, you would not have believed them. The city had suffered only minor damage, and Cyrus had repaired that. No looting, pillaging, rape, or murder; it had been the least violent transfer of power imaginable.

The three men entered the Throne Room. The 120 new satraps were present, along with Daniel, Darius, the treasurer, Mithredath, and several city officials. Cyrus had built a new larger throne of gold and ivory on which he sat, and Darius sat on Nabonidus's smaller throne to his right.

Cyrus rose from his throne. "Follow me," he commanded everyone. "There is something you need to see."

Cyrus wound his way through the palace until he came to the massive doors of the Treasury, guarded by six men. The guards bowed and stepped to the side. Cyrus and his entourage entered the Treasury, a massive room filled with gold and silver, gold and silver cups, bowls, lampstands, jewelry, and ingots. The jewelry had precious stones, and several bowls containing loose stones sat next to the jewelry, diamonds, rubies, sapphires, emeralds, amethyst, opals, and pearls. The Babylonian kings had been busy stripping conquered territories of their wealth. Kia had expected to see this, and then Cyrus led them to an annex Nabonidus had recently constructed. In the annex was statue after statue of gods, some more than forty feet tall. Kia was shocked.

"King Nabonidus decided to strip the territories to the north of the Tigris of their gods before we conquered those territories," said Cyrus. "And in this roped-off section are the treasures Nebuchadnezzar took from the Temple in Jerusalem before he destroyed it. Mithredath has an accounting of these items."

Mithredath cleared his throat. "There are 30 gold basins, 1,000 silver basins, 29 censers, 30 gold bowls, 410 silver bowls, and 3,901 other gold, silver, and bronze vessels for a total count of 5,400 items.[33]" Mithredath folded his parchment and looked at the king.

"I will not countenance this," said the king. "I decree today that these gods will return to their place of origin and that the people enslaved from those territories are free to return. I have also sent the following proclamation to all the territories of Babylonia: 'Thus says Cyrus king of Persia: The Lord, the God of heaven, has given me all the kingdoms of the earth, and he has charged me to build him a house at Jerusalem, which is in Judah. Whoever is among you of all his people, may his God be with him, and let him go up to Jerusalem, which is in Judah, and rebuild the house of the Lord, the God of Israel—he is the God who is in Jerusalem. And let each survivor, in whatever place he sojourns, be assisted by the men of his place with silver and gold, with goods and with beasts, besides freewill offerings for the house of God that is in Jerusalem.'[34] I have decreed this today, and you will carry it out immediately."

The assemblage returned to the Throne Room, and Cyrus dealt with all the questions and petitions of the new satraps. In the background, Daniel and the two other Babylonian overseers gave subordinates orders to publish the decree throughout the kingdom. They drafted copies and sent them with runners to Akkad, Nippur in Sumer, Borsipppa, Mari, Ashur, Nimrud, Nineveh, Haran, and Tayma. Runners went as far west as the ancient Hittite cities, south to Riblah in Israel, and west to Ur. They blanketed the kingdom with Cyrus's decree.

When the Magi had heard enough, the three men backed silently from the room. "Where to next?" asked Manoah.

"A visit to Lem seems the place to start," answered Omid. "We need to understand how he intends to help the Israelites."

Daniel had moved back into his old quarters in the palace, and they found Lem copying documents. "Have you heard?" asked Omid.

Lem smiled. "I have heard. The king met with Daniel late yesterday and had him draft the decree."

"What will you do next?" asked Manoah.

"I need to talk to some children who went through your training and leadership program. I need to see what help they need in organizing the return and who intends to return to Jerusalem."

"What do you mean?" asked Kia. "Do you think some will not want to return?"

Lem patted Kia on the shoulder. "You have never been a slave, have you? Slavery does horrible things to people. We are dealing with people born into slavery. They have never known freedom. They have never been outside of Babylonia. You must remember, none of the people taken captive seventy years ago will be making this trip. Those people are either dead or too old, like Daniel and me. We will die in Babylon. No, we are asking their children who never saw Jerusalem or the magnificence of the Temple to return to a devastated land and rebuild it. That is not an easy decision. Many will choose not to return. So, it's time to find out who's going and who's not." Lem put on his robe, and the Magi followed him from the palace into the street.

Criers were spreading through the city. They were on every street corner holding the decree and reading it aloud. Small groups gathered around them and gaped in wonder at Cyrus's decree. To some, it meant freedom; to others, economic ruin. What would Babylon do without these slaves? People ran in every direction carrying the news. It spread like locusts through a wheat field.

Lem and the Magi continued walking. They began to see individuals, then small groups on their knees giving thanks and praise. It was not just Judah going home; slaves taken from every conquered territory were free to return their gods to their homes. They walked past a construction project and saw a Hebrew slave grab a whip from an overseer's hand and throw it on the ground. The two men stood glaring at each other. Overseers would not be returning to Judah.

Lem turned into a shop selling leather goods, where a man was organizing the merchandise. He was tall with a dark curly beard, approximately 40 years old. He turned to greet the customers. "Lem, Manoah, Omid," said the man, his face lighting up. "How good to see you. I had heard the news; I had expected it for weeks. Cyrus is now king, and our seventy years are over. It's time to go home. Everything Isaiah, Jeremiah, and Ezekiel prophesied has come true. Praise God."

"Yes, praise God," agreed Lem. "You are the first person we have seen since the announcement, Zerubbabel." Lem turned to Kia. "Zerubbabel is the grandson of King Jehoiachin, Kia, and he is one of the men who will lead the Judeans in their return. Zerubbabel, this

220

is Kia. He is one of King Cyrus's generals from the Magi Family in Persepolis."

"It is nice to meet you, Kia. I have been busy," said Zerubbabel. "My uncle Sheshbazzar is the senior Judean returning, but he asked Mordecai and me to plan the return. I have appointed ten men to help me. We have contacted most of the children, well, no longer children, and so far, I know approximately 30,000 who will return. We do not know how many will return from other cities in Babylonia, but I hope it is a substantial number. It will take a large group to repopulate Jerusalem and rebuild the city and Temple. It seems a daunting task, but I feel God's pull. He is calling us home. Mordecai is responsible for logistics, food, clothing, transportation, building supplies, and weapons. Now that we have Cyrus's decree requiring the Babylonians to assist us, our planning will be easier and faster. We are moving a large group; there is no way we will be ready to go in less than a month. But what is one month after seventy years?"

Lem smiled. "I should have known you would have things under control. Excellent, Zerubbabel. Let me know if you need anything or if any Babylonians are reluctant to help. I am sure Daniel will be able to point out the error of their ways. We are off to see Jeshua. Knowing him, he is as far along as you in his planning."

They left Zerubbabel, crossed the bridge to west Babylon, and found Jeshua at an old warehouse the Israelites had converted into a synagogue. Jeshua sat at a table copying a section of Deuteronomy. He looked up and rushed to greet Manoah and Lem. He hugged them and kissed them on each cheek.

"My friend," Jeshua greeted him, "I just heard the word. We are going home. What wonderful news, and thanks to you, I have a full set of Scripture. I am finishing the last book of the Law, and you have provided me with a copy of the Prophets and Writings. Thanks to you, we have a complete Tanakh."

"Complete to this point," said Manoah. "God is not done with Israel. There is much still to write, and you will be part of it. How I envy you. Now I have a favor to ask. You know my son, Payam?"

"Yes, of course," said Jeshua. "I have met him several times. A fine young man. Why do you ask?"

"He wants to travel to Israel with you. He is eighteen and desires to be part of rebuilding Jerusalem and the Temple. I am proud that he wants to do this. The Magi have been part of Israel's history for 200 years. I would love one of us to see God's plan fulfilled and His city and Temple rebuilt. If I were his age, I would be going with you."

"Of course, he may come, and I will take responsibility for him. When my father left Jerusalem, he had a brother in Bethlehem. If his family is still alive, Payam may stay with him. We have no idea how primitive and dangerous things may be in Judah. Payam will stay in Bethlehem until I am sure it is safe for him to come to Jerusalem."

"Zerubbabel tells us his plan for the return is fairly complete, and Mordecai is working on logistics," said Omid. "How are your preparations?"

"In Babylon and in the territories with which I have contact, I have commitments from 4,289 priests in the 4 priestly families, 341 Levites including 128 singers of the sons of Asha, and 392 temple servants[35]. We have enough to bring the worship of God back to Israel. God has worked miraculously to preserve His people."

"Do you need anything from us?" asked Lem.

"Not at this time," said Jeshua. "I will send someone to the palace if I think of anything. As we prepare to leave, Daniel will be critical to Israel. The wealthy are not happy they are losing their free labor, and not only are they losing their slaves, but Cyrus has also commanded they assist us financially. I am sure there will be push-back. We will let you know if anything arises that looks like it could impede our return."

Four weeks after the announcement, the king summoned Kia to the Throne Room. The king had also summoned Zerubbabel's uncle, Sheshbazzar. Daniel stood next to the king and pointed to Sheshbazzar. "This is the senior member of the Judeans, my King. His name is Sheshbazzar."

Cyrus looked at Sheshbazzar. He didn't look like much, a short man, mid-sixties, hair and beard gray, a slight bend in his back, but his eyes were clear and bright. "I understand your people are ready to leave tomorrow."

"They are, my King," replied Sheshbazzar in a strong, clear voice. "We have everything we need. The citizens of Babylonia have been exceedingly generous. We have wagons, horses, mules, camels, and more than 6,000 donkeys. It is early spring, and we will be across the desert before the heat of summer. King Cyrus, you have been most kind to your people, and we will never forget it."

"You lack two things for your return, Sheshbazzar. You lack an official position. I name you the Prince of Judah. You are responsible for the Israelites under the governor of Mizpah. In addition, you need the sacred vessels you use in your worship. I am returning them to you today. Mithredath, my Treasurer, has loaded them in wagons outside the palace and has a detailed inventory for you. Now, you have everything you need."

Mithredath handed Sheshbazzar the list of the Temple's vessels, and Sheshbazzar's knees began to buckle. Kia was next to him and grabbed his elbow to steady him. Tears were in Sheshbazzar's eyes.

Sheshbazzar stood tall, straightened his crooked back, and looked at the king. "May the Lord God Almighty, Creator of heaven and earth, bless and keep you now and forever, King Cyrus, for the honor you have shown Him this day. You have blessed His people. The Lord God blesses those who bless His people and curses those who curse them. Thank you."

"Go Sheshbazzar, go home, and rebuild Jerusalem and the Temple, and may your God protect you."

"General Kia," said the king, "you will take a cavalry company and escort the Israelites to Jerusalem. You are responsible for their safety. Ensure the area around Jerusalem is secure, and report back to me."

Kia snapped to attention and saluted the king. "From the oldest to the youngest, I will deliver everyone to Jerusalem safe and sound. Thank you, my King."

Kia left the throne room with Sheshbazzar. As promised, four large wagons loaded with the Temple's vessels were outside the palace. The Persians covered the wagons with large tarps to protect the items from the elements.

"Make sure your men understand that these vessels are not just valuable; they are holy. Only the priests and Temple servants may touch them. Jehovah is a jealous God, and He protects what is His. I'm not concerned about theft,' said Sheshbazzar. "I am concerned about their safety. They may become curious and want to see the items. Tell them never to lift a corner of the covering to look at them."

"I will give the command," replied Kia, "and I will seal all four sides with wax and my signet. The coverings will not come off till you arrive in Jerusalem."

"I'm sorry you must endure such a long trip to ensure our safety, General."

Kia smiled. "This trip fulfills the greatest longing of my life. My son, Azad, commands a cavalry company and will lead the cavalry for this trip. We have read the Scriptures and believe Jehovah is the God of all creation. The opportunity to see Israel and Jerusalem is our greatest desire. We will be ready to leave tomorrow."

Kia ran from the Temple grounds to the cavalry barracks.

"Azad," he said as he ran up to his son, "there is not a moment to lose. The king has ordered us to accompany the Israelites on their return to Israel; inform your men. Tell your supply people they have one day to prepare for a six-month trip."

Azad laughed, hugged his father, and kissed him on both cheeks, then walked through the barracks yelling, "Up, get up, we leave for Israel tomorrow. Get moving. Prepare your armor and weapons and see to your horses. Get moving. There is not a moment to lose. Any man not ready to ride by tomorrow morning will find himself sweeping streets in Babylon for the rest of his life."

It was like hitting a bee hive with a stick. Men flew in every direction. The supply people were frantic. They had less than twenty-four hours to gather food and supplies for a six-month trip; it couldn't be done. They had to count on being able to gather things in Mari and other major towns to augment what they had on hand.

Babylon – 538 Bc

A caravan of more than 30,000 people stretched for almost 5 miles on the road outside Babylon. They had 100 wagons and hundreds of horses, mules, camels, and donkeys. People were excited and ready to begin. A few looked at the massive walls of Babylon with trepidation. They looked at the road stretching north and the vast open countryside and desert, and their hearts sank. Babylon had been their home their entire life. It was the only world they knew.

Kia and Azad rode along the caravan and saw those staring at Babylon wistfully. Kia talked to them and reassured them. Kia described the trip they were facing and reassured them he and Azad would be with them every step of the way.

The Magi Family was there to see the Israelites off, along with many of the citizens of Babylon and the Israelites who had either chosen to stay or were too old to make the trip. It was a massive noisy throng.

Omid, Manoah, Lem, and Daniel stood with Sheshbazzar, Zerubbabel, and Jeshua. Kia and Azad joined them. The men stood in a circle, and Daniel raised his hands and his face to heaven and prayed a blessing over the departing Israelites: "Jehovah, Yahweh Yireh, El Shaddai, Yahweh Shalom, El Elyon, The Great I AM; we know you by many names. You are vast and all-powerful. You have rightly judged Your people, and You have brought about their redemption through Cyrus, Your servant. I call your blessings on Your people. A long journey and a large task lay before them. Yet You will provide the strength, the materials to rebuild Jerusalem and the Temple, and the courage and strength to accomplish everything You have called them to do. Thank you, Father. We glorify and praise You and look to the day we will stand in the presence of Your Messiah, the Son of David. Until that day, give Your people strength, patience, and Your Spirit to accomplish everything you would have them do, and give them hearts that desire and worship You and You alone."

The men embraced, and Kia and Azad rode to the head of the departing caravan. The two men looked back at the Magi Family, not knowing if this might be the last time they would see them. The Family was leaving for Persepolis in a few days, and after their trip to Israel, Kia and Azad would campaign with Cyrus in Egypt. Kia wiped a tear from his cheek as he looked at Omid and Manoah, thankful the Family was in good hands. Kia turned and faced north; they had a long trip in front of them.

Jerusalem

Kia rode into Mari. They had been on the road for three weeks, and to this point, water and grazing had been adequate. Now they would face the desert. Kia had talked to some of his men familiar with this area. They would set a course for Tadmor, then west to the coast.

The governor of Mari met Kia at the city gate. "Are you leading the Israelite caravan?" he asked.

"Yes, I am General Kia. Sheshbazzar, the Prince of Judah, leads the Israelites and is riding up now."

Sheshbazzar joined them.

"Greetings, Prince Sheshbazzar. I am the governor of Mari, and I am thankful you are here. Approximately 20,000 Israelites and others from western and Northern Assyria have gathered to accompany you to Israel. They are about to eat us out of house and home. It is worse than a locust plague. Will you be leaving soon?"

Sheshbazzar looked shocked, and Kia felt his jaw drop. "We were hoping to resupply before departing. Did you say 20,000?"

"You heard me correctly," replied the governor, "and if the merchants have anything left, you are welcome to resupply. You should be able to find enough to get you to Tadmor. The rest of your party camped on the bank of the Euphrates. They are ready to cross."

Kia and Sheshbazzar thanked the governor, rode out of the city, and led their caravan around the city to the Euphrates. Waiting for them was a caravan almost as large as theirs. Kia's heart sank. *How am I going to get 50,000 people from Mari to Jerusalem?*

Kia and Sheshbazzar met with the new caravan's leaders, introduced themselves, and took responsibility for this new group. They remained on the Euphrates for two more days. Fortunately, several caravans of traders arrived during their stay, and they could buy more than enough food to get them to Tadmor and beyond.

It took them almost a week to get everyone across the river, and the trek across the desert began. Miraculously, they had several days of cloud cover and cooler temperatures, and every oasis and well they found had water. God had prepared everything for their return.

Azad and one of the Scouts rode point as they approached Tadmor. Suddenly a group of fifty bandit raiders rode from behind a dune to their left, charging straight at the two of them. *Apparently, these idiots had failed to scout the caravan, or they wouldn't be doing* *something this stup*id, thought Azad. He blew his ram's horn, and he and the Scout galloped back toward the caravan. Before they reached it, 500 Persian cavalrymen galloped straight at the bandits.

Too late, the raiders saw the cavalry. They attempted to rein and turn, but by then, the Persians were on top of them. In a minute, every bandit lay dead, and the Persians hadn't suffered more than a sprained wrist – one of the men had forgotten to release his spear after impact.

"Drag these bodies into the desert," commanded Kia. "I don't want the children to see this mess."

The Persians looped ropes around the raider's feet and dragged them far from their route. Others dismounted and kicked sand over blood-stained areas. Before the caravan arrived, they had erased all signs of the battle.

Zerubbabel rode up to Azad. "What was all the commotion?"

"A minor dust-up with a few of the locals," lied Azad. "They ran off when they saw us. Nothing to concern your people; we have handled it."

Zerubbabel smiled. "It is a great comfort having your cavalry along, Azad. I would have hated to make this trip without you."

"Speaking of which," said Azad, "Kia and I talked last night. Once you have settled in Judah, we will leave. You must be capable of defending yourselves. So, it is time for your young men to begin military training. At the end of each day, we will begin weapons-training classes for every man between the ages of twenty and thirty-five. We have 500 trainers. By the time we finish the journey, we will have trained your people.

"You must prepare for war. Israel still has enemies, and there will not be a Persian outpost closer than Damascus. You will be on your own. We will also train 500 cavalrymen, and they will ride with us until we reach Jerusalem. It's not much, but it's a beginning."

"Sheshbazzar or I should have thought of this," said Zerubbabel. "We have got to stop thinking like slaves. We are so used to someone else feeding and protecting us that we have stopped thinking for ourselves. I am afraid of the other things we may have failed to consider."

"Fear not, Zerubbabel. God will bring to mind everything you need to know. His Spirit rests on you and Jeshua. He will reestablish His people; He has promised it."

Zerubbabel smiled. "Which of us is Jewish?" he asked. "It seems you remember God's promises better than me. Thank you for reminding me, Azad. And thank you for offering to train our people.

We will be ready to start tonight."

That night, and for the remainder of the trip, the sound of sword against sword filled the camp—men trained with the sword, javelin, spear, bow, and sling. Israel once again had an army.

A few days later, they arrived in Tadmor, rested and resupplied, and they began the short journey to the coastal mountains. There, they turned south into Syria. The trip through Syria was without incident. They followed the mountains south, averaging ten to fifteen miles daily because of the heavy wagons, young children, and pregnant women.

After three months of traveling, they reached Damascus and. again, they rested and resupplied. Kia visited with the commander of the former Babylonian garrison, now Persian, stationed there. Kia updated him on everything in Babylon as of three months ago and sought information concerning their route south. The garrison commander said there was a height about thirty miles to the south from which the people would have a magnificent view of the Promised Land. Kia thanked him for the information, and the next day the Israelites continued south.

Two days after Damascus, they arrived at the small mountain described by the commander. They left the wagons, animals, and those who could not make the climb, and the people climbed to the heights, with Kia and Sheshbazzar leading.

They reached the summit, and the view in every direction was breathtaking.

Kia stood on a large rock and described what they were seeing. He spoke loudly, but not loudly enough for all to hear. People relayed his message through the mass of people. "Back to the northwest is Lake Huleh, and the gorgeous valley below the lake is the Huleh Valley." He paused for the word to pass. "To the southwest is the Sea of Galilee, famous for its fishing. It's small, but in strong winds, it becomes very violent." Pause. "We passed Mt. Hermon coming through Syria," he said, pointing northeast, "and Israel is now in view; just above and below the Sea of Galilee is the Jordan River. We will cross it, and when we do, we will be in Israel, which leaves us 100 miles from Jerusalem."

As Kia's last words passed through the crowd, a roar began to build. People laughed, hugged, and clapped each other on the back, and spontaneously a song spread through all the people. They sang the Song of Moses:

"I will sing to the Lord, for he has triumphed gloriously;
the horse and his rider he has thrown into the sea.

The Lord is my strength and my song,
and he has become my salvation;
this is my God, and I will praise him,
my father's God, and I will exalt him.
The Lord is a man of war;
the Lord is his name..."[36]

When the people finished the Song of Moses, they sang the Song of Deborah and Barak:

"That the leaders took the lead in Israel,
that the people offered themselves willingly,
bless the Lord!
"Hear, O kings; give ear, O princes;
to the Lord I will sing;
I will make melody to the Lord, the God of Israel.
"Lord, when you went out from Seir,
when you marched from the region of Edom,
the earth trembled
and the heavens dropped,
yes, the clouds dropped water.

The mountains quaked before the Lord,
even Sinai before the Lord, the God of Israel..."[37]

The people walked down the mount as the last strains finished. Spirits were high, but they would not be much longer.

They forded the Jordan River and twelve days later arrived in Jerusalem. But the nearer they came, the worse things looked. All through Samaria, they saw small villages and farms, hardscrabble places, barely capable of eking a living. In Judah, hillsides once covered in vineyards were now bramble and briar patches housing wild goats.

Then early one morning, they arrived in Jerusalem.

Kia wasn't sure what he had expected, but this was far worse than anything he could have imagined. King Nebuchadnezzar had reduced the city to rubble. The Babylonians had scattered stones from the city wall everywhere, and within the city, charred timbers evidenced the fires that had raged. The travelers did not go up to the Temple Mount; there would be time enough for that later.

The immensity of the task ahead immobilized Sheshbazzar but not Zerubbabel. He split the people into groups. "Do we have any farmers?" he asked. The people from Assyria and areas west raised their hands. More than 2,000 people. "We passed several valleys, coming in." Zerubbabel pointed to one man. "You will lead this group.

Pick the best areas for grains, set up a camp there, and tomorrow begin clearing land. There are three wagons with agricultural implements and with grain seeds. Take those and distribute them among the people. We need crops in the ground as quickly as possible.

"Do we have traders or men with negotiating skills?" Zerubbabel asked.

A smaller group stepped forward.

"We have gold," said Zerubbabel, "but we will need food come winter. Return to Damascus, discover where they trade and negotiate with traders willing to make the trip to Jerusalem regularly."

"Any well diggers or people with engineering skills?"

Again, a small group stepped forward.

"You will check and verify all the water sources available in and around Judah. Water is our number-one need, then food, then shelter. Clean out the wells, and verify what water is safe to drink and what is not. Mark all areas of drinking water after you have verified them."

Zerubbabel selected fifty healthy young men remaining and appointed one leader, saying, "Sanitation is critical. You will find an area close to the camp, but not too close, dig latrines if necessary, or clear and improve existing ones. You will designate and mark the latrine areas. We will expel anyone from the camp who fails to use the designated areas."

"Where are my warriors?" Those who had trained during the trip and whom Zerubbabel had not selected for other duties stepped forward. Zerubbabel selected 500 men. "Select weapons and armor from the wagons. You will ride with Kia tomorrow. Talk to those who remained in Judah, and see if anyone has been raiding in this area. You will find the raiders and discourage them." Zerubbabel looked at Kia, who nodded yes.

"Who are the best cooks?" asked Zerubbabel. Every woman not selected to this point stepped forward. Zerubbabel laughed. "Dumb question." He used his hands to designate one-fourth of the women. "You are the camp cooks and will also be responsible for the children." He chose one woman and instructed her to select five areas for cooking and communal meals.

Most of the people remained. "We are responsible for shelter," he said to this group. "I will lead you, and we will start now. I will designate a house that looks repairable, and fifty people will work on it until it is fit for habitation. Who has carpentry and or stone-mason skills?"

More than 3,000 men stepped forward. He divided them into

four-man teams. "One team will work with each group of builders to direct and train."

The group began to walk through the city. When Zerubbabel found a house with a usable foundation and partial walls on each side, he assigned a group of 50 people and one tradesman team. By sundown, he had designated 600 houses, and people had begun the process of removing rubble and finding suitable building material.

The people, who had been overwhelmed with trepidation in the morning, were now filled with hope. They had a plan, a leader, and a God who would strengthen and protect them.

Over the next few weeks, Kia and his small army found several groups who had been raiding Judah and strongly discouraged them from continuing their poor behavior.

A month after they'd arrived, Kia knew he had done as much as possible. He formed the cavalry and prepared to depart. Sheshbazzar, Zerubbabel, Jeshua, Manoah's son Payam and the other leaders gathered to say their goodbyes. Kia and Azad embraced the men and said farewell.

"Write to your mother, Payam; she will worry," said Kia. "Take care of yourself, and remember you are Magi. Record everything you see and hear, and send it to the Family in Persepolis. We are counting on you, and you will train your sons to do the same thing, and you will remind them they are Magi of the Family of Magi."

"I will, Kia. I will never forget, and neither will my sons. We will record everything of importance that we see and hear."

"I know you will."

Kia mounted and led his men north. He did not look back. An hour after leaving Jerusalem, they topped a rise, and then Kia and Azad looked back. They could barely see the outline of the city.

The two men turned back and rode on. Kia wiped his cheeks with the back of his sleeve and looked at his son. "Israel is home, Azad. Israel is home."

Magi Camp – Day 148

Liyana looked out at the children. "This has been a long journey, and Rahim and Pari have taught you the history of the Magi Family. Which of you will become adults next year?"

Five children stood. Liyana smiled at them. "Tell us one thing you have learned on this trip and how it made you feel."

One of the boys stepped forward. "Baildan, Baildan, **Baildan**..."

Liyana tilted her head to one side and narrowed her eyes.

The boy stopped chanting and looked embarrassed. "Baildan is my favorite. It is always hard for me to choose between him and Benjamin, but Baildan teaches me many things. He knew nothing about Jehovah, but he heard the Word of God from his brother, Meesha, Rachael, and Benjamin. Then he saw the Angel of the Lord pass through the camp of Assyria and kill 185,000 men in one night. He gave himself to God, started the Magi school, and founded the Magi Family. His courage and devotion are why we are in Jerusalem looking for the Messiah."

"Excellent," said Liyana.

One of the girls stepped forward. "My favorite is Meesha. Like Baildan, he heard the Word of God and believed. He studied with Isaiah's disciples and recorded the Tanakh and the first scrolls of the Magi Family. At the end of his life, he helped Baildan form the foundation of the Magi Family in the Nineveh compound. Whenever you unroll the scrolls, I think of Meesha."

The next child said, "My favorite is Jeremiah and King Josiah. I love King Josiah. He was only eight years old when he became king, and Scripture says he loved God with all his heart and soul.[38] God sent Jeremiah and Josiah to Israel to give them one last opportunity to repent, and they were both faithful and did all God commanded. I hate the scene where King Josiah dies; it always makes me cry."

"It made me cry too," agreed Liyana.

The next stepped forward. "My favorite is Natan. He was a man of great courage. He sent his family to Babylon to save them from the siege of Jerusalem, but he stayed. He was willing to suffer and die if necessary to bring us the story of God's wrath. He willingly submitted himself to the wrath of God. I don't know of any of the great warriors in the Magi Family who had more courage than Natan."

The last child stepped forward. "My favorite is Navid and Tiz."

Liyana was puzzled. "I asked about what you had learned."

"Not everything I learned on this trip is in the scrolls – yet, but they will be. My father told me when we began the journey, Navid was against it. He did not want the Family to go. He did not believe God would guide and protect us. Despite his objections and lack of faith, he led us. Every day he was the point of the spear, riding in front of the Family, protecting us from harm." He nodded at Navid. "Now look at him. He fought the Uxians at the Gate, he married Ava, the love of his life, he faced the Immortals without flinching, and in the power of the Spirit, he fought the slave traders with his bare hands. He submitted himself to God, and God changed him. God changed Tiz, too. We all know Tiz is a quiet man, always willing to follow. He never wanted to lead, but he led his men at the Gate, he faced a crocodile in the Euphrates to save a child, and he led 10 people against 200 slave traders. The most important lesson I learned on the trip is not in the scrolls. I learned that God changed and used Navid and Tiz, and He will do the same for me if I give myself to Him."

Liyana left the platform and hugged each child. *One day, my child will sit among these children.*

Liyana was about to dismiss the children when someone suddenly cried, "Look."

Everyone turned to the north and looked where the person pointed. There was a star, stationary over Galilee, that had not been there a few minutes before. A gasp went through the Magi Family.

THE MESSIAH

Hugav – Day 148

Fardad convened an emergency Family Council. "What are our options?"

"We have two options," said Jahan. "The Family breaks camp, we travel through the night and rest during the day until we reach the star, or we send our fastest rider to find the location of the Messiah."

"I'm for sending the fastest rider," said Navid. "It would be too great a strain on the Family traveling at night and moving flocks and herds. Too dangerous."

The Council agreed with Navid.

"It is settled. We will send two riders," said Fardad.

"Why two?" asked Jahan.

"They will be traveling at night on mountain trails, and they will be riding fast. If a horse is injured, the other rider can continue," said Fardad.

"You are right, Grandfather," replied Navid. "Hugav and I will go."

Jahan shook his head. "We need two men who can cover 200 miles in the shortest time possible. We are talking about twenty hours of hard riding. None of the horses could handle your weight. It's Hugav and Esmail."

Navid wanted to argue, but he knew his father was right. "You are right, Father. Hugav can ride Anosh."

Ram spoke, which startled everyone. "No, they will ride the Turkomans."

Jahan smiled and clapped Ram on the back. "Brilliant, of course, the Turkomans. The descendants of Bareil's great horse will run to find the Messiah. Fitting, Ram. Are you sure the son is up to it?"

"The dam is five; she is in her prime. She will have no problem. The son is two and a half, and I have been running him. He is ready. They are perfectly suited for this. Their smaller hooves are an advantage in the mountains, and none of our horses can match their speed and endurance. Most of our horses can sustain a pace of seven miles in an hour; the Turkomans can average ten."

"Ram, get the horses ready. Navid, bring Hugav and Esmail," said Fardad.

The two men left, and Navid returned, bringing Hugav and Esmail.

"Has Navid explained what we need?" asked Fardad.

"He has, Fardad," replied Hugav. "On the Turkomans, we will be back tomorrow night. We will mark the home of the Messiah, rest, water, feed the horses, and then return."

"You won't find the Messiah standing here," said Jahan. "Let's go."

The Council walked to the corral with Hugav and Esmail. Ram had the horses tacked, and he handed the riders two saddlebags. "One bag has cheese and bread for you; the other has barley, diced boiled chicken, dates, and mutton fat for the horse. Their diet is different from the other horses. It is best you carry their food with you."

The two men mounted and put heels to the horses, and the Magi Family gathered to watch them leave. The Family ululated, beat shields, and cried encouragement. Tonight, was the night. God was leading them to the Messiah.

Hugav and Esmail rode north, following the star. God had given them the star and a bright moonlit night, moonlight enough for Hugav to see. Hugav led, and Esmail followed.

The horses ran hour after hour. When they reached Shechem, Hugav remembered the well outside the city. They gave the horses a breather at the well, watered them, and gave them a few handfuls of feed. When the men remounted, the horses were breathing normally and were barely sweating. Hugav rode the son, and Esmail the dam.

Hugav's eyes constantly moved, watching for danger to the horse, to Esmail, or himself. The moonlight cast long shadows, and frequently, the shadow of a predator—owl, hawk, or falcon appeared as the bird flew between the moon and Hugav.

It was cool but not cold, and there was a gentle breeze. It was a beautiful night to ride, and Hugav wanted to relax and enjoy the ride but knew he could not. He fought sleep and yelled to Esmail periodically to ensure he was awake. He didn't want to turn around and find a riderless horse behind him. The fourth watch was the most difficult. The men worked together to keep each other awake. Muted shades of pink and red were peeking above the eastern horizon, but the star still shone brightly.

Hugav dug his heels into the big dam, and she responded with a powerful surge. When he looked back, Esmail and the two-year-old were matching the dam stride for stride, and as they topped a small rise, a town appeared. The star was directly over the town.

Hugav went to a gallop in his excitement. The two horses thundered down the rise, and the two-year-old pulled even with his mother. He was flying, but the old girl was not about to be outrun by a youngster. She flattened, her stride lengthened, and they were pulling away from the young stallion. The two men whooped and celebrated as the city's outskirts drew near.

Soon, they had to slow the horses to a walk, not wanting to wake the village. The light of the star engulfed one home. Hugav and Esmail dismounted, fell to their knees, foreheads to the ground, and gave thanks. They had found the Messiah.

Hugav looked around, memorizing the house and its surroundings, but to be safe, he searched and found several small rocks and built an altar, unobtrusively, on the side of the house. Without a word, he and Esmail walked their horses out of the town and rode a short distance to the north. They found a well on the outskirts of the city, where they watered and rested the horses and fed them the remainder of the feed. The men waited till they saw people stirring and rode into the town, stopped the first person they met, and asked, "Can you tell me the name of this city?" The man replied, "Nazareth."

Magi Camp – Day 149

The family ate the evening meal. Everyone was in a state of restlessness, anxiousness, peacefulness, or some other-ness.

"They should have been back by now," said Jahan, pounding his fist in the palm of his hand. "I should have known better than to send those two."

Navid shook his head. "Father, they need twenty hours of travel time, plus time to rest, water, and feed the horses. It's not time yet. They will be here, and we did pick the two best men, and you know it."

"You should be ashamed of yourself, Jahan," said his wife.

Jahan was not giving up that easily. "All I know is if I had made the trip, I would have been back by now."

Asha narrowed her eyes and looked at her husband. "If you had ridden the Turkoman, it would have died of exhaustion hours ago!"

Navid, Tiz, and Utana snorted but managed to stifle the laugh under Jahan's withering glare.

"I would have ridden a real horse, not one of those skinny runts."

"And you would have been back two days from now," said Fardad, bringing that discussion to a close.

Liyana wrung her hands. "I am so nervous I can barely stand it. I don't know if I can wait much longer."

Pari stroked her back. "It will be fine, Liyana. Hugav and Esmail are the two best riders in the Family."

"Long-distance riders, she means," Navid corrected.

"But of course." Pari smiled warmly. "Everyone knows that Tiz is the best rider."

Tiz waved both hands in front of him. "Whoa, whoa, whoa, don't drag me into this. I'm perfectly happy sitting here being ignored."

Asha looked at Pari and Fahnik. "It appears we have many things to celebrate today," she said. "Do you two have something you want to tell everyone?"

"Not again," said Pari. "What do you know that we don't know?"

"You missed your normal cycle, didn't you?"

"Five days ago," said Pari, "That's not all that unusual."

"It may not be," said Asha, "but you are with child. With you, it is easier to tell. Your sister was harder for several reasons, but she is also expecting."

Tiz and Utana leaped up, hugged, and began dancing.

Fahnik elbowed Utana in the shin. "I'm the one having your baby, not him. Get back down here and kiss me."

Utana dropped back next to his wife, grinning from ear to ear, and kissed her as commanded.

Tiz didn't wait for instruction; he picked up Pari, held her in his arms, and kissed her.

Ava put her hands on her hips and glared at Navid, who knew that look meant: "What about me?" And he kissed his beautiful and already-expecting wife.

Asha put her hands on her hips and looked at Jahan, "Well?"

Jahan had a shocked look on his face. "No, you're not?"

Fardad shook his head. "What a bonehead."

Hugav – Day 149

The two men rode out of Nazareth shortly after sunrise and headed south. They passed Shechem, stopping for water once again, and then continued. They were holding to a steady ten-mile-an-hour trot. The Turkomans were not tiring, and they ate up the miles. In the heat of the afternoon, the horses sweated heavier, and Hugav and Esmail lay their heads on their horse's necks listening to their massive hearts hammering. Their breathing was sound, and they showed no signs of stress. So, they rode on.

They were in the foothills past Bethel when six riders rode out from a group of rocks, blocking the road. Hugav reacted immediately and yelled, "Split." Hugav jerked his reins to the right and headed west. Esmail saw the move and went east.

The thieves split up with half going in each direction. Hugav looked back. Esmail had a good start and was easily outdistancing the men following him. Hugav noted one man in the group following him who rode a big Arabian with excellent short-distance speed. The rider was closing the gap between them and had his sword drawn. Hugav hated doing it, but he removed his sling and a bag of smooth stones from his sash. He removed a stone from the bag just as the dam leaped over a small crevice. The stone fell from Hugav's hand when she landed. Hugav fumbled for another stone and put it in the sling's pouch. The thief was twenty feet behind him. Hugav twirled the sling above his head, then turned, pointed his finger at the Arabian's neck, and released the stone. The stone hit with a sickening thud. The Arabian reared, dumping its rider, then staggered backward, crushing the man. The other two riders broke off pursuit.

Hugav rode west a short distance before finding a trail south again and resumed his ride to Bethany. Ten miles from the village, he saw a rider trotting in front of him and put his heels to the Turkoman. He closed the distance and rode up beside Esmail.

"Where have you been?" Esmail asked casually.

"I wasn't as fortunate as you," replied Hugav. "That big Arabian almost caught us. I had to put a stone in its neck. The horse reared, dumping the rider, and then trampled him. What a waste, but he left me no choice."

Esmail grew serious. "I'm sorry, Hugav. None of us like unnecessary death, but the rider chose a career in which death is a hazard. He met the wrong man today."

The two men reached the Magi Camp as the sun was setting, and when they were a mile from camp, they heard ram's horns sounding. *Good to see the sentries are on their toes.*

When they arrived, the entire Family was at the entrance to the camp. Ram came running up and grabbed the horses' reins. Esmail and Hugav dismounted as Ram went over every inch of the horses, checking them for injuries.

"We're fine, Ram," said Hugav. "Thank you for asking."

Ram scowled at Hugav and led the horses to the corral.

"Well," said Jahan. "Don't just stand there, say something. Where's the Messiah?"

Hugav wagged his finger. "You are the most impatient person I know. Aren't you going to ask us how we are or how our trip went?"

Jahan took two steps forward, stopped an inch from Hugav, looked down, and growled.

Hugav swallowed. "The Messiah, of course. We found Him; He is in Nazareth in Galilee. The star led us to His home. I marked it with a small stone altar on the side of the house. We take the same route that we took coming into Israel. We can be there in eight days if we start in the morning."

Jahan smiled and crushed Esmail and Hugav in an embrace. "That's my boys. Good job. Excellent. How are you?"

Both men were turning purple and gasping for breath.

Asha walked up and smacked Jahan on the back of the head. "Let them go before you kill them. You would think by now you would have learned how to give a gentle hug. But, oh no, you still hug like an angry mother bear."

Jahan looked down and saw the distressed look on the men's faces. "Oh, I'm so sorry," he said as he released them. "I forget myself when I get excited."

Hugav took a deep breath. "We're fine, and so are the horses. The Turkomans were magnificent. I'm sure Ram is giving them a special reward, which they deserve. We ran into robbers on our return. Unfortunately, I had to kill a man, but it was him or me."

Jahan shrugged. "He chose a bad profession. You did what you had to do. I'm glad it was him, not you."

The Family surrounded Hugav and Esmail, hugging them and showering them with food and wine. The two men were staggering from exhaustion and lack of sleep, and Navid and Tiz helped them to their tents.

Well before the first light, the Family was up, eager to start the journey, and they traveled until dark. They had waited 500 years to meet the Messiah and would not wait one day longer than they had to. They had passed Bethel the day before, and Fardad did not want the Family to stop. He climbed the mount alone, worshipped God, and returned to the caravan.

"I'm glad you had a chance to visit the mount again, Father," said Jahan.

"I will never see it again," replied Fardad. "But imagine, God has let me worship here twice. I am the least of all the Magi leaders, yet He chose me for this great honor. What glory, and now I am about to meet His Son."

"God does not make mistakes, Father. You have always been God's man. You are the leader of the Magi at this moment because you were the person God wanted to lead us to worship His Son. You were born for such a time as this."

Fardad buried his face in Jahan's chest and wept. "Have I told you how much I love you? You are the greatest gift God ever gave me. Thank you for your faith in me, Jahan."

"No, Father. It is me God has blessed. I have a father who loves me and taught me to love God and my fellow man. I am truly blessed."

The two men caught up with the Family, and the journey continued.

They arrived on the outskirts of Nazareth on the evening of the seventh day, Day 156. They made camp and sat down to eat.

"There will be enough light for us to meet the Messiah tonight," said Navid.

Fardad shook his head no. "No, the Family will meet Him tomorrow. We will worship Him properly. The area in which we meet the Messiah is Holy Ground. I want the clearing swept in the morning. After we have prepared the area, the Family will bathe and put on our white ceremonial robes. When we are ready, Jahan and Asha will ride into Nazareth, tell Mary and Joseph why we are here, and ask them to meet with the Family."

Everyone understood and nodded their heads in agreement. Tomorrow they would meet the Messiah.

Jesus

Jahan and Asha dressed in their finest clothes, oiled their hair, and put on perfume.

"How do I look?" asked Asha.

Jahan was about to reply casually, but he saw the concern on his wife's face. He stepped back, looked at her appraisingly, and said, "Honestly, you have never looked more beautiful."

He took her in his arms and kissed her gently. "Come, we have a Messiah to meet."

They exited the tent. Navid was outside with his father's horse, a white mule for Asha, and a mule carrying gifts for the Messiah, jars of frankincense, myrrh, and a chest filled with gold.

Asha hugged Navid. "We will be back shortly. We will return as soon as we can. Tell the Family to be patient."

Asha and Jahan mounted and rode into Nazareth. People were in the street, a few gave them quizzical looks, but no one stopped them. Hugav had drawn a detailed map of the city, which Jahan had memorized. Hugav's map and description were perfect. Jahan found the house and saw the small stone altar beside the house. He and Asha dismounted. Asha carried the two jars, and Jahan carried the gold chest. Asha knocked on the door, and a young woman answered.

"Yes, may I help you?" Mary asked.

"I am Asha, and this is my husband, Jahan. We are Magi from Persepolis, Persia. We saw your Son's star when He was born, and we have come to worship Him. Is Joseph home?"

Mary was speechless. "You have come from Persia to worship my Son? Why would you do that?"

"May we come in?" asked Asha. "We will explain everything to you."

"Yes, of course," said Mary. "Come in."

She stepped aside, Asha picked up her jars, and she and Jahan entered. They saw Jesus sitting on the floor, contentedly playing with a wooden spoon. Asha and Jahan fell to their knees with their heads on the floor and thanked God and His Son. They remained prostrate for several minutes, both of them praying silently.

They rose and rocked on their heels. Jahan looked at Mary. "We are Magi and are members of a Family of Magi that began 734 years ago. The founders of our Family are from Nineveh, Assyria. One of our founders, Meesha, was ambassador to Judah in the days of Kings

244

Ahaz and Hezekiah. He learned about Jehovah, and he believed. He also learned about the Messiah from Isaiah, and Isaiah taught that 'the ends of the earth shall see the salvation of our God,'[39] and he also said, 'so shall He sprinkle many nations.[40] Your Son, Jesus, has come to bring salvation to all mankind. That is what we believe."

Asha continued, "The day Jesus was born, we saw His star. We have watched the night skies for 500 years looking for the sign, and 157 days ago, we saw the star. The same night we saw the star, an angel of the Lord visited our Elder, Fardad. The angel told us we were to come and worship and that we were to bring gifts of frankincense and myrrh." Asha presented the two jars to Mary.

Jahan handed her the gold chest. "The angel didn't tell us to bring the gold. That is from us. The gold is more than 700 years old and belonged to one of the founders of the Family, Benjamin."

"I know we have just met, Mary, but you can trust us," said Asha. "Were you a virgin when you became pregnant with Jesus?"

Mary looked as if she were reeling inside. "How could you know that?" asked Mary, "We have not told anyone that."

"Isaiah said you would be a virgin. God is Jesus' Father. It had to be so. You have confirmed everything we ever believed."

"Where is Joseph?" asked Jahan.

"I'm sorry, Asha asked earlier; I forgot. Joseph is a carpenter. He is away on a building project."

"We have a favor to ask," said Jahan. "There are 200 people in the Magi Family who want to worship Jesus, and they will not fit in this room. I am also sure you don't want to draw that kind of attention to yourselves. Would you accompany us to our camp?"

Asha felt a tug on her hand and looked down to see Jesus smiling up at her and tugging on her finger. Asha's heart melted. She picked Him up, held him to her chest, rocked, and cooed to Him. She was holding the Messiah.

Mary smiled at Asha. "Of course, we will come to your camp." She stood, put on a robe, wrapped Jesus in a blanket, and followed them outside. Jahan put Mary and the baby on the white mule that had carried their gifts, and they rode back to the camp.

Tiz placed Pari on the platform in the clearing and sat next to her. They had talked again last night about their decision to remain in Israel, but Pari was filled with anxiety this morning. She and Tiz would be alone for the first time in their lives. There would be no one to help with her care. Tiz would become a carpenter and work all day, then have to gather food, cook, clean, and care for her. She was terrified. She could not put that kind of burden on Tiz. She bowed her head and prayed; she lifted her voice to God and asked Him to give her peace with the decision.

Pari opened her eyes. An older man with a donkey was approaching. *Why wasn't anyone stopping him? What were they thinking?* The Family had swept the area, taken off their shoes, and put on white robes in preparation for meeting the Messiah, and now they were letting this man and his donkey walk right through the clearing. The man stopped in front of her.

"Pari, El-Roi, Yahweh-Rapha has sent me, fear not, He sees and hears you." The man reached out his hand and touched her legs.

Pari saw a pure white light and heard a rushing wind, and warmth like a summer rain coursed through her body. The light faded, and when she could see again, the man was gone.

"Tiz, where did he go?"

Tiz tilted his head and looked at her. "Where did who go?"

"The older man and his donkey. They were right here. Where did he go?"

"Pari, I saw no one," said Tiz.

"But he talked to me; surely you heard him," she insisted.

Tiz pointed; Mary and Jesus rode into camp with Asha and Jahan. "We will talk about this later."

The Family was in the clearing. They had drawn a large circle and swept it clean. Everyone's shoes ringed the circle. The Family sat in the circle barefoot, wearing their white robes. This was Holy Ground. Navid met his parents at the circle's edge. They removed their shoes, stepped into the circle, and donned their white robes. The Magi were ready to worship.

Jahan led Mary and Jesus to the speaker platform, where Pari was on the platform sitting on her cushion next to Tiz. The Family knelt and pressed their heads to the ground without a word. They offered silent prayers to God.

Jahan heard a low murmuring of those who offered spoken prayers. The Family remained motionless and prayed for more than thirty minutes. Mary sat Jesus on a cushion, so he could see the people, and His little head rotated from side to side as He watched everyone. He never made a sound.

People finished praying and sat up, one by one, until everyone had completed their prayers.

Pari said, "Children, you may come up and meet Jesus, but remember He is a baby. No touching." The children rushed to the platform, and Jesus cooed and laughed. He crawled to the edge of the platform and sat. Every child had the opportunity to stand before Him. Some held out their hands, and Jesus would pat them or pull their fingers. Others bent down with their faces close, and Jesus patted faces, ears, noses, and anything that caught His interest. He laughed, and the children laughed. Many children brought their favorite toys and laid them at Jesus's feet. Nura gave Jesus the dreidel Navid had bought him in Jerusalem. Pari's heart burst with pride when she saw him lay his toy next to Jesus.

After the children, the adults came. They smiled at Jesus, but their gazes were intent. They were memorizing everything they could. They wanted to remember every detail about Him. Pari knew that they would discuss everything they remembered every day after this. Their combined memories painting a complete and perfect picture. Pari saw Tiz with his sketchpad. Tiz would not rely on memory; he was sketching the Messiah as he saw him. Pari knew whatever he drew would be wonderful.

Everyone came, Fardad, Navid, Tiz, Utana, Fahnik, Liyana, Gul, Ava, Dara, Delara, Esmail, Hugav, Farida, Habib, Kevan, Marzban, Ram, Vasil, Adel and Aref. They all came. Young and old, Council member and shepherd, men and women, they all came. Five hundred years culminated in this one wonderful moment as the Magi worshipped their Redeemer.

Asha was near Mary. "I am sure He must be hungry by now," said Mary.

"Of course, what are we thinking? You can use my tent," said Asha.

"Mother, may I come with you?" said Pari. "There is something I would like to ask Mary."

Asha looked at Mary. "That will be fine," said Mary.

Pari signaled to Tiz. "Would you take me to mother's tent?"

Tiz bent to pick her up. "What in the world," he mumbled.

Pari shot him a sharp look. "Just pick me up. We'll talk about this later."

Tiz bent his knees a little deeper and lifted Pari. He carried her to Asha's tent. Mary, Jesus, and Asha were in the tent. Tiz bent to put Pari down, but she jumped nimbly from his arms and stood before them.

Asha smiled; Tiz fell on his rump, his knees too weak to hold him.

Pari lifted her robe to her knees. Her legs were well muscled and fully restored. She was not standing on withered legs.

Tiz stammered, "What? How? How can this be?"

"The 'what' is God has healed me by His Grace and Mercy; the 'how' is an angel sent by God," said Pari. "From the moment we began this trip, I had prayed God would heal me. I believed. Before you arrived, Mary, I saw an older man with a donkey. He walked up to me and said the God who sees, El-Roi, and the God who heals, Yahweh-Rapha, had sent him. He told me not to be afraid and touched my legs. I felt the rushing of the Spirit of God. It was like warm rain, but on the inside, and I knew God had healed me in that instant."

"It's wonderful, but it is also a problem," continued Pari, "The Family cannot know about this. They will think Jesus had something to do with my healing, but He is a baby and was not involved. Unfortunately, some people will believe Jesus was the immediate cause of my healing, regardless of what we say. It would be horrible if word of my healing got out. It would put terrible pressure on Mary, Joseph, and Jesus. No one can know."

"What can we do?" asked Asha

"My solution is that Tiz, Nura, and I will remain in Nazareth. Tiz and I have talked about this several times, and God has taken the decision out of our hands. We must stay in Nazareth where no one knows or has seen us. Our children will grow up with Jesus, and I will write the Family and tell you about everything happening in Jesus's life. I believe God brought about my healing for this very purpose."

"How will Tiz make a living?" asked Mary.

"He is an artist, a skilled tradesman, and a carpenter. He can make a living. Tiz and I have not talked since God healed me, and the final decision to stay or go must be his."

"Joseph always has more work than he can do. I am sure he would love it if Tiz could help him," said Mary, "and you can stay with us until you get settled. Tiz, has a priest circumcised you?"

Tiz put his hands on Pari's shoulders and looked into her eyes. "We will stay. You know I hate being a warrior. All I have ever wanted to do is work with my hands. No one in Nazareth knows me. They don't know my violent past. We will grow old together in Nazareth and watch our children and the Messiah grow up. Can you imagine anything more wonderful?"

Tiz turned to Mary. "We are staying, and yes, Ram circumcised me, not a priest."

"It doesn't matter as long as you are circumcised," said Mary. "You and Pari need to develop a background story. You cannot claim to be Israelites. You cannot prove descent from one of the twelve tribes. You can claim to be a descendant of those who could not prove descent when Israel returned from Babylon. There are many such Temple worshippers. No one thinks anything of that."

"Thank you, Mary," said Tiz. "While you feed Jesus, I will find Jahan and him you are ready to return to Nazareth. Pari, I suggest you have a seat. We will explain everything to the family after Jahan and Asha return from Nazareth."

As they rode toward Nazareth, Jahan asked, "Mary, will it be all right if the Family spends a week here? Our animals need rest, food, and water. It also gives us more opportunities to see Jesus and meet Joseph."

"It is fine, Jahan," Mary replied "My only concern is people will ask questions if I make too many trips to your camp."

"I understand," Jahan agreed. "We will limit it to two visits at the most. Is that agreeable?"

"That will be fine, Jahan."

They arrived at Mary and Joseph's home. Jahan and Asha each hugged the baby, rode back to camp, and entered their tent. Their family was seated in the tent, including Gul and Liyana.

"Is there some reason for this gathering?" asked Jahan.

"You might want to sit down, Father," said Pari. "Tiz and I have something to tell everyone."

Jahan and Asha both sat, and Pari stood. It was a good thing everyone was seated.

"What?" And "How?" was echoed by everyone simultaneously, and then Gul fainted.

Asha revived Gul, and Pari continued, "The answer to *how* is: God's grace. An angel of the Lord visited me before Jesus arrived, and he healed me. The answer to *why* is that God has a new plan and purpose for Tiz and me. We will be staying in Nazareth. The Family must not know about my healing. People will think that Jesus was involved in my healing, so the only safe thing to do is ensure the Family does not find out about my healing. If word got out, it would be disastrous for Mary, Joseph, and Jesus. Also, by staying, our children will have the opportunity to grow up with Jesus. I will write to you frequently and describe everything we see and hear. In the best tradition of the Magi, we will record the most significant event ever to occur, the life of the Messiah."

"But what about the Family's children?" asked Liyana. "Who will teach them?"

Pari walked over to Liyana, lifted her to her feet, and hugged her. "You will teach them. God has been preparing you. He always has a plan and purpose for those who seek Him. You will teach until you reach Resafa, and then you and your husband will teach. I cannot think of anything more wonderful."

Navid looked longingly at his sister, tears coming to his eyes. "But what will I do without you? You are like a glimmer of sunshine on a dark day. You are a bird song in the gloom of winter. I cannot imagine life without you."

"Ava and your new child are all the sunshine and song you need. God has been preparing both of us, Navid. You for fatherhood and leadership, and Tiz and me for service to the Messiah. We each have a role to play, Navid. No one's role is greater or lesser than another. We each serve God as He sees fit. Now, Tiz will carry me to the clearing, and we will eat together. There will be no talk of my healing. Agreed?"

Everyone agreed, went to the clearing, and the Family ate together. The Family talked of only one thing, the Messiah. They were blessed and thankful. They had seen the Messiah, the dream of the men and women who had preceded them for 500 years.

Fardad went to Navid's tent the following morning. "Navid, gather the Council and come to the Meeting Tent."

"What is it, Grandfather? What has happened?"

"Gather the Council, Navid, and I will explain everything."

Fardad turned and went to the Meeting Tent. It took Navid a while to gather everyone, but finally, everyone was present.

"I was visited by an angel last night," Fardad said without preamble. "The angel said we are to leave Israel immediately. We are not to tell Herod the location of the Messiah, and we are to take a different route home. Herod intends to kill the Messiah if he can. He does not want a competitor for his throne. What a monster."

"The Scouts know how to eliminate monsters," offered Navid.

"Not this time, Navid. God is clear. He wants us to leave and leave now."

"The Family will be disappointed," said Jahan. "They were looking forward to continuing their worship of the Messiah."

"I know," said Fardad, "but we came at God's call, and now we will leave at His command. Blessed be the Name of the Lord. Navid, tell Tiz and Pari they need to prepare for their move to Nazareth. Gather anything you believe they will need to start their new life. Jahan, ride into Nazareth and ask Mary if she and Jesus can come to the camp. The Family can worship one last time and say their goodbyes. Also, tell her the warning I received from the angel; she and Joseph need to know."

The shoeless Family sat in the circle in the clearing, wearing their white robes one last time. Mary and Jesus ascended the platform, and prostrate, the Family worshipped again.

After a reasonable period, Fardad ascended the platform. "It is time for the Magi to return home," he said. "It is less time in Israel than I had hoped for, but God has made it clear. It is time for us to leave."

Fardad bent and picked up the Messiah. He held him high for all to see. "**BEHOLD YOUR KING.** And his name shall be called Wonderful Counselor, Mighty God, Eternal Father, Prince of Peace." Fardad cradled his Savior in his arms and lifted his eyes to heaven. "Jehovah, you are the God who sees. You are all-powerful and all-knowing, and You have sent your Son into the world to redeem all mankind. We do not deserve such a precious gift, yet He is here. Guide Him, protect Him, and grow Him in wisdom and knowledge. We thank You that all He purposes He will accomplish. No one in heaven or earth can stop Him from accomplishing Your Will. We love You, Father, and thank You for letting us see and worship Your Son. We would have traveled 2,000 more miles for this opportunity. Bless your children as we travel home. Keep us safe, and prepare our hearts and minds for the things your Son will reveal. We love You, Father, and we love Your Son."

AND ALL THE PEOPLE SAID, "AMEN."

Mary, Jesus, Tiz, Pari, and Nura left for Nazareth, and the Family went west to the seacoast and followed it north to leave Israel as quickly as possible. On the third day of their journey, one of the men found an unusual block of wood in one of the wagons and showed it to Navid. It was the piece of African Mahogany Tiz had received in Jerusalem in exchange for his carved eagle. Navid discussed with Jahan returning the wood to Tiz, and he agreed that Navid should take it and then catch up with the Family. Navid walked to the corral to get Anosh and was surprised to find Fahnik sitting astride the Turkoman stallion. Utana stood beside her, holding the reins to the white mule Mary and Jesus had ridden. Utana had strapped the block of wood to the mule.

"You didn't think you would get to see Pari and Tiz alone, did you?" asked Utana.

"If you're going, I'm going," said Fahnik, "things happened so quickly in Nazareth that I barely had a chance to say goodbye to Pari and Tiz."

Navid smiled, "I'm glad for the company, and I know they will be thrilled you came. Why don't you come, Utana?

Utana smiled back, "No, this is brother and sister time. You two haven't been alone since the slave traders captured you, Navid. This is your time. I'll be here when you get back."

Navid tacked Anosh, hugged Utana, and led the way south to Nazareth.

They made the return to Nazareth in one day and rode to the home of Mary and Joseph.

Navid knocked on the door, and Pari greeted them.

"Navid, Fahnik," she beamed. "Come in; how wonderful to see you. What are you doing here?"

Navid pointed to the large piece of African Mahogany strapped to the mule. "Tiz forgot that, and I knew he would want it." Navid saw Tiz on the floor playing with Nura. "Where are Mary and Jesus?"

"Joseph returned the day after you left," said Tiz. "He was visited by an angel of the Lord who warned him that Herod wanted to destroy Jesus. The angel told him to take Mary and the child to Egypt and remain there until Herod died.[41] I have taken over his carpentry business and will run it until he returns."

Navid and Fahnik spent the night, and he rose early the next morning. Nura was sleeping. Pari and Fahnik had made tea. The two women had been talking for the past two hours. Navid marveled as he saw Pari walking and preparing the morning meal with Fahnik. His mind still had difficulty processing this miraculous change.

"Sit and eat with us," said Tiz.

"I cannot; we need to catch up to the Family. We will take some cheese and bread with us for the trail."

Pari had planned on this and had baked an extra loaf. She put the bread and cheese wrapped in cloth in Navid's saddlebag. It was more than enough for Navid and Fahnik.

Navid and Tiz gripped each other's right forearms and embraced. "Take care of your family and the Messiah, Tiz. Remember, if you ever need me, I can be here with a group of fast riders in less than a month."

"I think we need your prayers more than your sword, brother. You and the Family will be in my prayers every day."

Tiz hugged and kissed Fahnik, "I want a detailed description of my niece or nephew," he said, "I need to be able to see them in my mind so I can paint of picture of him or her for Pari."

Fahnik promised she would.

Navid hugged and kissed Pari. His cheeks were wet, "I love you with all my heart, sister. Life will be hard without you. You better write, and you better write often. The Family will want to know every detail about your life and the life of the Messiah. We will look forward to reading your letters."

Fahnik and Pari hugged, cried, and whispered to each other. Fahnik kissed her one last time and walked from the house. Navid followed her.

They left the white mule for Tiz and Pari, and the two mounted and headed north to find the Family.

"That goodbye was harder than the first one," said Navid.

"Not for me," said Fahnik, "we left so fast there were many things left unsaid. I am thankful Tiz forgot that wood."

"I wonder now if he forgot the wood."

"Do you think he left it on purpose?" asked Fahnik.

"Tiz is a wise man, Fahnik, and he doesn't make many mistakes. Yes, I think he forgot it on purpose. He knew we would come. I am in his debt."

"So am I," said Fahnik, "now it's just you and me, brother. One day grandfather and father will be gone, and then we will be the Magi. We will lead the Family along with our children. Does that scare you?"

"Not for a minute. God has prepared us for that time. When it comes, we are ready. We are the Family.

"We are," said Fahnik, "but today it's just you and me, brother, and a wide-open road before us." Fahnik laughed and kicked the Turkoman hard. Navid laughed and gave Anosh his head. They were flying. Navid saw Fahnik racing along the narrow track, wheat growing on either side, the tops swaying in a gentle breeze. Fahnik's hair streamed behind her, her robe flapping in the wind. Fahnik sat erect, her strong, young legs gripping the horse's barrel. She leaned her head back and spread her arms wide. Navid rode up next to her, leaned his head back, and spread his arms wide. Brother and sister, riding into the future.

APPENDIX

Credits

Sherry Garner, my wonderful sweet wife, tolerates my strange writing hours and proofs my books. Her edits make me reexamine many things when what I think is obvious isn't.

Olivia Han (韩慕柔) for being the most brilliant 6th-grade editor imaginable. Olivia has edited two books of Magi Journey and is an integral part of the story. Olivia's questions have led to several additions for added clarity. Olivia attends Community Christian School and Trinity Baptist Church in Norman, OK.

Lt. Colonel Bill Terry, who assisted me on books one, and two, was again invaluable in editing book three. I love running across the street and brainstorming with Bill. He is both a mentor and friend. Bill is a member of Bethel Baptist Church in Norman, OK, and his faith and spiritual guidance are invaluable.

Larry Toothaker, Ph.D., a member of Trinity Baptist Church, performed invaluable detail edits and was very encouraging in all my efforts. I have loved sitting with Larry on Wednesday evenings over the church dinner, reviewing his feedback on Magi Journey. Thank you, Larry

Ronnie Rogers, the senior pastor of Trinity Baptist Church, has discipled me since 1998. Thank you, Ronnie, for leading me in the way of all truth.

Maps

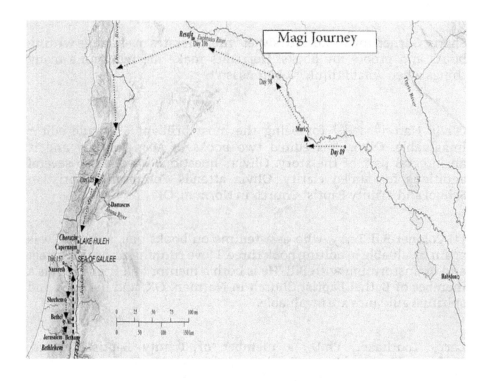

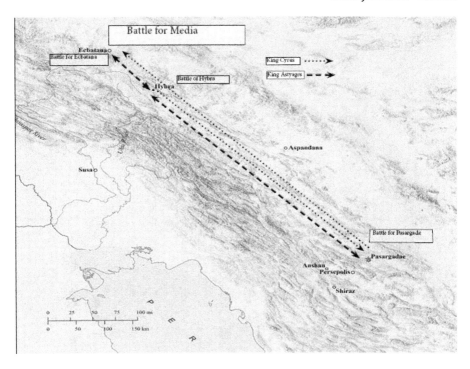

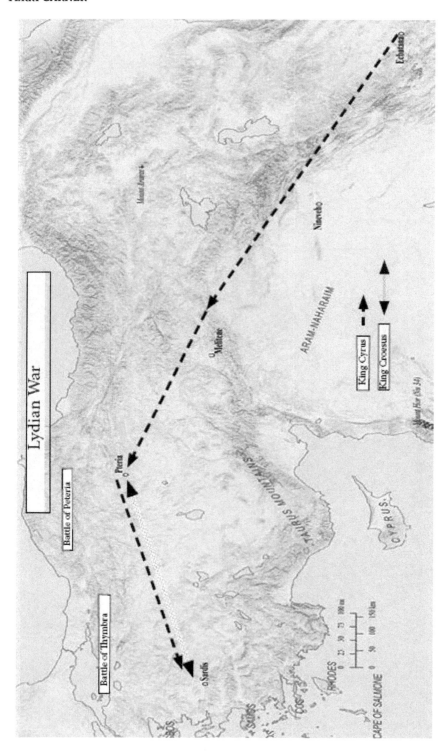

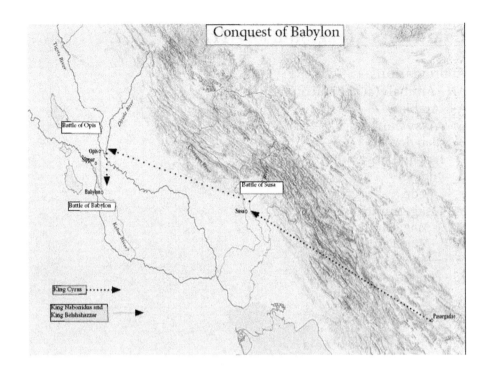

Characters – Magi Journey Trilogy

Abbreviations –
AN - Animals (at the end of listing)
AR- Arabian
AS - Assyrian
BY - Babylonian
IS - Israeli (Ephraimite)
JD - Judean
ME - Mede
MF - Magi Family
MFA - Magi Family Assyria
MFB - Magi Family Babylonia
MFJ – Magi Family Judean
PS - Persian
SL - Slave Trader
SY - Syrian

MFJ - Abigail - Wife of Zaia
MF - Adel - Leader of the right flank on the march
JD - Adin - A disciple of Isaiah
PS - Agradates - the name of King Cyrus II until age 10
JD - Ahaz - King of Judah
JD - Ali - A Judean, who rode with Eliya
PS - Alibai - AnUxian shepherdess
SL - Ammar - A survivor of the Magi raid
MF - Aref - A member of the Scouts
ME - Artembares - The best friend of Prince Astyages
SL - Asaad - A survivor of the Magi raid
MF - Asha - Wife of Jahan and mother of Navid
AS - Ashur - Second in command under Baildan
ME - Astyages - Prince of Media, became king in 585 BC
MF - Ava - Wife of Navid
MFB - Awa - Seena's aide
MFB - Azad - Son of Kia
MFB - Babak - Courier for Pera
MFA - Baildan - Leader of a troop of 100 cavalry, son of Domara

PS - Baraz - Satrap of southeast Persia, father of Leyla
MFB - Bareil - The 22-year-old son of Seena and serves as his military aide – Babylon

BY - Belshazzar - Co-Regent of Babylon with his father King Nabonidus

MFJ - Benjamin - Judean, son of Rachael, rescued by Baildan

PS - Cambyses I - King of Anshan, father of Cyrus II
PS - Cambyses II - Son of King Cyrus II and future king of Persia

PS - Cassandana - Wife of Cyrus II, mother of Cambyses II
ME - Cyaxares - King of the Media 625-585 BC
ME - Cyno - Wife of Mithradates
PS - Cyrus I - King of Anshan, father of Cambyses I
PS - Cyrus II - King of Persia, son of Cambyses I and Mandana, Grandson of King Astyagaes

MF - Danial - Leader of the dissidents
MF - Dara - Father of Utana
MFJ - Davi - The 15-year-old son of Natan
MF - Delara - A 5-year-old girl, very energetic
ME - Diomede - Captain of King Astyages's guard
MFA - Domara - The Patriarch of the Magi Family, counselor to Tiglath-Pileser III

MFA - Eil - Nineveh Magi, who founded The Scouts.
AS - Eilbra - Signal caller under Baildan
MFB - Elham - Wife of Omid
AS - Eliya - Servant of Meesha
MFB - Elka - The Daughter of Davi and Sarah
MF - Esmail - A member of the Scouts
MF - Fahnik - Daughter of Jahan and Asha, wife of Utana
MF - Fardad - The Leader of the Council, father of Jahan
MF - Farida - One of Rahim's best students, rambunctious
ME - Fravarti - Son of the nobleman Artembares - Median
MFJ - Gilad   The armor-bearer of King Josiah
MF - Gohar - Dissident, father of Mahsa
MF - Gul - The servant to Asha
MF - Habib - A member of the Scouts
JD - Hahn - A disciple of Isaiah
SL - Haider - A survivor of the Magi raid
MFJ - Hano - Wife of Meesha
ME - Harpagus - Cousin to King Astyages – Median, General under King Cyrus

MF - Hayat - A 13-year-old girl

JD - Heber - A Judean slave in Babylon
MF - Heydar - Conspirator
JD - Hezekiah - King of Judah
MF - Hosh - Military leader and father of Ava
MF - Hugav - A Scout, the Family's best climber
ME - Hyroeades - Found a way into Sardis for Cyrus
JD - Isaiah - The Prophet
MFJ - Jacoba - Wife of Natan
MF - Jahan - A member of the Council, son of Fardad
AS - Jamal - A member of Baildan's cavalry
MF - Jangi - Subordinate to Hosh
MFJ - Javed - Son of Zaia and Abigail
JD - Jehoahaz - King of Judah for three months, son of King Josiah

JD - Jehoiachin - King of Judah, son of King Jehoiakim
JD - Jehoiakim - King of Judah, son of King Josiah
JD - Jeremiah - Prophet in Judea from 626 BC – date of death unknown.

JD - Jeshua - Levite, who leads the return to Judah
JD - Josiah - King of Judah, son of King Manasseh
JD - Kadri - A disciple of Jeremiah
AS Karim Servant/armor-bearer of Baildan
JD - Kedem - A Judean slave in Babylon
MF - Kevan - A member of the Council, head of military training.

SL - Khalil - A survivor of the raid, who spied on the Magi
MFA - Khannah - Wife of Domara, mother of Baildan and Meesha

MFA - Khonayn - Family military leader - Nineveh
MFB - Kia - Son of Seena, leader of the Magi Family in Persepolis.
MFB - Lebario - Family military leader – Babylon
JD - Lem - Daniel's disciple.
PS - Leyla - Daughter of the Satrap Baraz
Other - Liyana - Slave captive who joined the Family from southern Africa

SL - Malik - A survivor of the Magi raid, was wounded.
MF - Mahsa - the daughter of Gohar
ME - Mandana - Daughter of Prince Astyages, wife of King Cambyses I of Anshan, mother of Cyrus II.

MFB - Manoah - Son of Davi and Sarah
AS - Mardokh - Member of Baildan's troop
MF - Marzban - A member of the Council, son of Kevan

MFJ - Meesha - Son of Domara, representative to the court in Jerusalem.

MF - Mehr - Mother of Utana
PS - Mirza - Servant of Baraz, horseman, Husband of Leyla
ME - Mithradates - Cattle manager Harpagus - Median
PS - Musa - Queen of Persia from 2 BC to 4AD, co-ruler with her son Phraates V.

SY - Nabil - Commander of the Syrian forces combined with Ephraim.

BY - Nabonidus - King of Babylon
BY - Nabopolassar - King of Babylon 626-605 BC
AR - Nadeem -Sheikh of Arabian spice traders, father of Taalib

SL - Naila - A serving woman of Sheikh Malek
MFJ - Naomi - Benjamin's wife
MFJ - Natan - Ambassador to Judah under King Josiah
MF - Navid - A member of the Council, leader of the Scouts, son of Jahan and Asha.

BY - Nebuchadnezzar - King of Babylon 605-562 BC
MFJ - Negar - Daughter of Zaia and Abigail
MF - Nura - 6-year-old child, adopted by Pai and Tiz
PS - Oebares - Cyrus II aide and general
PS - Omid - Sister of Satrap Baraz
MF - Pari - Daughter of Jahan and Asha
PS - Parviz - Leader of the Immortals
MFB - Payam - Son of Manoah, grandson of Davi
IS - Pekah - King of Israel, Northern Kingdom from 737–732 BC

MFA - Pera - Grandson of Benjamin, head of the Family in Nineveh

PS - Phraates V - King of Persia from 2 BC to 4 AD, co-ruler with his mother, Musa

MF - Rahim - A member of the Council, teacher of the children.

MF - Ram - A member of the Council, livestock manager
SL - Rashad - A survivor of the Magi raid, the son of Sheikh Malek.

MF - Reza - Dissenter
SY - Rezin - King of Syria, ruled from 754–732 BC
MFJ - Sabra - The 13-year-old daughter of Natan
PS - Safa - A friend of Leyla, her father is a court official

AS - Samir - Commander of fifty under Baildan
AR - Samsi - Queen of Arabia in the 730s and 720s (exact dates are not known)

JD - Samuel - Judean, who rode with Eliya
MFB - Sarah - Wife of Davi
MF - Sasan - Son of Fardad, chief counselor of Queen Musa
MFB - Seena - Head of Magi Family in Babylon
SL - Sheikh Malek - Sheikh of the Bedouin slavers.
JD - Sheshbazzar - Prince of Judah, leads the return to Judah

AS - Sin-sharra-ishkun - King of Assyria 627-612 BC
PS - Taghi - Leader of the Uxians
AR - Taalib - Son of Sheikh Nadeem, husband of Hayat
AS - Tiglath-Pileser III - King of Assyria from 745–727 BC
MF - Tiz - A member of the Scouts and caretaker of Pari
PS - Trdat - Prince of Ctesiphon, subject of Queen Musa
MF - Utana - A member of the Scouts, husband of Fahnik
MF - Vasil - Father of Hayat
MFB - Walita - Twenty-year-old wife of Bareil
MFB - Wardeen - Teacher of the Family in Babylon
SL - Yara - One of Sheikh Malek's wives
MF - Yusef - A 12-year-old boy, the son of Danial
MFB - Zaia - Son of Meesha and Hano
PS - Zard - Uxian shepherd
JD - Zedekiah - King of Judah, the son of King Josiah
JD - Zerubbabel - Leader of the Judeans returning to Judah

IS - Zichri - Military champion of Ephraim
SL - Zora - Sheikh Malek's favorite wife
AN - Anosh - Navid's warhorse
AN - Arbella - Baildan's favorite horse
AN - Arsha - Navid's war dog
AN - B - Tiz's war dog
AN - Bendva - Navid's war dog

Time Line Magi Journey

734 BC-Isaiah prophesies Israel will cease to be a people in 65 years

734 BC-Syro/Ephraimite War

734 BC-King Tiglath-Pileser III's (Assyria) first campaign against the Coastal levant.

733 BC-Tiglath Pileser's campaign against Israel.

732 BC-Tiglath Pileser's campaign against Syria

729 BC-Hezekiah becomes King of Judah (Co-regent)

724 BC-Fall of Samaria, the captivity of King Hoshea by Shalmaneser V

701 BC-King Sennacherib's campaign against Judah

669 BC-Death of King Esarhaddon, completion of 65-year diaspora prophecy (734-669 BC).

626 BC-King Nabopolassar begins to reign in Babylonia

626 BC-King Sin-sharra-ishkun begins to reign in Assyria

616 BC-Babylonia begins a campaign against Assyria

615 BC-Babylonia defeats the Tigris division

614 BC-Babylonia and Media defeat Ashur

613 BC-Babylonian campaign against Suhu

612 BC-Babylonia and Media defeat Nineveh

609 BC-King Josiah of Judah is killed at Megiddo by the Egyptians

609 BC-Jehoahaz – son of Josiah, reigns for three months

609 BC-Jehoiakim – son of Josiah, becomes King of Judah

605 BC-Prince Nebuchadnezzar defeats remnants of Assyria and Egypt at Carchemish

605 BC-Death of Nabopolassar, Nebuchadnezzar become King of Babylonia.

604 BC-King Nebuchadnezzar takes the gold from the Temple in Jerusalem, and the Prophet Daniel is taken captive.

600 BC-King Cyrus is born in Ecbatana, Media

598 BC-King Jehoiakim is murdered, and his son Jehoiachin is made king.

597 BC-King Nebuchadnezzar lays siege to Jerusalem, Jehoiachin is taken captive, and 10,000 Judeans, including the Prophet Ezekiel, are taken captive.

597 BC-Zedekiah becomes King of Judah

588 BC-King Nebuchadnezzar lays siege to Jerusalem for 18 months

586 BC-Jerusalem falls to Babylonia, the city and Temple are destroyed, and King Zedekiah is taken captive to Babylon.

580 BC-Death of Cyrus I, Cambyses I becomes King of Anshan

556 BC-Daniel prophecies in chapter 10 the rise of the Persian Empire.

553 BC-Cyrus becomes King of Persia

550 BC-Cyrus defeats Media at the Battle of Pasargadae.

546 BC-Cyrus defeats Lydia at the Battle of Thymbra.

539 BC-Cyrus defeated Babylon and created the Persian Empire.

538 BC-The first group of Israelites returns to Jerusalem

530 BC-Death of King Cyrus II, Cambyses II becomes king.

516 BC-The Temple is rebuilt 70 years after its destruction in 586 BC.

-0- AD-Birth of Jesus Christ, the Messiah.

Bibliography

Statements of Time-Spans by Babylonian and Assyrian Kings and Mesopotamian Chronology, JSTOR, November 11, 2021, https://www.jstor.org/stable/4200220?Search=yes&resultItemClick=true&searchText=Assyrian+kings&searchUri=%2Faction%2FdoBasicSearch%3FQuery%3DAssyrian%2Bkings%26acc%3Don%26wc%3Don%26fc%3Doff%26group%3Dnone%26refreqid%3Dsearch%253Ae5a8b91aa68b2c5f08f847bb12b0a3fb%26so%3Drel&ab_segments=0%2Fbasic_search_gsv2%2Fcontrol&refreqid=fastly-default%3Acc938798fdb6eeac4a83af94dcc96128&seq=1#metadata_info_tab_contents

Old City Maps, imgur, November 10, 2021, https://i.imgur.com/MnuIZyN.png.

Map of the Assyrian Empire, UCL, 11/16/21, https://www.ucl.ac.uk/sargon/images/glossary/map-large.jpg.

Nebuchadnezzar the Warrior, JSTOR, November 18, 2021, Nebuchadnezzar the Warrior: Remarks on his Military Achievements on JSTOR

map-syria.jpg (1260×962) (geographicguide.com)

List of Assyrian kings | Religion Wiki | Fandom.

Wood, Leon J., (1986) *A Survey of Israel's History*, Grand Rapids, MI: Zondervan.

Merrill, John, and Shanks, Hershel, (2021) *Ancient Israel – From Abraham to the Roman Destruction of the Temple*, Washington, DC: Biblical Archaeology Society.

Beaulieu, Paul-Alain, (2018) *A history of Babylon – 2200 BC-AD 75*, Weinheim, Germany: John Wiley & Sons Ltd.

Kriwaczek, Paul, (2010) *Babylon – Mesopotamia and the Birth of Civilization*, Great Britain: Atlantic Books.

Ellerbrock, Uwe, (2021) *The Parthians – The Forgotten Empire*, New York, NY: Routledge.

Herzog, Chaim & Gichon, Mordechai, (1997) *Battles of the Bible – A Military History of Ancient Israel*, New York, NY: Fall River Press.

Freeman-Grenville, G.S.P. (1993) *Historical Atlas of the Middle East*, New York, NY: Simon and Schuster.

Isbouts, Jean-Pierre, (2018) *Atlas of the Bible – Exploring the Holy*

Lands, Washington, DC: National Geographic.

Gabriel, Richard, (2018) *On Ancient Warfare – Perspectives on Aspects of War in Antiquity 4000 BC to AD 637*, Yorkshire, PA: Pen & Sword Books Ltd.

Dando-Collins, Stephen, (2020) *Cyrus the Great*, Nashville, TN: Turner Publishing Company.

ENDNOTES

[1] Stephen Dando-Collins, *Cyrus the Great*, Nashville, TN, 2020, Turner Publishing Company, pg.25.

[2] Psalm 4:4 "Be **angry**, and do not **sin**; ponder in your own hearts on your beds, and be silent. Selah"

[3] Isaiah 44:28 "28 who says of Cyrus, 'He is my shepherd, and he shall fulfill all my purpose'; saying of Jerusalem, 'She shall be built,' and of the temple, 'Your foundation shall be laid.'"

[4] Jeremiah 29:10-14 "10 "For thus says the Lord: When seventy years are completed for Babylon, I will visit you, and I will fulfill to you my promise and bring you back to this place. 11 For I know the plans I have for you, declares the Lord, plans for welfare[b] and not for evil, to give you a future and a hope. 12 Then you will call upon me and come and pray to me, and I will hear you. 13 You will seek me and find me, when you seek me with all your heart. 14 I will be found by you, declares the Lord, and I will restore your fortunes and gather you from all the nations and all the places where I have driven you, declares the Lord, and I will bring you back to the place from which I sent you into exile."

[5] Daniel 3:4-6 "4 And the herald proclaimed aloud, "You are commanded, O peoples, nations, and languages, 5 that when you hear the sound of the horn, pipe, lyre, trigon, harp, bagpipe, and every kind of music, you are to fall down and worship the golden image that King Nebuchadnezzar has set up. 6 And whoever does not fall down and worship shall immediately be cast into a burning fiery furnace."

[6] Daniel 3:26-30 "26 Then Nebuchadnezzar came near to the door of the burning fiery furnace; he declared, "Shadrach, Meshach, and Abednego, servants of the Most High God, come out, and come here!" Then Shadrach, Meshach, and Abednego came out from the fire. 27 And the satraps, the prefects, the governors, and the king's

counselors gathered together and saw that the fire had not had any power over the bodies of those men. The hair of their heads was not singed, their cloaks were not harmed, and no smell of fire had come upon them. [28] Nebuchadnezzar answered and said, "Blessed be the God of Shadrach, Meshach, and Abednego, who has sent his angel and delivered his servants, who trusted in him, and set aside[f] the king's command, and yielded up their bodies rather than serve and worship any god except their own God. [29] Therefore I make a decree: Any people, nation, or language that speaks anything against the God of Shadrach, Meshach, and Abednego shall be torn limb from limb, and their houses laid in ruins, for there is no other god who is able to rescue in this way." [30] Then the king promoted Shadrach, Meshach, and Abednego in the province of Babylon."

[7] Daniel 3:28-29.

[8] Psalm 49:13-15 "[13] This is the path of those who have foolish confidence; yet after them people approve of their boasts. *Selah* [14] Like sheep they are appointed for Sheol; death shall be their shepherd, and the upright shall rule over them in the morning. Their form shall be consumed in Sheol, with no place to dwell. [15] But God will ransom my soul from the power of Sheol, for he will receive me. "

[9] Proverbs 23:13-14 "[13] Do not withhold discipline from a child; if you strike him with a rod, he will not die. [14] If you strike him with the rod, you will save his soul from Sheol."

[10] Jeremiah 25:8-12 "[8] "Therefore thus says the Lord of hosts: Because you have not obeyed my words, [9] behold, I will send for all the tribes of the north, declares the Lord, and for Nebuchadnezzar the king of Babylon, my servant, and I will bring them against this land and its inhabitants, and against all these surrounding nations. I will devote them to destruction, and make them a horror, a hissing, and an everlasting desolation. [10] Moreover, I will banish from them the voice of mirth and the voice of gladness, the voice of the bridegroom and the voice of the bride, the grinding of the millstones and the light of the lamp. [11] This whole land shall become a ruin and a waste, and these nations shall serve the king of Babylon seventy years. [12] Then after seventy years are completed, I will punish the king of Babylon and that nation, the land of the Chaldeans, for their iniquity, declares the Lord, making the land an everlasting waste."

[11] Daniel 4:24-34 "²⁴ this is the interpretation, O king: It is a decree of the Most High, which has come upon my lord the king, ²⁵ that you shall be driven from among men, and your dwelling shall be with the beasts of the field. You shall be made to eat grass like an ox, and you shall be wet with the dew of heaven, and seven periods of time shall pass over you, till you know that the Most High rules the kingdom of men and gives it to whom he will. ²⁶ And as it was commanded to leave the stump of the roots of the tree, your kingdom shall be confirmed for you from the time that you know that Heaven rules. ²⁷ Therefore, O king, let my counsel be acceptable to you: break off your sins by practicing righteousness, and your iniquities by showing mercy to the oppressed, that there may perhaps be a lengthening of your prosperity." ²⁸ All this came upon King Nebuchadnezzar. ²⁹ At the end of twelve months he was walking on the roof of the royal palace of Babylon, ³⁰ and the king answered and said, "Is not this great Babylon, which I have built by my mighty power as a royal residence and for the glory of my majesty?" ³¹ While the words were still in the king's mouth, there fell a voice from heaven, "O King Nebuchadnezzar, to you it is spoken: The kingdom has departed from you, ³² and you shall be driven from among men, and your dwelling shall be with the beasts of the field. And you shall be made to eat grass like an ox, and seven periods of time shall pass over you, until you know that the Most High rules the kingdom of men and gives it to whom he will." ³³ Immediately the word was fulfilled against Nebuchadnezzar. He was driven from among men and ate grass like an ox, and his body was wet with the dew of heaven till his hair grew as long as eagles' feathers, and his nails were like birds' claws. ³⁴ At the end of the days I, Nebuchadnezzar, lifted my eyes to heaven, and my reason returned to me, and I blessed the Most High, and praised and honored him who lives forever."

[12] Daniel 4:36-37 "³⁶ At the same time my reason returned to me, and for the glory of my kingdom, my majesty and splendor returned to me. My counselors and my lords sought me, and I was established in my kingdom, and still more greatness was added to me. ³⁷ Now I, Nebuchadnezzar, praise and extol and honor the King of heaven, for all his works are right and his ways are just; and those who walk in pride he is able to humble."

[13] Deuteronomy 30:19 "¹⁹ I call heaven and earth to witness against you today, that I have set before you life and death, blessing and curse. Therefore choose life, that you and your offspring may live,"

[14] Isaiah 7:14 "**14** Therefore the Lord himself will give you a sign. Behold, the virgin shall conceive and bear a son, and shall call his name Immanuel."

[15] Isaiah 9:6-7 "**6** For to us a child is born, to us a son is given; and the government shall be upon[d] his shoulder, and his name shall be called[e] Wonderful Counselor, Mighty God, Everlasting Father, Prince of Peace. **7** Of the increase of his government and of peace there will be no end, on the throne of David and over his kingdom, to establish it and to uphold it with justice and with righteousness from this time forth and forevermore. The zeal of the Lord of hosts will do this."

[16] Isaiah 53.

[17] Leviticus 16:1-10 "The Lord spoke to Moses after the death of the two sons of Aaron, when they drew near before the Lord and died, **2** and the Lord said to Moses, "Tell Aaron your brother not to come at any time into the Holy Place inside the veil, before the mercy seat that is on the ark, so that he may not die. For I will appear in the cloud over the mercy seat. **3** But in this way Aaron shall come into the Holy Place: with a bull from the herd for a sin offering and a ram for a burnt offering. **4** He shall put on the holy linen coat and shall have the linen undergarment on his body, and he shall tie the linen sash around his waist, and wear the linen turban; these are the holy garments. He shall bathe his body in water and then put them on. **5** And he shall take from the congregation of the people of Israel two male goats for a sin offering, and one ram for a burnt offering. **6** "Aaron shall offer the bull as a sin offering for himself and shall make atonement for himself and for his house. **7** Then he shall take the two goats and set them before the Lord at the entrance of the tent of meeting. **8** And Aaron shall cast lots over the two goats, one lot for the Lord and the other lot for Azazel.[a] **9** And Aaron shall present the goat on which the lot fell for the Lord and use it as a sin offering, **10** but the goat on which the lot fell for Azazel shall be presented alive before the Lord to make atonement over it, that it may be sent away into the wilderness to Azazel."

[18] Isaiah 53:1-12 "Who has believed what he has heard from us? And to whom has the arm of the Lord been revealed? **2** For he grew up before him like a young plant, and like a root out of dry ground; he

had no form or majesty that we should look at him, and no beauty that we should desire him. ³ He was despised and rejected[b] by men, a man of sorrows[c] and acquainted with[d] grief; and as one from whom men hide their faces he was despised, and we esteemed him not. ⁴ Surely he has borne our griefs and carried our sorrows; yet we esteemed him stricken, smitten by God, and afflicted. ⁵ But he was pierced for our transgressions; he was crushed for our iniquities; upon him was the chastisement that brought us peace, and with his wounds we are healed. ⁶ All we like sheep have gone astray; we have turned—every one—to his own way; and the Lord has laid on him the iniquity of us all. ⁷ He was oppressed, and he was afflicted, yet he opened not his mouth; like a lamb that is led to the slaughter, and like a sheep that before its shearers is silent, so he opened not his mouth. ⁸ By oppression and judgment he was taken away; and as for his generation, who considered that he was cut off out of the land of the living, stricken for the transgression of my people? ⁹ And they made his grave with the wicked and with a rich man in his death, although he had done no violence, and there was no deceit in his mouth. ¹⁰ Yet it was the will of the Lord to crush him; he has put him to grief; when his soul makes[h] an offering for guilt, he shall see his offspring; he shall prolong his days; the will of the Lord shall prosper in his hand. ¹¹ Out of the anguish of his soul he shall see[i] and be satisfied; by his knowledge shall the righteous one, my servant, make many to be accounted righteous, and he shall bear their iniquities. ¹² Therefore I will divide him a portion with the many, and he shall divide the spoil with the strong, because he poured out his soul to death and was numbered with the transgressors; yet he bore the sin of many, and makes intercession for the transgressors."

[19] Psalm 107.

[20] Isaiah 9:1.

[21] Micah 5:2.

[22] Isaiah 9:6-7 "⁶ For to us a child is born, to us a son is given; and the government shall be upon his shoulder, and his name shall be called Wonderful Counselor, Mighty God, Everlasting Father, Prince of Peace.
⁷ Of the increase of his government and of peace there will be no end,

on the throne of David and over his kingdom, to establish it and to uphold it with justice and with righteousness from this time forth and forevermore. The zeal of the Lord of hosts will do this.

[23] Joshua 8:33-35 "³³ And all Israel, sojourner as well as native born, with their elders and officers and their judges, stood on opposite sides of the ark before the Levitical priests who carried the ark of the covenant of the Lord, half of them in front of Mount Gerizim and half of them in front of Mount Ebal, just as Moses the servant of the Lord had commanded at the first, to bless the people of Israel. ³⁴ And afterward he read all the words of the law, the blessing and the curse, according to all that is written in the Book of the Law. ³⁵ There was not a word of all that Moses commanded that Joshua did not read before all the assembly of Israel, and the women, and the little ones, and the sojourners who lived[c] among them."

[24] Genesis 12:8 "⁸ From there he moved to the hill country on the east of Bethel and pitched his tent, with Bethel on the west and Ai on the east. And there he built an altar to the Lord and called upon the name of the Lord. **AND** Genesis 13:² Now Abram was very rich in livestock, in silver, and in gold. ³ And he journeyed on from the Negeb as far as Bethel to the place where his tent had been at the beginning, between Bethel and Ai, ⁴ to the place where he had made an altar at the first. And there Abram called upon the name of the Lord."

[25] Genesis 28:11-19 "¹¹ And he came to a certain place and stayed there that night, because the sun had set. Taking one of the stones of the place, he put it under his head and lay down in that place to sleep. ¹² And he dreamed, and behold, there was a ladder[b] set up on the earth, and the top of it reached to heaven. And behold, the angels of God were ascending and descending on it! ¹³ And behold, the Lord stood above it[c] and said, "I am the Lord, the God of Abraham your father and the God of Isaac. The land on which you lie I will give to you and to your offspring. ¹⁴ Your offspring shall be like the dust of the earth, and you shall spread abroad to the west and to the east and to the north and to the south, and in you and your offspring shall all the families of the earth be blessed. ¹⁵ Behold, I am with you and will keep you wherever you go, and will bring you back to this land. For I will not leave you until I have done what I have promised you." ¹⁶ Then Jacob awoke from his sleep and said, "Surely the Lord is in this place, and I did not know it." ¹⁷ And he was afraid and said, "How

awesome is this place! This is none other than the house of God, and this is the gate of heaven." [18] So early in the morning Jacob took the stone that he had put under his head and set it up for a pillar and poured oil on the top of it. [19] He called the name of that place Bethel."

[26] Numbers 6:24-26.

[27] Daniel 5:10-12.

[28] Daniel 5:18-28.

[29] Luke 2:10-14.

[30] Luke 2:8-40 [8] And in the same region there were shepherds out in the field, keeping watch over their flock by night. [9] And an angel of the Lord appeared to them, and the glory of the Lord shone around them, and they were filled with great fear. [10] And the angel said to them, "Fear not, for behold, I bring you good news of great joy that will be for all the people. [11] For unto you is born this day in the city of David a Savior, who is Christ the Lord. [12] And this will be a sign for you: you will find a baby wrapped in swaddling cloths and lying in a manger." [13] And suddenly there was with the angel a multitude of the heavenly host praising God and saying, [14] "Glory to God in the highest, and on earth peace among those with whom he is pleased! [15] When the angels went away from them into heaven, the shepherds said to one another, "Let us go over to Bethlehem and see this thing that has happened, which the Lord has made known to us." [16] And they went with haste and found Mary and Joseph, and the baby lying in a manger. [17] And when they saw it, they made known the saying that had been told them concerning this child. [18] And all who heard it wondered at what the shepherds told them. [19] But Mary treasured up all these things, pondering them in her heart. [20] And the shepherds returned, glorifying and praising God for all they had heard and seen, as it had been told them. [21] And at the end of eight days, when he was circumcised, he was called Jesus, the name given by the angel before he was conceived in the womb. [22] And when the time came for their purification according to the Law of Moses, they brought him up to Jerusalem to present him to the Lord [23] (as it is written in the Law of the Lord, "Every male who first opens the womb shall be called holy to the Lord") [24] and to offer a sacrifice according to what is said in the Law of the Lord, "a pair of

turtledoves, or two young pigeons." ²⁵ Now there was a man in Jerusalem, whose name was Simeon, and this man was righteous and devout, waiting for the consolation of Israel, and the Holy Spirit was upon him. ²⁶ And it had been revealed to him by the Holy Spirit that he would not see death before he had seen the Lord's Christ. ²⁷ And he came in the Spirit into the temple, and when the parents brought in the child Jesus, to do for him according to the custom of the Law, ²⁸ he took him up in his arms and blessed God and said, ²⁹ "Lord, now you are letting your servant[e] depart in peace, according to your word; ³⁰ for my eyes have seen your salvation ³¹   that you have prepared in the presence of all peoples, ³² a light for revelation to the Gentiles, and for glory to your people Israel." ³³ And his father and his mother marveled at what was said about him. ³⁴ And Simeon blessed them and said to Mary his mother, "Behold, this child is appointed for the fall and rising of many in Israel, and for a sign that is opposed ³⁵ (and a sword will pierce through your own soul also), so that thoughts from many hearts may be revealed." ³⁶ And there was a prophetess, Anna, the daughter of Phanuel, of the tribe of Asher. She was advanced in years, having lived with her husband seven years from when she was a virgin, ³⁷ and then as a widow until she was eighty-four.[f] She did not depart from the temple, worshiping with fasting and prayer night and day. ³⁸ And coming up at that very hour she began to give thanks to God and to speak of him to all who were waiting for the redemption of Jerusalem. ³⁹ And when they had performed everything according to the Law of the Lord, they returned into Galilee, to their own town of Nazareth. ⁴⁰ And the child grew and became strong, filled with wisdom. And the favor of God was upon him.

[31] Matthew 2:1-9 "Now after Jesus was born in Bethlehem of Judea in the days of Herod the king, behold, wise men[a] from the east came to Jerusalem, ² saying, "Where is he who has been born king of the Jews? For we saw his star when it rose[b] and have come to worship him." ³ When Herod the king heard this, he was troubled, and all Jerusalem with him; ⁴ and assembling all the chief priests and scribes of the people, he inquired of them where the Christ was to be

born. ⁵ They told him, "In Bethlehem of Judea, for so it is written by the prophet: ⁶ "'And you, O Bethlehem, in the land of Judah, are by no means least among the rulers of Judah; for from you shall come a ruler who will shepherd my people Israel.'" ⁷ Then Herod summoned the wise men secretly and ascertained from them what time the star had appeared. ⁸ And he sent them to Bethlehem, saying, "Go and search diligently for the child, and when you have found him, bring me word, that I too may come and worship him." ⁹ After listening to the king, they went on their way.

[32] Daniel 6:1-2 "It pleased Darius to set over the kingdom 120 satraps, to be throughout the whole kingdom; ² and over them three high officials, of whom Daniel was one, to whom these satraps should give account, so that the king might suffer no loss."

[33] Ezra 1:9-10 "⁹ And this was the number of them: 30 basins of gold, 1,000 basins of silver, 29 censers, ¹⁰ 30 bowls of gold, 410 bowls of silver, and 1,000 other vessels; ¹¹ all the vessels of gold and of silver were 5,400. All these did Sheshbazzar bring up, when the exiles were brought up from Babylonia to Jerusalem."

[34] Ezra 1:2-4.

[35] Ezra 2:36-58 "³⁶ The priests: the sons of Jedaiah, of the house of Jeshua, 973. ³⁷ The sons of Immer, 1,052. ³⁸ The sons of Pashhur, 1,247. ³⁹ The sons of Harim, 1,017. ⁴⁰ The Levites: the sons of Jeshua and Kadmiel, of the sons of Hodaviah, 74. ⁴¹ The singers: the sons of Asaph, 128. ⁴² The sons of the gatekeepers: the sons of Shallum, the sons of Ater, the sons of Talmon, the sons of Akkub, the sons of Hatita, and the sons of Shobai, in all 139. ⁴³ The temple servants: the sons of Ziha, the sons of Hasupha, the sons of Tabbaoth, ⁴⁴ the sons of Keros, the sons of Siaha, the sons of Padon, ⁴⁵ the sons of Lebanah, the sons of Hagabah, the sons of Akkub, ⁴⁶ the sons of Hagab, the sons of Shamlai, the sons of Hanan, ⁴⁷ the sons of Giddel, the sons of Gahar, the sons of Reaiah, ⁴⁸ the sons of Rezin, the sons of Nekoda, the sons of Gazzam, ⁴⁹ the sons of Uzza, the sons of Paseah, the sons of Besai, ⁵⁰ the sons of Asnah, the sons of Meunim, the sons of Nephisim, ⁵¹ the sons

of Bakbuk, the sons of Hakupha, the sons of Harhur, [52] the sons of Bazluth, the sons of Mehida, the sons of Harsha, [53] the sons of Barkos, the sons of Sisera, the sons of Temah, [54] the sons of Neziah, and the sons of Hatipha. [55] The sons of Solomon's servants: the sons of Sotai, the sons of Hassophereth, the sons of Peruda, [56] the sons of Jaalah, the sons of Darkon, the sons of Giddel, [57] the sons of Shephatiah, the sons of Hattil, the sons of Pochereth-hazzebaim, and the sons of Ami. [58] All the temple servants and the sons of Solomon's servants were 392."

[36] Exodus 15:1-18.

[37] Judges 5:2-31.

[38] 2 Chronicles 34:31 "[31] And the king stood in his place and made a covenant before the Lord, to walk after the Lord and to keep his commandments and his testimonies and his statutes, with all his heart and all his soul, to perform the words of the covenant that were written in this book."

[39] Isaiah 52:10 "The Lord has bared his holy arm before the eyes of all the nations, and all the ends of the earth shall see the salvation of our God."

[40] Isaiah 52:15 "so shall he sprinkle[c] many nations. Kings shall shut their mouths because of him,
for that which has not been told them they see, and that which they have not heard they understand."

[41] Matthew 2:13-15 "Now when they had departed, behold, an angel of the Lord appeared to Joseph in a dream and said, "Rise, take the child and his mother, and flee to Egypt, and remain there until I tell you, for Herod is about to search for the child, to destroy him." [14] And he rose and took the child and his mother by night and departed to Egypt [15] and remained there until the death of Herod. This was to fulfill what the Lord had spoken by the prophet, "Out of Egypt I called my son.""

Made in the USA
Middletown, DE
29 October 2022

13740349R00159